William Smethurst is a director of a ~~~~~~~~~~~~~~
and the author of four previous novels, *Night of the Bear*
(written jointly with Julian Spilsbury), *Bukhara Express*,
Sinai and *Pasiphae*. He lives in Warwickshire with his
wife Carolynne and daughter Henrietta.

Woken's Eye

William Smethurst

HEADLINE
FEATURE

First published in 1999
by HEADLINE BOOK PUBLISHING

First published in paperback in 2000
by HEADLINE BOOK PUBLISHING

10 9 8 7 6 5 4 3 2 1

ISBN 0 7472 6147 4

Typeset by Avon Dataset Ltd, Bidford-on-Avon, Warks

Printed and bound in Great Britain by
Mackays of Chatham plc, Chatham, Kent

HEADLINE BOOK PUBLISHING
A division of Hodder Headline
338 Euston Road
London NW1 3BH

www.headline.co.uk
www.hodderheadline.com

For Margaret and Daphne

Part One

1

Electronic Intelligence (ELINT) Section, National Security Agency, Chicago, 1962

The photographs had been taken by a spy plane over the Ciego de Avila mountains as the sun went down and the shadows lengthened. The quality was poor because they'd been sent by landline from Miami, but there was no possibility of mistake. Crude white lines superimposed on the negative showed oxidiser tanks parked in the tall sugar canes, tracked prime-movers in the thick undergrowth of palm forest. There was the menacing shadow of a missile erector, its thick cable snaking behind it to the firing pit.

A young intelligence operative stood at the back of the room, behind the experts, and stared up at the screen. He wondered what his folks in Scott City, Kansas, would think if they knew Fidel Castro was now able to launch MRBMs against the USA. He pictured a missile landing on his Scott City high school, and mused fleetingly on the romance of his final year, with a girl who might soon be reduced to carbon atoms. A girl from Kansas had enough to cope with, he told himself in the cool, sophisticated, city manner he was cultivating, without Fidel Castro blowing her to bits.

When his break came he got himself an iced Coke and went outside and sat on the fire escape. It was humid, with only the faintest breath of air coming in off the lake. 'And when it's sleepin' time, we start to swing . . .' sang a gaggle of drunken voices from far below.

They'd been to see Sinatra at the Villa Venice. The young operative had been there himself, a couple of nights back. 'Me and my pals always used to have sleepless nights here in the Windy City,' Sinatra had said, 'but then we'd get rid of the broad and sleep a little better.'

The young operative smiled, but only for a moment.

Sinatra would be truly sleepless tonight – him and Dean Martin and Sammy Davis Jnr – if they knew what he knew.

Other night-shift operatives were also on the fire escape: smoking, drinking coffee, savouring the occasional movement of cool air from Lake Michigan, looking at the sodium lights shining through the trees along the lakeside drive, and discussing the crisis. The talk was of an invasion of Cuba and a conventional war in Europe. That was why military traffic was three times its normal level, they argued. That was why so much stuff was moving across the Atlantic. Three airborne brigades were being sent to England. Berlin would be the battleground.

Berlin . . . the young operative from Kansas rolled the word off his tongue, as if he'd been there a hundred times, as if Germany was his own backyard. But when he went back inside he was startled to find a signal from USAF Command Westphalia on his desk.

It said that an American aircraft from Germany was missing over the English coastline. When it disappeared at 0200 GMT, it had been heading for a USAF base in Lincolnshire.

The aircraft was an RPV with a speed of Mach 4 equipped with electronic intelligence-gathering transceivers, standard infra-red linescan, and a Carl Zeiss 3-lens reconnaissance camera. It also had on board an un-named explosive device. Non-nuclear but experimental in nature.

'What do I do with this?' he asked the senior operative at the next desk. The operative read the signal and said, 'Tell SIGINT, then tag it as active till we find out what's happened.'

Signals flowed. The humidity fell before dawn. Just before the night shift ended somebody came down the row of desks, a look of shock on his face, saying, 'Have you heard?'

The young intelligence officer felt the blood rush into his head.

The war had started!

But the news was from California and told of a personal tragedy, albeit one that would shock the world.

He went off duty. The signal concerning the lost aircraft was still tagged as active, left on his desk to be swept up with a thousand other signals and processed by the filing clerks.

By 0100 hours in Chicago, 0700 hours in London, the CIA had warned the US embassy of a possible disaster on English soil. The ambassador was awakened and told that RAF Coastal Command could not be asked to mount a search because the RPV's flight did not have UK government authority to land in Britain. He asked why the US was flying experimental weaponry into the UK without permission, and was told that the device was most secret, en-route for the

US, and was landing in Lincolnshire only for refuelling.

The embassy, by that time, was already monitoring the BBC. The lead story of the early morning news was that Marilyn Monroe was dead: found naked in bed in her house near Hollywood, clutching a telephone receiver.

At 0800 hours the BBC was still leading on Marilyn Monroe. John Huston was quoted: 'Her great enemy was sleepless-ness.'

At 10 am two CIA agents from London Embassy arrived at Wormby on the Lincolnshire coast, the place directly under the RPV's flight path when it lost contact with its escorting Lockheed A-12. They had made good time on the roads, it being a Sunday with little early traffic. They reported a fine, hot morning now the early mist had cleared.

They parked their car by the Wormby Flats Holiday Camp and climbed the sea wall, up through aromatic grasses, following a sandy path worn by countless holiday makers, bird-watchers, and courting couples. From the top they looked out over the salt flats. To the north was a low, grey cliff that receded into the misty distance. To the south was the earth wall that protected thousands of square miles of Lincolnshire from the North Sea.

A group of girls were sunbathing.

One of the agents, a man in his forties, muscular but overweight, sweating slightly in his city suit, went over to them and said, 'Hi.'

They were lying on their fronts with their bikini tops undone. They stared up at him expressionless, not moving.

6

'Nice day,' said the agent, smiling genially, pretending not to notice their hostility. He left them and wandered along the sea wall. The tide was out. Below him was a small beach of pebbles and shingle before the start of the mud. Families were settling themselves lazily for the morning's sunbathing: mums rubbing sun cream on small children, dads putting up sunshades or reading the *Daily Express*. Skinny teenage girls in swimsuits, not yet old enough to holiday alone with their friends, were stretching themselves on towels, sulky and bored. Sometimes small brothers threw balls that hit them, and they screamed in irritation. The CIA agent could smell sun oil mingling with the scent of grasses and the tang of the sea, and felt a moment of nostalgia for his divorced wife and estranged children. A transistor radio played: Bob Dylan's voice floating tinnily over the dunes, wondering how many seas a white dove must sail.

The agent joined in, singing quietly to himself on this fine, lazy morning of maximum peril, wondering how many cannonballs would fly before they were forever banned.

He looked up at the hazy, pale blue sky. According to Dylan the answer was blowing in the wind, but what did that mean exactly? A cloud of Strontium 90, borne on the breeze?

The other agent, a younger man, had gone back down to the car. He drove back across the flat, black-loam fields of potatoes to a village. He phoned London Embassy and said, 'Negative.'

At 11 am he was back outside the Holiday Camp. He turned on the car radio and heard that Marilyn Monroe's last words had been 'Goodnight honey,' said to her housekeeper

Mrs Eunice Murray. Her last words to the world had been to *Life* magazine: 'Everybody is always tugging at you. They would all like sort of a chunk of you.'

The agent sighed and shook his head. Then he left the car and went into the holiday camp. He collected some leaflets, pretending that he was interested in a family holiday (he'd rather have given bone marrow without anaesthetic) and looked at a notice board which had *Entertainments Today* written over it in blue and pink spangly letters. *Lolita* was playing in the cinema at Boston. There was a poster of Sue Lyon sucking a lollipop, but he was unmoved. All he knew or cared of *Lolita* was that it was shot by Kubrick with two alternating aspect ratios, 1.66:1 and 1.33:1.

He noted that there was bingo in the camp theatre in the afternoon, and in the evening a professional mind-reading act.

The two agents met up on the sea wall. 'I've walked for the best part of two miles,' said the older man. 'There's a café, full of bird-watchers. If we stay around we may catch sight of a North European redbill. If you see a toad with yellow stripes it's a natterjack, and you will have something to tell your grandchildren in future years. Oh, and *Lolita*'s showing in Boston in case we're here overnight.'

'Yea,' said the other agent, 'I know.'

'I saw it in Leicester Square, but I don't mind seeing it again. Jesus . . .'

He shook his head, thinking of bikini-clad Sue Lyon in her heart-shaped sunglasses, licking her lollipop.

They walked to a quiet spot and sat in the sun, looking out over the sea. The older agent, who liked girls, watched some. The younger agent, who liked film-speed ratios, watched the tide and worried about non-nuclear experimental explosive devices.

'Maybe it went down in the sea.' he said.

'The guys on the A-12 say not.'

'Do we know what sort of device it is?'

The older agent shook his head.

'If it's non-nuclear, maybe it doesn't matter if it leaks.'

'What did London say?'

'They said to stay here awhile.'

'That's fine by me. If you don't want to see *Lolita* maybe we can go to a dance in the holiday camp.'

'Sure, if you're into the cha cha cha.'

'They've not caught on to the Twist in these parts? They've not heard of Chubby Checker?'

'There's a mind-reading act. A clairvoyant.'

'Maybe we can take him on the strength. Get him to locate the objective. Maybe we ought to suggest it to London.'

They chuckled. They went back to the holiday camp and bought themselves ice creams, and again climbed up on the wall. They took off their suit jackets and sat on the grass in their short-sleeved shirts, with their crew-cut hair and gold-rimmed glasses.

They ate their ices and watched the mud flats of Black Buoy and Gat Sand as they were covered by the tide, the water creeping in surprisingly quickly, through a maze of channels and streams.

The fat man watched a girl in an imitation leopard-skin bikini, her brown legs, the swell of her breasts.

The younger man watched gulls swoop and cry over the mud, over something that flashed for a moment, silvery, then was gone. A dead fish, he decided.

Eventually they went back to their car. They drove to Holbeach, found a public phone box, different from the others they had used, and reported to a London number that there was no evident alarm in Lincolnshire.

No aircraft had crashed. No device, nuclear or otherwise, had exploded.

Or if it had, nobody knew. Nobody saw it happen.

2

Lincolnshire, AD 1216

A cry of alarm from the mists ahead. A curse and a choked scream.

Something was wrong.

A flurry of air – the sea mist shivering, then clearing – a runner revealed, splashing back from the varward division, fear on his face, crossing himself.

Sand demons, bogeys – whatever they believed in, in this country (his accent was thick, much of what he said incomprehensible) – somehow a sumpter horse had been frightened, led astray and lost its footing, had stumbled. A sergeant had given its keeper a bloody head. The horse was lost.

The army commander looked up at the sky. What hour was it? Past None, for certain, he thought; nearer Vespers. It would be dark before they were at the Fosdyke. For safety they should have bivouacked on the Holland shore, crossed the causeway at dawn, with the low tide – but the King was in a fury to get back to Lincoln, to find Alexander's army and destroy it. He was waiting, now, somewhere ahead, sending back a stream of messages, every one the same: *Hurry, hurry!*

The column was moving again. Channels bubbled on

every side of the causeway, rivers that formed and re-formed themselves, cutting their way through the sand and mud. Sea birds wheeled overhead – gulls and oystercatchers, tempting for the archers, but poor eating at the end of the day, and a man might drown to secure the carcass. 'Quicksands,' the guides called, 'quicksands, quicksands,' their hoarse voices like a kind of sea bird, their warning cries imitated in subdued, mocking tones by the foot soldiers. But the men walked carefully nonetheless; the sands were only inches from the hidden path.

Now the varward division was in mid-estuary. The Commander stopped his horse and looked back, and swore impatiently, for the Poetevin mercenaries of the rearward division were only just reaching the sea wall, the old Roman *vallum*. He sent a message urging them to move speedily – as if this army did not always move with speed – then watched as the single-horsed carettes and the long cart of the *garderoba* lurched down to the sands, followed by the wagons with grain and kindling, and finally the drabs, for even an army moving as fast as this picked up drabs like lice, and it seemed that half the whores of Lenne were journeying north.

A woman trudged past, clinging to a packhorse that had a linen shirt over its rump, spread to dry, steaming gently. She was Florence the laundress, an old campaigner. She winked at him and grinned, and he smiled and called her an old harlot. Tramping beside her was a man of middle years, his peasant clothes at odds with his neat, shoulder-length hair, its sides brushed in loose waves after the manner of the Gascons. William the *Aquarius*; the king's bathman, the only man of his calling, perhaps, in all of England.

A warning cry from the scouts. The Commander turned sharply.

More mist . . .

Thick, this time. Cold and white, rolling out over the waters from the fens.

How far out would it spread? How much time did they have?

He should have waited until tomorrow's dawn. Or he should have taken the Wisbeche road – but this was cursed country for an army: a land of bogs and running streams, of great sluices and channels. Risegate Eau and Byker Coln, Laften Lode and Old Bech – every one to be laboriously crossed before they reached the Kyme Eau, and even then there would have been a two-hour march to Swinehead.

And the French were less than a day's march away, he thought wearily, and moving to join with the Scotch army that was ravaging the north; to cut the kingdom in two.

He sat his horse and watched the slowly spreading mist, and thought back again over this year of disasters for the English. Of the navy's futile efforts to destroy French transport ships at Dieppe and Fecamp. Of the army that had mobilised on Barnham Down to oppose the invasion: gathered too soon, and in the wrong place.

Of the surrender of London to the French. Of Louis, proclaimed *Rex Anglorum* on the steps of St Paul's.

A year of shame. And it was only October, sweet Christ. And the English army, what was left of it, could not even oppose the French besieging Windsor. They were being forced north into the fens and flood lands of The Wash, crossing out of Norfolk, trying to catch the Scotch and kill them, but in truth seeking safety.

'It's getting thicker,' said Ferrers, commander of the main-battle division.

The distant Lindsay shore had disappeared. Only a few bunches of withies stood in drifting pools of white. The crossbow-men guarding the treasury were being swallowed up like ghosts.

Now the column had stopped again.

There were shouts from ahead.

The Commander said, calmly, 'Find out what is happening.'

A runner went forward, past the dim shapes of the carettes.

A cry came back. A wagon was lost – it had missed the path and was tipped half in the quicksand. The column could not get past.

Ferrers said, 'Fuck.'

There was a call for ropes. Then a scream of pain, followed by a confusion of shouting voices.

It was the knights, said a messenger from the mist, a young squire of Sire Rogier, his voice high-pitched with indignation: they were pushing men from the causeway.

The Commander nodded. Knights would kill to save their horses. A knight's horse cost eighty marks, which was more than a villein would earn in a lifetime. A knight without his horse was nothing.

Another messenger: the King's chapel was stuck in the sands.

The Commander suddenly realised that the voices ahead were crystal in their clarity – that he could even hear cold rasp of an iron blade being drawn from a scabbard – that the waters around them were no longer rushing and gurgling.

It was low tide. A moment of stillness before the waters rushed back.

He looked up at the sky, searched for the orb of the sun.

'Get me the master guide.'

A guide came running back, the long white pole of his office balanced on his shoulder, his felt-wrapped legs slopping through the waters.

'What of the King's chapel?'

The guide did not know one wagon from another.

'How far are we from safe ground?'

Not far, said the guide, eagerly, ingratiatingly.

'How long before the tide turns?'

The guide shrugged. He did not count in hours.

Ferrers said, 'It's clearing.'

A wind, chill, from the sea.

The mist moving in wraiths.

The guide said, suddenly, loudly, 'An eagre.'

Ferrers said, 'What?'

The guide said again, 'An eagre!'

The Commander was disorientated. He thought for a moment that the water bubbling round his horse's feet was the Welande, flowing out to the Wash.

Then the remaining mists were swept away like a veil.

He saw the army stretched across the sands, the varward division still struggling up the Fosdyke, the main-battle division close behind them. He saw the Holland shore, and the red orb of the sun falling over the Roman wall.

And then, from the sea, the eagre came.

3

Lincolnshire, the present day

A feeling of terror, of sudden panic, swept over him as the road curved and then ran straight as an arrow alongside the River Nene.

There was a heat haze over the fens, and out of it a big lorry was coming towards him. He felt the electromagnetic field round his body tighten, and a crawling sensation brushed over his skin as though unwanted attachments – as Julia would say – were clinging to his aura. 'Raiders at three o'clock!' he said to himself, breathing deeply, calmly, holding the air in his lungs and then expelling it slowly.

He pulled up on the burnt grass verge.

Heal and release, heal and release . . .

The lorry thundered past, blasting hot air and dust through the open window of his car.

It felt like soil falling lightly over his head.

These are the people most vulnerable to possession:

People with an illness involving a high fever.

People who are low in spirits or who lack self-esteem.

People who have suffered a violent impact to the body or mind so that their aura is torn. These last are the most vulnerable of all, because the distortion flares – like a beacon across time and space – and attracts visitors from other dimensions.

Silence.

He looked up at the vast, milky-white sky.

Dared he to go on? His spirits were low, his self-esteem in tatters. His mind, some might say, was disturbed.

But at least, he told himself, he did not have a high fever.

He sat for a moment watching coots, or moorhens – he wouldn't know the difference – bobbing on the shining water.

Then he turned the ignition, and went eastwards again, along the straight road.

At Spalding he stopped at a supermarket for a pot of tea.

'It says here,' said Ray Monkman, perched on a stool in the Dreamboat Café and reading from a letter, 'that he worked at Wormby once before.'

'So he knows about compering the bingo then?' said Normandie, the blonde girl behind the bar. 'And about waiting at table in Hell's Kitchen?'

'Christ, Christ,' said Ray Monkman rapidly, 'will you please try to be constructive and stop undermining my business?'

'But everybody calls it Hell's Kitchen.'

'No, no they don't.'

'Ray, there are teenagers here who have been calling it Hell's Kitchen since they were five.'

'Where else will you get scampi and chips for three quid?'

'Mablethorpe.'

He looked at her, stunned.

'So have you told this guy, this mystic,' Normandie went on, sounding increasingly like his second wife, 'about his other duties?'

'He hasn't got other duties. He's an entertainer.'

She looked at him sadly.

'Oh Ray,' she said.

'I'm not saying you're not, but he's been on television – he's been a great name in his time.'

'That time being long past?'

'Ah well . . .'

All the best things in life, his tone implied, were long past. The Clitheroe Kid. Gerry and the Pacemakers. Donny Osmond. He looked at his watch. 'If he doesn't turn up you'll have to put a lace cloth over your head and call yourself Mystic Myra.'

'No chance.'

'Just a joke, petal. I sometimes wonder about your sense of humour.'

She thought she might tell him something about her sense of humour, and why it wasn't in evidence as much as it had been. Instead she drank from a mug of tea and thought about eating a biscuit. Ray said suddenly, 'I'm not touching a drop till six,' and she said, 'Very wise.' After a moment he said, with conviction, 'I don't need it, it's only habit, and anyway I can't afford to drink Scotch these days,' and she knew that he was going to bang on about Fantasy World at Skegness. Sometimes, but not often, she felt sorry for him. His photograph in the Wormby Flats brochure showed a tanned, jolly face with a beaming smile. In real life he was grey and pouchy, with a rat-like expression. A man in his mid-fifties, she thought, with a bubble coming out of his head saying that failure was his friend.

'Imagine what would happen if I opened a dolphinarium, eh? If I opened the biggest dolphinarium this side of Florida?'

'Nobody would come to Wormby Flats to see dolphins.'

'Well of course they bloody would!'

He rambled on. It was hot and humid. Outside, children were screaming in the kiddies' pool. The extractor fan was rattling, because he wouldn't pay to have it fixed. There was a smell of stale beer because nobody ever cleaned up the sticky pools or drip trays. A subversive student waiter had phoned the environmental health officer, but nobody had come to check.

But then, nobody would come to Wormby Flats, she told herself, not from choice, not unless they'd owned a caravan here since the year dot, or were beguiled by Ray's small ads (*Wormby – Queen of Lincolnshire's Caravan Resorts*) in Yorkshire's local papers.

Only two couples were in the bar: oldies, caravan-owners from way back, sitting quietly over their bottled stout. Through an arch that was modelled in plaster like a Spanish hacienda, a sorry attempt to make holiday makers at Wormby think they were on the Costas, she could see a small, plump, homesick Australian girl, Chrissy, laying tables in the Conservatory Restaurant. Beyond the conservatory was a small garden of sea pinks, plastic windmills and dusty gnomes, and beyond that were rows of caravans that ran up to the sea wall. None of the caravans had a view of anything but each other, but at least the wall protected them from the east winds. People sat on little wooden balconies they'd built, or lay on rugs on the dry brown grass. When they weren't doing that they walked over the sea wall and sat on the small pebbly beach, or took a trip to Boston or Skegness, or went for a drive to look at Lincolnshire village churches. In the evenings they sat in the bar and listened to the disco, and watched the young folk prance about.

But these days not that many teenagers came, by choice, to Wormby Flats. There wasn't much drunkenness; very little trouble. The heats of the Miss Wormby Flats contest were on a Wednesday, the finals on a Friday. More weeks than not, the Miss Wormby Flats sash and cup (both returnable by Saturday lunchtime) adorned a fourteen-year-old with a flat chest and braces on her teeth.

There was bingo in the afternoons. An old-tyme sing-along on wet Wednesdays at 3 pm. Quiz nights Thursday. Karaoke Friday.

Generally speaking, it was all as quiet as the grave by midnight.

'You OK?' Ray Monkman asked.

'I've got a headache.'

'Oh,' he said, unsurprised.

She wished he'd go away. But where would he go? This was the Dreamboat, and he was its captain; and this bar, this confection of varnished pine, dusty mirrors, and sticky optics, was his bridge. Over his head recipes for cocktails were felt-tipped on fluorescent pink-and-yellow stars. *Sex On the Beach* said one, offering Bacardi, vodka, gin, brandy and grenadine over ice. *Slow Comfortable Screw ('There's no favourite like an old favourite' says Capt'n Ray)* said another.

'Ray,' she said. 'I want a different caravan.'

'You can have any caravan you want at this rate, petal.'

He was still on about the bookings.

'I'm dying of sleep starvation.'

'You'd know about sleep starvation if you had my worries.'

'Listen, you rat,' she said, suddenly losing her temper, 'I am an entertainer, an artiste. I was never supposed to work in the bar and unless I get a caravan where I can sleep without Mad Morag shagging her boyfriend six inches from my head I am not doing another single shift, all right, amigo?'

'What's with the Italian?'

The door opened and Jude came in. She was another Australian, far from home, but unlike Chrissy was tall, leggy and fierce. 'And here,' she said brightly, 'we have the boss.'

'Oh yes, where's the boss?' said Normandie. 'Are you the boss?' she asked the man who had come in behind Jude. 'If so, I want a word about my caravan.'

'She's suffering from sleep deprivation,' said Ray. 'She's such a party girl.'

'You're such a sod,' said Normandie.

'Shut it,' said Ray, with a note of menace. 'OK, who wants a BMW? Come on, there's a BMW going to anybody who wants one.'

'Oh God,' said Normandie.

'Nobody?' He looked round enquiringly. 'Oh well . . .'

He helped himself to the optics.

'Bacardi,' Jude explained to the man, who was smiling politely. 'Malibu and whisky.'

'You are, I take it,' said Ray, 'the Astounding Felix, our mind-reader extraordinaire?'

'Clairvoyant,' the man said, gently chiding, but entering into the spirit of things. 'Reciter of monologues and, dare I say it . . .' he paused whimsically, 'comedian.'

He wore a purple suit. His sky-blue shirt was made out of some kind of shiny material. Its top buttons were rakishly undone, showing a wrinkled old chest.

'We've enough comedians in this place already,' said Ray.

'But no clairvoyants,' said Jude, 'else we'd none of us have come here.'

'Ha, ha,' Ray laughed, sipping his drink and feeling better. 'OK, chum, let's get you settled in, show you the ropes. What I'm trying to do at Wormby Flats is to recreate the British seaside holiday of the past. Nobody really wants tacky Eighties theme parks. Sea and sand and ice-creams, that's what they want, and good old-fashioned entertainment in the evenings.'

The Astounding Felix nodded, looking at Ray attentively.

'Mind-reading tonight, monologues and comedy tomorrow afternoon in the conservatory lounge, and if your jokes are on the blue side, run them past me first. Now let's see, did we ever talk about you calling the bingo?'

They gave him fish and chips for his tea. Then Normandie led him along the rows of caravans, to the one in which he was staying. She said it was horrible, but at least he'd got it to himself. He said he was an old campaigner and she said, 'See you at eight-thirty.'

The caravan smelled faintly of old vomit. He opened his suitcase and took out his dinner jacket with the wide lapels, and his black cape with silk lining, and hung them up. He

23

took out his several pairs of shoes, black and shiny, and placed them neatly in a row.

He found, to his surprise, that the gas cylinder was not empty, and that there were teabags in the cupboard, and milk in the fridge. He made himself a cuppa, then lay down on the bed until eight o'clock, when he roused himself and dressed.

He entered the Dreamboat precisely thirty minutes before his act. He had never missed the 'half' in fifty years – no stage manager, he proudly claimed, had ever been thrown into a panic wondering where the Astounding Felix had got to. He saw Normandie standing by the tiny stage, wearing a low-cut dress, ready to strut her stuff, to enjoy her one moment of glory in the long and sordid day. She was with the boss, Ray Monkman. She smiled and waved. He waved back, gallantly, and edged his way towards the bar.

'Doesn't he seem a bit odd to you?' said Normandie.

'Weird,' said Ray. 'But mind-reading is a weird thing to go round doing. I wouldn't want people reading my mind.'

'No,' said Normandie. 'I wouldn't, either, if I had your mind.'

'You might be in for a few surprises,' he leered.

Three-in-a-bed, obviously. Him, her, and his favourite waitress. 'Staff member of the month', she reflected, had a meaning all of its own at Wormby Holiday Village.

'How much are you paying him?' she said, watching Felix order a large whisky.

'Now, petal, you know I can't discuss personal contracts.'

'I expect it's the Equity minimum.'

'Equity?' said Ray comfortably. 'What's Equity?'

Poor old sod, she thought. Ray had probably offered him a tenner a show and here he was, spending it in the bar.

'I had a talk to him while he was having his tea,' she said. 'He told me this was a proper holiday camp in the Sixties. There was a real theatre, with tabs and changing rooms, and a stage manager to say "OK, you're on, love." '

She spoke of a sweet world, lost beyond recall.

'Things move on,' said Ray.

'What exactly does that mean?'

It hadn't been meant to mean anything. He was only making conversation before her act. But women were all nasty and sharp nowadays, he told himself. It had been different in the Sixties, the time of his youth. Nobody ever heard Cliff's livin' doll answering back.

'Ray, Ray,' she said, 'are you there, Ray?'

Not that he minded them sassy, he thought, remembering Pamela from the last season but one.

The lad on the organ finished playing selections from *Evita*. Normandie turned on her mike. Ray leaned behind a curtain and turned on her stage lights. She started to sing 'Autumn Leaves'. He'd told her and told her that she ought to start her act with an upbeat number, something hot and snazzy, but she wouldn't listen, and what could you do?

She had nice tits though, he thought, as he always thought at this stage in the proceedings.

While she sang he looked round the club, noting the lads who would be trouble after three bottles of premium lager, and the retired steelworkers from Sheffield who would drink ten pints and still not fall over. He waved, discreetly, at a waitress, who tossed her head scornfully: but that didn't mean anything, he'd found.

He wondered if Psychic Sid ought to be drinking quite so many large whiskies just before his show.

'Thank you, thank you, everybody . . .'

The lights dimmed. The lad on the organ played scary music.

'Tonight,' said the DJ, who at other times worked as a sound-engineer with Radio Lincolnshire, 'we have with us a man who will probe the darkest secrets of your mind.'

He paused and stared round. There was a ripple of interest; polite, good-humoured.

'A man who will lay bare your innermost thoughts – hello, there's someone who doesn't want his thoughts laid bare.'

It was a lad, creeping off to the Gents.

'And *laid bare* is not perhaps an inappropriate choice of words.'

A table of girls shrieked. The lad blushed and grinned.

Ray, who had made his way to the bar, nodded happily. He gave Felix, who had drained his glass and was deep-breathing to strengthen his aura, a hearty pat on the back.

'Ladies and gentlemen' said the DJ, 'the man the LA police department call in when they've a crime they cannot solve – the Astounding Felix!'

He swirled out on the stage.

'I am the music master,' he said. 'I am the dreamer of dreams.'

He flicked back his black cloak lined with scarlet silk. He

smiled out into the sea of faces. He started into a story of
Doris Stokes, his great friend and mentor. It gave him time
to get the feel of the audience, to pick up the vibrations, to
isolate the auras: the muddy greens and browns that meant
unhappiness, disease, worry. The trick, as always, was to
spot the psychos, those on the edge: the women – it was
nearly always women – who might tumble into hysteria or
threaten suicide.

'Doris would always say that three was the most magical
of numbers. All things come in threes. Tragedies, deaths,
major events . . .'

Five minutes gone, and some of the punters were getting
restive.

'Now, if some young lady would kindly step forward . . .'
a slight pause, a meaningful tone, 'I should like to feel her
aura.'

A ripple of laughter. It was going well. It was going fine.
He couldn't think why terror had seized his old heart when
he passed Cambridge, and the great vista of the fens had
opened before him.

'Please! This is a serious scientific experiment! The aura,
ladies and gentlemen, is part of all living things. Every plant
has an aura, every blade of grass, every flower – as the
Prince of Wales himself was telling me only last week at
Highgrove, when he called me in for a consultation. Joking?
Sir, I never joke about the aura, or about the Royal Family.'

He led a woman out from the audience. He told her that
her aura was rose-coloured, which was the literal truth. He
told her that her brooch of moss agate would bring her riches,
happiness, and longevity.

He invited other ladies in the audience to come forward with unusual brooches or rings. He told one that lapis lazuli would endow its owner with courage and beauty. The moonstone, he told a plump girl of eighteen, promised a long youth, fruitful dreams, and successful dieting.

He talked of Soul Retrieval, that became necessary when subtle bodies split over this or other lifetimes, leading to trauma and bewilderment.

Twenty minutes gone. But now there was a buzz of conversation at the back of the room. The audience was losing interest. They wanted tricks. Three of them wanted to communicate with the dead.

And why not?

He stopped and stared out.

He held up his arms.

'There are those with us tonight,' he said, 'who would make contact with the souls of those who have passed before.'

Silence. Even at the bar, at the back of the club.

'It is the most reasonable thing in the world to want.'

A pause.

'You loved them and you want to know that they are safe and happy. You want to feel sure that they are no longer in pain.'

He had spotted the three, sensed them: two women, both middle-aged. An elderly man.

'Yes,' he said, after a moment. 'Yes, it is possible to communicate with those who have passed on. I have communicated with thousands who are now beyond the grave. But first, a word of warning.'

He was counting himself down into Alpha, feeling the

thud of his pulse, the slowing beat of his heart.

'Remember that the departed are no longer of this world. They are in a far distant country, and although it is possible to contact them – although I might be able to contact them for you now, tonight . . .'

He stared round, slowly, milking the moment.

'They may not respond. Not because they do not love you. But because they are trying to tell you something. Trying to tell you that you must learn to let go.'

Another pause. Suddenly, 'You, madam.'

The younger of the two women.

'You have lost a sister.'

Wrong. He was not far enough into Alpha, his intuition was playing him false. She was looking confused, wondering if she ought to say yes out of politeness.

'Wait. It's your mother you have lost, not your sister. That is the message I am getting. You were like sisters, and you are finding it very hard to cope, to accept your loss.'

She was nodding.

'I have a message for you, Joan. It is Joan?'

He was deep in Alpha, feeling weightlessness, focusing on his Third Eye, still counting down to slow the brainwaves.

Again the woman was nodding, her face drained of colour. A man next to her took hold of her hand.

'You have lost your mother, after nursing her through a year of cancer.'

Her mouth was open with shock.

'There is something she wants to say to you.'

He was down almost as far as Theta now, in the dangerous potent place, his Third Eye aching.

'She says to tell you that she is in a land of great peace and tranquillity. She is at peace—'

The shock came suddenly, breaking the barriers, smashing the protocols.

He was falling, falling down into Theta.

A voice in his head; low, wheedling, demanding.

It had happened forty years ago. And now it was happening again.

4

Nottingham, AD 1216

A day and a night on the road from Gloucester, riding fast along the Fosse with three horses for every man, and only a solitary scout to warn of Frenchmen raiding from Mountsorrel. Then they were clattering over the Trent at dawn with Nottingham castle floating over the mists and the first thing Lacy saw, while Cantuar screamed for the drawbridge to be lowered, was Crok the troubadour, a sly, winsome look on his catlike face.

He was hanging over Fitz Baldwin's new moat-tower and swinging a bag that contained – he called out, temptingly – the head of one of Alexander's army.

He would sell it, he said, for a shilling.

'He came with the rabble from Newark,' said Phillip Mark, Sheriff and Castellan, leading Lacy past the fires that burned in the outer bailey. 'They say he was with John when he died. For a penny he'll tell you the king's dying words, which were that he, Crok, and a washerwoman called Florence should each have a pension of twenty marks *per annum* from the demesne of Stow.'

The castle was preparing for siege. Firewood – massive tree trunks brought in from the forest – was piled high against the curtain walls. Cattle and poultry were in pens. Over a stone drain were hung sides of meat, slaughtered though it was not Martinmas, not the killing time. In the inner bailey, men were unloading grain from carts brought in from the monasteries. In the keep, in the great chamber, thick wooden shutters stood ready to replace windows that had been glazed at enormous cost.

The King was three days dead and the world was awry.

'Well?' asked Mark, turning to him as the door slammed shut.

'The Prince is at Devizes. Thomas Sandford is sent to get him. He'll be crowned in Gloucester in a week.'

'Who by? Langton's in Rome.'

'The Bishop of Winchester.'

'What of the Earl Marshall?'

'He goes to meet the Prince and the Queen at Malmsbury.'

'Earl Ranulf?'

'Marches to Gloucester.'

'And your father?'

'The same.'

Phillip Mark strode back and forth, up and down his hall, wondering which way the wind blew.

'As does William Brewer,' said Lacy, watching him.

'Yes?'

The Sheriff turned, eagerly. Brewer brought in Devon and the West. Earl Ranulf commanded Chester and the North. William the Marshall was Earl of Pembroke and ruler over Striguil and Lenster. The Lacys themselves brought in Ludlow and the Marches.

'And Fawkes de Breauté,' Lacy added.

'That madman.'

32

'He holds Cambridge.'

'He's insane. More crazed than Nicolaa de la Haye. You know I'm made joint Sheriff of Lincoln?'

'With the Lady Nicolaa?' said Lacy, startled.

'John did it hours before his death. It was done for her, mind, not for me – I'm to protect her from wolves.'

The Sheriff poured wine. Lacy sat on a bench by the fire and drank gratefully. It was good wine, not sour or greasy as it usually was this far north. October sun shone through the glazed windows, through the motes of dust and the thin, sharp, sweet-smelling smoke. The walls were hung with new tapestries – woven with vivid reds, blues, and golds. He was a man of some taste, the Sheriff of Nottingham, a clever man, despite the songs that were sung.

'You have heard what killed him?'

Lacy shook his head. Accounts to reach Gloucester had been garbled and contradictory. A midnight rider from Sire Rogier. Another from the Lady Nicolaa, begging the council to send her aid to pursue the Scotch king. They would know more of John's last days here, not twenty miles from the place where pitiless death – as a friar had exulted in Warwick market place – had pressed finally upon him.

'Burning gut,' said the Sheriff.

'The monks say this?'

'Who else? He went at midnight, as a storm rattled the roof tiles. There was also a grey fur in his throat, they say, that the medicants could not pull free. Others say he was poisoned by the Abbot of Swinehead – you know of his whoring with the Abbot's sister? Yet others say he died of rage, when his chapel and treasure was lost in the sands of Lenne.'

'There were those on the road,' said Lacy, thinking of the friar at Warwick, 'who say it was God's hand.'

'And there are those,' said Phillip Mark, 'who will now make their peace with Louis.'

A pause. The Sheriff stared into the fire, seeking pictures. 'But not I,' he added.

And it was true that he had ever been John's man.

'The corpse is being taken to Worcester,' he went on, 'all except his gut, which the Abbot of Croxton carried away as a prize. Poor John, eh? The monks had him at the end of it. But he is released from much bitterness of mind, from many disturbances.' He stared into the fire and sighed. 'From so many vain labours.'

He was mourning the loss of Normandy.

'He was a plunderer of his people,' said Lacy, drinking down his wine.

'Yet he was loyal to his friends,' Mark said softly. 'A king who paid his debts, and when did the world last see one of those?'

The wine was warm in Lacy's belly; his eyes were closing. He heard a distant bell toll the hour of Terce.

'You are on your father's business?'

The Sheriff was looking at him, curiously.

He shook his head: the Lacys held no lands in the East.

'Well then?'

He stirred himself. He stood up. 'You know Lindsay and Holland?'

'No more than I can help.'

'According to Sire Rogier, the Confessor's crown was lost along with the King's holy relics. I'm to find it before the French do and take it to Gloucester.'

Mark stared at him, then smiled faintly and nodded.

The Confessor's crown, his expression said, was a matter of little concern.

He himself was a Norman, a civilised man who cultivated roses. The Normans would have a lean time of it, whether England or France was the victor.

They went out on to the battlements and looked east. Lacy was from the Welsh Marches, and was unused to this flatness, filled as far as the eye could see with trees. Mark said, 'Tell Earl Ranulf and the Marshall that I cannot withstand a siege if they bring up engines from Windsor.'

Lacy nodded, staring out over the forest. 'I will tell them.'

Mark would hold Nottingham as long as his honour demanded it. But his thoughts, as the world knew, were already on his lands in Gascony.

'I daresay,' the Sheriff added wryly, 'that Nicolaa de la Haye will promise to hold Lincoln till Domesday.'

Lacy went down to the outer bailey, seeking the castle steward and ostler, looking for his men through the smoke of the campfires. The garrison was swelled with foresters from Sherwood and with masterless soldiers from John's army. With them were also portly men of middle age, *petit* knights of the shire, called from the comfort of their homes to render service for their land, sitting woefully over porridge and slivers of meat, drinking the thin ale brought round by castle servants.

'A shilling,' said a wheedling voice, 'is poor enough pay for a Scotchman's head.'

It was Crok, John's troubadour, though some called him by other names.

He had a bruise over one eye. He was filthy but wearing a scarlet, fur-lined pelisse, the pickings of Newark, no doubt. What songs did a troubadour sing when his master was cold clay? Who then paid his daily wage?

'You were on the sands of Lenne?' said Lacy.

'I marched with the army,' said Crok, slowly swinging his bag.

'You don't march with it now.'

Crok looked pained. The King, said his reproachful eyes, was dead.

But why had he not followed John's corpse to Worcester? Why was he not clinging still to the remnant of the court, the household?

'You know where the wagon of relics was lost?'

Crok looked at him cautiously, then nodded.

'Come with me,' said Lacy, 'and I will give you maintenance.'

Crok smiled and swung his bag – then, on a thought, his eyes darted eastwards, towards the postern gate and the vast, endless forest.

'Six men-at-arms will deal with Robin Hood,' said Lacy.

They left Nottingham an hour before Sext, riding fresh horses, heading into the east, through Sherwood, the sun at their backs. For several miles a forester guided them, then it was left to Cantuar, the King's Messenger. The road was Norman built to Belevedoir and well maintained by the forest stewards – wide enough for sixteen knights to ride abreast, or for two oxherds to touch the tips of their goads – but beyond that it was a track, fit only for packhorses.

An hour after None the mists began to fall. They reached the forest edge at dusk. Ahead lay the fens where the King's writ had never run and that were now the heartland of the rebels, the *Norrenses*. This was where John had come with sword and fire, sweeping through the eastern counties then moving swiftly away before the French in London could rally: a feint towards Windsor, a forced march to Lincoln to relieve the Lady Nicolaa de la Haye, then to Lenne to cheer the loyal defenders.

Scrubland. Black soil. A distant light that flickered for a moment.

Cantuar scouted ahead. He returned, and reported a burned-out village. Its ashes were scarcely cold, for John's army had come south less than two weeks ago. There were signs that men, outlaws most likely, had been picking over the debris.

They were too late to reach the monastery at Folchingham. They found a stream to water the horses and slept in the open. Lacy, as he lay on a bed of bracken, heard Crok the troubadour grumble under his breath. But Crok was an army man and should have been used to crawling under a hedge with his cloak wrapped round him.

Lacy slept and dreamed, of Stretton and the Roman house where they had rested on the road north after they hit the Fosse, and where his squire William had disturbed an adder in the tiled runnels beneath the floor: the adder, in his dream, was weeping for the King's death. Then he was in the castle chamber at Newark and John on his deathbed was crying out for his crown that was lost in the waters of Welland or Welstreme, and the Abbot of Swinehead was asking him if he repented of having slept with his sister.

A noise woke him in the night. Crok in his sleep, whimpering of Eustace, the black monk who commanded the French fleet.

But the traitor monk was at Sandwich still, according to intelligence.

Lacy remembered that Crok had a reputation as a seer, a necromancer.

Was the troubadour peering into the future? Was he picturing King Louis, seated on his throne in Westminster Hall, while messengers from the *Norrenses* told him that the crown of England was lost in the Wash?

Was King Louis even now ordering the French fleet to sail north to find it?

The troubadour suddenly cried out: 'The French are at Bury!'

Cantuar stirred, his hand reaching for his knife. A soldier, dragged out of a deep sleep, said, 'Fuck.'

The French were at Bury . . .

But it didn't need a seer to tell them that.

Crok was mumbling again of the black monk, the *nigro monacho*.

His reason had left him, Lacy decided. His wits were gone.

5

Wormby Flats, Lincolnshire

'Bloody marvellous! I won't pretend I know how you did it, but bloody hell!'

Faces – friendly, awed, curious – were crowded round him. Ray Monkman was waving to the barmaid, ordering drinks. 'Can you see into my mind, now?' he went on. 'Can you tell what I'm thinking?'

Somebody passed him a whisky and said, 'Here you are, mate, spirits for the spiritual.' He gulped it down.

Ray said, 'Well, what am I thinking then?'

'Leave him alone,' said Normandie, coming up, looking anxious. 'He's just done a performance, he doesn't need this. Are you all right, Felix?'

It was the smells that lingered after the faces had dissolved and his memory had been wiped by an unseen, probably mischievous, hand. Wood smoke and crushed bracken – the stink of unwashed bodies huddled close for warmth. Sour smells that filled him still with terror . . .

'Come on now,' said Ray. 'Tell me what I'm thinking about at this minute.'

'For God's sake, Ray . . .'

He stirred himself.

'You hope to have sex with a girl tonight,' he said, with

39

deep and rising malice, 'but you are not confident that you will succeed. You are worried by the figure fifteen.'

A moment's silence, then uneasy laughter. The tall Australian girl, Jude, said, 'Can't you always get it up then, Ray babe?'

'You go to bed with fifteen-year-olds,' Normandie said severely, 'and you'll get put in prison.'

'Oh Christ,' said Jude. 'He's here again.'

A boy was in the doorway, looking round, his eyes hurt and resentful.

'Listen. I have never, ever,' said Ray earnestly, 'had a go at a fifteen-year-old.'

Felix said, 'Excuse me,' and pushed his way out through the crowd.

He stumbled through the darkness. His mind was still fuzzy, still half in the Otherworld. He thought of phoning Julia but he had no mobile, and anyway he was too tired to speak to Julia. Inside his caravan he gulped down a glass of water, then took off his clothes and crept, exhausted, under the blankets. Soon he heard people making their way back from the Dreamboat. He heard the contented murmuring of the middle-aged; the long, shouted good-nights of children who were being forced to go to bed.

Later, still wakeful – scared of sleep and what it might bring – he heard the waiters and kitchen workers as they came back to the staff caravans. A girl gave a scream of anger and a boy laughed a stupid laugh. He drifted into a doze, only to be awakened by two people having an argument outside his window, six inches, it seemed, from his head.

'I just don't understand what you're saying.'

'Jesus, Simon, I don't know any other way to say it.'

'Everything was fine on Saturday. I don't understand what can have happened between then and now.'

'Nothing has happened. I just want to be on my own for a bit, OK?'

'I think you owe me an explanation.'

'I don't fucking owe you anything.'

'Just tell me what I've done wrong!'

'You've done nothing wrong.'

'I'm coming into your caravan.'

'You try it, and I will unscrew your head and drink your brains.'

Felix, in the dark, shuddered.

'If I've done something wrong I'm sorry . . .'

They moved away. Felix lay in the silence.

A sea bird called in the night.

Soon he was back in 1962.

Girls were Glam. Young bodies danced to the Twist.

There was a girl, a young chanteuse, who had a passion for Kunzle Cakes, the cake in a chocolate shell. Each day they drank frothy coffee together, served in glass cups. One afternoon they went to Boston, in his yellow bubble-car, to see Sue Lyon in *Lolita*.

Later they made love, on the beach at Wrangle as the sun went down.

Afternoons in her chalet, listening to Adam Faith and Bob Dylan.

Nights on stage in the camp theatre – *the Astounding*

Felix, as seen on Commercial Television!

Then he'd had his attack.

Epilepsy. Just like Napoleon and Julius Caesar, they told him at the hospital.

But had Napoleon and Julius Caesar been summoned by the dead?

Really summoned – not just chatted to by characters who were, in a manner of speaking, part of the act? Not just by the spirits of Red Indians, who by rights ought to be members of Equity?

He woke in the early dawn, startled by the silence, the absence of traffic roaring along Hanger Lane. For a second he thought he must be in digs somewhere – back in the old routine, with a landlady's breakfast of fatty bacon and tinned tomatoes to look forward to; a day reading newspapers in some provincial library. Then he remembered where he was and why, and his old heart began to thud.

At eight he got up and dressed, made a pot of tea, and then went to the phone outside the club.

'It's happened.'

The weather had changed during the night and a sea mist swirled round the caravans. The kiosk was beaded with moisture.

She said calmly, 'The same as last time?'

'If anything, stronger.'

He felt the morning chill seep into his bones.

'And did you find out what you wanted to know?'

She was using her professional voice, the voice she used when she spoke to little ladies who came to her for soul retrieval, or when she gave Hopi-ear therapy sessions at the BBC in Shepherds Bush.

'No.'

A pause. Perhaps a faint sigh down the line.

'How much do you remember?'

'Very little.'

He watched drops of rain fall into the cold waters of the kiddies' pool. The wind, an unseen hand, sent shivers over the water.

'There was a forest.'

'Anything else?'

For a moment before his eyes, the knight, grey-faced with exhaustion, the white cross on his surcoat filthy with mud.

'A knight,' he said. 'Anxious about something.'

'It may be that you are projecting your own anxiety. I can see a scabbard. Did the knight have a scabbard?'

'I don't know.'

'When will you try again?'

Not 'Is it wise to try again?' Not 'Think of the dangers before you try again.' She *wanted* him to try again – basically, of course, she wanted him out of her front room; him and his sadness, his worries that lurked (despite the space clearing and the little tinkly bells she hung over the doorway) in the dark corners and behind the furniture.

'I've my comedy routine tonight. Then I'm booked for mind-reading again on Saturday.'

'But you have another two mind-reading sessions next week?'

'Yes.'

'Well then. Take it slowly. Do you feel anything from around you?'

He looked out at the rows of caravans, the sea wall grey through the misty drizzle. There was a small, curious-looking garden by the entrance to the club. It had concrete paths and little grottos with windmills on them, and heathery plants, and garden gnomes that fished or held Bambi deer in their arms.

'No, nothing.'

'No feeling,' Julia went on, 'for the past?'

'I know that I have been here before.'

'1962,' she said, dismissively.

'Before that.'

There was another pause.

'What are you doing today?'

'This morning,' he said, looking at the leaden skies with a small stirring of professional satisfaction, 'I am engaged for poetry reading and comedy in the Conservatory Lounge.'

'What will you give them?'

'Hilaire Belloc. Kipling.'

'If you can keep your head,' said Julia.

'Yes,' said Felix.

His head. His mind. His brain.

'I'm not sure,' she said cautiously, 'about your comedy routine.'

'I have studied a new poem,' he said, firmly. ' "A High Tide on the Coast of Lincolnshire".'

A pause.

'Take care,' she said, then added with false warmth:

44

'Remember that if you change your mind, you can always come back to the put-u-up.'

Later he made his way through the sea mist to the Conservatory Lounge. A notice by the Spanish adobe arch told him that yesterday at this time there had been the pre-Teens Disco, and tomorrow there would be American Line Dancing. Today, though, it was entertainment for the old folk, for the wrinklies. About twenty of them were drinking tea and eating slices of buttered malt loaf. The conservatory was glass on three sides and the whiteness outside, through which nothing could be seen, gave the proceedings a surreal quality. It was as if the Dreamboat had become a ghost ship, sailing through foggy Arctic seas.

'Today, ladies and gentlemen, we have with us the man who can make you tingle,' said Ray Monkman, holding a fat slice of malt loaf and looking casual in a knitted cardigan. 'No, love, don't get all excited, the milkman hasn't come on holiday.'

The wrinklies cackled, there being nothing like an old 'un.

'One day this man can make you shake with fear, and the next with laughter. Ladies and gentlemen, to bring back the monologues of yesteryear and show us the lighter side of life – the Astounding Felix!'

The boy on the organ played 'Happy Days Are Here Again'. Felix strode out, a smile on his face, a jaunty bounce to his step.

'When I went to my digs in Wormby the landlady asked me if I could make my own bed. "Certainly," I said, so she gave me a hammer and a piece of wood . . .'

Silence. Then a little boy, brought by his grandma, laughed. 'Thank you, thank you,' said Felix warmly, pretending that the applause had been universal, but after only a few more gags he abandoned the comedy, and stood before them looking solemn.

'Ladies and gentlemen. I would like to recite for you an old Victorian favourite from this part of the world. "The High Tide on the Coast of Lincolnshire".'

He began powerfully, with maximum energy, surprising them all, making them stop chewing at their malted loaf and listen.

> 'The Old Mayor climbed the belfry tower,
>> The ringers ran by two, by three.
> "Pull, if ye never pulled before;
>> Good ringers, pull your best," quoth he.
> "Play up, play up, O Boston bells!
> Play all your changes, all your swells,
>> Play up *The Brides of Enderby*." '

He stopped and looked round. Suddenly the wind howled round the Conservatory Lounge, and the sea mists swirled, and rain splattered against the glass. One or two women – perhaps putting it down to his psychic power over the elements – gave a nervous laugh. He lowered his voice.

> 'Men say it was a stolen tide –
>> The Lord that sent it, He knows all;
> But in mine ear doth still abide
>> The message that the bells let fall . . .'

Afterwards, Ray Monkman said, 'Can I have a word?'

They went into the bar.

'They're a good-natured lot,' Ray said, 'and I'm not saying it's not been good patter in its time – that line about there being a dirty great crack down your bedroom wall but you couldn't read it because it was in Welsh, was a new one on me. But the world's moved on.'

Felix nodded. He knew as well as any man how the world had moved on.

'When you wrote and said you were available for a fortnight, I thought well why not give it a go? I've been trying for some time to turn the Dreamboat into a popular local night spot. A stroll along the beach, a few drinks, a meal from our exciting new menu – have you seen our exciting new menu?'

Felix hadn't.

'You can have goujons of sole,' said Ray, 'followed by deep-fried vanilla ice cream with honey.'

Felix looked impressed.

'And after they've eaten, the idea is to give them live entertainment that's more than just a local DJ belting out disco music. Sophisticated food and sophisticated humour. Something to bring in the punters from Wisbech and Boston. You with me?'

Felix nodded.

'The monologues and poems – well, the old biddies liked them, and I'm all for a bit of culture. It's the jokes that are the trouble. We were going to try a spot of comedy in the Dreamboat tonight, weren't we?'

Felix nodded again.

'Perhaps we ought to have a rethink. Telling the punters you're staying in a two-star hotel and can see both of them through your bedroom ceiling is very funny, I laughed like a drain myself . . . but it's not sophisticated.'

'No.'

Ray punched him lightly on the arm, which hurt. 'Clairvoyance, tonight, chum. That's what you're here for, that's what you're good at.'

He tried to phone Julia again, but there was only her answer phone, with its message of peace and serenity. He tried to lie down and rest, but was overcome by panic and got up again and went outside, and paced up and down the grass, smoking a cigarette.

Clairvoyance tonight . . .

It was why he had come to Wormby, after all.

Was his courage going to fail now?

Sea birds overhead – a cloud of gulls, screaming suddenly, for no obvious reason. A memory, fleeting, came and was gone.

He turned and walked away from the staff caravans, finding the path that went up to the dunes, up through the marsh grass and sea pinks. He reached the sea wall, his mind still confused with shadowy memories – of 1962, certainly, but also of another time: other seashores, perhaps, other places. The mist had cleared and the sun was shining with surprising heat. Eastwards, the salt marshes gave way to grey mud that stretched to the sea. There was a smudge of smoke from a distant ship. The smell of salt on the warm, damp wind.

His eyes filmed over. He searched for echoes in his mind. Nothing.

He turned and looked inland.

A flat, empty landscape under a vast sky. A metalled road running by a dyke. Closer, a field path, and a little wooden footbridge in a froth of white flowers. A solitary farmhouse.

His eyes lingered, for a moment, on the farmhouse.

He looked to the west, to the holiday village – its lines of caravans huddled against the sea wall like an army encamped in the fold of a mountain – and in the far, far distance, the tall tower of Boston church.

' "All fresh the level pasture lay," ' he muttered, turning south and walking rapidly along the sea wall, his head down. ' "And not a shadow mote be seen –

> Save where full five good miles away
>> The steeple towered from out the green;
> And lo! the great bell far and wide
> Was heard in all the country side
> That Saturday at eventide." '

'Hiya,' called Normandie.

She was lying in the sand dunes in a bikini, sunning herself. 'I'm getting away from Ray Monkman for a couple of hours,' she said, smiling up at him. 'How are you getting on, then? Come and join me if you like.'

He was confused; half in another world, another time.

'It's very kind of you, but I thought I'd go for a walk. I feel –' he added, not wanting to seem discourteous – 'in need of some exercise.'

Two teenage lads, scouting through the long grass in search of topless girls, stared up at him in disbelief.

'You're doing a show tonight?' she asked.

He nodded.

'Listen. Don't take any notice of Ray. He's a bastard. He's the same to everybody.'

He said, bravely, 'I've known many a bastard in my time.'

'I'll bet.'

She smiled again, warmly, then turned and lay on her back. He walked on. Behind him one of the teenage boys said something, daringly, and he heard Normandie reply, 'In your dreams, little boy.'

He walked rapidly along the sea wall until he came to a sign pointing down to a path – the path that ran across the fields, past the farm and over the little bridge. He went down it. By the farmhouse was a paddock containing a pony and a small, modern caravan. 'I know what they *claim*,' said a voice through the caravan's open window as he passed, 'but my readings are significantly different. We're just lucky that Janus-configured, Broadband ADCPs provide two independent methods of observation . . .'

He stopped to look at the farm. It was redbrick and utilitarian. It had metal-frame windows with the paint curling off them and a vast satellite dish attached to a chimney. A concrete-covered yard had weeds pushing up through cracks and was stained with engine oil.

A woman was hanging out washing while a girl pretended to help. He caught the girl's eye. She was sixteen or seventeen and he had seen her before. His heart thudded suddenly. She looked at him and smiled, then turned away.

He remembered: she had served him his whisky last night in the club.

'How was your walk, then?'

Normandie was sitting on the step of her caravan. The thin, fair-haired boy, Simon, sat next to her. He ignored Felix and said, 'At least she ought to have the common decency to give me an explanation.'

'Yes,' said Normandie, 'she certainly ought to do that.'

'I mean, why can't she?'

'I don't know.'

He stared moodily at the ground, then abruptly stood up and walked away. Normandie said, 'Young love. You OK?'

He nodded.

'I heard your poetry reading was great.'

'I'm afraid that Mr Monkman thought otherwise.'

'He's not called Mr Monkman, is he, Jude?'

Jude was loping down the line of caravans, peering from side to side like a Red Indian.

'What do we call Mr Monkman, Jude?'

'We call him Bastard,' said Jude. 'Has Simon been about?'

'You've just missed him.'

'Oh God.'

'Let's go inside have a cup of tea.'

'So long as he hasn't seen me,' said Jude. 'If he finds me, I don't want to be trapped.'

They went inside the caravan. It smelt of soap and perfume. 'He can't understand why you've suddenly changed,' said Normandie, making tea, opening biscuits.

'It isn't sudden. I've spent nearly a week letting him down

51

gently. But it's no use. If I'm snogging Pierre he thinks it's just because I want to hurt him. He can't get it into his head that we're finished. What am I going to do?'

She looked at Felix as if at the Wise Old Man of the Mountains.

'I once had a yellow bubble-car,' said Felix. 'And a girl covered it in pink lipstick hearts.'

'Did you care for her?'

'I did at the time,' he said, remembering her warm lips, her hair in his face.

'Men,' said Jude.

He said suddenly, 'I shouldn't have come back here.'

They both looked at him, surprised.

Normandie said gently, 'Why not?'

'Because this is an unlucky place for me.'

'Are we still talking about the girl and the bubble-car?' said Jude, curling herself on the bed, her long brown legs tucked under her, ready for a story.

They both looked at him expectantly.

'I'm sorry,' he said. 'I shouldn't have spoken. There are many perils,' he went on, trying to sound ironic and humorous, 'for those who would delve into the secrets of the human mind.'

'Is it to do with your act?' said Normandie.

Her aura was gold, the colour of success and of the occult.

He nodded.

Outside a voice said, 'Jude?'

'Shit.'

Jude slid down under the table.

'Jude?'

'Tell him I'm not here.'

Felix said, 'Excuse me,' and got up.

Jude, from under the table, said, 'Will you please tell him I've gone to Paris?'

When the light began to fade he drank two glasses of whisky, put on the second of his freshly laundered, carefully folded dress shirts, then his black dinner suit and his cloak. He walked along the hard parched path sniffing, like an old hound, the smell of chips and beer. Suddenly there was another scent in his nostrils – dry grass on the summer night air – and he heard the sound of a girl singing, and in his mind saw the moon glimmering on the sea, and the froth of waves on a pebble shore.

1962 again, he thought with a pang of loss, of regret.

He looked up, sharply, sensing a movement, a shadow – something casting itself over his mind.

But it was only a bird, sweeping silently over his head, heading inland to its nest.

In the club bar he ordered another whisky. The barmaid was the girl from the farmhouse who had helped her mother with the washing.

Where had he seen her before?

'Some other place,' Julia would say, matter-of-factly, 'some other life.'

Julia was always meeting people she knew from previous incarnations.

'Your change.'

The girl spoke mechanically, not looking at him, turning to another customer.

He drank it in one gulp, feeling his head buzz, knowing, even as he swallowed the liquor, that drugs and alcohol weakened the will, leaving the body defenceless, open for a stronger will to capture. Behind him, the Fab Fifties Hour was ending with a burst of 'Jailhouse Rock'.

'Elvis. The King. Is he dead or isn't he?'

It was the Brylcreem DJ.

'Perhaps we can get a message from him – here tonight in Wormby. Are you out there, Elvis?'

The lights were going down. The lad on the organ was playing spooky music.

'Those of you who were here last night know what it is to have your minds read. You girls, eh?'

He paused, staring round at the girls, not without effect.

'Who'd have thought what was in your minds?'

They tittered politely.

Felix felt a hot spurt of anger. Little sod. Sending an artiste up, seconds before his act. Ruining the atmosphere.

Christ, who was this leaning against him, whispering sweet nothings?

'A woman with a pink blouse, a big woman.'

It was Ray Monkman.

'She's from King's Lynn and she's got a cat called Little Beth. Perhaps you can have Little Beth pining for her mistress, eh? But not pining too much,' Ray went on beerily, 'or she might bugger off.'

He punched Felix on the arm, a whimsical habit of his, increasingly painful to its recipients, and disappeared.

Felix looked round for the girl who had served him his drink. He pointed to the optic and waved his glass.

'Ladies and gentlemen, the man who's already the talk of Skeggy...'

Too late.

'The Astounding Felix!'

Alpha could provide protection. It would alter the state of consciousness, of course, and heighten the state of psychic perception. It would increase the dangers, as Julia had warned him, but it would also protect against them.

Elementals rarely appeared to someone in an Alpha state. And if they did you could deal with them, say the words of power – *Go to your true place now as I am in mine. I accept no evil thought, word or deed. I send it back to its source.*

He counted himself down into Alpha as he swept out onto the stage and turned to face the audience.

6

Woken's Eye, AD 1216

'Woken's Eye,' said Cantuar, reining in his horse.

A sea wall, built by the Romans. A ruined watchtower. A causey running back through the swamps towards Moulton Second and Quaplode. A village, churchless, built half on the silt and half in the wet mud. Three small fields, ditched.

They sat their horses, on the earth wall, looking out into the falling darkness. A cold wind blew from it, from the void.

'The end of the world,' said Cantuar, a king's messenger who knew all the world that was to be known.

They built a fire. The wood was damp and smoke billowed, and the Sweet Christ knew how long it would take for meat to cook, though William skinned the conies with the urgency of a boy of twelve who has not eaten since daybreak.

The men drew lots. Four fell asleep while the other two mounted guard. Cantuar disappeared towards the village. Lacy climbed up the crumbling masonry of the tower, taking Crok the troubadour with him.

Wings flapping overhead: geese or shrikes roused by the sentries. There was the cry of a bird, as there always was at daygate, when the last of the light was gone. There was no moon, yet, but he could make out a faint luminescence to the east. By it, he could see black water running through mud banks.

Crok, beside him, shivered in his fur-lined pelisse. Was he thinking of the *nigro monacho*? If Eustace and his fleet were in the bay, they would know nothing of it – not until they heard the splash of oars. Roman sentries, Lacy thought, must have stood like this, watching and listening for the barbarians. Their marks were still on the stones, dog-Latin, carved in the long hours of idleness.

He remembered that Crok had Latin, which meant that he must have been a cleric of some kind in his early days.

'Well?' he said. 'Was this the place?'

Crok nodded. He was staring out to the sea, his face to the cold wind.

'What happened?'

Crok knew little. He had been with the King. They had travelled ahead of the army after leaving Wisbeche. They had waited – King and bodyguard, seneschal and chamberlain, the clerks of the chancellery – at the Roman camp, a mile beyond the shore.

Messengers had gone back and forth. A wagon was lost, men were drowned. He, Crok, had eventually gone down the track to the Fosdyke shore and found Florence the washerwoman, and Ferling the huntsman, and had asked if Thomas de Porkericiis and the hounds were safe – and William the *Aquarius*, though if an aquarius could not survive the sea then who could?

They had laughed at that.

'But this,' said Lacy, abruptly, 'was where the army came?'

Crok nodded. There was a hidden track across the estuary:

the guides would mark it out with poles in the morning, when the tide fell.

'Where are these guides?'

Crok shrugged. He had never been of the commissariat, he had never served with the scouts. The guides would perhaps have been killed when the wagons were lost: or more likely they would have melted into the fens and still lurked there.

'Like the Eorl Hereward,' he said.

Lacy said, 'Eorl Hereward was in the time of the Conqueror.'

Crok said nothing. Then he tittered in the darkness.

Lacy wondered about him, this killer of Scotchmen, this singer of ditties, this necromancer. Was he laughing still at his joke about the *aquarius*? Or could he truly see Hereward the Wake, a ghost still walking the fens?

They clambered back down the tower. It had a single room, still serviceable though the peat roof was rotting. In it were the horses, the worst rounceys that the Sheriff of Nottingham's bailiff could palm off on them, but worth three pounds apiece even so.

Cantuar had returned from his scouting. 'There's a path, though they use punts for the most part.'

'Is there a manor?'

'Of sorts,' said Cantuar. 'Everyone is fled.'

In time they ate: the three coneys, a hind quarter of pig. Two men were posted as sentries, to guard the horses from thieving villagers. The others went back to sleep again. Lacy sat with his back to the wall, wrapped in his cloak.

Crok was curled asleep, his arms round his loathsome bag.

How much of John's treasure, Lacy wondered, had been lost in the quicksands? How much had been looted in the chaos of Newark?

Crok had his pelisse, but had clearly not looted the treasure chests or he would not have drifted penniless to Nottingham. Where had he killed his Scotchman? The Scotch army had disappeared into the north when John raised the siege of Lincoln . . .

A sentry came rustling back through the undergrowth. Horses were approaching: he could hear them across the still waters, see a man with a torch lighting their way.

'Well?' said Lacy, turning to Cantuar.

Cantuar hesitated. '*Norrenses*, maybe, moving north from Bury.'

Norrenses. Northern earls who had thrown in their lot with the French – but it had become the slang word, these days, for any rebel troops.

His men were on their feet, reaching for their bows. They threw earth on the fire. The archers found places for themselves in the ruins of the tower and along the bank: they would fall back into the one secure room with the horses, if need be.

Soon Lacy could hear them: horses and riders, moving quietly for the most part, an occasional sharp word in French but that meant nothing. Then an English voice, loud and alarmed:

'Ware, ware!'

They had seen the fire or, more likely, caught the smell of wood smoke.

Silence.

Lacy could hear a rushing, gurgling noise. It was the sea: the tide sweeping in across the salt marshes, running up against the wall, beating gently against it.

An age passed. Unbelievably he found his head nodding, his eyes closing. He had been three days and nights on the road from Gloucester.

On the fire, which had been only partially doused, a branch fell. A flame spurted and his head jerked up.

A horse and rider, motionless on the edge of the undergrowth.

It was a woman. Her ox-skin cloak was worn with the hair on the outside, after the way of country people, but was fastened with a gold clasp. Her hair was gathered into a gold *crespine*.

She edged her horse into the firelight.

'Madam,' he said, and stood up slowly and carefully, for her men would have their crossbows wound and at this distance a bolt would take away a man's stomach. He slipped back his cloak to show his knight's red tunic, on it the white cross of England.

He did not need to ask her name. She was Nicolaa de la Haye, Castellan of Lincoln, friend, and sometime lover, of King John.

The fire flamed suddenly: pig bones and fat catching fire.

Black smoke billowed round her head.

Crok, in the darkness, tittered.

7

Wormby Flats, Lincolnshire

He fell to his knees and lay panting, grasping hold of the rough sea grass, squeezing it to feel the pain of reality. In his nostrils was the smell of sea buckthorne, its leaves crushed, and the acrid smoke of burning meat.

A movement.

A figure, dark against the salt marshes.

He flattened himself: petrified, having forgotten how to breathe.

A voice – but all he could hear at first was the thud, thud of his old heart.

'Are you all right?'

After a moment he looked up.

A man, silhouetted against the sky. A dim, bearded face. Bare, muscular legs. Shorts and sandals, and a jumper against the night chill.

He gave a little laugh. 'I'm fine,' he said, and staggered up, lurching so that the man put out a hand to help him.

'Oops,' said Felix, stumbling again, looking along the shore for reassurance – then his heart stopped, for in the distance a fire blazed.

'Are you staying at the camp? Or, as perhaps I ought to say, the holiday village?'

After a moment, Felix said, 'Yes.'

'I'll walk back with you.'

Solicitous, kindly.

'There's no need.'

'I'm heading that way. My landlady's daughter works in the clubhouse.' He held up a bottle of whisky. 'I'm invited to the staff barbecue.'

Felix remembered being told about the staff barbecue.

They walked along the wall and then down a path to the shore, jumping over the rock pools, the channels of mud that still ran with water from the receding tide. Eventually they came to the small pebbly beach and the figures round the driftwood fire. One of them was Normandie, who said, 'What happened to you then?'

'I felt the need of some fresh air.'

'We were terribly worried when you walked out like that.'

'Just like a zombie,' said the tall Australian, Jude. 'Everybody thought it was part of your act and that you'd come back wearing a Dracula outfit. You remember that woman you asked to think of a number? Well, she's probably still thinking it. I don't think Ray was happy.'

'Good,' said a voice.

'The important thing,' said Normandie, 'is that you're all right.'

He felt a sudden warmth that somebody cared: then a stab of self-pity, for nobody had said anything like it in a long time.

'Come and sit down by me,' she said. 'You can have a hot dog in a minute.'

He sat by the fire. The young man who had found him in

the dunes sat down between two girls and grinned through his bushy, piratical beard, and opened his bottle of Scotch. The staff of the Dreamboat said 'Ooh,' appreciatively, then looked at Felix, waiting for him to produce something to drink.

Normandie said, 'Felix is my guest.'

'Welcome to the Mid-season Staff Party, Felix,' said a boy, passing him a can of beer.

He was still in another world, still half expecting to see the watch tower silhouetted against the sky, the flicker of torches along the causeway – a woman with gold glinting in her hair . . .

'Cheers,' he said, gulping down the warm lager.

Sausages and lamb chops cooked over the makeshift grill. There was a large tray of bread rolls and sliced ham.

'If you want to know what the Bastard contributed,' said a voice, 'the answer's sod all.'

'So Vicky helped herself.'

'You told me to do it,' said a girl, defensively.

'Vicky, we said get *some* ham, we didn't say get *all* the ham.'

'He won't know it was me, will he?' said Vicky, panicky.

'He always knows it's you, Vicky.'

'Oh my God,' she cried.

'You'll have to go into Boston early tomorrow and buy ham. Lots and lots of ham.'

'Will somebody come with me?'

'I will,' said the camp organist, a lad known as Penguin because of the dinner jacket that Ray made him wear in the cause of sophistication.

'Oh, right,' Vicky said without enthusiasm, for Penguin was considered creepy.

Simon, the rejected lover, sat by Jude. He tried to imply, by his protective proximity, that they were still together. Her body language said that they were not. He passed her a can of beer and she said 'Thanks,' in a voice as far away as the moon.

A girl played a guitar and sang about home.

'But, Chrissy, you don't want to go home,' said Jude. 'Your parents keep trying to make you go back to Australia and you keep refusing to go.'

'It doesn't mean I don't love them!'

'Well, of course it doesn't.'

'It's my little sister's birthday. They'll be having a picnic in the Grampians. I'd just like to be there, you know?'

'A barbie under the eucalyptus trees,' said Jude, heartlessly.

'Yes, yes, we used to go and pick olives,' said Chrissy, sniffing.

Somebody passed Felix the bottle of whisky. He took a huge gulp, then another. They all stared at him. He passed the bottle on with a smile of apology.

The girl from the farm was holding her hands out to the flames. A boy leaned over and kissed her.

Where had he met her before?

The boy was fumbling with her shirt. Another girl pushed him hard and said, 'Don't do that here, please.'

'Let me get it right,' Normandie was saying to the bearded man from the beach. 'You're a marine physicist but nothing to do with the Environment Agency?'

'God, no. MAFF is responsible for coastal defence.'

'So you're MAFF?'

'Well, no, but they're the people who've given the contract to CCMS.'

'Which is?'

'The Centre for Coastal and Marine Sciences.'

'And that's you?'

'Ultimately. At the moment I'm seconded to FORCE.'

'FORCE?'

'We forecast the progress of coastal evolution.'

'A marine physicist with FORCE. It's obviously a cover. If you take over the world, I hope you'll be kind to the little people.'

The little Australian girl was playing her guitar again, singing a song about a park in old Kalgoorlie, where the bougainvillaea grew. Tears ran down her face. She was not used to whisky, to its propensity to cause melancholy.

'Oh Chrissy,' said Jude. 'You've never been to Kalgoorlie in your life. How can you get nostalgic about somewhere you've never been?'

Later a group of children appeared, teenagers from the Holiday Village looking for a midnight adventure.

One of them said, 'Got any beer, then?'

Normandie said, 'Sorry, kids.'

They sat on the fringe of the circle, like little animals.

'This is one hell of a party,' said a sad, student voice.

'Why don't we go and trash the gnomes?' said another.

'No, Pierre,' said Normandie. 'Please don't.'

'At the end of the day,' the marine physicist was saying, as he had been saying, it seemed to Felix, for some time, 'a coastline is a balance between factors like geology, engineering intervention, storm surges, and changes in the mean sea level.'

'You make it sound convincing,' Normandie said, 'but I know an alien when I meet one.'

'All FORCE does,' he laughed, 'is develop methods to identify areas at risk in terms of flood protection.'

'I'm not listening. You're the man who came out of the night.'

The girl from Western Victoria was sobbing. Jude said, 'Hey, come on, Chrissy. You don't want to be back there.'

But she did. She really did.

The wind was rising, chill and damp, carrying drops of rain. The fire flared and spat. Felix looked across the flames again, to the girl who had served him behind the bar, the girl from the farmhouse. Her name, he had discovered, was Karen Tymoor. She was asleep, leaning against her boyfriend, while he held her in the crook of his arm. How old was she, sixteen, seventeen? Younger than the others. Too young to be groped in the dark by a boy.

Wood smoke swirled suddenly and filled his eyes and his nostrils. He could smell burning herbs and meat fat.

A dark, dirt-streaked face. Sinews of flesh pulled through white teeth.

The firelight shining on her brooch.

'Come on,' said Normandie, her arm round him, for he was swaying, 'let's take you home.'

The marine physicist helped her. They supported Felix back

up the path through the dunes, and then down the Heritage path to the caravans.

'I shouldn't be here,' said Felix at one point.

'None of us ought to be here,' said Jude, coming down the path behind them.

'We're going to sing outside the Bastard's caravan,' said a voice. 'Anybody coming?'

'Oh don't, please, Pierre,' said Normandie, who would bear the brunt of Ray Monkman's rage the following day. But they were gone, leaving her with Felix and the marine physicist.

'Are you all right, Felix?'

'I'm fine, sweetie.'

He didn't sound fine.

'Just a bit of toothache,' he added.

They helped him to his caravan. He went inside and determinedly shut the door.

'Well,' said Normandie, after a moment. 'Fascinating though anthropogenic pressures and multi-spectral scanners are, and cool though this party has been, I have to go to bed.'

'I'll walk you home,' said the marine physicist.

'I am home, pathetic though that might sound.'

'I'm in no hurry. I can't go to bed till I've downloaded some stuff from the satellite at two.'

'Still, you ought to be there. They might send it early. Night, and thanks for your help.'

She left him. The mist had thickened. There were one or two lights scattered among the caravans, otherwise the world was in darkness. She could hear him behind her.

'Oh,' she said turning, pretending surprise. 'It's you. I wondered who it was.'

'I forgot to tell you my name,' he said. 'It's Michael.'

'Oh, right, Michael. Well, goodnight.'

She went quickly into her caravan, fearful that if she didn't move fast he would start talking again about sediment transport in combined waves and currents. She said, 'Morag?' but Morag and her boyfriend were in his caravan, thank God, though how she could do it with three other blokes lying there only inches away Normandie couldn't imagine.

She cautiously looked out through the window but the man from FORCE had gone.

Felix woke in the night. His head throbbed: a pain behind his eyes. Dehydration – a sinus attack. He fumbled with the sheet that had wound itself tightly round his body, and tumbled out of his narrow bed. He drank the warm, chemical-tasting water that trickled out of the plastic tap. His pyjamas were damp with sweat. He would have liked a clean pair – laundered and smelling of lavender, for he had a taste for cleanliness – but he had no clean pyjamas and would wear his sweaty ones again tomorrow night, unless he found his way to a launderette (very unlikely), or paid a chalet girl to do some washing for him. He was too old for this, he told himself, staring out through the grimy window, his eyes pricking with self-pity. There was a faint luminescence in the sky, motorways and street lights reflected from twenty miles away. Nowadays the sky was never truly dark in England.

Not as it once had been.

His left eye throbbed, the blood pumping round the veins of his body. He drank again, feeling sick.

Something was with him.

Something in the caravan.

Not a manifestation – it was in his mind. It was probing the frontiers of his consciousness. It was examining him.

Curiosity killed the cat, he wanted to say – and having formulated the thought, of course, he had said it.

'Curiosity killed the cat!'

He had said it, though his mouth had not opened, and not a sound had been made. The thought, the words, existed now as chemicals, as atoms of electricity, in the warm blood-filled crevices of his brain.

He felt a terrible heaviness. A perspiration broke out on his skin.

He had been detected again. Spied from the watchtower.

He climbed back into bed, pulling up the sheet, the blanket, trying to count himself down into Alpha, his place of safety.

Too late.

Now it was a voice in his head.

The King's justice . . .

Then again, louder.

The King's justice in eyre . . .

8

Moulton Church, AD 1216

'The King's justice in eyre . . .'

But which king's justice? Or to put it another way, thought Crok, the justice of which king?

He sat on the edge of the dais and cracked pignuts with the sokesmen of Woken's Eye and Moulton Second, and laughed to himself, despite his ravening hunger.

He pictured King John's corpse, that was even now being born to Worcester. This, he told himself, was a king in a coffin. A king who was a *supplicant* for justice, not a king who *dispensed* it. He sniggered and cracked another nut, while his mind's eye glided south down the Severn, and found in the forests a woman, the pale fair Isabelle of Angoulême, and her son, the young Prince Harry, hurrying north to escape the French with only Sir Thomas Sandford and four knights of the household to protect them.

This was a king uncrowned. A king not yet knighted even – and who would knight him, indeed, now his father was dead? That would be a knotty problem for the Council, thought Crok, staring round the church and chomping nuts.

The hundred jury of Ellowe Wapentake is called to stand and be sworn before Nicolaa de la Haye, the King's High Sheriff . . .

* * *

His mind's eye winged its way eastward to London, where Hobregge, the Dean of St Paul's, had preached that Louis of France was the true King of England, legitimised through his marriage to Blanche of Castille, descendant of King Henry the Second.

How John had railed at Hobregge! How he had yearned to put his eyes out, to sear with a burning brand his traitorous tongue!

Louis of England! *Rex Anglorum!*

Now here was a true king. A king on a throne. A king with an army at his back, and with London at his feet. A king whose French knights held the Cinque Ports, and whose admiral, the black monk Eustace, held the Channel.

What was Louis, *Rex Anglorum*, thinking this fine October morning, as he sat in Westminster Hall on the day before the feast of Crispin and Crispian?

The Petty Lord of Woken's Eye, a man called Pilche, was bringing forward a villein, John de Quyercubus, who it seemed had been singing for the love of certain women who were standing in a field when Hugh Weston, who was immensely drunk and hated John because he sang so well, took a naked sword and cried out that he would kill him. At which John went down on his knees and raised his hands asking God's peace, but Hugh ran at him with the sword, so John drew his knife and killed him instantly.

Ha, ha, laughed Crok, who liked to be with the King's Sheriff in court, who liked to watch how the world turned.

He giggled and chomped, and felt a sharp stab of pain in his tender molars. He stopped chewing and cautiously probed his teeth, of which he had nine, with his tongue.

John de Quyercubus pardoned for homicide at the instance of the Lord of Woken's Eye.

Crok's mind went back to Worcester, and the remnants of the army that bore the King's corpse to its resting place. Was Thomas de Porkericiis still running with the King's hounds? Was Ferling the huntsman still in attendance, with the hawks sent to England by the King of Norway? Was Florence still marching to the drum? She could wash and wash, and scrub and scrub the royal shirts – but the king would never again wear them. And William, his friend the *Aquarius*, could prepare baths by the score, but John would never again sink his flesh into the hot, perfumed water. Crok snickered and bit a hazelnut shell, and yelped as a pain shot again through his jaw. He spat out bits of rotted tooth.

'Be quiet,' said Nicolaa de la Haye from above him.

He sat, still and quiet as a mouse.

An essoiner in his clerk's black robe crept forward to the dais.

Robert Hauteyn had solemnly espoused Alice at the church door, and they had lived together for sixteen years and had three children. Then came one Joan, of whom he had previously begot a son named Richard, and this Joan claimed Robert Hauteyn as her husband, though they had never been espoused at the church door. The Bishop of Peterborough had pronounced Alice and Robert divorced, but on Robert Hauteyn's death an inquisition post mortem had failed to decide on his heir.

'Well, it's not Master Richard,' mused Nicolaa, turning to Lacy, the King's officer, who sat beside her, 'for Joan was never espoused at the church door. Nor the sons of Alice, for he and Alice were divorced by Holy Church. His heir can only be his brother Thomas. Do you not say so?'

'I say there is not time for this,' said Lacy curtly, 'and no safety in it.'

'I am Sheriff and they want justice.'

'They have wanted justice a long while.'

'They had it from John.'

'There was no law, madam,' said Lacy, dogged and angry, 'under King John.'

They would never get on, these two, thought Crok. The Lacys had stood with the Northerners at Runnymede. Sir Walter Lacy, this young knight's father, still had a fine of five hundred pounds to pay to dead King John by feast of St Michael. It was a wonder the Lacys were not in London Town, warming their hands at King Louis's fire.

'You mean,' said Nicolaa, enjoying herself, 'that the barons who broke their oath would accept no law?'

'He broke the law himself when he annulled the charters.'

'Fuck the charters.'

Crok cocked his ears and chewed his nuts, and winked at the sokesmen.

'Sweet Jesu,' Nicolaa went on, amazed, 'you dare talk to me of the charters!' She leaned close. 'I'll tell you what,' she said softly, using, as she often did, the common tongue, 'I'd

76

rather have John's war than Richard's peace – or that of his father before him.'

She turned away before he could reply. She said to the Undersheriff, 'I have six women brought by the priest for coupling outside the marriage bed. What is the custom hereabouts? Shall they do penance, or pay Legerwite to the lord of the manor?'

'And which did you do, madam?' Lacy asked in a low voice. 'When you coupled with the King?'

'Well, I'll tell you what,' she said, turning back to him, 'I did not walk in my shift through Lincoln.'

Crok laughed and laughed. The sokesmen, uneasy and bewildered, laughed with him.

Cecily Holt of Holbeche Hurn is called for fornication at the instance of the priest of Moulton.

Crok looked lasciviously at Cecily Holt but, on examination, she was an ill-looking woman. He turned back to covertly watch Nicolaa de la Haye, this most famous of John's loyal barons. He wondered how old she was. She had married de Camville when she was twelve or thirteen, and the same year had famously gone to Barfleur to meet King Richard and demand the Castellanship of Lincoln that her father, and her forebears Picot and Coleswegan, had held before her. Now her husband was dead. There was a son called Richard in honour of *Coeur de Lion.*

She wore a cote of green velvet, edged with fox, close fitted to her slender body, the neck low to show her chemise. By the firelight of the King's chamber – which was where

Crok had usually seen her – she had seemed young. But by daylight there were lines round her eyes, silver hair in the gold net of her *crespine*.

She was more than thirty, he thought. She was an old woman.

'Well, troubadour?' she said, turning to him, mocking as ever. 'What would you do with this Cecily of Holt, who couples in the fields?'

Crok made a crude gesture with two fingers, and the sokesmen laughed.

'Madam, I am sent by the Council,' said Lacy angrily, 'to find the crown of England.'

'Then find it.'

'It lies in the sands of Welande.'

'Then turn back the waters, if you can, like Canute.'

Crok sniggered. It would be another day before the neap tide, when the sands would be uncovered. Why else was Nicolaa de la Haye, the King's Sheriff, concerning herself with women who coupled out of the marriage bed?

Lacy was speaking urgently. 'The world knows that we are at the coast. There are troops of *Norrenses* beyond Crowland – the Deeping Fen is full of rebels driven into hiding by John. Will you send to Lincoln Castle for more men?'

'And risk the castle itself?' Nicolaa was now speaking rapidly herself. 'You know full well that Lincoln town – may it rot – is in league with the French.'

'And the French are at Bury,' said Lacy. 'And could be here by tomorrow daygate.'

Nicola said, 'Then fight them.'

He stared at her. He had six men-at-arms and a boy.

9

King's Lynn, Lincolnshire

He lay back in the chair while the dentist peered and probed,
and warned him about the infection risks of exposed gums.
Then they took an X-ray, and sent him back to the waiting
room where Normandie was reading old copies of *Hello!*.
After the next patient, they called him back into the surgery,
and the young, efficient dentist scraped around a bit more in
a puzzled, investigative sort of way, saying: 'If there's any
sensitivity raise your hand, but don't try to speak.'

A bright beam of light penetrated the crevices of his
mouth.

'I don't want you biting my finger off,' the dentist added,
as though Felix were an Alsatian.

Tap, tap, against his teeth.

A puzzled pause.

'OK,' the dentist said with decision, 'the X-ray isn't
showing anything but I think there may be a bit of infection
in the gums, so we'll try antibiotics. Have you had antibiotics
before?'

He had, and without adverse reaction. But he did not have
gum infection. The pain was in his jaw. It was in the bone.

'Pain travels,' said the dentist, curtly. 'You can think
you've a poorly tooth on one side of your mouth, when the

problem is somewhere else entirely.'

The surgery was decorated with posters of Teletubbies, all waving toothbrushes.

'What you need to get to grips with,' said the dentist, looking at him wearily, 'is all this plaque, getting under your gums and irritating them. Why should I bother about your teeth if you don't?'

They went to a teashop that sold aromatherapy oils, mystic brooches, and greetings cards made out of paper from sustainable sources. Normandie ordered coffee and cakes. She looked at him in his grubby purple suit, his rumpled dirty shirt. She said, 'What are we going to do with you, then, eh?'

'I seem to have been in the wars a bit lately,' said Felix, pathetic but brave.

'Last night you said it was dangerous for you to be at Wormby. What did you mean?'

A girl was chalking lunchtime specials on a blackboard: puzzling over the spelling of mussel in the mussel-and-prawn lasagne.

Normandie was looking at him.

'It's dangerous,' he said, 'to be anywhere these days.'

'Why is Julia a stupid cow?'

What else had he said to her when she helped him back to his caravan?

'You mustn't take any notice of the things I say when I'm pissed.'

'But were you pissed?' she said, puzzled. 'You seemed more, well, exhausted.'

'Who wouldn't be, working at Wormby Flats?' he said then, cunningly changing the subject, 'However did the Bastard get you here?'

She looked at him, undeceived, then sighed. 'I was going to Israel. Six months singing in a club on the Red Sea. The flight was paid, it was an Equity contract, everything was great, except that the Equity contract was never actually signed and nobody mentioned till we were at the airport that the club was really in Lebanon. So I came here. I claim I'm a singer and entertainer, Ray Monkman claims that I'm his assistant manager, also known as dogsbody. It's what makes the entertainment world turn, of course. Middle-aged men deluding sweet, vulnerable, and frequently achingly-lovely young girls.'

Two ladies at the next table, who had been listening with interest, nodded to each other. They too had once been young, deluded by men and, possibly, achingly lovely.

'You mustn't be cynical,' said Felix, though God only knew he had suffered from theatre managers in his time.

'Oh, Ray Monkman's only a small sort of bastard in the scheme of things. He never mentioned that I'd be serving in the bar every night and in charge of the Junior Disco, but fair's fair, he only wants me to go topless, he hasn't drugged me senseless and sold me by the hour to Korean business-men.'

The ladies ate their fruit scones and listened intently.

'Anyway, there's only ten weeks to go to the end of the season. How's your toothache?'

He had taken paracetamol and antibiotics with his café latte and was feeling better.

'It's easing off, thanks, quite a lot.'

Just a dull ache, but a reminder that his body was not his own.

'Do you know what Ray wants now?' she said. 'Blue Heaven Night. Blue cocktails – he experimented with those for a week – a blue comedian from a club up the coast, and lap dancers wearing blue feathers – that's me, Jude and Chrissy. You know Chrissy? She's the little Aussie girl with the big,' she dropped her voice, making the shopping ladies strain forward, 'tits. What a life, eh?'

'What a life,' said Felix, though which life he was talking about, he was far from sure.

'So how did you start in the game?' she asked.

The ladies' eyes flickered with interest.

'Variety.'

'Max Miller and all that?'

'No, not Max Miller, I'm not a hundred. But in the early Fifties, as a young man, I had a moderately successful act. That, of course, was before television. Clairvoyance is not an entertainment suitable for television. A medium probing the frontiers of the human psyche cannot provide the instant gratification that television demands, and besides, I never enjoyed the mechanical illusions – sawing people in half, catching bullets in one's teeth.'

'Can you do that?'

'Oh yes.'

'What, proper flying bullets?'

'Indeed.'

'Gosh,' she said, impressed.

He would not like to do it now, he thought, not with his aching, sensitive gums.

'So what happened when the theatres went dark?'

He smiled faintly, but it was a telling phrase. 'Butlins in the summer. A season at Wormby Flats in the early sixties.'

The slow steady decline in the number and quality of his professional bookings. The agent that he walked out on and the agent that went bankrupt owing him money. The agent who told him that changes in the entertainment industry presented an invigorating challenge – and that he was letting go of any act that couldn't get a booking on *Six Five Special*.

His last agent, Jimmy (most of them had been Jimmy), had sent him on tours of the bleak north; round and round the working men's clubs. After that had come the sessions for psychic societies in the remoter parts of South London, that he didn't tell his agent about, more from a sense of shame than to save the agent's share of the booking fee.

Seances on wet afternoons in Dulwich.

'I'm an entertainer,' he always said. But there was nothing entertaining about small rooms filled with lonely widows who wanted to speak to their dead husbands, or mothers who wanted to send their love to children who had died of leukaemia.

Normandie was deep in her own thoughts. Red Sea night-clubs, he guessed, not needing to use his psychic powers: cruise ships anchored by coral reefs. The M&S ladies reluctantly departed to make their husbands' lunches, and to recount what they had heard about the way some people live and the things they get up to.

His jaw, which had been quiescent, started to throb.

For a moment he wanted to tell her what was happening to him. But how could he say *I am being contacted from beyond the grave* when for forty years he had been making his living by doing just that?

'Sometimes I think I've been a bit of a fraud,' he said, preparing to confess everything, ready to astound.

Normandie said, 'Well, look at those two.'

Stepping out along the pedestrianised street were Jude, wearing her little black waitress's skirt, and the bearded marine physicist called Michael.

They left the café. 'Why have you been a fraud?' Normandie asked, and he said, 'Oh, nothing.'

'Hi,' said Jude.

'Hello,' said Normandie, smiling sweetly.

The four of them walked down the High Street. Michael Boulding, it seemed, had come into town for provisions. 'I found him buying stuff in Woolworths,' said Jude.

'Do agents of FORCE use Woolworths, then?' said Normandie.

'What's this?' said Jude.

'Something secret,' said Normandie. 'Something it would be dangerous for you to know about.'

'Oh, right,' said Jude brightly but looking annoyed.

They went along King Street to the river, and sat on a wall by the Custom House, and looked out over the muddy waters of the Great Ouse. Felix had fallen behind and was staring intently at an old building.

'I brought him in to the dentist,' Normandie said. 'He woke up in the night with terrible toothache.'

'You mean with a hangover,' said Jude.

'He wasn't drunk, he just wasn't well.'

'He said some funny things,' said Michael Boulding.

'Like what?' asked Jude.

'Never mind,' said Normandie feeling protective.

'He's creepy. What's he peering at?'

'He's just looking in a shop.'

'Don't you find him creepy?'

'No,' said Normandie.

'That first night in the club was totally creepy. You should have been there, Michael. He sort of froze halfway through his act and stared at this woman. He didn't seem to be looking at her but through her. Seeing things.'

'Of course he sees things,' said Normandie. 'What use would a clairvoyant be who didn't see things?'

'Well, I spoke to her afterwards and she was really, really frightened. They'll never come to Wormby again, I can tell you. And he prowls round the dunes at night. But then, so do you, Michael.'

'But I'm allowed to.'

'Hush,' said Normandie. 'Or she'll find out, and then she'll have to be killed.'

'What?' said Jude.

'Never mind.'

'Why do you keep on being mysterious?'

'Am I being? I'm sorry.'

'It's part of my job to monitor the tides at night,' said Michael Boulding, looking confused.

Felix joined them.

'Did you find something interesting?' asked Normandie.

'The building is late medieval,' said Felix, 'but behind the facade are the arcaded gable walls of a twelfth-century stone house.'

'Twelfth century,' said Jude. 'What happened in the twelfth century?'

'Henry the Second and Thomas à Becket,' said Normandie, who had read medieval history at university. 'Richard the Lionheart and Bad King John.'

She drove Felix back to Wormby Flats. Ray Monkman was sitting on the terrace by the Magic Garden, stopping the gnomes from being pinched, although they were all concreted firmly in place, particularly the fishing gnome that was the most frequent target of teenage hooliganism.

Normandie said, 'Hi,' and he said, 'Where've you been then?' and she told him. He looked at her reproachfully, as if nobody ever offered to take him to the dentist, though Jude and a dozen others would have taken him three times a day with pleasure, and would have sat patiently for hours listening to the drill.

'You can't just bugger off,' he said, scowling at Felix, who was staring about him vaguely, looking embarrassed and shifty, his purple suit repellent in the sunshine. 'Anything might have happened.'

'Did anything happen?'

'There was a French chap here looking at my *Negés de jardinière*.'

'Your what?'

'My gnomes.'

'Oh, the goblins.'

'Yes, ha ha, I'm laughing.'

'She ran and ran,' said Felix suddenly –

> 'As if she feared some goblin man
> Dogged her with gibe or curse.
> Or something worse.'

'Pardon?' said Ray.

'A poem by Christina Rossetti.'

'There,' said Normandie. 'Christina Rossetti knew all about goblin men like you.'

'Ho, ho,' said Ray heavily. 'Ho, ho, ho.'

'Goblins, Ray, goblins,' said Normandie wittily, 'not dwarves.'

'That was hey ho,' said Ray, 'thimble brain.'

Felix grinned eerily and wandered off to the telephone kiosk. Ray said, 'I'm going to have to sack him.'

'What?'

'Your chum. The Incredible Felix.'

'The Astounding Felix.'

'He isn't, though, is he? Other than being astoundingly and incredibly awful. Look how he upset that woman the very first night he was here.'

'You told him he was a bloody triumph.'

'I've had her husband on to me.'

'Your very words. "A bloody triumph, Felix old cock".'

'She couldn't sleep a wink afterwards.'

' "Bloody marvellous, squire," you told him.'

'She kept having nightmares.'

'How could she have nightmares if she couldn't sleep?'

'Living nightmares. Some bloke in an iron helmet out of *Star Wars*. Her husband's threatening to see his solicitor. And what about last night, eh? All that stuff about auras again, and magic numbers, then he just walks out into the night. And his jokes are terrible. And his poems go on too long. God knows, I welcome a bit of culture, but going on and on about pirates eating cold fish isn't culture in my book.'

'The pirate was a cat. It was one of TS Eliot's comic poems.'

'Yes, I gathered that, petal, but did anybody else? It's romantic poems the women want, poems about love. A nice sentimental poem about a cat called Fluffy would be all right, but he just doesn't understand his audience.'

From inside the club came the sounds of the Junior Disco; the voice of Uncle Simon: 'For Christ's sake, I told you *not to do that*!'

Ray said, 'This is supposed to be a place where cares and woes are banished. One visitor's been terrified out of her wits by an entertainer, a load of food's been nicked from the kitchen, and bastard hooligans have had another go at the garden ornaments. What's happened to innocence? What's happened to the British family holiday?'

'I don't know,' she said.

Certainly he'd done his best. The shop had paper Union Jacks for sale, and plastic buckets and spades. Some visitors even bought them for their children – you saw the tiny tots later on the beach, pudgy and determined as they tried to make sandcastles out of pebbles.

'But I think Felix is very good.'

'You thespians stick together,' said Ray, a wise old bird.

The Junior Disco ended. Simon came out and said, 'Have you seen Jude?' He'd been thinking about her, thought Normandie, all through the disco, while the wicked girl had been in King's Lynn, picking men up in Woolworths.

'She's gone to her caravan.'

He hurried off.

'Listen,' she said, 'I think that when Felix offered to come here – well, I think it was to get over something that happened years ago. Some kind of therapy.'

He looked at her.

'I think something happened here back in the sixties – something he hasn't been able to come to terms with.'

'You think he got raped?'

'Oh Christ, Ray . . .'

'Because they didn't have male rape in the sixties, I can tell you.'

'Don't be stupid, of course they did. But I think Felix had some kind of a psychic experience.'

'It's his job to have psychic experiences.'

'Yes, all right,' said Normandie, wearily.

'Basically, you think he's a nutter.'

'No!'

'That's it. He's going.'

'You're all heart, aren't you, Ray?'

'I've got responsibilities. You'll know what that means, one day, petal.'

'Give him another chance,' said Normandie. 'Please.'

Ray savoured the moment. He sighed.

'Well, just for you,' he said, not unconscious of the

expensive 'Spookie Night' ads he'd taken in the Spalding free sheet.

He stared at Felix, hunched secretively in the phone kiosk, looking like a man making calls of an obscene or bizarre nature.

'When will you try again?'

'Tonight.'

'Be especially careful when you are in Theta.'

'I won't go into Theta.'

'Don't be too eager, even in Alpha. Remember the dangers that exist for those who have an overwhelming desire to speak with the Other World.'

'Yes,' he said, knowing that the greatest danger, because it had no moral value, was an inordinate desire for wealth, and knowing – with a sudden contraction in his stomach muscles – why he was in Wormby.

'Do you think it could be the knight?'

Felix thought for a moment.

'No.'

'But the knight was there on all three occasions?'

'Yes.'

'I told you I saw a scabbard.'

'It isn't the knight.'

'The lady?'

'No.'

'How much is still clear?'

'Very little. Almost nothing.'

'I am concerned that it came to you in your caravan. It's clearly more powerful than you are.'

He didn't say anything to that.

'I am sensing your aura,' she said. 'Your energy is low. There is a blockage.'

'There has been a blockage for forty years.'

'You are facing it and fighting it.'

'Yes.'

'Remember,' she said, trying to bolster him up, 'that if your intentions are honourable you will have the universe and all of its powers to aid you.'

'Yes.'

She was thinking of other things. In a week's time she was off on her cruise round the Mediterranean, and then to stay with friends in Devon. The date on which she would return to London had not been mentioned and Felix had been too proud to ask.

'You will take care?'

'Yes, Julia.'

He put the phone down.

He took what precautions he could. He went through the formulae he had so often practised and so little regarded. He sat and meditated, and allowed his consciousness to leave the earth plane and project itself out to the mental plane, seeking the mysterious light that marked the entrance to the astral world.

He spoke to his guides. He asked for other guides and felt himself carried upwards, and his body lightened and began to float like flotsam on a beach, moved by the incoming tide, in that half-world where the astral world and the physical world met. He wanted to break free entirely – but was aware, even as he soared, of the thin, transparent silver cord that connected his astral double to his physical body.

He breathed slowly, as he had been taught, and as he had taught others. He imagined leaving his old, tired body and entering the Other World. Of becoming a body of purest light – a pure spirit on the vast astral plane, free from the burden of his mortal self, the cumbersome weight of chemical existence. Free of aches, pains, weariness.

Free of the disappointments of life. Of the burden of weight that he carried.

At dusk he got to his feet, still alive, his old bones stiff and complaining. He changed into his dress suit, fixed the cape round his shoulders, and stared at himself in the tiny, dusty mirror.

His toothache had gone, the ache in his jaw.

Outside, the neon *DREAMBOAT* was an electric blue against the darker sky.

Music from the sound system smashed into his eardrums. The DJ faded it down to say, 'What do you call an Essex girl with two brain cells?' and then back up again as the audience roared, 'Pregnant!' At the bar Ray was perched on a stool like one of his gnomes. He waved to Felix, calling him over.

'There's a big party from Spalding, so you've got to go for it,' he shouted over the din. 'I've had a word with the lad.'

Felix looked at him, puzzled.

'With him – Penguin.'

He waved at the lad on the organ.

'If Hiawatha comes on, he's going to play Red Indian music.'

He punched Felix on his arm, hurting him.

Felix said, 'You really want me to raise people from the dead?'

Ray looked at him enquiringly, cocking his head to one side.

'You really want me to summon spirits,' said Felix loudly, angry at the foolishness and ignorance around him, 'from the Other World?'

'From a happy place,' Ray shouted, slowly, into Felix's ear. 'Don't go and upset anybody.'

The noise cut.

'And now,' said the DJ, 'for tonight's live entertainment at the Dreamboat Café.'

He counted himself into Alpha, his place of safety, mentally reciting the spell, 'Go to your true place now as I am in mine.' His Alpha kingdom had altered little since he had first been told by his teacher: *Imagine a place of peace and contentment.* There was the lake with its reedy shore. There was the waterfall and the forest of dark conifers. There were the snow-peaked mountains. He had described it once to Julia, who had said, 'Everyone has a lake and mountains, but it doesn't matter.'

'Ladies and gentlemen,' he said, facing the audience, 'in an article I wrote for the *British Journal of Psychiatry* in 1986, I warned against the danger of foolish people who meddled with psychic forces. People so ignorant of the powers that exist in the Other World that they risked their souls and sanity. People stupidly curious to see what ought not to be seen. People who sought to profit financially from the loneliness and distress of those who were left behind.'

He looked meaningfully at Ray Monkman at the bar.

'It is only those who have a genuine spirit of enquiry, and who approach this great matter with humility and in peace, who can safely lift the veil between this and the Other World. Who can face the unknown and speak with spirits that have gone before and – yes – peer into the future.'

'When am I going to win the lottery?' – a voice from the back.

'You, sir,' he replied, 'are not going to win the lottery.'

Cries of shame.

'But there is a person here tonight who is.'

'Yeah, ten quid.'

'No, not ten quid. A great deal of money.'

He had their attention now. There was no more chattering, no more shouted drinks orders from the bar, no rude teenagers clattering in front of him while he was trying to do his act. His eyes moved slowly along the line of faces, from table to table.

They were frozen in anticipation.

'I know who will win the lottery and how much they will win. It is one hundred and forty thousand pounds.'

It was the right amount. There was no point talking millions to people who thought ten grand was enough to retire on. They stared at him intently, spending the money.

'One hundred and forty thousand pounds, give or take twenty quid. And it will happen within six months.'

Suddenly he shook his head. He took a deep breath.

'But I am reluctant to say more. I have a responsibility

here. If I say who the lucky person is, the person concerned might very well hand in their notice at work.'

A small murmur of amusement.

'They might start to indulge in a life of luxury and fast living.'

A few laughs. But they were watching him greedily, waiting for the hand to point down at them from the stardust sky.

'All in anticipation of what is to come in six months' time. But anticipating the future, ladies and gentlemen, is full of risk. A prediction is accurate *providing nothing is done to change the essential circumstances*. If the government abolished the lottery, for example, my prediction would fail.'

A groan of disgust. They didn't believe that one.

'Or the person who is going to win might drink himself – or herself – to death before their winning number came up – the excitement, you understand. Or they might kill themselves by riding around in sports cars. Or take up sky diving and plunge to a horrible and grisly death. You, madam—'

He pointed at a portly lady who shrieked.

'Might run away from your husband in your excitement and get eaten by a tiger.'

More shrieks.

'No, please, this is not funny, ladies and gentlemen. It is a dilemma I must ponder during the remainder of my show tonight . . .'

He didn't need psychic powers. He was an entertainer.

'Tell us who it is. Tell us who it is . . .'

They chanted, banging their glasses on the tables. At the

bar Ray Monkman raised his own glass in a toast, a tribute. Behind the bar, staring at Felix intently, was the girl from the farmhouse, Karen Tymoor. Did she think that she was going to win the money?

'I must consult,' he said, 'with my conscience.'

It was time to go into empathy, to read a mind, to sense its sorrows and joys. To pluck a name from the air, and watch a member of the audience gawp with shock. He counted down further into Alpha.

'Tell us, tell us, tell us . . .'

Already he was in his own place, his kingdom, his happy land. He was by the waterfall with its rounded, mossy rocks, looking over the grass sward running down to the lake, the distant mountains with their snowy peaks, the thick pine forests.

Nobody could come into Alpha without invitation. No living person and, more importantly, no after-lifer, other than his personal guides. In his Alpha kingdom he was safe so long as he did not try to attempt *visualisation of the dead*.

And he wasn't going to try that. Not tonight. Not in Wormby.

'Ladies and—'

Something was wrong.

The sun was still bright on the peaks. It still glinted on the cold, clear waters of the lake, shining on the green grass.

But he was no longer alone.

There was a presence in the dark pine forests. In Alpha, his place of safety.

It was not one of his own guides – not Bright Running Water, or Little Tibetan Flower, or Amun.

It was in the forest, in the dark. He could feel its eyes on him.

His jaw throbbed.

'Tell us, tell us, tell us . . .'

Greed. Avarice. It was around him, and it was inside him. The greed around him was trivial – it was for an end to worries over the gas bill, for a new caravan, or a holiday in Florida. Inside him it was for much more. It was urgent, sharp, and cruel.

'*Tell us, tell us, tell us . . .*'

'Cousin,' said a voice in his head.

The air was fuggy and hot, smelling of stale breath, and of decomposition.

10

Woken's Eye, AD 1216

'Cousin, what happened?' said Nicolaa de la Haye softly –
though Pilche, the Petty Lord of Woken's Eye, was no cousin
of hers, being a sokesman who fed his own pigs while his
daughter milked the kine.

Yet Nicolaa had always had courtesy, thought Crok, warm
in his pelisse, drowsy on new cider. He remembered how she
had charmed William the *Aquarius*, so that he was forever
offering her the gift of a hot bath (though Nicolaa, not
infected by Eleanor of Aquitaine's madness, rarely indulged
him) and how she had charmed rude Florence, who had
gladly washed her fine linen shifts, and hung them out with
the King's shirts, to the amusement of the soldiery.

Crok drank deep and belched with contentment. The hall
was less of a pigsty than might have been expected on this,
the furthest edge of the world. A peat fire burned and tapers
were lit. In the gloom were the peasants and sokesmen of
Quaplode, Moulton, and Woken's Eye. With them, and
indistinguishable from them, was the priest of Moulton, he
whose passion was to catch and chastise women that
fornicated in the fields.

Pilche, the Petty Lord, looked round hesitantly.

The army had come north from Tydd, he said, in the

vulgar tongue of the fenman. The estuary guides had been summoned. The causeway was passable, to those who could find it, an hour after None.

The army was in a hurry, the commanders impatient.

Nicolaa nodded faintly. She looked across the smouldering fire at Lacy.

There had been a mist – it was the mist, said Pilche, that panicked the carters, who were hired men from Lenne: the mist and the water running fast through the runnels of Black Buoy. There had been a cry from the soldiers that the *tide was not yet out* – but it stood to reason that though the tide was out, the river still ran seawards. 'You can't stop the river running,' the guides had told each other, amazed at the stupidity of the men of Lenne.

'And the holy relics?'

She did not mention the gold crown, Crok noted in amusement. Nor the white gold cups, or sapphire-encrusted basins. There was no mention of gold staffs studded with rubies, or of the famous bedewin stone, or the Sword of Tristram.

He watched the faces of the sokesmen, the villeins. There was a sullen look on the face of the girl – Pilche's daughter – who was fifteen, perhaps sixteen. Crok noted with interest a shadow of anxiety, of fear.

'What happened to the King's relics, cousin?' asked Nicolaa again.

A driver had panicked.

'For what reason?' asked Lacy abruptly – his eye not moving from the doorway, his ears alert for the jingle of harness, the cry of a sentry.

Who could say? Perhaps the guide was lost for a moment in the mists. Perhaps the wagon driver was demon-led, and thought the shore was sea and the sea was shore, and the waters of the Welande running out were in truth the sea waters returning. There had been an eagre.

'An eagre?'

A tide that turned before its time. A stolen tide. There had been the sound of horses, screaming as horses did when the ground gave way beneath them. Panic had spread back along the causeway, where men waited with the waters running around their feet. A knight swore loudly that his horse had cost him eight hundred marks: he tried to canter forward to dry land and was swallowed, man and beast, by the sands, though many had tried to pull him free. A guide had seen two sumpter horses, heavy laden, disappear. He had tried to loose one of the saddlebags.

'Tried?' said Lacy sharply.

Pilche nodded. His eyes were red and rheumy, his thoughts seemingly far away.

Crok looked at the girl, Alison, his daughter.

Again he noted the look of fear.

'How many carts and horses were lost?' asked Lacy.

Only the army commissariat knew that. At daygate, when the army was on shore and messengers were flying back and forth to the King at Swinehead (Crok remembered it well) a count had been taken, but even then troops were confused about their numbers. Two of the King's household knights had been lost.

'The sons of Sire Rogier and John Monmouth,' said Nicolaa sadly.

There was a pause. A woman sobbed with pity for the high-born lads, swallowed by the sands.

That night, said Pilche, guides had led out men with burning brands, and ropes and nets, to recover the lost treasures. There had been a hunter's moon (Crok had seen it from the Fosdyke shore: the colour of Leicester cheese, sitting on the edge of the sea) but nothing had been found of the King's chapel.

'The holy relics,' the priest of Moulton said loudly, 'are lost.'

There was a murmur of dismay round the hall.

'The true splinter from the cross of Calvary,' the priest called out. 'The stone from the gut of Saint Peter.'

A low moan welled up.

Crok laughed.

What, was the stone from the gut of Saint Peter now a pebble on the Lincolnshire beach? Was the true thorn from Christ's right hand, and the true splinter, cedar of Lebanon from the cross of Calvary, now lying in cold mud? Was the morsel of bread from the feeding of the five thousand (which was certainly a true piece and not a false morsel like that held by the monks of Peterborough) gobbled up by a fish – the fish perchance, to be eaten any day now by a Lincolnshire villein?

He hooted with laughter.

Or by a priest!

Again he hooted, for it was a joke that John would have relished.

'Be still,' said Nicolaa, and Crok was still as stone.

In the shocked silence he thought of the other things

wrapped in the saddlebags. The communion cups of white gold, studded with rubies. The gold shrine, its cross studded with three huge sapphires. He saw, with his mind's eye, John in the hunting lodge at Feckenham, holding up a white-gold cup to the candle light.

The blue fire of the cut stones.

The fire billowed blackly. It was only a hut, this hall. They were behind the times in these parts. There was no tile vent in the roof to suck up the smoke, which hung in a choking fog. There were no screens even, no *chancelliere* to stop the draught running in through the doors. On the other side of the wattle wall he could hear cows and could smell their stench. Or perhaps it was the Lord of Woken's Eye's nocturnal stench, he thought, looking down at the caked rushes at his feet. He huddled in his fur pelisse, and turned up his fastidious nose.

But he was hungry and his flesh sagged. And despite the comfort of the cider there was an ache in his jaw.

'With tomorrow's tide we will recover the holy relics,' said Nicolaa crisply, rising to her feet. 'It is not God's will that they should lie on the sea bed.'

But she was not thinking of relics, thought Crok, cackling again, amused, forgetting his teeth.

'Be quiet,' said Nicolaa, turning to face him, 'or I will have you whipped.'

He was as still as a mouse.

The soldiers at the door watched him uneasily. Crok's mind had been turned at Rochester, it was said, when he decapitated six Welsh servants of Cadwallon and the king gave him a shilling for each head. Now he had a hunger for shillings and was grown careless about how he got them. A poor soldier might wander off into the forest for a shit and not be seen again: not outside Crok's bag.

King John, they told each other, might have pulled the beards of the Seven Kings of Ireland – but Master Crok would do better than pull beards, given a sharp knife.

Crok settled to sleep with the donkeys. He scratched his lice-infested hair, and wondered whether William the *Aquarius* had truly gone north to Worcester, or had run away to be an outlaw with Little John and Will Scarlett. He thought of Florence and the merry times they had had; the songs they had sung to William's whistle. He got up eventually and went in search of food. The two guards exchanged glances as he passed. One drew a hand across his throat.

Crok was off to do mischief.

Pity the poor soldier who fell in his path.

He searched the soldiers' saddlebags, but to no avail. He found an apple and ate it. He plodded the squelchy track along the dyke, and climbed the wall, and sat next to the Roman tower and looked out over the writhing sands by the light of the old, dying moon. In due time he heard the sound of horses screaming as the earth sucked them to its bowels.

But it was not horses that the sea-demons wanted, he told himself, fancifully. Nor was it the splinter from the true cross, or the stone from the gut of Saint Peter.

It was the Crown of Edward the Confessor. It was the Sword of Tristram. It was the white-gold cups studded with rubies and the gold shrine studded with three great sapphires.

In particular, it was the gold shrine and the sapphires.

He went down to the beach and along the shore. There was a chill wind and he shivered despite his pelisse as he crawled and jumped across the slimy stones. Hunger gnawed at his stomach. He smashed the shells from mussels and ate the gritty meat.

The moon went behind the clouds.

He sat, patiently, and waited.

When King Richard had died a galleon had been seen in the sky, complete with full-rigging, marvellous to behold. When King Henry died fishes had jumped from abbey pools in Normandy, and had fought in the air and killed themselves, to the amazement of the monks.

For John, poor John, the slate tiles of Newark had tumbled down in a storm.

He snickered.

The moon came out. He saw a movement, the gleam of pale hair, almost white.

Somebody was on the sea wall.

It was the girl Alison, the Petty Lord's daughter.

A shadow moving – somebody come to meet her, perhaps. Yes . . . now she was climbing down to the mudflats, her and her shadow.

He saw them again, a moment later, in amongst the rocks.

They were looking in a pool. Then they were both gone.

He went slowly along the shore, prising the flesh from cockles, looking for samphire to eat, thinking how he might beg a brand from the guards, make a fire, get something hot in his stomach. The moon shone in the rock pools and he peered into them, seeking soft crabs. He climbed slowly towards the place where the girl had been with her shadowy friend.

He stared down into the water. It was at the high-water mark, he reckoned. Covered twice a day, but only just.

Perhaps they had been trying to read the future – seeking pictures by way of moonbeams: it was a common fallacy that moonlight on still water had magical properties.

No, not that . . .

He slipped his hand into the pool. His fingers scrabbled over the sharp rocks. After a few moments, delving under an overhanging stone, he found something soft and sodden.

It was heavy when he lifted it.

In the yellow moonlight, among the dark pulpy mass, a small jewel danced.

He looked back at the dark, hidden shore. He wondered what else the sokesmen of Woken's Eye had pulled from the maws of the sea. He wondered where they had hidden it.

11

Wormby Flats, Lincolnshire

Ray said, 'I want a word.'

He led Felix to a corner of the Conservatory Restaurant, by the window, and sat him down in the gloom. It was black outside: midnight, and a mist rolling rapidly down over the sea wall. The windows were covered in condensation, giving a soft, romantic aura to the red and green glow of the Magic Garden.

'Fancy a Scotch?'

Felix nodded.

Ray padded back into the club, through the Spanish arch with its trail of plastic vine leaves. He came back with two large ones.

'Right, then,' he said heavily.

A girl, Chrissy, came into the conservatory hoovering. Ray called out, 'Just bugger off and clean somewhere else, eh love?'

She gave Felix a look of sympathy then went back into the club.

'I know you've been a bit down on your luck,' Ray said. 'I knew that when I booked you.'

Felix sipped his whisky.

'I wasn't expecting Paul Daniels.'

Felix smiled politely.

'Not on the money I'm paying, eh?'

He laughed. Fair was fair. He was a reasonable man.

'OK. So you can't really communicate with the spirit world. Am I falling off my chair in shock? No. Neither's anybody else. Most of the punters realise, deep down inside, that it's a load of bollocks. They know there's no such person as Little Tibetan Flower – you did tell us you had a spirit called Little Tibetan Flower?'

Felix nodded.

'They know Aunty Jane isn't sending messages back from the Other World. But just for a few minutes they want to think it's true. They want to be given a little shiver of excitement. Basically, they want you to do tricks they can't work out.'

Felix nodded again.

'They don't like it,' Ray leaned over the table and spoke quietly, 'when the act isn't trying. When it's bloody obvious that the only spirit he can raise comes inside a little glass.'

Felix nursed his glass.

Ray leaned back. He took a drink himself. He sighed. 'I gave you that woman from Wisbech. Told you the name of her cat. You didn't make use of it.'

Felix said, 'I don't cheat.'

'Well, perhaps you should.'

'I'm a clairvoyant.'

'I'll believe you.'

'An entertainer.'

'No,' said Ray sadly. 'No, you're not, mate.'

The girls were turning the club lights out. They stood

by the vine-wrapped Spanish hacienda arch and looked at the two figures sitting in the cold, dark restaurant. 'Good night,' they called. After a moment, getting no reply, they left.

The refrigerator behind the bar rattled and hummed in the silence.

Ray seemed lost in his own thoughts, looking out through the window at the lights in the Magic Garden. Then those lights also went off: gnomes and fairies were hidden in their sandy home, safe from prying eyes.

The wind was moaning gently round the conservatory. The weather had turned again. It was a terrible August, everybody said so.

'What I'm trying to say is,' said Ray, and then stopped and had another drink from his glass.

Felix was surprised, and touched, that Ray found it difficult.

'If you would rather we curtailed my contract?' he said, gently.

'I think, squire,' said Ray, 'it would be for the best.'

The digger's engine cut in a cloud of diesel smoke, instantly whipped away by the wind. The driver peered forward. The claw had caught on something – half pulling it out of the mud. It looked as if it was metal: the wing of an old car, maybe.

He looked round for his boss, who was operating one of the other two diggers that were busy dredging out the tidal channels, piling up earth behind massive boulders on the new sea wall. They were a small outfit. They got work by undercutting the opposition; by being on the job at first light and not taking two-hour dinner breaks.

A bloke was sitting on the sea wall, watching them. He'd been there when they arrived at six-thirty and must by now be frozen to death – the sun was shining in a blue sky but the wind was bracing, a proper Skeggy wind straight from Siberia. He didn't look like a twitcher – he had no binoculars, no camera. He sat huddled up, miserable: a man waiting to drown himself when the tides came in.

The driver looked down again at his digger's claw. Bent metal. Could it be a Saxon shield? If it was they'd be held up for a month, sitting in their digs in Holbeach while the archaeologists ferreted about. He'd dredged up some stuff in his time and it was always bad news. Medieval burial sites, Roman villas – before you knew it television cameras were all over the shop.

He jumped down from his cab.

It was more likely a bit of an old car.

A flap of metal, aluminium, attached to something that was still buried. He grimaced and put his hand down into the clammy mud that he knew to be full of little red worms. He tugged and the metal moved slightly.

Some kind of curved casing. He wiped away the mud and saw numbers impressed on bright metal.

Sweat beaded his forehead.

He could hear his boss's digger bearing down like a beach buggy, vibrating, he thought, like hell.

He straightened and ran. The beer he'd had last night made him gasp for breath, but he leapt the runnels and rocks – his mates told him later – like a fucking ballerina.

* * *

110

Felix watched the man running and waving his arms, and the other two drivers stop their diggers and jump down. Then all three moved quickly away, their vehicles abandoned.

Felix stared out over the sands, watching the tide as it came in.

Eventually one of the drivers came along the path behind the sea wall and told him that there might be an unexploded bomb on the beach.

'Or it might just be Des wanting some excitement,' he said matily. 'Can you stay here for a bit and tell people to keep off the beach – just till the police arrive?'

Felix nodded. The man went back along the path.

Felix stared at the excavators, abandoned at the base of the sea wall.

His jaw throbbed and he nursed it with his hand.

Jude clambered over the rocks in her white bikini and flip-flops, her deep-bronzed body goose-pimpled by the brisk wind, her nipples – thought Normandie – far from obscure.

'Shit! Ow!' she cried. 'You'll have to help me, Michael.'

She was after him, thought Normandie, amazed. Perhaps it was his legs, which were thick, muscular and brown.

Michael laughed and stood with muscular legs akimbo, and held out his hands. Jude took them and jumped down.

'Thanks,' she said, not letting go.

'Simon was looking for you earlier,' said Normandie.

'Simon?' said Jude vaguely, as though they had never been the Beatrice and Benedict, the Juliet and Romeo, of Wormby Flats.

'Yes,' said Normandie. 'You remember Simon.'

'Not really, no. What exactly is it you're doing on the beach, Michael?'

They had found him taking readings from a black box that contained, he said, a sensor linked to a buoy out in the bay.

'Well, my *primary* function,' said Michael, 'as I was saying to Normandie the other night, is to examine the interactions of hydrodynamic, sedimentological, and bio-geochemical processes on Wormby Flats.'

'That right?'

'The impact on sediment transport of currents and waves. Trying to improve understanding of sediment processes at turbulence and intra-wave time scales. It's called near-bed profiling.'

'Bed?' said Jude, latching on to a word she understood.

'Sea bed,' said Normandie, as Michael bent over a second black box. 'He means sea bed.'

'It's amazing the things Michael knows about,' said Jude. 'What did you say you were a PhD in, Michael?'

'Marine physics.'

'I've often thought I'd like to do a PhD.'

'What?' said Normandie.

'You don't know anything about me,' Jude said defensively, 'I don't know why you think you do. Perhaps I'm a late-developer. Would you say that I'm a late-developer, Michael?'

'If you are,' said Michael with unexpected smoothness, looking at her with frank appraisal, 'it has done you no harm.'

'Why are they building up the sea wall?' asked

Normandie, who had had enough of this. Ahead of them on the empty beach were three bright yellow excavators, seemingly abandoned, looking like mechanical dinosaurs in an arrangement of modern art.

'Because this part of the world is sinking into the sea.'

'Global warming?'

'To the extent that the ice cap melts and the sea level consequently rises, yes.'

'That's just terrible,' said Jude. 'But I expect you know how to deal with it.'

'Actually, it doesn't have to happen. In my opinion, we could just as easily be in for another little ice age.'

' "Little ice age" sounds cosy and comforting,' said Normandie. 'What would it mean though?'

'A few glaciers on the top of Scotland, perhaps. The weight of ice would depress sea levels and pull East Anglia up.'

'Wormby Flats would turn into Wormby Cliffs?'

'Not very big cliffs, but something like that, yes.'

'Ooh look,' said Jude. 'Hasn't he been sacked?'

A figure was wandering through the mechanical dinosaurs, looking like the sort of man parents warn their little children about.

'Yes,' said Normandie, who had wondered where Felix had got to.

'I'm not surprised,' said Jude. 'Did he just go to sleep halfway through his act, or what?'

'I think he's having personal problems.'

'If he's sacked,' said Jude, 'why is he still here?'

'Ray said he could stay in his caravan till the end of the week.'

'Well, I have to be on my way,' said Michael Boulding. 'Make sure some stuff's downloaded itself OK from the sat.' He looked conspiratorially at Normandie. 'Stuff from FORCE HQ, know what I mean?'

'Ha, ha,' said Normandie politely.

'Listen,' said Jude, 'do you really think I could be a marine physicist?'

'Why not?'

They were approaching the excavators.

'Hi, Felix,' Normandie called.

He was peering into the deep ruts made by one of the digger's wheels.

'I'm sorry you're leaving. Ray's such a bastard.'

He looked up and smiled, and nodded vaguely. He was wearing his terrible purple suit. His sparse hair was hanging down untidily over one ear. He needed somebody to take care of him, she thought. To brush back his hair and apply a good gel.

'OK, so when am I going to be invited to tea at your caravan?' Jude said to Michael Boulding, abandoning the subtle approach.

He looked surprised.

'Tomorrow if you like.'

'Great.'

Felix was bending over, examining the soil exposed by the digger, prodding at something.

'What's that you've got?' said Normandie.

He held up an oval shape, dark grey, slightly smaller than his hand.

'Can we have a look?'

He passed it to her. She scraped at the surface with her thumbnail. It was black under the hard crusted sand.

'It looks to me like a bit of old tar,' said Jude. 'Tar that's solidified.'

'Can I see?' asked Michael.

'A chunk of tar, washed in by the tide.'

'No,' said Michael. 'There's a design on it. Look. What do you make of that?'

They made nothing of it.

'You ought to drop this in at the county museum,' said Michael.

'What?' said Jude. 'A bit of old tar?'

'It might be something of interest. Something off a ship, perhaps. I can take it into Boston for you if you like, Felix.'

Felix had turned away and was peering round again.

'Yes, you take it,' said Normandie, watching him, troubled – though why she should feel responsible for him she couldn't say.

'Right then, I'm off.'

'Till tomorrow,' said Jude.

He went, up the sea wall, over the dunes.

'I got him to ask me to his caravan,' Jude said, 'but don't think he fancies me.'

'You should put yourself forward more,' said Normandie. 'It's no good being a shrinking violet.'

'If you want something in this life you have to go for it.'

'And you really want him?' asked Normandie, amazed.

'He's OK.'

'He's very possibly the most boring man in the universe.'

'That's why you share secrets with him is it?'

'What secrets?'

'The man from FORCE, stuff.'

'It was just a stupid joke. You want him, you have him.'

'I don't know why you have to be snobby.'

'No,' said Normandie sincerely. 'I don't either. I'm sorry. Felix, do you want to go for a coffee? You look frozen.'

Felix's face was mottled by the cold, the skin blotched with grey and dark red patches.

'Look at that bloke,' said Jude.

A man was standing on top of the sea wall, waving, but they couldn't hear what he said because the wind was blowing off the sea.

'Is he shouting at us?' said Normandie.

'If he is, it's probably something obscene. Felix, do you want to go to the twitchers' hut for a drink?' Jude went on, speaking slowly, as if to a five-year-old. 'Would you like a coffee or a Bovril?'

Michael Boulding had made his way up through the dunes, and was talking to the man on the wall.

'Felix, are you listening?' said Jude, then, to Normandie, 'Talk about away with the fairies.'

'There's something wrong,' said Normandie.

Michael was running back down the path, waving his arms urgently, gesturing to them to move away from the excavators.

Felix had fallen to his knees and was delving in the mud again.

'Felix, we've got to go!'

He was lifting something. A piece of metal. Flat, sharp, a jagged edge.

'Felix, there's a bomb – we've got to move!'

Felix held up the metal over his head. He stared out over the pewter sea, the tide running in fast now through the mud flats.

'I'm off,' said Jude.

They left him. Seagulls gathered, attracted perhaps by the bright metal that flashed in the air like silvery fishes – and that was, Felix called out loudly, the great Sword of Tristram, that had once slain an Irish dragon.

12

Woken's Eye, AD 1216

The sea birds wheeled and cried and swooped for oysters. The world was sand and mud and water that ran through a million runnels. Ahead went the guides with their white wands, leading the way along the ridges of marsh grass that squelched under the horses' feet. In single file behind them came Lacy and then Nicolaa de la Haye, on her grey stallion, and behind her on a pony, Alison, the daughter of the Petty Lord of Woken's Eye.

Then, with the men and their nets, came Crok on his rouncy, his head down, his eyes on the wet sand. He was hearing in his head the songs of the Poivetians: following still the path of the army, following the drum.

The guides spoke to each other softly. As they went, they stuck white wands in tufts of marsh grass.

They were far out in the estuary. Behind them the Roman wall was a black line running east until it disappeared in mists. Ahead, on the Fosdyke shore, a packhorse train could be seen setting out across the sands.

War or no war, you would never stop the packmen, Crok thought, with their pots and their pans, their bales of cloth, their razors and needles. He sometimes had it in mind to be a travelling merchant himself.

'*Skins* of Shrewsbury, the *ferry* at Tilbury,' he sang quietly, his eyes restlessly darting from tuft to tuft of marsh grass, seeking the shape of a corpse in every mound of mud. '*Robbers* of Alton' – (he was thinking about the landlord of the Dragon – a man who charged 2d for a flea-ridden bed) 'and the *Archers* of Wales.'

Was it only this summer that the army had been in the land of Llewellin, burning the crops of those same Welsh archers? Taking succour to Robert de Viperi in his castle, and shooting cranes on the banks of the Severn? Was it such a short time ago?

There was a faint sun, silver through the thin clouds. The waters of Welande were draining out across the sands before them, and the guides were knee-deep in water, following a hidden line to the next island of marsh grass.

Now the guides had stopped and were talking amongst themselves. One of them crossed himself. They turned, solemn and sad, and looked up at Lacy and Nicolaa.

Lacy took a small sack from his pommel, brought for the purpose. He rose in the saddle and threw it up into the air. It came down on the muddy sand and was swallowed instantly.

'Sands *qui vivus dicitur*,' said Lacy.

'Jesu have mercy,' said Nicolaa.

Saltmarsh and sodden reeds and runnels of flowing water. Birds, attracted by the gleam of harness, alighted on the sands called quick. How plump would a little bird have to be, Crok wondered, before it was swallowed for a sand-creature's supper?

'Hereabout is Sire Rogier's boy,' Nicolaa said loudly. 'And John Monmouth's son. Here lies Sir Walter Clifford.'

Lacy said, 'There's something.'

The sands were newly ridged at every low tide by the flowing waters of the fen rivers. Ancient tree branches, brought down in last winter's floods, were lodged still in the thick mud. But yes, there was something that might be the grey wood rim of a wheel.

'Can you get to it?' asked Lacy.

The guides looked doubtful.

The packhorse train approached, the quiet jingle of harness carrying across the still air. Nicolaa called, 'What news, masters?' though merchants rarely admitted to knowing anything beyond the price of saddles, or why Jervaulx cheese was now being called Wensley.

'Orford is besieged.' said a packman. 'And the French march north from Bury.'

Crok's eyes nervously scanned the shore.

'To where do the French march?' asked Nicolaa.

The packmen looked blank. Mountsorrel, perhaps? The French kept a hold on Mountsorrel.

They sat their horses a moment and considered the state of the world.

'They say Willikin has slain a hundred Frenchmen,' said one, brightly. 'The corpses are all eaten by dogs.'

Sir William Cassingham had stayed in Kent when the invader landed. He had taken his peasants to the woods, armed with knives and bows. Now all England knew of his exploits: *Willikin of the Weald*, who fell like a wolf on French convoys as they made their way to London from the Cinque Ports.

The packmen passed on their way. By nightfall they would be in Lenne.

'Lacy?' Nicolaa said.

Lacy stared at the grey curl of wood, just visible in the ooze, like the back of a sleeping serpent.

'You think they march to Mountsorrel?'

'It's likely enough.'

Certainly King Louis was no longer in London, chewing the fat with the Archbishop's brother. He might be marching to Mountsorrel, or he might be marching further east. By nightfall, perhaps, French raiders would be in Moulton Second, Holbeche, and Woken's Eye.

'Well, we can't stay here,' said Nicolaa abruptly, her eyes on the sea bank behind them.

Lacy said, 'A hundred marks to the man who recovers the wagon.'

It was as much as a sokesman would earn in his lifetime.

Rope was wound round a lad's waist. Rushes were thrown out over the sands. The boy, who had butter-yellow hair, wriggled first on his stomach, then rolled himself forward over the rushes. His hand reached out to catch the rim of the wagon's wheel. He began to sink.

'Ware, ware!'

It was the Petty Lord's daughter, Alison.

The boy had grasped the rim of the wagon. He tried to rest his weight on it, to pull himself up out of the sand.

The wheel itself began to sink.

'John!' Alison cried.

'Pull him back,' said Lacy.

The rope was taunt: it was not moving. The boy was sinking, rolling over, pulling the wagon wheel down into the sand with him. He gave a startled cry and then a convulsive lunge. He had the wit, Crok noted, to fill his lungs with air. Lacy took the rope from the men and wound it fast round the pommel of his saddle. He called for a guide to lead him, but his horse was in more than a foot of water, itself sinking and almost beyond control. He jumped down and grasped its bridle and pulled it forward.

The boy's mouth was under the sand but his eyes were clear and wide open. Then there was only his butter-coloured hair. He was gone. Alison cried a terrible cry.

'Pull! Pull!' yelled Lacy.

The men grabbed the rope. They pulled but their feet sank into the sands and slithered on the marsh grass. The rope did not move.

Above them sea birds cried and circled.

The girl cried out again.

There was a movement in the sands, like a serpent writhing in the depths. Then waves of mud, black and dank, rose to the surface, and with the mud came a black mud demon, hauling itself hand over hand on the rope. The men leaned forward, knee-deep in the treacherous sands themselves, and pulled him free. The girl jumped down from her pony and knelt and wiped the mud from his caked, closed eyes, and from his mouth.

They threw water over him. He breathed.

She kissed him.

She wept and called him *Valentine*.

Crok looked on, interested. Was this the lad, he wondered, she had met last night by the shore? He wagered himself a penny that it was. He wondered how much loot, how much *booty* the two of them had squirrelled away. Why, he wondered, was the lad risking his life to please the Lady of Lincoln. To be rid of her? To disarm suspicion? They were cunning enough, these sokesmen, he knew that.

'The warren of *Walton*,' he sang quietly, thinking how he would enjoy a fat, warren-bred coney roasted with garlic. '*Warwick* for cord . . .' How much capital did a travelling packman need to set himself up with Thaxted knives, and with Leicester razors and Coventry soap?

It was something to ponder on.

Cantuar, the King's Messenger, whose eyes never left the dangerous shore, said, 'There's a rider on the sands.'

He was a messenger from Savary de Mauléon, who had been left in Lenne to ship the army's winter corn north to Grimsby. The French were moving north from Orford, he said dramatically, and would be on the coast by daygate.

They returned to the shore, to the reed, mud, and wattle huts of Woken's Eye, to the lord's hall.

Nicolaa said, 'How many days to Gloucester?'

'Three,' said Lacy, whose men were saddling their horses.

'Have a care round Mountsorrel,' she said.

'I'll go north.'

She nodded. They would travel together to Nottingham. 'Alison, your father will send you to Lincoln,' she said, 'after the Feast of the Blessed Virgin.'

She would turn the girl into a lady.

Alison curtseyed, prettily enough – but her eyes, Crok saw, were on the mud-caked lad saved from the maws of the sand demons.

Lacy and his men were already mounted. He said curtly,

'I want to be out of the fenland by dusk.'

Nicolaa mounted her grey horse. She said loudly and clearly, 'My Lord, do you swear your oath of fealty to Henry, by the Grace of God, King of England, Lord of Ireland, Duke of Normandy and Aquitaine?'

Pilche, Petty Lord of Woken's Eye, looked at her in astonishment. Then he rose to the occasion (Crok told himself, giggling) by sinking to his knees in the mud.

'*Guardé*,' said Nicolaa, daughter of la Haye, descendent of Picot, setting off down the causeway towards the old Saxon shore.

Crok scurried quickly over to his rouncy. When mounted, he bowed graciously to the villagers, all of whom were thieves and traitors.

Along the causeway, past the islands of drained fields, over the sluice gates. Through Cowbit and Moulton, and now there was firm dry ground underfoot. Through Crowland, with its burnt-out fields, its abbey church with broken door, for Savary de Mauléon had raided Crowland a week back. In Crok's ears was the jingle of the harness, and in his head the beat, beat, beat of the drum. In the corner of his eye he could see Ferling ranging alongside with the hounds, and hear the King lay bets with William Brewer on a couple of coneys escaping the dogs.

'*Whores* of Charing,' he sang to himself, though it was two years since Charing drabs had given pleasure to any but Frenchmen.

'*Scarlett* of Lincoln' – Nicolaa in her castle, flying the white cross of England on its field of Christ's blood, though the folk of Lincoln town were happier with green, the colour of outlaws, John having filched too much of their money (the Mayor, even now, was held hostage in Oxford). '*Thieves* of Grantham, and *Merchants* of Lenne . . .' he crooned, thinking of the thieves of Woken's Eye, and what they still had hidden. But he was content enough. In his bag were fourteen small jewels, torn from the satin bag he had found in the rock pool, and this was more than Sir Walter Lacy's son, or Nicolaa de la Haye, had to show for their pains.

He mused, as they trotted at speed through Hoylande and the Deeping Fen, on plans to set himself up as a pedlar. The air was sweet and his pony fat on beechnuts and samphire, and the sun warm, and for a brief moment his jagged tooth scarcely ached at all.

Part Two

13

Electronic Intelligence (ELINT) Section, National Security Agency, Chicago

The signal that found its way to Trudy Pierce's screen was from the CIA.

Part of a US aircraft – type as yet unidentified – had been found on the Lincolnshire coast of England. Incomplete serial numbers were stamped on a section of casing. War Department records showed that they had been issued in June 1962 – the numbers grouping allocated, for the most part, to Ryan company Firebees, or craft from Boeing plants in California. There was nothing relevant in CIA records, but the computer had thrown up a reference to a file *Lincolnshire, UK, August 5th 1962*. Could ELINT Records help?

The signal was low grade but flagged urgent. Trudy Pierce saw no NSA involvement and ignored it. An hour later she got a call from a CIA desk officer in Maryland.

'I just don't see why you're talking to us,' she said, more confident and aggressive than she felt, but bruised by the number of times crap jobs were being dumped on her desk. She was a year out of Chicago State, with a masters in English literature, for which she had done a thesis on repression in *Mansfield Park*.

'This is simply not NSA business,' she said firmly, thinking how, in *Mansfield Park*, heroine Fanny was forever being sent on wasteful errands in the summer heat.

The boy in Washington – she was betting he was little more than a boy, somebody her own age but more streetwise, no doubt – said, 'There's an NSA tag on the file.'

'On the computer file?'

'What other file is there?'

Both operatives were too young to remember files made out of paper.

'OK, but why us, why don't you call Fort Meade? It's only four blocks away from where you're sitting.'

'Honey, it's no more difficult to call Chicago than to call Fort Meade.'

Honey? Honey? What was this, a Doris Day revival?

'And the tag,' he went on, 'belongs to you.'

'I don't see how the NSA could have been involved in a plane crash in England.'

'We don't see it either.'

Bored but polite. A Harvard boy she guessed, with an MSc from MIT or Berkeley. They were all over Wilmington and Fort Meade, all wearing the same type of shirt, taking the same type of girl out to eat the same kind of authentic *Korean peasant cuisine* of an evening.

'Not,' she said, 'unless you have reason to believe the aircraft was carrying some of our equipment.'

'Basically, I want to sort this and go eat,' said the CIA boy.

'You realise Koreans eat dogs.'

'What?'

'Nothing.'

'Nobody eats Korean food any more,' he said. 'And nobody's talking about plane crashes. This is about two pieces of aluminum, the smaller bearing the serial numbers, the larger being about five feet long, curved at one end. According to the British military, it's some kind of missile vane or fin.'

'It's part of a bomb?'

'Not that we can find out. But the Brits have evacuated a holiday beach and they're pressing for some answers.'

'What about Air Force Intelligence?'

'They have no record of the serial numbers, though the original signal did originate with AirINTEL.'

'I'll run a check, but I still don't see how the NSA gets involved.'

'Can you call me at around three o'clock?'

'It won't take that long.'

'I told you, I need to eat.'

'I thought you said the British had evacuated a beach?'

'Yea, but if you could see the chick I'm taking to lunch . . .' he said in a funny drawl, possibly trying to sound like David Schwimmer from *Friends*, which meant that he was quite old and not so sophisticated after all. 'Anyway,' he went on, back to his normal voice, 'I guess it may take longer than you anticipate.'

'You think so?'

'Just a guess. What's your name by the way?'

'Trudy Pierce.'

'Hi, Trudy. I'm Rob Marguerie.'

'Three o'clock,' she said, coldly. 'Please give me the serial numbers and the number of the tagged file.'

* * *

She was a home girl, an only child. Each morning she took the commuter train in from the western suburbs. At midday, when it was fine, she and two girl friends ate their lunch baskets by the Buckingham Fountain in Grant Park. When it rained they went to the Fine Arts Building café where real live struggling artists served them with Athenian salad and home-made tomato rice soup. In the evening, while other young operatives in ELINT headed to great little apartments round Wells Street, she caught the train back to Lake Forest. While others spent their nights in Jilly's Retro Club or Butch McQuires, she ate supper with her parents, watched TV, or in summer sailed on the lake.

But appearances were deceptive. She had applied to NSA for romance, for excitement. One night a week she did weapons training in a club in the West Loop, and on another learned unarmed combat in a gym in Greek Town. This time next year – she vowed every time she walked through Union station and had to resist the temptation to jump on board trains with Santa Fe and New Orleans on their destination boards – she would be an agent in the field, tracking illegal immigrants from Mexico, or drugs shipments from the Caribbean. The only reason she didn't want an apartment in Wells Street was because she didn't intend to be a desk officer in ELINT long enough to enjoy it.

In the meantime she traced lost NSA files in a Chicago office tower, and sat out on the fire escape as so many young operatives had done before her, gazing out over Lake Michigan and dreaming dreams.

It was twelve thirty. She thought of her friends waiting

with their lunch boxes by the Buckingham Fountain. She thought of the English beach, where it was now early evening, and where the cops on duty would want to go home.

Should she let them stand in the cold and rain (she knew all about summertime in England) missing their evening meal? Not able to put their kids to bed with a story, just so that she, Trudy Pierce, could lunch in Grant Park with her friends?

Yeah, well, why not? It was a tough world, baby, as her father so often told her, a world full of people not as nice as the people in Pinewood Bay.

But then she imagined the CIA boy in Wilmington, coming back from his long lunch with his girl, and saying in his David Schwimmer voice, 'Nothing? In three hours? OK, now here's what you need to do, *honey* . . .'

She sent a gopher to search SIGINT A Group because of its involvement with Former Soviet Bloc targets and its liaison role with service CSS components, reasoning that any electronic surveillance stuff from 1962 was likely to have been directed against the Reds. She put out a general retrieval request on the serial numbers taken from the aluminium vane, but nothing showed. She duplicated the process already carried out by the CIA guy, and got the same result: FILE LIVE.

An NSA tag.

The name of an officer: Charles Rowlands.

Personnel records showed that he'd retired in 1990.

She got herself a coffee and thought it through. Then she accessed COMINT, the unit that evaluated electromagnetic intelligence and stuff encrypted from foreign sources, though there was no way the NSA should have been monitoring British communications from airborne devices over the English North Sea.

A security query on her screen.

The gopher had burrowed its way into E-systems in Dallas, the world's third-most-powerful computer site. It had been stopped dead inside one of the system's seventeen Cray C916/16515 machines.

She spent thirty seconds trying to get it loose, but the electronic cop had banged it up inside an intruder trap. Another thirty seconds – why the delay? – and internal security in Fort Meade was on her screen wanting to know what the hell she was looking for and why. She copied the CIA request, marked it priority, and was satisfied to see the gopher released after another thirty seconds.

She opened her lunch box and ate the sandwich her mother had made for her.

The gopher was at Greenville: *depot maintenance of electronic equipment and systems* which sounded like a cover although it might be something to do with RIVER JOINT and other airborne SIGINT systems. The NSA had more invested in Dallas than was publicly revealed; a large Federal Building downtown was, she knew, comparable to the ELINT unit at Chicago, originally part of the nuclear threat dispersal programme of the late fifties, designed to keep National Security at work when Maryland was too hot to handle.

She pulled the gopher out; it was ferreting to no purpose.

She was warming up now, getting involved.

The gopher was intuitive, but it wasn't as intuitive as she

was. No way was the answer to this one going to be found in E-systems. She pulled it out and set new parameters: a) which files from 1962 had been stored on hard disk b) which were on floppy c) at which location were they stored. As an afterthought she queried microfilm, which had been a sort of craze in the Sixties, so her mother told her, like mini-skirts and The Beatles.

She sent another gopher deep into Boeing and Ryan company records.

She found nothing in two hours.

It was weird. An NSA LIVE tag meant the project was operational. That the file had not been closed. So why was there no record of it? Why, given that what they were talking about here was a piece of US aircraft on a distant foreign shore, was the Air Force Intelligence Agency's computer coming up with a negative?

She accessed the AirINTEL database at Fort Meade and requested a further search of the AirINTEL computer. Another negative. She sat and thought for a few moments, then, gently, her fingers softly stroking the keyboard, she circumvented the defence protocols and slipped in through the back door.

She'd had the ability to do this for the past three months – she'd had the ability, in all probability, since she was around seven. It was this ability that had made her the star candidate out of the thousand or more college graduates who applied to NSA in the summer of 2000.

She keyed in the NSA tag number and the serial numbers

on the chunk of aluminium dredged from an English shore. She sent her request into the electronic ether.

Her screen dissolved then reformed.

She was inside the High Security Net.

She suddenly realised what she had done and broke out in a sweat.

'Go for it!'

She looked up in alarm, her heart thudding – but it was only the two duty operatives, on the far side of the room, eating bagels and playing Dungeons and Dragons.

Otherwise the huge office with its grey and pink walls, its chilled water fountains, its seventy square feet of office space per operative, its bronzed anti-intrusion windows, was empty in this summer lunch-hour.

She was trembling. What was the penalty for this kind of thing? She had a feeling it was a six-months' jail sentence, mandatory, and instant dismissal. That would make a stir on Lakeside.

Have you heard about little Trudy Pierce? Oh my Lord . . .

She pictured the Ladies Guild ladies baking her cakes.

A bleep on the screen.

She was being switched through to Kelly Air Force Base in Texas, home of Air Intelligence Agency HQ, of rapid radio relay, and of control and communications countermeasures.

A password demand.

Rejected.

One more mistake and the electronic cops would freeze the link.

She typed in a revised code sequence to bypass the logic

gate and pressed the pad. As she did so the true, stupid reality of what she was doing overwhelmed her and she cancelled. Sweat was pouring down her face, into her eyes, down between her breasts.

A roared 'Yes!' of triumph from the guys playing Dungeons and Dragons.

On the screen, a millisecond before the link was cut by security police, the words: *File A-TCAE377.b Aug 5th 1962. Lincolnshire England. Refer 694th Int Grp Archive Wichita.*

When the guy from the CIA, Rob Marguerie, called at 3.30 pm, she was out taking a late lunch. A message told him she'd failed to locate the tagged file.

14

Wormby Flats, Lincolnshire

'And now for a summary of the news from Radio Lincolnshire. Police cleared the beach at Wormby for several hours today after a bomb scare. A Ministry of Defence spokesman said later that two pieces of metal found by excavators reinforcing the sea wall were now believed to have fallen from an aircraft, possibly an American plane coming in to land at RAF Wisbech. An investigation is continuing. At Skegness, Fantasy Island 4 has attracted a record attendance for the third week running—'

Ray Monkman turned off the radio. He looked through the little window that connected his office to the kitchen, his eye on the number of scampi-shaped fish balls in the Capt'n Ray's Seafood Platter, the amount of chocolate sauce on the deep-fried vanilla ice-cream. The servery girls knew nothing of running a business. He sometimes thought of serving the sauce up in small china pouring jugs, the only effective means of portion control, but how many of the jugs would get nicked if he did? The phone rang. He said, 'Wormby Flats Holiday Village,' in his confident, sunny voice, and a woman said, 'This is Lincolnshire County Archivist's Office,' which meant nothing to Ray, unless she wanted to book a table in the Dreamboat Café for the archivists' annual outing.

She said she would like to speak to Felix the entertainer.

'So would I,' said Ray.

'Pardon?'

'Felix the *entertainer*. I am querying your use of the word *entertainer*.'

The archivist didn't know anything about that, but she wanted to talk to a man called Felix. Ray said he'd pass on a message. Normandie came in. 'Your chum Felix is so old,' he said, wittily, 'that the archivists want him in their museum.'

'What?' she said, rattily.

'To remind people, I expect, of the days when he was an *entertainer*.'

'He's old, Ray. And he's ill. And you've sacked him.'

'Funny that, because he's still here.'

'He's got nowhere to go.'

'Unless, of course, it's a supernatural thought-form I'm seeing about the place.'

'He also happens to be genuine clairvoyant.'

'I'm genuinely pissed off, I'll tell you that, petal.'

There was no need to ask what he was pissed off about. Caravans and the people who came to stay in them, and the people who had to be employed to look after them. People who demanded money off him and people who failed to pay him. Policemen who closed his beach and frightened the punters into thinking they'd be blown up any minute. It was everything really.

'When's Spookie going then?' Ray asked, leafing through a pile of bills.

'I don't know. You said he could stay till the end of the

week. For God's sake, it doesn't cost you anything.'

'It's just that you wanted a different caravan, to get away from Morag shagging her boyfriend six inches from your head, and I thought you could have the Incredible Spook's caravan. That was all, petal.'

'You're such a bastard.'

'I was just feeling sorry for you. Isn't it time for Kiddies Fun Hour?'

'You're the one who'll be sorry.'

'I doubt it,' he said, not asking about what – there were so many things she could be thinking of.

'He's a true clairvoyant,' said Normandie, getting her blow-up dolphin and brightly coloured inflatable balls out of their cardboard box. 'Somebody who sees things that others cannot see.'

'I wish he'd see something for me,' said Ray, with a tired but leery grin.

Something cuddly and obliging, she thought, with tits. 'What did you mean,' she said, 'about archivists wanting him?'

'She's from Boston and she wants to measure him up for his stand,' said Ray, deciding his joke would run a little longer.

'Actually, I think she might want to talk to him about something that he found on the beach.'

'What, on my beach?'

'Don't worry about it.'

'Whatever it is, if it's on my beach it's mine.'

'I doubt that very much.'

'Well, what was it?'

'Just a casket full of Spanish doubloons, ha, ha. The archivists' office are dating them for him, before he sails off to the Bahamas on his new yacht.'

The door opened. A small thin man peered in.

'Hello Jack,' said Ray, not without warmth. Jack Fountain was chairman of the Caravanners' Committee. He represented the easy-life faction, as opposed to the Let's-have-a-row-with-the-site-owner faction. There had been a ferocious battle, from what Ray had heard, before he had emerged as the caravanners' leader.

In truth, Ray didn't care which faction won. Threats of a mass migration – flocks of geriatric caravans heading north to the sandy shores of Mablethorpe – left him cold. Few of the owner-occupied mobile homes could have been moved without falling to bits, no matter how much he charged for groceries in the site shop. 'I'm a little man, I can't compete with Tesco's,' Ray would explain in the owners' club newsletter and the threatened revolt would slowly collapse.

'There wasn't a bomb, then?'

'No, there wasn't a bomb. It was some bit that fell off a Yank plane.'

'Have you got the judges organised yet then, Mr Fountain?' asked Normandie.

'We thought perhaps Ray and you, love.'

'I'm not sure if I altogether approve of beauty contests.'

'Now then,' said Jack, 'no feminists at Wormby.'

No, thought Normandie, blowing up Donny Dolphin. No anything much at Wormby, really.

'I wanted a word about the sign,' said Jack.

'What about it?' said Ray, glumly.

There were two signs at the site entrance. One said: FAMILIES AND COUPLES ONLY. The other said: TOURERS WELCOME. Nobody ever wanted a word about the second sign.

'Southern Breeze on Avenue Four. Two girls.'

'Well that's a couple, isn't it?'

'A couple of what?'

Ray started shuffling through his box file. Normandie said, 'See you when I see you,' and left with her arms full of dolphin and inflatable balls.

'It says here,' said Ray, 'that they're cousins.'

'Oh dear,' said Jack, shaking his head from side to side.

'Look, Jack, we have to move with the times. Live and let live is my motto – and anyway there are laws, these days.' Ray was getting excited. 'Sexual equality and equal opportunity!'

'Nobody's saying they're lesbians.'

'What then?'

'Well, we can discount them being professional trophy-hunters. Not when we bear in mind the largesse involved in the Miss Wormby Flats first prize, as kindly donated by the management.'

'Twenty quid is twenty quid,' said Ray warmly.

'And we're grateful. But about these tarts.'

'Now,' said Ray, 'you don't know that.'

'They're working the site.'

'Judge not,' said Ray. 'Lest ye be judged.'

'They've had a fourteen-year-old's pocket money off him.'

'Bloody hell,' said Ray, startled.

'That was twenty quid an' all.'

143

* * *

Jack Fountain went and Ray toiled to finish the weekly accounts, for he had dispensed with a book-keeper on grounds of economy. He'd also dispensed with a groundsman, and every day went round himself collecting up litter. He also weeded the bed of French marigolds by the car park and the plants in the Magic Garden. He'd end up doing every job on the site at this rate, he thought wearily, looking through the bills. For a moment he pictured himself, serving pints of beer with one hand, playing the organ with the other, balancing plates of Capt'n Ray's Seafood Platter on his head like a seal and singing 'Autumn Leaves' in a spangly dress.

He decided to take a walk round. The national economy was picking up if prostitutes were moving in on the Holiday Village. And what in God's name were fourteen-year-old lads doing with twenty quid in their pockets?

He padded down the rows and found Southern Breeze. It was one of the newer caravans, circa 1985, that he used for the brochure photograph. He walked round it softly, and knocked on the door, but to no effect. He looked in at the window. Female clothing was all over the place: trousers, panties, little tops. They were an untidy couple, he knew that.

He peered in for a few moments, inquisitively, then remembered the message for Felix and went to the staff caravans, an area of the site he normally chose to avoid. These were the oldest caravans of all. He reasoned, not without justice, that young people would turn the nicest caravan into a pig sty, so they might as well have pig sties to start with.

He looked in through the window of Felix's caravan.

Felix was sitting on the floor, Buddha-like.

Ray watched him for a few moments, fascinated, then went back to the club house. Normandie had finished her Kiddies Fun Hour and was deflating dolphins. She said, 'Did you tell Felix?' and he said, 'No, his mind was on another plane and I was frightened to cut the thread in case it floated off and never found its way back.'

'I've just been on the phone to Michael Boulding, the marine physicist guy who took the artifact into Boston.'

'The who who took the what?' he asked, confused.

'The thing Felix found on the beach. It turns out that it's a seal.'

Ray's eyes fixed themselves on Donny Dolphin. It was funny, he thought, that he'd been thinking only a few minutes ago about seals balancing things.

'No, Ray, not that sort of seal. This is the sort of seal you put on documents and it's almost certainly medieval in origin. What do you make of that? Your heart's beating a little faster, eh?'

He looked at her.

'To me, I hope, it's the spirit of historical enquiry, the romance of the past. You no doubt can see little cash-machines with their numbers whirring up, up, up.'

Donny Dolphin gasped its last. Into the box it went. The door opened and Jack Fountain said, 'We saw you having a look at Southern Breeze.'

'What do you mean cash-machines whirring?'

'Think about it. Medieval seals, medieval treasure chests?'

'Hookers,' said Jack Fountain, 'whores, as we used to

say. My gran could put more meaning into the syllables "whoooer" than you would think possible. They used to parade up and down Candle Alley.'

'See you,' said Normandie.

'Candle Alley being so named,' said Jack, who liked to reminisce, 'because the folk there couldn't afford gas or electricity.'

Ray followed her outside. 'Are you saying this seal thing is valuable?'

She leapt up the sandy bank, taking the illegal, well-worn path through the lavender hedge that bordered the Magic Garden. He leapt through it after her. 'Ooh you hypocrite,' she said shocked. 'You shout at little children who do that.'

'Tell me about this seal.'

'He found it where the excavators are working. Next to where the bit of American plane was found. It was uncanny. He sort of homed in on it using his psychic powers.'

She set off again, along the path to the dunes and the sea wall.

'Hang on,' he yelped.

'Sorry.'

'But why should it set cash-machines whirring? Will you stop!' he cried, leaping after her and grabbing her arm.

'Ray, between three and six in the afternoon I am off duty, right?'

'Yes, but why might it be valuable?'

She looked at him. She relented; or perhaps she didn't.

'It probably isn't. But if Felix is a seer – a mystic who has a special skill at finding things – if he can rootle out buried stuff from the past – well, it's just a shame you sacked him, isn't it? Particularly when you think how the Crown Jewels of England might be buried on your bit of seashore.'

She ran off along the path.

He returned to the office. Jack Fountain was watching trays of food pass out into the café. 'According to the menu,' he said, 'the deep-fried ice-cream is smothered in chocolate sauce. From where I'm sitting there isn't enough to get your toe wet.'

'What do you know about the Crown Jewels of England?' Ray said. 'They're in the Tower of London, aren't they? Why should they be buried on my beach?'

'Are they buried on your beach?'

Ray thought for a further milli-second about what Normandie had told him. 'No,' he said. 'I don't suppose so.'

'Strictly speaking, the beach between high and low tide belongs to the Queen.'

'You mean I'm a Holiday Village by Royal Appointment?'

'Not,' said Jack Fountain, still watching food being taken into the café, 'unless that's Prince Andrew I can see ordering a jumbo sausage with curry sauce.'

He laughed a bit. Ray said, 'Yes, yes, very funny.'

'It's not just your beach that belongs to the Crown. It's every beach.'

'It's come in useful, hasn't it, Jack, all those years reading the *Reader's Digest*?'

'Aye well, if you don't want to know . . .'

'I do want to know.'

'It was King John who lost the Crown Jewels of England.'

'Where?'

'Here.'

Ray stared at him.

'Somewhere in Lincolnshire any rate. In the quicksands of The Wash.'

'Bloody hell.'

Jack said, 'About these tarts.'

But Ray was already out of the door, through the magic garden, and leaping, with surprising agility for a man of his stocky build, through the hole in the hedge.

Felix's caravan was empty.

Ray went to the beach, only the second time he had ventured beyond the sea-defence wall this season, the first time having been the previous day, when there had been the unusual interest of an unexploded bomb. The bomb had been a fantasy just as no doubt the buried treasures would be a fantasy, but it was, he reflected, a time of heady excitement for a small stretch of pebbles and rock that's only trick was to submerge itself in water twice a day.

He passed caravanners sunning themselves and said mechanically, 'Hi, enjoying yourselves, are you?' A mother said, 'Our Cindy should enter the beauty contest shouldn't she, Mr Monkman?'

'I should say so,' he said, hurrying past, thinking of sparkling jewels and golden crowns. The sun was warm on his forehead. There was a gentle breeze from the south. He could smell the sea and the scent of sea grasses. The tide was in and for once the ocean was a hazy blue, stretching to the horizon. He told himself that he ought to do this more often, it would help him to relax, cope with his irritable bowel syndrome.

He looked along the shore. The excavators had been moved. The policemen had gone, and with them the blokes from army bomb disposal and the RAF. It was difficult, now, to say exactly where the bits of aeroplane had been found.

He looked for a lone figure in a purple suit, picking up vibrations from the astral plane, or consulting with Red Indian guides.

But Spookie was nowhere to be seen.

15

Wormby Flats, Lincolnshire

It was Michael Boulding, out checking his beach sensors, who found him. He was sitting in the tall grasses on the sea wall, looking northwards towards the Fosdyke and the distant smudge of Gibraltar Point.

Darkness fell as they walked together back to the holiday village, to the Dreamboat Café. They stood at the bar and watched Normandie finish her act. Jude came past and said, 'Hi, Michael,' and then, 'Thanks for the tea.'

'Any time,' said Michael, politely.

'You waiting for Normandie?'

He nodded. She sighed extravagantly and passed along to the conservatory with her tray of fish suppers.

'Felix wants to talk to us,' Michael said quietly, when Normandie joined them.

'Do you, Felix? What about?'

He looked unhappily round the crowded bar.

'It's complicated,' said Michael. 'Shall we go to my place?'

She hesitated. She didn't know if she wanted to go to Michael's place. Anyway, she was on duty, it being Ray's night off, the night he went to Spalding Conservative Club, or to drink with his horrible mates in a pub in Holbeach.

She looked at Felix again. He looked seedy. Ill. She remembered him on the beach, waving the bit of the American plane, while the digger driver and the policeman shouted at him.

In the end she left Simon and Pierre to close the bar and lock up.

The car jolted slowly along the track to the Tymoors' farm. For a moment its lights illuminated the farmhouse, shining through the aluminium window frames, playing over the bedroom ceilings. Normandie wondered if Karen Tymoor was lying awake, listening, watching the shadows. The car turned into a track by the paddock and pulled up beside the caravan.

She got out of the car. There was a snuffling noise in the darkness; Karen Tymoor's horse had come to see what was happening. Michael said softly, 'Hello, old girl.'

Normandie stroked the horse's nose. There was the heavy smell of dew on grass, the scent of straw that had been baled in a neighbouring field.

'OK,' Michael said.

They went inside. He lit a gas lamp that hissed comfortingly, reminding Normandie of her days in the Scout Guides, sitting in the dormitory at the Cader Idris Mountain Centre discussing the boys they'd snogged. Felix's purple suit was almost black in the lamplight. He sat at the table and peered down into the shining yellow sphere, every inch a magician. Normandie said, 'I think we ought to take you shopping, Felix. Buy you some new clothes.'

He smiled gallantly. She thought again how ill he looked.

'Right,' said Michael, sitting down. 'I've explained to Felix that the thing he found on the beach is a seal, several centuries old, badly distorted and eroded by the sand.'

A shadow of pain crossed Felix's face.

'Are your teeth all right?' Normandie asked. 'Have you been taking your antibiotics?'

A sudden flicker of irritation . . .

'Sorry,' she said.

He stared down, into the yellow flame of the gas lantern.

'So what did you want to tell us?' she asked, gently.

After a moment he sighed. 'I am being summoned,' he said, 'by the past.'

He looked up, expecting shock, astonishment.

They were waiting for him to go on.

After all, he was clairvoyant. A seer.

'Summoned by what in the past?' asked Normandie.

Silence.

'You told me on the beach that you needed protection against something with a black aura,' said Michael, after a moment. 'What would have a black aura?'

Felix sighed gently. Anything that was negative. Anything that was evil. Vampires, werewolves. Succubus, incubus.

'An aura in medical terms,' Michael went on, 'is something that causes people to hallucinate and find that their memories are disconnected. There is a clouding of consciousness.'

'I think that in the psychic world,' said Normandie, 'an aura means something different. Felix, are you frightened by what is happening to you?'

Frightened by the eyes in the pine forest? Frightened he

would slip unconsciously into Alpha – or, worse, be taken there against his will? Frightened that he would be pulled downwards into Theta, and then to the terrible place below Theta where all would be revealed, but from which he would never escape, never wish to escape: the place of the catatonic, of those who had given up all hope?

'Is there some connection with the seal?'

For a second the mists parted and he felt the wind sharp against his skin – and there was fur round his neck, wet and chilly to the touch, and his jaw throbbed, and his mouth was full of salt and gritty sand, and in his stomach was the weight of sea creatures torn from the rocks.

'It was the bag,' he said. 'The bag was sewn with tiny jewels. He threw the seal away. It was no use to him.' He stared down into the gas sphere, as though it was a crystal ball. 'The French were at Mountsorrel. John was dead.'

The mists fell. The picture was gone.

Normandie and Michael looked at each other.

'Felix,' said Normandie, softly, after a moment, turning back to him, 'is this King John we're talking about? King John who lost the Crown Jewels?'

'The wand with the head of a dove,' he said. 'The Sword of Tristram.'

'What's that?'

Silence. For a moment he looked puzzled.

'You said something about the Sword of Tristram on the beach the other day. When you picked up the bit from the American plane.'

He blinked at her, confused.

'Was the sword part of the Crown Jewels? The treasure that King John lost?'

He nodded. Another pause.

'And do you think you can find this treasure?' asked Michael.

'Why else do you think I came back to Wormby,' he said, 'after all these years?'

Moths batted against the windows, attracted by the flame, anxious to burn their wings.

Michael got up. He filled the kettle and put it on the stove.

'As I understand it,' he said, 'the story is that King John crossed over the Wash with his army. Basically, he misjudged the tides and his wagons got swallowed up by quicksands. Nobody knows where it happened.'

'Do you know, Felix?' asked Normandie.

He shook his head.

'But there is some kind of spirit that is leading you it?'

He nodded, though spirit was an imprecise word to use.

'And this spirit first, well, manifested itself in 1962?'

Again he nodded.

'Can you tell us what happened?' said Michael, sitting down again, speaking in a scientist's sort of voice.

He smiled faintly. Michael Boulding was not a believer.

'I was doing my act in the camp theatre. I had gone into Alpha, which is something you may or may not understand, but it involves absorbing the psychic power from around you and allows you to see things clearly...'

To see, not always accurately, into the mind of your subject.

'Visualisation in Alpha is a potent tool but not as potent as visualisation in Theta. It is in Theta that you utilise the mass psychic collective consciousness, that you reach out to those in the Other World.'

He stopped.

After a moment Normandie said, 'Did you go into Theta?'

He nodded.

'And?'

'I collapsed. The girl who was stage-managing in the theatre – if stage-managing is not too grand a term – called for the camp ambulance. This was a pukka holiday camp in those days, a sizable place. They used to get television stars on a Sunday night – Frankie Howerd, I remember – many famous crooners. But the camp ambulance was busy going round the bars collecting the night's takings and the switchboard refused to put out a call for it, because it might have alarmed the happy campers. Or crappy hampers as the boys and girls on the staff called them.'

'Oh Felix,' said Normandie, 'the way artistes are treated!'

''Twas ever thus, sweetie. Eventually I was taken to my chalet and a doctor was called. He decided that I had had an epileptic fit. But the truth was that, for a moment, standing there on the stage, I had been possessed.'

The kettle began to boil.

'By this spirit from the time of King John?' said Normandie.

Spirit . . . it sounded like something from *Aladdin and the Forty Thieves*.

He nodded.

Michael got up. He made tea in three mugs. He said,

'Felix, have you ever taken part in any scientific experiments? Experiments into the nature of psychical reality?'

'There was a parapsychology study at Croydon. Run by the Spiritualists League.'

'Right, OK,' said Michael carefully, rattling mugs. 'Anything more, shall we say, academic?'

Felix shook his head.

'Nothing connected with the phenomenon of consciousness as it relates to contemporary engineering systems and human-machine technologies?'

'Michael,' said Normandie, 'he sees things.'

'Yes,' said Michael. 'But how?'

'Through his psychic powers. He's clairvoyant.'

Felix's eyes roamed round the caravan. He liked a couple of biscuits with his tea late at night. Abernethies for choice; a poor man's luxury, he used to tell himself.

'Felix,' said Normandie, 'is there any way that we can help you?'

In the corner of the caravan a green light was blinking, a small green eye.

'I don't know how, sweetie. The "spirit", as you so quaintly call it, is trying to guide me, but there is nothing here from the past, nothing to hold on to. All is changed, changed utterly.'

He turned his head abruptly. There were several lights now, the gentle hum of an electrical motor.

'It's the computer downloading from the satellite,' Michael said. 'It tells me the wave height out at sea, shows how the surface currents are running in the bay. I have to go to the beach later to check the buoys.'

Felix said, 'I'm sorry but I'm very, very tired.'

His hand, its skin mottled by the haemorrhage of tiny blood vessels, rubbed at his jaw.

They took him back to the Holiday Village. There was a note from Ray Monkman stuck to the door of his caravan. He didn't have to leave the site on Saturday. He was welcome to stay for his second week and give some more poetry recitals. Perhaps he could do a bit of bingo calling in the afternoons and be a judge in the Miss Wormby Flats heats. 'Let's have a pint and talk about it,' wrote Ray.

Felix smiled in the darkness.

'Goodnight, sweetie. Goodnight, sweet prince,' he said, obscurely, vanishing into the dark interior of his caravan with a bottle of whisky to frighten away the demons. The site was silent, except for the low beat of music from one of the staff caravans, the kitchen lads partying the night away and very likely inhaling noxious substances.

'Well, what do you think?' said Normandie quietly.

'Think?'

'About Felix!'

'He's an entertainer. He tells people they've got interesting auras and does magic tricks.'

'You saw him on the beach! Something led him to the seal – something psychic. What if next time he's led to King John's lost treasure?'

She had found her way in the darkness into the Magic Garden. She sat on a little goblin table that shone palely in the starlight. She could smell lavender from the valiant, bruised hedge. There was a distant humming noise, a plane somewhere. She looked up and saw its navigation lights winking, way out over the loom of the sea wall, over the ocean.

She said, 'I'll go to King's Lynn tomorrow. See what I can find out about King John and the jewels.'

'Good idea,' he said, absently, putting his arm round her and kissing her.

In the caravan, Jude stirred and said, 'Where've you been?'

'Nowhere. Where's Morag?'

'With her bloke. I'm hiding from Simon. Was that Michael?'

'Yes.'

'Was he trying to come in with you?'

'Yes.'

'He seemed very determined.'

'Yes.'

'I went to tea this afternoon but he just talked about you all the time. He wanted to know about your last boyfriend and why you'd chucked him.'

'Oh.'

'Then he talked science stuff.'

'Yes.'

'Stuff about hydro-whatsit things.'

' "Hydrodynamic, sedimentological and biochemical processes." '

'Yes, those things.'

'It's his field.'

'He likes you,' said Jude, sadly, 'because you're clever. But I thought you said you didn't fancy him?'

'I don't.'

'Why were you snogging him then?'

Why indeed?

'Night.'

She got into bed and instantly fell asleep. She was woken up by Jude shouting at her to answer the phone, then by Jude slithering out of bed, swearing loudly, and brutally thrusting a mobile into her ear like a corkscrew.

A voice said, 'I've been looking on the Internet.'

'What?'

'It's me, Michael.'

'I know it's fucking you, Michael.'

Jude groaned loudly and pulled her pillow over her head.

'I didn't want you to think I wasn't interested in helping old Felix.'

'What do you mean, *old Felix*?'

'Well, he is old.'

'You don't have to patronise him about it.'

'OK, sorry. Look, I've found out that there's a lot of research into clairvoyance been done in the States, mainly at Princeton, but also in Texas.'

'What?' she said. 'What?'

'Tell him,' said Jude loudly, 'to go away.'

'Was that Jude?'

'Yes.'

'Say "Hello Jude." '

Christ Almighty.

'Mind you, they don't call it clairvoyance. They call it analytical methodologies for quantitative assessment of remote perception data.'

'Michael, go away.'

'It may be that I can come up with some sort of test –
something to tell us if he's faking it or not.'

'He isn't faking it.'

'I know he doesn't think he is. Look, perhaps we could
meet up tomorrow and talk about it—'

She turned off the phone. She looked out thought the
caravan window. There was the faint light of the false dawn.
For a moment she thought she saw a shadow move and dance
in the dark window of Felix's caravan – but she was
exhausted; wherever she looked she saw shadows move and
dance. Donny Dolphin, screaming children.

She fell back into bed and sank into oblivion.

16

Wormby Flats, Lincolnshire

Normandie overslept and almost missed the Kiddies Fun Hour. She ran to the office and found Ray struggling to inflate Donny Dolphin. 'I overslept, OK, because I'm so tired,' she said, going on the offensive. 'Tired, tired, tired, of working till midnight and being woken every day at dawn by screaming kids.'

She was tired because of all the shagging, said Ray, following her out to the kiddies pool, his arms full of inflated plastic balls. After all his years running a caravan site he knew what it was that gave waitresses dark smudges under their eyes.

'I am not a waitress,' she turned on him.

'Well I don't know what you actually are, love, in that case,' he said, and escaped rapidly to talk to the two tarts in Southern Breeze, give them another warning. One more 'Hello, sailor' to passing schoolboys and they were out, he didn't care if one of them was the niece of Wormby Flats' oldest caravan-owner and they couldn't help being friendly.

In the afternoon there were the weekly heats of the Miss Wormby Flats contest. Ray had worried about some of the mums objecting to Felix as an adjudicator (grinning ghoulishly in his purple suit) but everybody clapped him politely.

Being judged by old theatrical goats was, it seemed, part of the beauty-queen tradition.

The sun blazed down. Skylarks sang. The smell of the sea mingling with the smells of sun lotion and ice cream, and Ray, with two pints of Stella inside him, was for a moment happy. He had made this happen. He had brought all these people together. Without him (and his redundancy money from the *Daily Star*) the Wormby Flats Holiday Village would have ended up a graveyard of caravans, a rusting vacation city for the oldest of old-age pensioners.

Instead, just look at it . . .

A British family seaside resort, with a restaurant serving deep-fried ice-cream, a Magic Garden that brought gnome afficionados from as far away as Munich, and – for this one week of high season at least – every single caravan occupied.

'And now the contestants!'

They were mainly skinny fourteen-year-olds. They wore swimsuits with little frills and flounces. They giggled and blushed. Some of them pirouetted like fashion models, and made their mums and dads laugh. To Ray, this all helped to give the occasion its air of childhood innocence. He sat at the judges desk, smiling as the girls paraded under a string of Union Jack bunting and the sound system played the hits of the sixties.

'Sonia Ecclestone from Penkridge,' said Jude, who could be his personal Miss Wormby Flats any night of the week were it not for her vile temper and shrewish tongue. 'Tell us who your favourite pop group is, Sonia.'

The sun shone. A whiff of hot fat from the kitchen mingling with the scent of the bruised lavender hedge. This is England, Ray cried out to himself, his heart swelling, the strong lager doing its duty.

'And have you got a boyfriend, Sonia? The truth now, or we'll get the Astounding Felix to look into your mind and tell us what he sees.'

Felix smiled and looked roguish and waved his little finger.

Next day was Wednesday – Normandie's day off. She said to Ray, 'Simon's going to do the bingo instead of Felix, so that I can take him out. Is that all right?'

'Where are you going?'

'Just out.'

They were chasing after the jewels.

'Hocum pokum,' he said. 'And you a girl who went to uni.'

'Went to *what*?'

'Oxford uni,' he said, uneasy but defiant.

She blinked rapidly then went. Jack wandered in to talk about the tarts in Sea Breeze, a subject which, Ray pointed out, was clearly becoming an obsession with him and not altogether a healthy one.

The phone went. It was the archivist woman again from Boston, asking for Felix. 'And can you please tell me his surname?' she said.

'He hasn't got one.'

She gave a little laugh.

'He's the Astounding Felix.'

'But Astounding Felix, presumably, is his stage name?'

'Who knows? Perhaps he astounded his mother at birth.'

Ray winked at Jack, who winked back.

'Perhaps,' he said, 'he did a magic trick.'

'Yes, very amusing,' said the archivist.

'It's the only name I'm aware of,' said Ray, knowing that Felix was really somebody else, though he couldn't remember who. 'Is it about the seal?'

'If you could please ask Mr Felix to ring me.'

'It's just that it was found on my land and we're all very interested, as you'd expect.'

'Oh. I see. Well, yes. We've had it looked at by an expert and it could date from the beginning of the thirteenth century.'

'Which would make it . . .?'

'Yes, I know. Possibly from the reign of King John. But don't get overexcited.'

'All right,' said Ray, dutifully.

'There's nothing whatsoever to connect it to lost baggage trains. It's far more likely to be a town seal, or it could be monastic, or even have been lost from a ship. Anyway could you ask Mr Felix to give me a ring? Perhaps, if you are claiming part-ownership, you would also like to come and see us.'

'Is it valuable? What would we be talking about? Just a ballpark figure . . .'

'I've really no idea,' she said, ending the conversation on what was, for her, a satisfactory note.

He put the phone down.

'Felix Shafto,' he said.

'You what?' said Jack Fountain.

'It's the Astounding Felix's real name, I've just remembered.'

'It doesn't sound very real.'

'No. Personally I call him Spookie.'

He thought for a moment. Then he got up and went outside. Normandie's car was just pulling out of the car park. Her scientist friend with the beard and the toothy grin was sitting next to her and Spookie, the purple ghoul, was sitting in the back.

Jack, from behind him, said, 'Anyway, getting back to business. Those two tarts are still at it.'

'As they have been, Jack,' he said, watching Normandie's little car make its way along the long, straight road through the fields of onions and cabbages, 'since the time of Babylon and of Sodom and Gomorrah.'

'But not at Wormby Flats.'

Too true, Ray thought, looking at his empire, his little kingdom by the sea. He'd explained to Felix, the night before over a fish supper and two lagers, that anything he found on the beach or in the caravan site should be brought to him, Ray Monkman, as the rightful owner. There'd be a fair divvy between them, he'd explained, of any reward that might accrue.

Felix had nodded, vaguely, the way he did, but hadn't said anything. Could he be trusted? Could anybody be trusted?

His eyes rested broodingly on a grassy mound at the far end of the rows of letting caravans. On it were the remnants of a wooden stockade, and a sign that said *Fort Wormby*, the words painted inside a cowboy lasso. When Ray had bought the caravan park the stockade had been called Wormby Castle, and knightly banners had flown from its two small turrets, and there had been a sign pointing to nonexistent dungeons. Then, when Fantasy Island opened at Skegness, Ray had launched the great Cowboys and Indians revival with Wild West barbecues and, for a couple of weeks, a singing cowboy on a horse.

But what, he wondered now – as he had pondered idly at times in the past – was a grassy mound, a hillocky lump, doing there in the first place?

'Noses, ears, belly buttons,' said Jack, standing next to him in the sunshine and still musing on the girls in Sea Breeze. 'I dread to think where else they've got themselves pierced.'

'You wouldn't know,' Ray asked, 'where I could hire a metal detector?'

'Bloody hell,' said Jack, impressed.

'OK, so where are we going?' asked Michael.

'To find the place where the Crown Jewels were lost.'

'That'll be interesting.'

'Yes, won't it?' she said coldly. 'Felix and I have had a long talk, and I spent two hours yesterday in King's Lynn library. There's a lot more known about it than you'd think.'

She stopped in Holbeach and bought ham, and rolls, and a cake for each of them. 'What sort of cake do you want?' she asked Michael. 'I don't mind,' he said, which made her think he really was an alien from another planet.

She drove them out to Holbeach Marsh, across the flat reclaimed land behind the sea wall, and then along the byways to Gedney Drove End and the estuary of the Nene. At the lighthouse guarding the Nene Outfall Cut, she stopped and looked at Felix who smiled back at her politely.

'Well, it wasn't here,' said Michael, looking at an Ordnance Survey map spread on his bare knees. 'This side of the river wasn't reclaimed until the eighteenth century, and the Norfolk shore not until 1846. In King John's day this was sea bed. As also, for that matter, was the coast at Wormby.'

'Could there have been a path across at low tide?'

'Not this far out to sea.'

'OK. Now, Felix, we know King John and his army left King's Lynn and crossed into Lincolnshire. Right?'

Felix, in the back seat, nodded.

'What we're going to do now is to drive inland and at some point in the next half hour we cannot help but cross the place where they forded the estuary.'

Again he nodded.

'Will you know when it happens?'

He shrugged sadly. He had an Other World look about him, or perhaps it was the heat. She didn't want him to doze off. He ought to have been in the front seat, next to her, but Michael had been in it quicker than a rabbit.

She drove slowly inland, along a narrow straight track. On the other side of the river, a group of ramblers tramped along the Nene Way. Michael, looking at the map, said, 'The next building we come to, by the way, is King John's Farm.'

They reached a junction and a farmhouse. Normandie pulled up by the side of the road. They turned and looked at Felix.

He looked at the building and shook his head.

'No,' said Normandie. 'It doesn't look very old, does it?'

It was getting hotter. There was a faint breeze; on it the

scent of honeysuckle. Bindweed grew in the hedges, huge white trumpets covering the hawthorn. 'They used to call bindweed Our Lady's Smock,' said Normandie. 'It's such a lovely flower really. All right to carry on?'

The track ran back towards the Nene, then inland again to the village of Sutton Bridge. 'There are those,' Normandie said, 'who claim the treasure lies somewhere underneath the local golf course. The tourist office has even set up a King John's treasure trail. Anything here, Felix?'

Apparently not.

'OK,' she said after a while. 'We have crossed the route that must have been taken by King John's army. I am now doubling back and taking us to the only place I know where there is anything physically left from the thirteenth century.'

She drove east, through the village of Walpole St Andrew. Then she turned up a small track and, after a few minutes, stopped. A low bank of earth divided two huge fields of cabbages.

They got out of the car and climbed it.

'This is all that remains – in this area at least – of the ancient sea-defence wall,' said Normandie. 'It was here in King John's day. It was here long before King John. It was built in all probability by the Romans.'

They sat on the ancient bank. In the distance, over the fields, they could see occasional flashes of reflected light, cars on the A17 caught in the sun. Michael fetched their lunch. They ate their rolls. Normandie poured coffee from a flask.

Felix ate his cake and wandered off.

'Now what's he doing?' said Michael.

'I don't know. He's a sort of psychic sniffer-dog. I think we just keep out of the way. The ancient sea wall is our last chance. If he can't pick up vibrations here, poor love, he's not going to do it anywhere.'

Felix had made his way along the bank. He was staring out over the sea of blue-green cabbages.

He turned and shook his head.

Sorry, sweetie, his expression said.

They drove back through Boston and out to Butterwick, to another stretch of ancient sea wall at Wrangle Flats. They sat looking out over the salt marshes. Felix again wandered off. Gone with the fairies, thought Normandie sadly.

'I suppose,' said Michael, 'that the jewels really were lost? It isn't just some sort of legend?'

She went back to the car and returned with a file and some apples.

'There are two contemporary accounts of what happened. OK?'

He nodded.

'The first is by Ralph, Abbot of Coggeshall, writing in his *Chronicon Anglicanum*. He described King John's last journey and said, "Moreover the greatest distress troubled him, because on that journey he had lost his chapel with his relics, and some of his packhorses with divers household effects at the Welstreme, and many members of his household were submerged in the waters of the sea, and sucked into the quicksand there, because they had set out incautiously and hastily before the tide had receded." '

'Say that again.'

'All of it?'

'No, about the tide.'

'*Quia incaute et precipitanter,*' said Normandie chomping her apple, '*se ingesserant aestu maris nondum recedente.*'

She passed him a sheet of paper. He said, 'This account only mentions chapel relics and household effects.'

'Very true.'

'No Crown Jewels.'

'Not even a little one.'

'You said there were two chroniclers. Who was the other?' She looked again in her file.

'Roger of Wendover, a monk at St Albans. He wrote something called the *Flores Historiarum* ten years after the disaster. In it he said, "Then, heading for the north, he lost, by an unexpected accident, all the wagons, carts, and packhorses, with the treasures, precious vessels, and all the other things which he cherished with special care; for the ground was opened in the midst of the waves, and bottomless whirlpools engulfed everything, together with men and horses, so that not a single foot soldier got away to bear tidings of the disaster to the King. The King, however, barely escaping with his army, spent the following night at the abbey called Swineshead." '

'Right,' Michael said, rubbing his hands in a piratical manner. 'Now we're talking. Treasures and precious vessels.'

'We're also talking a load of nonsense. "Not a single foot soldier got away to bear tidings of the disaster" – and yet the King, we are told, barely escaped with his army? Wendover was a fantasist. In another place he claimed that King John banged the Archdeacon of Norwich up inside a cope of lead, chained him to a wall, and then starved him of food until the cope crushed him.'

'So? It sounds likely enough.'

'Except that the Archdeacon in question, one Geoffrey of Norwich, outlived King John and became Bishop of Ely in 1225.'

'You're saying that Wendover made things up?'

'I'm not saying anything. But he does record, as a matter of historical fact, that a washerwoman who plied her trade on the Sabbath was sucked dry by a small black pig.'

Michael ate a crisp. 'Right.'

'And he also says, as historical fact, that a loaf of bread baked on a Sunday ran with blood when a knife was put into it.'

'OK. So what other evidence have you got?'

'None.'

'Wendover, our expert on washerwomen suckling small black pigs, is the only authority to tell us that the Crown Jewels of England were lost in the Wash?'

'As far as I know. There may be other sources, I'm not a medievalist. Until I went into King's Lynn library all I knew about King John was from a Robin Hood pantomime I was in. "Good King John was a Right Royal Tartar. 1215, Magna Carta." '

He rolled over on to his stomach, and started to tap tap tap into his laptop, accessing some computer somewhere, she supposed, that would give him a full inventory of King John's treasury, with a price tag on each item for insurance purposes. She lay back and listened to the skylarks.

He said, 'You know I said I'd try to find some sort of

scientific test? I looked into it but it isn't easy to prove or disprove retrocognition.'

She drifted into a doze.

'There's something called morphic resonance. They've done work on it in Texas. We think memories are stored in the brain because we can't conceive of them being stored anywhere else. But nobody knows *where* in the brain they are stored.'

He stared at the screen, then adjusted it slightly to avoid the sun's glare.

'The accepted belief is that memories are stored through synaptic modification – connections between the nerve cells, modified as electrical pulses. But the morphic-resonance guys say the brain is actually the hardware and downloads memories from outside. Memories from the past, laid down by others.'

He looked at Felix who was sitting, Buddha-like, on the ancient sea wall, staring over the fields. Was he somehow accessing the memories of a man who lived, and died, in the early thirteenth century?

He glanced at Normandie. She lay sleeping or pretending to sleep, her eyes closed, her brown hair half over her face, her mouth slightly open.

He went back to his laptop. The lights on his modem blinked.

Normandie said, dozily, 'The resonance he wants is from a physical connection with the past. Something from the thirteenth century. Perhaps we ought to take him to look at the crown of Edward the Confessor.'

So she had only been pretending to be asleep.

'I thought it was lost in the Wash,' he said, 'with the other Crown Jewels?'

'I think we can manage it,' she said, sitting up and looking at Felix, 'all the same.'

17

Worcester Cathedral

Evening light flooded into the quire, down through the high west windows. The choir in their stalls sang the Song of Simeon: *Lord, now lettest thou thy servant depart in peace.* Normandie wondered if King John, over whose calcified bones these words had washed every day for eight hundred years, was indeed truly departed, peacefully or otherwise.

The young voices soared.

For mine eyes have seen thy salvation.

The King's tomb was a few metres in front of her. She stared at his effigy with its thin, Angevin face; its neat but foxy beard.

Oh Lord, shew thy mercy upon us.

Once, in Lincoln Cathedral, he had sent a knight thundering up to the pulpit to tell the saintly Bishop Hugh to cut his sermon short because he, the King, wanted his dinner.

And grant us thy salvation.

Not a pious king, then. But when Hugh of Lincoln lay dying, John visited him and comforted him, and later helped carry his corpse to the grave. And on his own deathbed, at Newark, he had gladly received both the counsel of confession and the Eucharist. And his final request, the codicil to his will, was that his body be buried in the church of his

177

favourite saint, Wulstan, the only Saxon bishop to have survived the Conquest.

And they had borne him across the very cockpit of England, those foreign mercenaries of his small army; borne his corpse to Worcester out of love and affection – for they had no more silver pennies to look for.

Normandie glanced at Felix, sitting next to her in his purple suit, like some ancient, disreputable bishop. His gaze, also, was fixed on the Norman stone effigy.

Lighten our darkness, we beseech thee, O Lord; and by thy great mercy defend us from all perils and dangers of this night.

They had opened the tomb up once, measured John's bones and found him to be a shortish chap, only five foot five inches in height. Short and stout, fond of his food, an eye for a pretty face – more than just an eye, by all accounts: the Abbot of Swinehead was said to have poisoned him for having ravished his sister.

She looked at the stone crown on his head. Simple in design, almost Celtic. Huge holes for chunky jewels. A copy, faithful no doubt, of the true crown of Edward the Confessor that had been lost in the sands of the Wash.

Michael whispered, 'When are we going to sing a hymn?'

'We aren't. This is choral evensong.'

'I was hoping for "O come, O come Emmanuel".'

'Why? We're not in Epiphany.'

'It was my favourite at school.'

She wondered what sort of school he'd gone to, that encouraged him to chatter through prayers.

For the love of thy only Son, our Saviour, Jesus Christ.

'Amen.'

Felix still gazed intently on the tomb. Was he communing with John's spirit? Was he cleansing the dead King's aura?

She smiled faintly.

The choir was singing the anthem. She tried to imagine John's funeral on that day in late October. Had it been sunny and crisp, with blue skies and an early frost curling the bright golden leaves? Or dim and misty and cold, a day in sympathy with the mood of those gathered in Wulstan's church. 'A splendid service was held as was fitting for a king,' said the chronicle she had read in King's Lynn library. 'Thus the prophesy of Merlin was fulfilled, that said that he would lie between sovereigns. And this was the truth, for he lies between St Wulstan and another saint's body.'

She looked at the two white banners that now hung on either side of the choir: one dedicated to St Oswald, the other to St Wulstan.

The service was drawing to a close.

The grace of our Lord Jesus Christ, and the love of God, and the fellowship of the Holy Ghost, be with us all evermore.

'Amen,' said Felix, loudly, making one of the choirboys stare at him.

They remained in their seats as the choir and congregation left.

'A bit of a loser,' said Michael.

'Yes,' said Normandie, sadly.

'Didn't he give England to the Pope?'

'Not really.'

'I thought he did.'

'Only as a political necessity. Half the northern barons were in revolt and the French were threatening to invade. And anyway, it was meaningless, an empty gesture. Richard had already given England to the Emperor.'

'What emperor?'

'The bloke who captured him when he was on his way home from the Crusades. He was supposed to have locked him in a tower, where he wouldn't have been found for a hundred years if his faithful minstrel Blondel hadn't wandered all over Europe singing under dark castle walls until one day he heard his master sing back.'

'I think Blondel was the name of Hitler's dog,' said Michael.

'Whatever. The fact is, that although Richard was gay and highly prone to sing to minstrels wearing tight tights, he never was locked in a tower. When he was a captive he held his court in the city of Spires, transacted his kingly business, and even had his favourite hawks sent over from England. And to get his release he handed over England as a fief of the Empire, but does anybody ever criticise him for that? No. It was John who got blamed for everything.'

They got up and walked round the tomb. John clutched his sword with a fierce grip. His feet rested on a mythical doglike creature that gnawed his scabbard. Two tiny stone bishops crouched by his head like imps – crying, Normandie thought, *Repent! Repent!*

The sun's rays no longer came pouring through the west windows. The tomb was in shadow, the stone face cold and grey. A sign said: 'His tyranny led to the barons enforcing his signature of Magna Carta.'

'Poor John,' Normandie said. 'He had his dark side. But he administered justice painstakingly and judiciously.'

'So why was he so unpopular?'

'Because he had to contend with something that nobody had ever had to contend with before. Something nobody could see or comprehend but that brought terrible ruin and disaster.'

'Do you know what she's talking about, Felix?' Michael asked.

Felix smiled and shook his head.

'Inflation,' said Normandie. 'It came in from Europe. It was terrible, and nobody understood it because it had never happened before. The King's income stayed the same but everything was more expensive. It made him desperate for money. And of course,' she added, truth being important, 'he was greedy by nature.'

In the cathedral shop they bought Ray a present: a key ring that said on it RAYMOND, and explained that Raymonds everywhere were persuasive, resourceful and created their own luck. Normandie wanted a cup of tea but the teashop was closed. They walked down to the river and found a pub. It was six-thirty. Normandie said, 'How long is it going to take to get back?'

'The same as coming,' said Michael logically, going to the bar.

They wouldn't be back at Wormby Flats till gone midnight. 'Oh God, Felix,' she said dismally, 'when am I ever going to catch up on my sleep?'

'Young men,' he said, sympathetically, 'are demanding lovers.'

'He's not my lover!' A terrible thought struck her. 'He isn't going to be, is he? Felix, have you been seeing things?'

'You will meet a tall dark stranger,' said Felix mechanically.

'Not till I've had a good sleep I hope,' she said, for she was a girl who needed her sleep more than all the jewels in England's crown.

'Well, Felix,' she said gently. 'Was it any use?'

He looked at her enquiringly.

'Sweetie?'

She hesitated over how to put it. Had King John communed with him during evensong? Was King John his new guide in Alpha?

He smiled faintly, which she thought was pretty unfair. Few people, she imagined, could discuss discarnates as though they were as much a part of the physical world as Sainsburys.

Michael came back from the bar with drinks and crisps and three toasted cheese sandwiches.

'Is that all I'm going to get for my dinner?' she asked.

'Dinner?'

'It's all right. Don't worry.'

'I didn't know you'd want *dinner.*'

Why, she wondered, did he say 'dinner' as though it was something that consisted exclusively of larks' tongues and champagne, partaken of by plutocrats while the people starved?

'Has it helped, coming here?' Michael asked Felix.

'We've been through that,' said Normandie shortly.

'And?'

'No,' she said, but then remembered how Felix had stood, before the service began, with his hands on the cold thirteenth century marble of the coffin lid. 'Felix, was there an aura? Can you detect an aura from old bones?'

He thought for a moment then smiled ethereally. ' "Could storied urn or animated bust," ' he said, ' "back to its mansion call the fleeting breath?" '

She waited for him to go on. He sat in silence.

'Yeah, right.'

'There would have been a disturbance, certainly,' he said after a moment, 'if the King was the discarnate.'

'But there wasn't?'

He shook his head.

Michael said, comfortably, 'OK. We can't try to rush Felix. Whether he's picking up some kind of morphic resonance or whatever, it's got to work its own way in its own time.'

They ate their toasted sandwiches, and talked about inflationary pressures in AD 1200, and about some porcelain dinner plates that Normandie had seen earlier in the Royal Worcester Factory shop and that she would come back and buy if ever they found the Crown Jewels.

Felix listened and dozed and wondered what could have brought him to a pub in Worcester, being bought drinks and sandwiches by two strangers who wanted him to stir up old church ghosts. Certainly there had been dark, psychic forces in the cathedral choir, flowing against the high Norman arches; shades rather than apparitions, felt rather than seen (Julia would have seen them, mind you, in a flash). It was only what you would expect in a place of such spirituality, such emotional intensity. He had wandered alone down the nave, and had sensed something by the small, dark, tower stairs down which King Charles had hurried after seeing his army defeated by Cromwell. He had sensed something also by the steps to the Norman crypt – but it came, in the end, from the nearby tomb of Prince Arthur, the elder brother of King Henry the Eighth.

Had Arthur lived there would have been no Reformation, a cathedral verger had explained to a party of visitors, while Felix hovered round the chantry like an old purple ghost himself. There would have been no break with Rome, no dissolution of the monasteries.

The aura that he sensed was silver, and spoke of sweetness and sorrow. It was the sadness of old monks, Felix decided, that lingered round the bones of the boy prince.

Around John's tomb, there had been nothing. The bones were inanimate. He had attempted psychokinesis in the way of Uri Geller, generally an easy trick, but nothing had stirred, he felt certain. Which was hardly surprising, given the number of incantations spoken over the tomb down the centuries.

The peace of God which passeth all understanding . . .

'You all right, Felix?'

They were staring at him, gently, curiously. They were wondering what was going on in his head. It was a question, he thought with a sudden little lurch to his heart, that he often wondered himself these days.

She said, 'Shall we take you home?'

Home.

What a sweetie she was.

* * *

The M42 became the M6. The signs were to Coventry, Ashby de la Zouch, Nottingham – names that spoke of Medieval England. Felix slept for a while, then something began to trouble him – thought-forms resonating in his mind – and he opened his eyes. It was dusk and vehicles on the motorway had their lights on. He looked out at the juggernaut lorries and saw amongst them, though dimly, the shapes of mounted men.

Their car was crossing the path of an army. But why should this disturb his sleep? What road could you take, in the midland shires, that did not cross the path an army had once taken? This was England's cockpit, England's killing ground.

Banners like wraiths in the dusk. French, he realised, his heart thumping gently. A French army seeking the Fosse Way to Lincoln.

'I'm pulling in for a drink, OK?' Normandie said when they were on the A14 and swinging round Kettering.

'There's some bottled water in the back,' said Michael, busy with a laptop computer and mobile phone.

'I want to go to the loo, if you don't mind.'

They stopped at a Little Chef. Michael stayed in the car, absorbed in his calculations of tidal flows in the Boston Deeps, calling up his satellite that was somewhere over Greenland. 'I'm sorry,' said Normandie when they were in the café, 'but I must have sustenance. How about a hot Danish? This is on me, Felix, just sit down.'

They ordered. She said, 'You look terrible. Are you all right?'

'My joints ache. My gums bleed.'

He smiled, showing red hurt gums. 'Old age, sweetie.'

She felt a sudden chill, a crawling sensation.

'Felix, if all this is making you ill, maybe you ought to pack it in. Maybe you should go back to London.'

He looked out of the window, at the darkness.

'Do you know,' he said, 'about space clearing?'

'Pardon?'

'Negative energy is given out from the psyche during times of emotional stress, you see. And it gets stuck in the nooks and crannies of rooms and houses, and positive life-enhancing energies are unable to flow properly round it.'

'Really?'

She wondered what he was getting at.

'It's Julia's latest thing. She goes round people's houses, cleaning out these nooks and crannies like a spiritual Mrs Mop. The trouble is, she hasn't the time to do all the houses that need cleaning out, not with her lectures on Tibetan Singing Bowls. So she wants me to do it.'

'Don't you like living with Julia?'

'I don't live with her. I've been staying with her, temporarily, on her put-u-up, while I sort out my affairs. We have little to do with each other. If the truth were known we tend to avoid each other.'

'Right.'

'I've never had money,' he said, after a moment; implying, somehow, that this was because of absent-mindedness or carelessness, his mind having been on higher things.

'Nor me,' said Normandie, which was true enough, others having paid for her pony when she was eight, her new little car when she was eighteen.

'It was Julia who encouraged me to come to Wormby. I am at the end of my resources, we both agreed, and must find the jewels. But how to do it? Nothing is the same. I reach out to the Other World, but afterwards there is nothing but an image – or a few words in my head. The French,' he added softly, 'are at Bury . . .'

'Sorry?'

'Bury St Edmunds. The French are at Bury and the King's treasure is lost, and must be recovered. But how? I went into Theta and was led to the seal. Must I go into Theta again?'

Down to the emanations of darkness that he was unwilling to disturb. Down to the abode of the catatonic.

She looked at him. She was drawn into the blackness.

This way, she told herself, madness lies.

In the car she said, 'Hurry up, I want to get home,' and Michael looked up in surprise, and said, 'I've not been the one sitting feeding my face.'

'Please, Michael.'

He turned off his laptop and started the car.

She dozed, then surfaced as they crossed the A1 at Peterborough and swung round a roundabout and off the bypass. A bright red-and-yellow sign indicated a Formule 1 hotel, and she thought for a moment that Michael was taking them there, planning to put Felix in a room of his own and then try to persuade her into having sex.

'Oi,' she said.

They passed the hotel and headed into the city.

'Wrong cathedral,' said Michael.

'What?'

'We went to the wrong cathedral. Felix wants to look at this one.'

Peterborough Cathedral was black against the sky.

She looked at her watch. It was just coming up to eleven o'clock.

Felix said, 'I'm sorry.'

'That's all right, Felix,' she said, wearily.

They parked and walked through a dark passage and out into a brightly-lit shopping precinct. Teenagers sat in groups, eating burgers and chips. They found the entrance to the cathedral close. Felix disappeared inside it, into the darkness. She said, 'I'm so tired,' and sat on a bench. Michael sat next to her. He put his arm round her.

'I'd rather you didn't,' she said.

He took his arm away.

'I'm sorry.'

He muttered something indistinct, then sat and whistled carelessly.

'When he said he wanted to come to the cathedral,' she said, warm and friendly, but trying to adopt a professional ghost-hunter tone of voice, 'what reason did he give?'

'Just that he felt drawn to it.'

'Drawn to it? Did he say that?'

'It was what he meant.'

'I'm getting worried about him. I didn't like the way he was talking in the café. Do you want a cheeseburger?'

'God, no.'

'No.' She nodded. 'They're very fattening.'

'That's nothing to do with it,' he said irritably.

'What?'

'Whether they're fattening or not – it has nothing to do with it.'

Yes, he was an alien. He was from the Planet Og. On the other hand, he had a propensity to turn nasty when he didn't get his own way vis-à-vis sex, which was a very human male attribute. The programmers of Og, she decided, had known their stuff.

'There's a Waitrose in one of the malls,' she said. 'I came over one day with Simon and Jude and Pierre, and we bought loads of stuff and took it back and kept it on a shelf in the fridge in Hell's Kitchen. Microwaved ourselves a nice little lunch each day until some bastards started nicking it. Do you think we should go after him?'

'He didn't seem to want us.'

'But the cathedral must be closed. What can he be doing?'

She got up. He sighed irritably. He had obviously been helpful and good-natured, and driven all round the Wash and all the way to Worcester, just because he wanted to go to bed with her.

Well, tough.

'Come on, hurry up,' she said coldly.

They went into the close, past the cathedral café and gift shop, into the darkness.

Normandie called out quietly, 'Felix?'

The August sky above the two great towers was purple. There was the red gleam of a security camera.

'Perhaps he's gone back to the car,' said Michael.

'Of course he hasn't.'

The cathedral loomed over them, immense.

'What's that?'

'What?'

A siren – a police car perhaps – out on the bypass, the noise carrying in the summer night. Youths, whistling and calling out in the pedestrianised shopping area behind them.

He caught it: distant music, faint, then gone.

'Monks,' she said. 'Monks chanting.'

'Somebody's sound system.'

'Don't be stupid.'

'The cathedral's locked. It's empty.'

A movement by the great west door.

'Felix?' she called, doubtfully.

Whatever it was, it was gone.

There was a narrow passageway between the cathedral and the wall of the Bishop's palace. They went along it, their eyes slowly becoming accustomed to the darkness. The passage opened out again. There was an enclosed space, a lawn.

'Felix?' she called.

He was on the far side of the close, facing a high wall. Only his face and hands were dimly visible – his purple suit was lost in the blackness. She felt a sudden embarrassment, thinking that he was having a piss: but then she saw that he was rubbing his hands together, almost as if he had washed them and was holding them under a wall dryer.

18

Peterborough Abbey, AD 1216

Compline, the last office of the day. The monks in their
stalls, the abbot before the altar.

Sustinuit anima mea . . .

But who is this a-knocking?

Sir Fulk Fitzwarin the outlaw?

The crash echoed through the massive nave, through the
new-wrought arches of the West Front, their mortar scarcely
dry. The monks faltered for a moment in their chanting. In
the far gloom a monastery obedientiary climbed the scaffold-
ing and called down through a window before shouting,
urgently, back to the Abbot.

Then the door of pale new oak swung open and Crok
came in, thumping on it with his staff, laughing as the fat
monkish faces turned in their stalls.

Nicolaa shouted down the nave: 'What news, sirs?'

Lacy was behind her, his scarlet tunic with the white
cross glimmering in the light of the torches, his spurs
clattering on the cold stone. The monks' eyes were on him as
they sang: *Domine non est exaltatum cor meum: neque elati
sunt oculi mei . . .*

My heart is not exalted, neither are mine eyes lofty.

The Abbot, Robert of Lindsay, hurried down the nave,

servants running behind him with lanterns. King Louis was besieging Berkhampstead, he called out – and had demanded the homage of the Abbot of St Albans.

'Lincoln, my Lord Abbot, tell me of Lincoln,' said Nicolaa, taking off her cloak, unconcerned with the affairs of abbeys and monks.

The *false* Earl of Lincoln, said the Abbot nervously, had resumed his siege of Lincoln Castle.

'Jesu's blood,' Nicolaa swore.

'What word from Gloucester, from the Council?' asked Lacy.

There was no news from the west.

Lacy stood for a moment, grim-faced, then went with Cantuar to stable the horses. Crok followed him to see that his rouncy was fed, and to give it the best of the monks' summer hay. He found two crossbow-men eyeing his sack, which was tied to his rouncy's pommel. 'The last soldier to put his head inside,' he said conversationally, 'is still in there.'

He laughed and did a little dance and rolled his eyes, and they crossed themselves and fled. Not, he thought, that they would find anything of value in his sack: the sixteen jewels were safe in their velvet pouch, tucked safe inside his cote.

Back in the church he prowled along the aisles, looking for marvels. He climbed the little tower that contained the uncorrupted arm of St Oswald, and squatted by the guardian monk and peeked at the arm, which was in a silver casket lined with satin. It looked stuffed rather than uncorrupted, though the yellow fingernails, curling like rams' horns, looked genuine enough. He was contemplating the trade in relics when Nicolaa passed below him, walking up and down, down and up, with the Abbot, who had had a letter from the Prior of Belvoir.

'The ground opened up in the midst of the waves,' said the Abbot. 'Not one foot soldier escaped to announce the disaster to the King.'

Which was nonsense, thought Crok. They'd come pouring up to the Fosdyke, those sodden men of the rearward division, wailing of the disaster. But monks would say anything and these Peterborough monks were famously jealous of John's relics. They had spread rumours that the King's piece of bread from the feeding of the five thousand was a fake, and their own piece the only genuine piece in England. They had boasted that they – and only they – had a genuine part of Aaron's rod, and a true fragment of Christ's swaddling clothes.

' "*Auxit autem aegritudinis molestiam perniciosa ejus ingluvies*," ' said the Abbot, reading excitedly from the Prior of Belvoir's letter.

Nicolaa said nothing. Her Latin, Crok knew, was uncertain.

' "*Qui nocte illa de fructu persicorum, et novi ciceris potatione nimis repletus febilem in se calorem acuit fortiter et accendit*." '

So the King's death was all down to gluttony, was it? To the stuffing in of peaches and the drinking of new cider? It was not, then, due to those last ministrations of the Abbot of Swinehead's sister (desperately comforting him for the loss of his treasures) that had inflamed the feverish heat within him?

He laughed coarsely. Nicolaa looked up and said, startled, 'Jesu's blood.'

He vanished.

She called, 'Crok?'

He squatted by the guardian monk, as still as a mouse.

'Crok,' she said with ominous calm, 'come down.'

Down he crept, through St Oswald's little chapel.

She said to the Abbot, 'This man was John's troubadour. He was with the King at Newark. If he likes to, he will tell you the honest story.'

Then the monks were round him, plucking his sleeve, asking their monkish questions. He asked for ale and they led him out through the cloisters, past the newly built lavatorium where the monks washed their hands before they ate, and where each monk had a neat little towel on a shelf. Was it true, they asked, that John had been stabbed to death by his servants when he swore that bread would cost a mark for a quartern loaf?

The King died of a rotting gut, he told them, drinking deep. He had had it since Lenne.

He told them about the night at Wisbeche, of the King calling out in pain at the hour of Lauds, even as the monks chanted the morning offices. How John – grey-faced, his round fat belly shrunk – had been carried back and forth to the royal privy by William and Florence.

But – said the monks – if the King had not died by his servants' hand, had he then died of his sins?

No, he had died of the rotting gut.

But had he truly repented?

Crok heard the distant sound of the monks of Newark, on

194

the night when the end came. *Domine Jesu Christe, fili Dei vivi, pone passionem, crucem, et mortem tuam inter iudicium et animam meam.* John in his terror repeating the words, 'O Lord Jesus Christ, the son of the living God, set thy passion, cross, and death between thy judgement and my soul.'

The monks gazed greedily into his eyes.

Perhaps.

He pulled himself away in a panic, feeling for the packet of tiny jewel stones at his chest.

Unclean spirits, wise men said, cling round the monastery.

The way to banish unclean spirits is to take up St John's gospel, and they will fly away like so many birds.

'He was,' said Nicolaa loudly, a sob in her throat, drinking deeply of the abbey wine, 'a generous and a loving king.'

She stared round her, defying man or monk to say otherwise. 'A better king than Richard, who whored after boys and bled the kingdom dry.'

A ripple ran through the circle.

'John minded himself with England,' she said, 'and with the common weal.'

Only because he lost Normandy to the French, thought the monks.

'Well, I'll tell you what,' Nicolaa said, slowly, defiantly. 'He was a loyal friend to those that deserved friendship.'

And that was true enough, thought Crok, tears springing to his eyes, for he had drunk a deal of ale.

The aching in his jaw was gone. With his tongue he probed the jagged remnant of tooth. He would have to have it pulled out, he thought vaguely. He shuddered, for he himself pulled teeth, it being part of a minstrel's art. He drank deeply and felt the warmth stir his blood.

'A casket *casulam* of gold, a belt of gold fringe *auri frisio*,' the Abbot was murmuring to Lacy.

They were the treasures yielded up to John by Peterborough Abbey and now, presumably, lost in the sea.

'He gave you good law, Abbot,' Nicolaa said.

'Not so, dame,' said Lacy calmly. 'It was armed might that wrung the charter from him.'

'Shoes embroidered with pearls,' the Abbot went on nervously, 'a crystal vessel for incense, a mitre with precious stones.'

'And what, my Lord Abbot,' said Nicolaa, suddenly, wheedling, 'did his excellence the Lord Pope say about the fucking charter of Runnymede?'

The monks sat silent.

'Well?' she shouted.

The Abbott said, 'The world changes.'

'Did not the Pope say, "On behalf of Almighty God, Father, Son and Holy Ghost, and by the authority of Saints Peter and Paul we utterly reject and condemn this settlement?" Did not the Pope call the charter shameful and base? Illegal and unjust?'

The Abbot nodded.

'A king bound fast by a charter,' said Nicolaa, 'is no king. Is this not true?'

The Abbot moved uncomfortably. Lacy stared into the fire.

'And what did this charter say?' she went on. 'No man shall be imprisoned on account of the appeal of a woman concerning the death of any other than her husband. What is this? No woman, Lord Abbot, may appeal for justice against the murder of a son or daughter? Or of a father or mother?'

The Abbot wanted to say that she herself was a woman and ought to be seen and not heard, but the words would not leave his tongue.

Lacy said quietly, 'The charter said, to none will we sell, to none deny or delay, right or justice.'

Crok crept to the kitchen. Under the angry eyes of an ancient pittancer he scoffed down a cake and poured himself more ale. Back in the Abbot's hall he edged himself close to the fire, within the comfort of a chancele screen. He settled himself in straw and watched the sparks fly up and out of the roof. The talk was still of the charters, and the barons who might desert the French and return to Henry's good lordship if they were reissued. Crok drank. His head swam pleasantly. Soon he was marching again. He could hear the *beat beat beat* of the drum, the brassy trumpet of the levy marshal. He was back at Corfe on that summer's morning when the campaign first started, the varward division marching north along the dust-white road, the Queen and the young Prince waving from the keep. Where did they not go, swaying and rattling, in this last mad summer?

'*Coverchief* of Shaftesbury, *Plains* of Salisbury,' he hummed – though the army had been forced north round Old Sarum, Marlborough being in rebel hands – and then to the east, to harry the French at Windsor, which was where a messenger brought news that King Alexander was marching home to Scotland, after parleying with Louis to divide up the English kingdom.

How they had chased north, then, to catch the vile Scotchman! How the scouts had galloped to spread a net across his path! *March, march, march* from Clare to Stamford – the French so close on their heels that no business was done by the chancellery clerks that day – then twenty-six miles to Cambridge and a drunken night with Fawkes de Breauté, then forty more miles – forty full miles, sweet Jesu, had ever an army moved so fast? – before they limped (Crok limped for sure) into William of Aumale's castle at Rockingham. Then, that night as they lay exhausted, a messenger had come cantering past the sentries, the white cross of England on his surcoat lit by the blazing fires of the soldiery.

The Lady Nicolaa was in dire peril in her castle of Lincoln, hard pressed by Alexander's Scotchmen and by Gilbert de Gant, the false Earl of Lincoln.

'Help me, my Lord,' wrote the Lady Nicolaa.

And John, a portly man long past his youth, had leapt, scalded, to his feet though supper was about to be served (was this a man steeped in baneful gluttony, Sir Prior of Belvoir?) and sent messengers galloping back up the Fosse, and summoned the commanders of the divisions. Soon after midnight the trumpets rang out.

And in the darkness the army marched again to the drum. Scouts out in a screen, the varward division with the King and the Seneschal; the centre with the treasury and *Garderoba*'s long carts; the rearward with the whores and the kitchen drabs.

198

Fifty miles from Rockingham to Lincoln, and Crok's feet marked every yard, for when he tried to bury himself in the cooking pans of the pantry wagon he was thrown off by wicked Sergeant Holbeck. 'This isn't the time for singing and lolling,' said the sergeant (for Crok would buy his passage by singing vulgar ditties to the cooks). 'This is the time for marching and chop, chop, chopping.'

And the soldiers of the rear guard tittered, thinking of Crok's sack.

In the dawn they saw the distant walls of Lincoln Castle and the half-built spires of Bishop Hugh's cathedral. Before the monks had finished chanting Prime they were marching up the long hill from St Peter at Gowts to St Peter at Arches and then to St Peter at Moston (so fond were these folk of Lincoln of St Peter). Up the winding hill the varward division went, with its banners flying and the King at its head, past the Jews House and up the cobbled street to the castle.

The Scotch were gone in a mist and the false French Earl of Lincoln was away, hiding in the forest like Robin Hood.

Lady Nicolaa came out of the west gate. She offered King John the keys to the castle, which were due to him now because she had not been able to hold it without his succour. 'I am a woman of great age,' she said, not losing her taste for irony, 'who can no longer sustain so many labours and anxieties.'

John, the white dust of the road in his hair, and in his beard, kissed her and said, 'Nicolaa my Beloved.'

And he gave her back the keys.

* * *

Crok drank the last of his ale. Tears moistened his cheeks.

It had happened, all this, only ten days ago, just before the feast of St Denis. And now John was dead.

Nicolaa was staring at him. She was tipsy, he thought, which would make her malicious. He wished he could slither from sight.

'Cheer us,' said Nicolaa, 'or get out.'

Crok said toughly, 'The situation is bad, dame, but we should not repine.'

'No?' – soft as velvet, a cat preparing to pounce.

'Our own resistance weakens when things go all our way. And we grow soft, if life is one long holiday.'

She stared at him. Then she laughed.

The crash of a distant door. A man shouting: the clatter of armour.

A messenger from Fawkes de Breauté. Berkhampstead had fallen. The French army was moving against Norwich. The city of Lenne had declared for Louis.

'What?' shouted Nicolaa. 'The King gave Lenne his own sword – the King *died* for Lenne!' Then, abruptly, 'What of de Mauléon?'

The messenger looked frightened.

'Where is de Mauléon!'

De Mauléon was John's captain in Lenne. He was a proud, arrogant man. A great prince of Poitou.

De Mauléon had fled northward into the fens.

'Jesu's blood,' shouted Nicolaa.

The monks chattered. By the feast of St Martin (or for certain within its octaves) they told each other, the boy Prince would fly England like the Atheling had fled Duke

William. The Bishops would bow to the new conqueror as Stigand and Wulstan had bowed to the old. The Great Council would meet in Gloucester, no doubt, as the Witan had met in London in the last days of 1066, and there would be talk of summoning the armies of the Earl of Chester, and of Brewer in the west, just as the Witan had talked of calling up the Saxon armies of Mercia and Northumbria.

In those times there had been a young Atheling. Now there was a boy of nine.

Nothing, in the end, would be done.

John had been a tyrant king. He had delivered the Kingdom to the French.

Crok pleaded his clerical office and was found a cubicle in the monks' dormitory, a hot fug of a place with its windows newly glazed by the oversoft Abbot. They took his dagger, saying that no brother was permitted to wear his knife at night for fear that he might wound himself while he slept. They gave him a compress of herbs to rub on his broken tooth, and a syrup potion. He lay cosily under his fur pelisse, with wine fumes filling his head and a great numbness in his jaw. A curtain of sleep fell over him.

In the night he woke to find a sub-prior leaning over him, shaking him gently and inviting him to the *opus dei*. He closed his eyes tight and wished he had bedded himself down in the stables where the horses farted but did not shine lanterns in his eyes.

He was roused by the monks an hour before dawn.

'Well, my Lord Abbot,' said Nicolaa, standing on the

church steps fastening her cloak. 'You had best hurry and bury your treasures.'

The Abbot smiled palely. All night he had tossed and turned in fear that the French would come in fury, and the abbey's relics and treasure be plundered for the glory of Chartres and Notre Dame. Then the great west front of the cathedral would never be completed, and his plans for a ceiling of painted wood would remain an idle dream.

'Dig, dig, dig, my lord,' said Nicolaa. 'There's no time this day for chanting.'

But the monks were singing the Office of the Holy Cross, as they had on the day that King Harold fell at Battle, and the day that the Danes had come to plunder the abbey of Christ's golden crown and foot rest. As they had when Duke William had given the monastery to a Frenchman called Turold. The monks had sung the offices then, and their scribes had scribbled in secret places. *Eorl Edwin and Eorl Morkere fled away. But Hereward alone, and all that would follow him; he bravely led them out . . .*

Now another French king sat in Westminster. Would another Hereward come out of the fens to wake the kingdom with fire and sword?

The archers and crossbow-men were mounted. At their rear, on his rouncy, was the hunched figure of Crok, ludicrous in his kingly pelisse, his leather wallet and sack hanging from his saddle.

'Crok,' Nicolaa said. 'If you have stolen anything from the monks I shall send you back so they can beat you with Aaron's rod and strangle you with Jesu's swaddling clothes.

Well, Lacy, where do we go? South? Fawkes de Breauté still holds Cambridge.'

Lacy looked out over the fens to the south. De Breauté's allegiance was sure but his plight was desperate. He looked to the west but Ermine Street was patrolled by troops of the rebel Earls Robert FitzWalter and Robert de Vere, while in Leicestershire the French had long held Mountsorrel.

'Well?' Nicolaa said, impatiently. 'Do we sit and wait for them?'

The French would come from the east, along the road that ran like an arrow towards the dawn light: a causeway into the wildest of the fens, built by the Romans to conquer Boadicea.

'North, as before,' Lacy said.

The nearest castle held by royalists was Nottingham. The only safe road was through the forest.

It was a cold dawn, with a rime of hoar frost in the hedgerows.

The Abbot watched as they moved in a single line through the deer park and vanished into the grey mists that hung over the water meadows.

19

Wormby Flats, Lincolnshire

'Is that what you wanted Felix? Is that any help?'

They were back in the car, heading east. Normandie was using Michael's laptop, and had found the Peterborough Abbey site on the Internet. 'It says here that Abbot Benedict of Canterbury started the craze for relics,' she said, her face palely lit by the screen. 'He came to Peterborough in 1177 and brought with him the shirt stained with Thomas à Becket's blood. Felix?'

'Sweetie?'

'You were asking about relics. Is that what you wanted to know?'

He was exhausted; drained. He could not think what to reply. He had lost all feeling, he realised, in the palm of his left hand. He ran his other hand along it, gently, stroking it, but it remained lifeless, as though it did not belong to him.

'Well, never mind,' said Normandie, speaking now from a great distance. 'You just have a rest . . .'

He slept, rocked and soothed by the motion of the car, waking only when it stopped and its engine was turned off. There was a rustle of clothes and Michael whispered, 'It's OK, he's asleep.'

He was kissing her. Felix felt cautiously at his lifeless

hand again, pinching it to see if any feeling had returned.

Nothing.

She said, 'I've got to go to bed.'

'Not yet.'

'Michael, it's no use . . .'

They were kissing again.

It could go on till dawn, this.

He yawned softly, discreetly.

A rustle. The silence. He could feel them, peering at him, looking at the old man curled up on the back seat.

'Poor old sod.'

'Sshh . . .'

'All those years on Jennifer's put-u-up.'

'It's Julia, not Jennifer. And she's probably a very nice person if the truth were known. Do you think he's self-regressing?'

'What?'

'Back through the birth canal. Travelling in the spaceship of the psyche.'

'It's possible,' he heard Michael say, gravely, untruthfully.

'What was he thinking about, do you think? When he was staring at that wall?'

'God knows.'

'Was he conscious?'

'I think he was under some sort of self-hypnosis.'

'It's gone too far this, hasn't it?'

'In short, yes.'

A sigh.

'Felix?' she said, gently. 'Come on, wake up.'

He opened his eyes.

They were both looking at him intently. Had he been voyaging back in the spaceship of the psyche? Would he say, suddenly, where the Crown Jewels could be found?

He yawned again.

'Hello, sweetie,' he said.

Next morning he caught the bus into Boston. Vicky and Penguin, the boy organist, spotted him in a run-down shopping arcade where you could buy curry-sauce powder by the scoop and the sound system played Johnny Mathis. He looked vaguely distressed, Vicky would say later: ill, and fey, and *psychic*. He was staring at a sign that said *THINKING OF STARTING YOUR OWN BUSINESS? IDEAL UNITS AVAILABLE*. Was Felix thinking of opening a shop? What sort of shop? Sweeties? DIY?

Jokes and novelties, Vicky and Penguin decided, with fancy dress hire on the side. They watched him examine a pile of best caulis, two for two pounds fifty – would he be a greengrocer? – and a stack of cheap American videos that were dedicated to *MAN'S TWO GREAT OBSESSIONS: CARS AND BEAUTIFUL WOMEN*. Would Felix open a smutty video shop?

They lost him after that, because Penguin wanted a chip buttie with curry sauce, and a look at the videos of cars and babes, but they spotted him again in the town centre, going up an alleyway of boarded-up shops. Like sleuths, they followed him, there being very little else to do in Boston. A minute or two later, he vanished into a tiny cottage-like building under the walls of the church.

They went closer. Vicky squeaked in amazement: the shop

not only offered rare and exotic merchandise, together with a professional body-piercing service, but it was actually called SPOOKIES!

They went inside. Vicky pretended to look at Halloween masks. Penguin admired figurines of mythical warrior women with proud, naked breasts. Felix was gazing – stargazing, totally wrapt, Vicky would later say – at a selection of crystals in a glass cabinet. Then he asked the girl assistant if they had a fisherman's ball. She told him that she had never heard of such a thing. Eventually he rejected the larger, cheaper balls of lead crystal, and chose a small sphere of quartz.

When he had gone, Vicky bought herself a dream-catcher made out of feathers and tiny coloured stones and flints, crafted by the Red Indians of the American plains.

Felix closed the curtains in his caravan. He washed the crystal in soapy water. He took a flashlight he had bought in the Boston shopping arcade, and a sheet of cardboard, to the table. He made a slit in the card and, after some manoeuvring, managed to project a narrow beam of light down into the crystal. He sat for two hours, staring into the sphere.

It was his last, best hope.

Eventually the flashlight battery grew dim.

He went to the kiosk outside the kiddies' play-pool and phoned Julia.

'Oh, hello Felix,' she said with false warmth. 'I was hoping you'd call before I left.'

It was tomorrow that she went on her cruise.

'I was wondering,' he said, with lightness and humour, 'whether your new tenants would be needing a cat- or dog-sitter?'

'Actually I did mention you,' she said, after a moment. 'I tried to put in a word.'

(Julia, Julia, you of all people should know not to lie to a clairvoyant.)

'The thing is, well, they don't actually know you, do they, Felix?'

Not enough to provide him with a sleeping space, a pot of tea each morning, and a look at their *Daily Telegraph* before he went to Acton library. Down the phone he could hear the old, happy roar of traffic on the North Circular; smell the comforting, familiar scent of fusty velvet curtains.

'Felix?'

He told her that he had failed.

A pause. Then she said, 'Oh dear.'

'It's gone,' he said, 'whatever it was.'

'Have you tried to reach out?'

'Yes.'

'Well?'

He sighed. 'I felt something at Peterborough, in the cathedral, but here on the coast there's nothing.'

'What did you feel in the cathedral?'

'Panic. Fear.'

'You could try lucid dreaming.'

She sounded abstracted. She was in the middle of her packing.

'I bought a crystal.'

Another pause.

'And?' she said.

'Nothing.'

'When did you buy it?'

'Earlier today.'

'That's no use. You must let the moon shine on it through a window, at a time that is near the full moon.'

'Yes, I know all that.'

'Nothing will happen for several nights of course.'

She had cheered up. Several nights from now she would be on her cruise ship off Minorca.

'I can't wait for several nights, and it's all nonsense anyway, just ritual for amateurs. I am ill.'

'Ritual is important,' she said, trying not to hear what he was saying. 'You will see shadows at first, then scenes from your past lives will appear. Is it a sea crystal?'

'No.'

'It's probably as well, for they attract warlocks and witches. But you must have confidence and you must be patient. Why are you always so impatient? Remember how long it took for you to achieve the first and second levels?'

'Yes.'

At the first level he had mastered ventriloquism, protection from evil, and the detection of others' magic. At the second level he had become able to practise extra-sensory perception and, in theory, to levitate.

'Perhaps,' she said, 'you will need to achieve the third or fourth level.'

At the third level he would have the power to summon monsters and call into being wraith forms and walls of wind. He would be able to fly. He imagined himself flying over

Wormby, perhaps in a costume reminiscent of Superman. That, he thought, would be a treat for the patrons of the Dreamboat.

At the fourth level, the level of master, he would have power to summon a wall of fire, and to pass through the dimension door.

'You have always abhorred necromancy,' he said. 'The third and the fourth levels.'

'Well,' she said, sighing, resentful now, 'I don't know.'

'It doesn't matter. You must have a nice holiday.'

'I certainly need one.'

'Goodbye, Julia.'

'Be sure to recite the prayers of protection.'

'Yes, Julia,' he said, putting the phone down.

He sat in the dunes, staring out over the sea, over the old estuary. Holiday-makers were on the beach but they did not belong to the world that he was seeking.

If he wanted to see into the past world, he would have to draw on the life force of his audience.

He would have to draw them down with him, into Theta.

Dare he do it? He shuddered violently. His hands dug into the bank. He raised them and let the dry sands run out through his fingers.

People watched him curiously. Eventually somebody went up to him and said, 'You all right, mate?'

He nodded but did not speak.

Later, Normandie came to the sea wall. 'What are we going to do with you, Felix?' she said, anxious, caring.

He smiled. Who could say?

He gazed at the distant smudge of Gibraltar Point, far away over the estuary. Seagulls wheeled behind a coastal boat that chugged its way into the Haven and up to Boston town. If it chugged far enough, through the docks and along the South Forty Foot Drain, it would find itself at Swinehead Bridge and at Swinehead Abbey – except that the abbey was long gone, its dressed stones dispersed among a score of Tudor farmhouses.

He stared out, as he had so often stared in these last days, across the Cots and Frampton Marsh, seeking the sullen menace of Wybert's Castle, and the tiny figures of merchants gathered on the Fosdyke shore as they waited for guides.

There was nothing.

'Felix?' said Normandie. 'What are you going to do?'

Empower the mass psychic collective consciousness of Wormby Flats, sweetie, he thought, but did not say.

Reach out, with the most powerful weapon he had, to the Other World.

The outboard engine cut. In the silence she could hear the water lapping the prow.

'He's still trying to find the jewels. He's making himself ill.'

'Can you hitch the rope round the buoy?' said Michael.

At the third attempt she managed to lasso the bobbing plastic ball. 'Hurry up, I'm not a sailor,' she said, holding the rope tightly as the boat swung at its new anchor.

He lowered a thin metal rod over the side.

'What does that do?'

'Sends a signal down. When it beeps, it means that the

particles in the water are sending a signal back. It helps us see how the sediment is being dragged up. It's part of the near bed processing.'

'Ah, right, the near bed processing,' she said, hoping he wasn't going to give her an hour's lecture just because she asked one small innocent question. 'So what are we going to do about Felix then?'

'I don't see that there's anything we can do. Basically, he isn't our responsibility.'

She lay back. It was less humid here than it was on land. The sun was opaque in a pearl-grey sky. She closed her eyes, thinking that if she were alone, or even with Jude and the lads, she would take off her bikini top. The boat bobbed gently.

'I'm turning on the beacon,' said Michael.

'You do know we're the only friends he's got?'

'The high-frequency beam between here and the shore helps us examine the structure of waves and surface currents,' Michael said, his voice coming closer, the boat rocking gently, 'and the fine-scale acoustic profile helps us assess the amount of sediment.'

He was lying next to her. He was more confident on the ocean, she thought, than he was on shore.

'There's a lot of sediment down there on the sea bed,' he said. 'A lot of murkiness.'

He started to kiss her. She could move away, smartish, and say 'Shouldn't we be getting back?' in a voice from five billion miles away, or she could just lie where she was and put up with it. It was peculiar how he never seemed to get the message. Perhaps she did fancy him in a weird sort of way.

'Ow,' she said, as he tipped her against a marlin spike, or rowlock, or something equally pointed and nautical. He got up and – moving dangerously fast in so small a seagoing craft – went to the locker and pulled out a tartan rug.

She smiled pityingly and shook her head.

He spread the rug and she sighed and, after a moment, lay down on it. He lay half beside her, half on top of her, and started to kiss her again. The boat moved gently against the buoy, the water lapping. Occasional seagulls flew overhead.

She said, after a bit, 'About Felix.'

'Bugger Felix.'

'Don't be such a sod.'

He sighed. 'Look, I've spoken to a friend of mine who works at the Bohr Unit in Cambridge.'

'What's the Bohr Unit?'

'They investigate human consciousness, cognition, perception. Elements of clinical neurophysiology.'

'How can they help Felix?'

'They might be able to find out if he's genuine or not. They're tangentially into stuff like the explication of phenomena on fundamental grounds – quantitative assessment of precognitive and retrocognitive remote perception data, that sort of thing.'

'Why didn't you tell me about this?'

'I was waiting for my friend Rake to come back to me. Let's wait and see what he says, OK?'

He was pushing her gently down again.

'What a lot of things you know about.'

'Not really. I don't know your name.'

'What?'

214

'Your real name. You weren't christened Normandie.'

'Yes, I was. I was conceived, as it happens, in a cabin on the *Pride of Hampshire*, as it headed into the port of Le Havre.'

'Why aren't you called Hampshire or Havre then?'

'Because I have kind considerate parents perhaps?'

'If you were to conceive now, would we have to call it Wormby Flats?'

'Christ,' she said, 'I'd better not conceive now . . .'

The little boat rocked gently on the swell. A seagull came down to perch on the prow, then gave a great cry and took flight again, with a great flapping of wings.

Later she sat like a figurehead, bronze in the cloudy, troubled sunlight, as the boat curled slowly in the water and headed back down the necklace of buoys, towards the Environment Agency jetty.

20

Wormby Flats, Lincolnshire

'You need to take your mind off her,' said Ray, 'so I've come up with an idea to help you.'

He was wondering if he wasn't wasting his time. The boy, Simon, was dull and listless: sick with love.

'I've been going through the staff job-application forms. It seems you're the only student doing History at uni. Oxford, is it?'

The lad's eyes flickered about, looking for Jude. 'UWE,' he said.

'UWE,' repeated Ray, doubtfully, 'as opposed to uni?'

'University of the West of England.'

'Oh,' said Felix, unsurprised. 'Well, you know about the Astounding Felix finding that seal from King John's treasure hoard?'

Simon nodded.

'I want you to go to Boston library. Look up everything you can. How the treasure was lost. Where exactly – *exactly* mind you – it all happened.'

'What about the bingo and the Kiddies' Fun Hour?'

'I'll worry about those,' said Ray solicitously. 'It's more important to get you away from here for a few hours, give your brain a rest from thinking about your girlfriend.'

'Boston library's no use. I'd have to go to Lincoln.'

'All right then. Go to Lincoln. You've got a car, haven't you? You mustn't forget to tell me how much you spend on petrol.'

Simon went. It was mid-afternoon before he returned. At lunch time Jude said, 'What have you done with Simon?' and Ray said, 'He's gone to the pictures with his new bird.'

'Liar,' said Jude, but she looked uneasy and hovered about reception for an hour watching the car park. When Simon came back, Ray took him to a corner table in the conservatory, discreetly masked behind a yucca.

'It's a puzzle knowing where to start,' said Simon. 'You really need to understand the extraordinary socio-economic set-up in the fenlands in the early thirteenth century—'

'No I don't,' said Ray, his heart sinking; this was what came of teaching History at places called UWE. 'Never mind all that. Just stick to the jewels.'

'Well, basically, John's army was travelling north from King's Lynn. He had the Crown Jewels with him in specially constructed chests. He also had his own portable loo and a chap was paid two shillings for carrying it about. Wouldn't it be funny,' he added, a smile hovering over his face for the first time since Jude had taken the sun from his sky, 'if all Spookie found was a royal shithouse?'

'Ha, ha,' said Ray, despairing of the next generation. 'So what happened?'

'There was some kind of disaster when they were crossing the sands of The Wash.'

'What bit of The Wash?'

'In the estuary of the Wellstream, according to the monks

who wrote soon after the event. A historian called St John Hope did a paper on it in the early twentieth century, and decided it must have happened near Cross Keys. According to him, the army left King's Lynn on the 12th October 1216, hoping to cross the sands at low tide, which was about noon. He thinks they must have been delayed, and then tried to cross in a hurry without guides. His guess is that some of the carts fell into quicksands and blocked the passage for the rest of the army. Another historian, Fowler, says this is all nonsense, and that it all happened near Wisbech. Another chap, Holt, thinks it all happened at a ford halfway between the two.'

'Do any historians say it happened at Wormby Flats?'

'No.'

'So what was the sodding seal doing here?'

'Well now, I did come across something a bit interesting.'

He looked through his notes. A voice said, 'Hi.'

It was Jude, standing under the Spanish hacienda arch.

'Hello, Jude,' Simon said, abandoning his notes.

'Never mind her,' said Ray. 'You said there was something a bit interesting. What is it?'

Simon's eyes returned, reluctantly, to his notepad. 'There's a reference in Camden. In his *Britannia* in 1607, he said that King John "lost all his carriages and furniture near Fossdyke and Wel-stream, by a sudden inundation." '

'So?'

'The Fosdyke isn't anywhere near the Wellstream. It's near here, on the Welland Estuary.'

'Is it?'

'Yes. And what about this? It's from St John Hope's

investigation, but he didn't realise its significance. He was trying to establish where the hidden path across the Wellstream had been, so he wrote to the directors of the Great Northern Railway...'

His eyes were back on Jude, who was leaning against the Spanish arch, under the trailing plastic bougainvillea.

'Stop looking at her. Looking at her's no use.'

'The Great Northern Railway,' Simon said, again returning to his notes, 'had built a track from Cross Keys to Long Sutton. St John Hope wanted to know if they had come across evidence of a constructed causeway.'

He was looking at Jude again.

'Jude,' said Ray. 'If you've finished work, just bugger off, all right?'

After a moment she flicked her hair and went.

'I told her,' said Ray, confidentially, 'that you'd been to the pictures with a bird.'

'Yeah?' said Simon, brightening. 'What did she say?'

'Not a lot. Now about this railway.'

'Yes, well, the bloke at GNR replied on 30th December 1901, saying that the railway track had been made by the old Norwich and Spalding Railway company. You wouldn't think there'd have been a Norwich and Spalding Railway, would you?'

'Mate, I'd believe anything.'

'Anyway, he said the construction plans were lost. But he went on to say: "Judging from a similar road over the sands across the estuary of the Welland a little further to the north, which was in existence not so many years ago, I should imagine that there was no laid track or corduroy road across the estuary of the Nene. That over the Welland was without one and the sands are alike in both cases." Now you realise what this tells us?'

'No,' said Ray, honestly.

'It tells us that John's army not only had to get across the sands at the Nene estuary – or Wellstream estuary as it was then. It also had to get across the Welland sands, and what was more, it had to do it late in the day when the tide was coming in. I've also found another reference to the passage across the Welland sands . . .'

His voice trailed off. Jude was outside, looking in through the glass.

Ray said, 'For Christ's sake, stop looking at her, don't you know anything about women? Listen. Concentrate. I want to understand this. You're telling me that the Crown Jewels really could have been lost here in Wormby Flats?'

'I don't know. The chronicles say it was the Wellstream. But they didn't have maps in those days. Nobody knew for sure what rivers were called – most of them had two or three names. The locals would have spoken English with a Scandinavian dialect, the army commanders would have spoken English or French, the priests Latin. The Welland and the Wellstream both had the same source in the Deeping Fen near Crowland. It only needed one monk – who had never been near either – to confuse one with the other, and every other chronicler would have repeated the mistake. And it makes a hell of a lot more sense for it to have happened here.'

'Why does it make more sense?'

'Well, the chroniclers say that the King was with the army when it crossed the Wellstream and barely escaped with his life. But we know for a fact that he spent the night of the 11th October at Wisbech Castle – and so did his government officials, and his chancellery department.'

'So?'

'So he didn't need to go anywhere near the Wellstream sands. And if his chancellery department went to Wisbech with him, and his portable *urinalibus* and his personal featherbed and linen sheets, I'll bet his jewels and his holy relics went with him as well. Why shouldn't they have done? We know they were carried on packhorses because there's an item in the pipe roll for eightpence halfpenny given to a servant who looked after a sumpter of relics.'

'A what of relics?'

'Sumpter. It's horse used for carrying stuff. Sumpter horses could have travelled with John to Wisbech. And if that was the case, then they wouldn't have been lost in the Wellstream estuary at Cross Keys, would they?'

'Wouldn't they?' said Ray, lost.

'I've just explained! We *know for a fact* that the King and chancellery didn't travel that way. It's the one certain fact that we do know. Look, let me draw you a map.'

He was getting enthusiastic, forgetting about Jude, who was peering in at him indignantly. 'The army and the King *both* left King's Lynn. Right? They were heading north, back towards Lincoln. The army planned to take the direct route across the sands of the Nene, here . . .'

He drew an arrow.

'But the King came inland, here . . .'

Another arrow.

'To spend the night at Wisbech Castle.'

'With the Chancellor of the Exchequer,' said Ray, showing that he was taking it in.

'It's funny you should say that. King John, you see, had a screen called a chancele in his chamber to keep the draught out. His clerk used to sit behind it counting his money and keeping the books. And it was because he sat behind the little chancele screen that he did, in the end, become known as the Chancellor of the Exchequer.'

'You ought to send that to *Reader's Digest*,' said Ray. 'Can we get back to the jewels?'

'Yeah, right. The army crossed the Wellstream and the King left Wisbech Castle and at some point joined them. They must all have come across the sands of the Welland estuary, because they ended up at Swinehead Abbey. The chronicles say that John wasn't present when the disaster happened, so perhaps he and his entourage went ahead.'

'But they all came together through Wormby Flats? Through the caravan site?'

'If this was where the hidden path was, yes . . .'

Jude's face and body were pressed against the glass.

'Never mind her! How many jewels and crowns and things are buried on my beach?'

'I've got a list for you. It was compiled by a historian called Hilary Jenkinson in 1923. I've got to go now,' he added, getting up.

'You're being bloody stupid,' said Ray. 'It's no use chasing her, she's got to chase you. Remember the golden words: Treat 'em mean, keep 'em keen.'

But Simon had gone.

Ray started to read down the list.

A silver shrine set with onyx and other stones.
A jewelled gold shrine containing a cross with three
sapphires and a coral formerly belonging to the 'lord'
of Chester.
Silver vessels by the weight of 134½ marks, besants and
other gold by the weight of 3 marks 1½ oz.
Four great mazers with gilded feet and bands lately
belonging to 'our excommmunicate enemies' at
Colchester . . .

He wondered what a besant was.

After a bit he sighed, and stopped reading.

He went in search of Felix. The weather had turned humid again and he sweated just walking along the rows of caravans. He passed Sea Breeze. Tomorrow the two tarts would finish their week's holiday. They'd go back to Birmingham, back to their ceaseless toil, but strengthened, Ray hoped, by their week of sunshine, good food, and ozone.

It was only five o'clock but already getting dusky. Low clouds lay heavy on the flat, gloomy, Lincolnshire landscape. It was an awful place when the weather was like this: even Ray yearned for Skeggy's bright lights, for hot dogs and candy floss.

Felix was sitting on the steps on his caravan talking to Vicky. 'So you're really going?' Vicky was saying. 'I think that's such a shame. I thought your poems were lovely, particularly the one about the lion and the little boy.'

'But he got eaten up,' said Felix.

'Only because he poked it. It's good to teach respect for the natural world.'

Ray said, 'Afternoon one and all,' and sat on the steps. Vicky froze.

'Can I have a glass of water?' Ray asked. 'Can you get me a glass of water, little Vicky?'

'It isn't very nice to drink,' said Vicky, frightened by his benign humour.

'Just get it love, eh?'

She went into Felix's caravan and returned with a cup of tepid water. Ray drank it. He said, 'This weather.'

'There's thunderstorms coming,' said Vicky. 'Fortunately for us, each caravan will act like a Faraday's cage and protect those within.'

Ray looked at her, astonished.

After a minute she crept away into the gloaming.

'You're leaving us then?' Ray said.

Felix nodded.

Ray let go his hope of fabulous riches. He let it fly from its cage, flutter away to the wide blue yonder. But in truth it was already gone. Realisation had dawned as he read down the list of gold thuribles and phylacteries, of gem-studded crowns and sceptres, of cups of solid gold encrusted with diamonds. It was Disneyland Paris, this stuff; it was Fantasy World Tahiti. It wasn't Wormby Flats, Lincs.

He would go back to the old, faithful dream: a seventeen million win on the National Lottery, shiny new caravans that would make Jack Fountain gasp, and a new Magic Garden with subterranean tunnels and railways, all run by animated gnomes.

'It's a pity,' he said, 'things haven't turned out the way either of us hoped.'

Life, he was talking about. Life.

He closed his eyes. He'd been up since seven o'clock. He'd weeded the flower beds outside reception before the punters were about (it looked bad for the gardening to be done by the boss: the campers made jokes). He'd cleaned out the beer pumps before the bar opened. He done the bingo and unblocked the *pissoir* ('excuse my French, lads') in the gents. He'd helped serve up the punters' high tea because two waitresses were pre-menstrual and lying down.

Another month of this and the brokers men could move in and good luck to them.

Felix was saying something. Ray opened his eyes and said, 'Pardon, squire?'

'I would like to do my mind-reading act.'

'When?'

'Tonight.'

Ray smiled at Felix, kindly. 'I don't think so. It made you ill last time. You should have seen yourself.'

Felix said, 'I'd like to do it, all the same.'

Ray looked aimlessly down the regimental lines of caravans. The club sign shone brightly against the dull, heavy sky. Dreamboat Café. He wished somebody would send him a dreamboat to sail away in; over the seas to China.

'All right, if it'll make you happy,' he said, after a moment, yawning. 'And as long as you don't want any more money.'

It had been a slowboat to China, he remembered, not a dreamboat. But then again, he wasn't in any hurry. He sat with Felix, in the muggy heat, and tried to decide which of the waitresses he'd take with him.

21

Wormby Flats, Lincolnshire

Felix was in the brown water, down with the beavers, water filling his lungs. He woke retching, gasping for breath, jerking his head up, twisting from side to side so that he banged his forehead against the table and the pain made him cry out.

He lay back, trying to slow his breathing, his forehead beaded with sweat. Had it been retrocognition – a scene from a past life? Or had it been precognition – a glimpse into the future?

The air was dense with electricity, his caravan stifling and unnaturally dark. Outside he could hear two women talking about the weather, the likelihood of thunder, the number of summer storms they seemed to have on the Lincolnshire coast. He turned on the light and insects crawled all over it. He looked at his watch: it was just gone six thirty – he'd been asleep for less than half an hour. His head pounded and his jaw ached. He got up and splashed water over himself, then hung out his dress suit, and polished his black patent leather shoes. The effort of buffing the shiny surface made him sweat again.

He made himself a cup of tea, drank it, then went outside. The sky was low and leaden: the blue neon DREAMBOAT seemed to float in its own watery element.

He had an hour before he needed to change for his act. He walked along the path to the sea wall, and climbed through the dunes. A gust of warm wind buffeted him and then suddenly died. There was a flash of lightning, far out at sea. A few raindrops fell, but this storm was moving to the north: there were sheets of rain over distant Gibraltar Point.

A man was down on the shore. Michael Boulding, bending over one of his sensor devices. Felix watched him finish his task then walk back up into the dunes, along a path to his caravan by the Tymoors' farm.

Felix walked eastwards along the top of the sea wall, also towards the Tymoors' farm. In time he stood by one of the parked yellow excavators. A storm meant electrical energy. It was something he could use, perhaps – ask any medium and they would tell you that humid nights were good for a seance, quite apart from their theatricality.

Another fork of blue lightning, far out at sea. A group of holiday-makers, walking along the shore, cried out in excitement. One of them shouted at Felix, waving his arms, telling him to move away from the excavator. Felix waved back and did as he was told, touched, as he always was, when somebody cared about him.

A flock of birds wheeled overhead then came to rest in the long grass behind the sea wall.

'Redshanks,' said a voice.

A man was crouched in the dunes with his camera. 'It's always nice,' he said, 'to see our summer visitors.'

Felix nodded, expressed polite interest. He walked further along the sea wall, the warm wind at his back, then down the path through the dunes, towards the farm and the heritage path. He could hear a church bell in the distance, borne on the gusting wind, very likely coming from Boston Stump. He wondered why they were ringing the bells on a Saturday night.

' "But while the west bin red to see," ' he said, out loud. ' "And storms be none, and pirates flee, Why ring *The Brides of Enderby*?" '

A girl's voice, calling out.

After a moment he saw Karen Tymoor, standing at a field gate while the cows lumbered across the grass towards her. ' "Where the reedy Lindis floweth," ' he said, softly, under his breath. ' "From the meads where melick groweth. Faintly came her milking song." '

He was by the stile and the little bridge over the dyke, the place where the bank was covered in yellow and white blossoms of yarrow. The still water was surrounded by thick marsh sedge and reeds. It was black as ink. He peered down into it.

A plane came overhead, low over the fields of wheat stubble, slowly curling over the sea-defence wall, turning along the coastline towards the RAF bombing range. Looking up, he saw the winking red eye of the jet's guidance cone.

He looked down again. The surface of the water had been disturbed, the green scum torn. Looking down through the slit, through the torn surface and into the depths, he saw a man, twisted and crab-like, picking up something from a rock pool.

'Felix?'

It was Normandie, hurrying along the path from the caravan park.

'Are you all right?'

He nodded and smiled.

'What's all this about you doing your mind-reading act?'

'It's what we clairvoyant do,' he said bravely, 'to earn our daily crust.'

'Michael thinks you're being stupid. He thinks you're risking some sort of seizure – something to do with chemical neurotransmitters in your brain, I can't pretend to understand it.'

'Nor me, sweetie,' said Felix, who had given up trying to understand anything.

There was a flash of lightning, closer, the storm coming in from the sea. For a second the banks of creamy yarrow were as bright as day – but the inky waters of the dyke, he noticed, remained dense and solid.

'Listen, don't you think it might be dangerous?'

'Don't you worry about me,' he said, smiling stoutly.

'I worry that you don't know what you're doing.'

He smiled and waved his finger from side to side, cloaking himself in the mystery of his art.

She looked at him doubtfully.

'Take care, OK?'

He nodded.

'And hurry up, or you'll get wet.'

She was gone, running to Michael's caravan before the storm broke.

'I really think he's on the verge of some sort of breakdown.'

'I spoke to Rake again earlier. He seemed interested in the connection with the bits of American aircraft. I hope you'll like this.'

He had cooked her spaghetti, prepared meat sauce that wasn't out of a tin, gone to trouble. She sat and ate, worrying about Felix.

A light flashed on his computer. He picked up the phone. 'Boulding.'

She stood in the doorway of the caravan. Karen was leading her pony to a wooden shed at the end of the paddock. Her father was calling to her from the house, telling her that *Los Senoritas* was going to start. He was a television engineer, a fanatic about his trade who had festooned his house with receiving dishes. The family was hooked on soap operas from Brazil.

Michael said into the phone, 'On at least one occasion he has acquired information about geographical targets that are spatially and temporally remote and inaccessible by known sensory means. I know you've done experiments using digital scoring techniques. Yes, I spoke to Dr Rake. He's calling me back.'

She looked at her watch. It was nine o'clock. Felix would be starting his act. She said, 'I'm going back to the camp, OK?'

He said, 'Hold on.'

He'd made a pudding.

'I'll see you,' she said.

'Yes,' he said, into the telephone. 'Yes, he could have been exposed to a number of electromagnetic sources. I'm carrying out OSCR work on the beach with two high-frequency radar transmitting systems, working at a frequency of 50.75 megahertz . . .'

She ran back along the path by the farmhouse. Through an uncurtained window she could see Karen, her mum and dad and her two brothers watching television on a monster screen and eating convivially from large bags of crisps. She went over the dyke and over the stile into the caravan park. As she approached the club she heard a scream and the sound of a glass being smashed. Then the door was flung open and a family came out – a child clinging to its mother, crying, a man, thin-faced, thin-haired, not the sort of man who made a fuss, looking angry and frightened.

Others came out behind them. Two teenage girls were in tears. Another was starting to snivel. Her mother said, 'Don't you even think about it,' and yanked her by the arm towards the caravan lines, but she started to sob anyway.

Inside the club they were queuing three-deep at the bar. She pushed her way through. One man said, 'Is he some kind of nutter?' Another man agreed that, yes, he must be bloody raving. Vicky was behind the paella smorgasbord, looking pale and confused.

'It was Felix,' she said.

'But what did he do?'

'He asked some girls to think of something, then he promised he would astound them by showing how he'd written down what it was on a piece of paper. But instead of that he started talking to himself. It was really creepy. He just stood there, looking through people, talking out loud but not to anybody. Then Penguin made a crashing noise on the organ for a laugh.'

'A laugh?'

'He had to do something,' said Vicky, who did not find Penguin as loathsome as she was required to do by the sisterhood. 'Then this girl screamed and a man shouted at Felix, asked him what he was effing playing at. What am I going to do with all this stuff?'

She looked at the paella platter, ten quid a go, piles and piles of it.

'Eat it, I would,' said Normandie.

She found Ray in the office with Jack Fountain.

'It's just some girl who had hysterics,' said Ray determinedly, before she could speak. 'It wasn't Spookie's fault, except that he was boring the arse off everybody, standing like a wazzock speaking with tongues.'

'This is a family site,' said Jack Fountain. 'There were young children out there, Raymond. They'll be having nightmares and if you want my opinion—'

'Yes, Jack, your opinion is always highly valued,' said Ray unwisely.

'Don't be fucking patronising,' said Jack, showing a new side to his character. 'If you want my opinion, you'll get him off the site, now. Tonight.'

'He's an old man,' said Normandie. 'Where's he supposed to go at this time of night?'

'Just because a girl had hysterics?' said Ray. 'Just because some silly little cow wanted to show off?'

'Get him out of here.'

'He's a top bloody entertainer,' said Ray, 'and he's not going anywhere.'

Normandie looked at him in surprise.

'You think I'm joking,' said Jack. 'You think I don't count. You both think we're all shit, basically.'

'No,' said Normandie, 'no, please, that's not true.'

'We're just the poor sad bastards who pay the lowest rents on the coast for the shittiest site on the coast.'

Ray sat hunched at his desk, a whisky perspiration on his forehead, his hand clasping his glass. 'I've put my bloody life into this place,' he said. 'Redundancy money. Savings. Everything. But you're right about one thing. This place was shit till I came here.'

'A café that nobody can afford, caravans let to tarts, and a gnome garden,' said Jack. 'That's the sum total of what you brought to Wormby Flats.'

'Why?' Ray asked. 'Why did I bother?'

'Get him out, Raymond.'

A woman pushed open the door. She was in her thirties, solidly built, a mum with three children, the daughter of one of the committee members. 'Well? Have you told him?'

'It's all right Mrs Langley.'

'Is he going or not?'

'No,' said Ray, eager for conflict. 'He's not going anywhere.'

'Well, my kids aren't stopping here in that case. I think somebody should talk to the police. I reckon he's on a list.'

'What?' said Normandie.

'Have you seen the way he looks at little girls?'

'You stupid, stupid woman,' said Normandie.

'If you had kids . . .' said the woman, shocked.

Jack stood up. 'It's all right, Mrs Langley,' he said pushing her out gently, shutting the door.

'I won't do it,' said Ray.

'No,' said Normandie. 'Don't.'

'And I'll tell you why I won't do it. I won't do it because we're not in Alabama where mobs go round lynching people.'

'No, we're not,' said Normandie.

'We're not in Afghanistan where they string up blokes for not wearing a beard and stone women for having a shag. We're not in Italy where the Wops go round having screaming hysterics.'

Normandie didn't say anything.

'He's upsetting people, that's all I know,' said Jack, looking a bit confused. 'There are people who won't sleep tonight.'

'Do you know where we are?' Ray gulped a mouthful of whisky. 'Do you actually know where we are, Jack?'

'I know where I am. But where you are, Raymond? God only knows.'

Normandie said, 'Where's Felix?'

'England,' Ray was saying as she left. 'That's where we are, Jack, poor sodding England, and she's not finished yet.'

'You're pissed,' said Jack, sadly.

His caravan was in darkness. Two little boys, out for fun, were banging on the window. Normandie shouted at them sharply and they ran away. She knocked on the door and called his name, calmly, and waited for a moment. Then she went to her own caravan. Jude was sitting scraping wet sand off her legs. Normandie said, 'Have you see Felix?' but Jude had missed everything, having been in the dunes with her new bloke and not enjoyed it much.

Simon peered in and said, 'Hi, Jude.'

'Hello, Simon.'

'Simon, were you there tonight?' asked Normandie. 'Did you see where Felix went?'

'No. He just disappeared.'

'As in disappeared disappeared?' asked Jude who, like Vicky, took things literally.

'Simon,' said Normandie, 'please tell me exactly what happened.'

'Two girls were taking part in a mind-reading trick. Suddenly they both screamed. One of their dads wanted to knock Spookie's head off. I'd have disappeared myself if it had been me. Where did you get sand on your legs from then, Jude?'

'Where do you think, Simon?'

'He'll strangle you,' said Normandie, 'if you go on winding him up. Does anybody know why the girls were frightened?'

'He asked them if they could see some fruit on a kissing tree, and they said they'd try, expecting something sexy – you know, something a bit naughty.'

His eyes were back on Jude's legs, long and brown, muddy with caked sand.

'Well, go on,' said Jude.

'But it was two dead men hanging from a gallows.'

'Oh God,' said Jude, startled.

'They both saw the same thing?' asked Normandie.

'So they said.'

'That,' said Jude, 'is scary. Now that is truly scary.'

'We've got to find him.'

'Why?' said Jude. 'It's nothing to do with us, is it? You say "we've got to find him" as if we're Mulder and Scully and he's an alien, but even if that were true I'd still vote for shutting the door and sitting very quietly till it was all over.'

'In the dark,' said Simon.

'No,' said Jude. 'Not in the dark. In the light.'

'OK.' Normandie got up. 'I'll go and find him myself.'

'We'll help you,' said Simon. 'Come on Jude, don't be a cow.'

She looked at him in surprise. One of the waiters, a stolid lad, appeared in the doorway. 'The Bastard wants to know if Felix is here.'

'No, he isn't,' said Normandie. 'But we're going to try to find him.'

They trawled through the rows of caravans, not that there was anywhere he could be hiding other than in his own caravan, and if he was in there he wasn't letting on. They found Vicky and Chrissy with foil containers of paella smorgasbord, looking for a party. People were still wandering about, exchanging accounts of what had happened. Several complained to Normandie – it wasn't fair on the children, they said, meaning it wasn't fair on them having to cope with juvenile nightmares.

Jocantha Webster, one of the girls who had taken part in the mind-reading trick, was standing outside her caravan telling Ray and a crowd of sympathisers what had been so wickedly done to her. 'He told me to count slowly – well,

237

you heard him. To count slowly down from twenty to one and to try not to think of anything.'

'Did you find that difficult?' Ray asked solicitously.

'Then he said, "What fruit grows on the kissing tree?" You all heard him say that.'

Yes, they'd all heard, said those who had been in the club, corroborating her amazing story.

'Me and Shelley were supposed to say what sort of fruit, and then we were supposed to look at what he'd written inside his envelope.'

'Does anybody have his envelope?' asked Normandie.

Nobody had.

'Has anybody seen him?'

They hadn't, but if they did he wouldn't forget it in a hurry.

'What's that you've got?' asked Ray sharply, seeing Vicky and Chrissy with their silver foil containers.

'Nothing,' said Vicky and Chrissy, themselves disappearing into the night.

The warm wind was gusting down over the sea wall. Banks of cloud were moving down from the north, a solid wall of black against the blue ink of the sky.

Jocantha said suddenly, 'I can see their faces.'

'Shelley Barston saw exactly the same,' said a voice. 'Two men with blackened tongues and no eyes. It's her dad who's called the police.'

Ray said, 'What? What's that?'

Jude appeared in a yellow storm jacket, Simon and Pierre behind her. Normandie said, 'OK, let's go.'

* * *

They went along the path and up to the sea wall. There was a hazy light, enough to see Michael's buoys out on the water. A moment later the moon disappeared behind the wall of massed clouds. It started to rain: big fat drops, warm even as they fell, doing nothing to lessen the humidity.

'You have a look up that way,' she said to Jude and Simon, pointing northwards. Simon shot her a grateful look and off they went. Pierre followed Normandie south along the wall towards the excavators and the bird watchers' hut.

This was where Felix had come before, where he liked to sit in the rough marsh grass, staring out to sea.

Rain was falling steadily now, running down her bare legs. For a moment the moon reappeared through a rent in the clouds, and showed the tide flowing swiftly in through the salt marsh, bubbling through the mud channels.

She shouted, 'Felix?'

A shadow against the dunes, by the path that went down behind the wall.

'What is it?'

Pierre, close to her ear. 'A bird.'

'No way.'

He pointed. She saw it: a barn owl, hunched and tense as it flew low over the sand.

'I thought I saw something else.'

But what had she seen? Her skin tightened. She shivered. Then she felt Pierre's jumper round her shoulders. She turned to him, and he smiled. He was not wearing a shirt and his chest was very smooth, she thought – with whatever bit of her brain thought such things – considering the bristly stubble on his chin, his mop of black hair.

'Don't be stupid.' She tried to give him his jumper back, but he smiled again and ran down the path where it dipped behind the wall.

His brown body merged into the night.

'Pierre!'

She went down into the darkness after him, carefully feeling her way. Slowly she climbed up the other side, back to the top of the sea wall. There was the faint light of a ship out at sea. Along the coast, to the east, the lights of King's Lynn were reflected against the clouds.

She could see Pierre, some distance ahead. She walked towards him. Below her, she could hear the tide rushing along its constantly changing courses and inlets, through Blue Back and Black Buoy Sand, submerging the salt marsh as it had done with every tide for a thousand years.

She sensed the barn owl, again, flying low, seeking small mammals, perhaps, among the dunes.

'I think we're wasting our time,' she said as she reached Pierre. 'He wouldn't have come all this way.'

He was staring along the wall. Her eyes followed his gaze, but she saw nothing. The ship out at sea had disappeared, the lights of King's Lynn had gone. She turned to him. It was not Pierre. It was not Felix either, she realised as blind panic overwhelmed her and her lungs refused to breathe.

'Normandie?'

A call from a distance.

Eyes under a hood dripping with rain, staring at her, curious, wary, not unfriendly.

'Normandie?'

She closed her eyes. When she opened them there would be the light of the ship out at sea and in the sky over King's Lynn.

She opened them.

The face was closer, peering at her. There was a sour, terrible smell in her nostrils.

22

The Forest of Sherwood, AD 1216

'Crok?' said Nicolaa, sharply.

He had been whispering spells as he lay curled on the bracken, holding tight to his fisherman's crystal.

'What are you saying, Crok?'

He muttered to himself, then snored.

Pretended, being cunning, that he was asleep

After a moment they turned back to the fire, and started to talk again. He heard Nicolaa say, 'But did they not die together? Tristan and Isolde?'

'No, for she found him already dead of his wounds,' said Lacy. 'She lay beside him, and kissed his lips and face. Then she clasped him tightly in her arms, body to body, mouth to mouth, and so gave up her spirit.'

Now that, mused Crok, reminded him of King Richard's fearful law that a murderer should be bound alive to the corpse of his victim and then buried in sand.

'A noble end,' said Nicolaa, nodding softly, her gold crespine glinting in the firelight, 'for a most noble knight.'

'They were lovers,' said Lacy, 'embraced in death. Eternally inseparable.'

The two of them stared into the flames.

Aping King Arthur, of course, was the fashion among

young English knights. They had built themselves a round table in Winchester Castle (this being before the French took Winchester) and sat solemnly round it, and assured each other that it was the true Camelot table, fashioned by the wizard Merlin for Uther Pendragon and given to Arthur by Leodegrance of Cameliard as dowry of his daughter Guinevere. They called themselves by the names of Arthurian knights, and drank mead they claimed was from far Lyonesse, and got hog-drunk discussing the ideal of knightly conduct. When Fulk Fitzwarin was outlawed by John he went on quests to rescue damsels and slay dragons, though he later refused to say where he found them.

Perhaps Lacy thought he was on a quest now. Perhaps, when the young knights play-acted at Winchester, he had taken the part of Tristan. Perhaps he thought that Nicolaa was Isolde.

Crok snickered quietly in the bracken. They'd be coupling soon, for Nicolaa had always liked a king's officer with good harness, and everyone knew that talk of treasure inflamed the blood and encouraged lust (he had seen it happen with John a hundred times). And they liked each other, these two. It was only when they talked of charters that they spat like cats, but that was not surprising for charters were dreary things. There had once been an attorney at court (a puffed-up essoiner if the truth were known) called Groaning and Sighing, whose cock was inflamed by thoughts of charters and deeds from the time of King Edward, but he was the only man so affected that Crok ever knew of.

If William were here, or Florence, they might have a

wager on it. 'A shilling,' William would say, 'that they'll be coupling by Nottingham.'

And the three of them would think deep and chew the cud and cast gnawing anxious eyes on the young lord and his lady, pondering on the heat of their blood, thinking of what a shilling would buy.

Meat turned over the fire. A small roe deer, plumped-up on summer grazing. A little fat deer, Crok thought fondly. He could see the fat run down it, smell it as it sizzled. He moved slightly in the bracken, his saliva running.

Nicolaa's eyes were on him in an instant. 'He was there on the sands of Lenne,' she said. 'He was there with the army.'

Not when it happened, dame, not when the mists came swift and silent as a greyhound over the sands and the tide rushed in before its time.

'He knows what treasure John had. He was ever in the King's chamber when the chests were opened. He knows what remained and what went to the Jews.'

A terrible lot had gone to the Jews.

'If there were any spoils at Newark, he would have had them.'

There had been no spoils at Newark, not after the Poetevin mercenaries had helped themselves.

Crok thought of the tiny jewels bound tight to his chest. He lay as still as a young deer in the tall grass when Ferling passed with his hounds. As silent as a songbird when de Porkericiis was hunting with his hawks.

She was watching him, broodingly.

'And he's a seer,' she said.

Lacy said, 'I wondered what he was.'

Soldiers sitting round the fire grinned. They were unshaven and filthy, with stumps for teeth and fetid, meaty breath.

'Crok?' she said. 'Where is your bag?'

'You don't want to see in his bag,' said Lacy.

'He's got a crystal in it.'

The men looked shifty.

'In his bag,' said Lacy, 'he has a Scotchman's head. Or at least he has somebody's head.'

The soldiers, simple souls, tittered and showed their brown stumps.

'Crok?' said Nicolaa. 'Alexander is at Lincoln now, pounding my walls. I'll give you a shilling for your Scotchman.'

He had left the Scotchman's head on the kissing tree, it having become full of white maggots. She knew this; she had seen him stick it there. But women were naturally malicious. *There is no head above the head of a serpent; and there is no malice above that of a woman.* They had their sweetness (he thought, fleetingly, of little Alison de Pilche, who cried 'Ware! Ware!' and loved her Valentine) but their sweetness was gooseberries from among thorns, or, as the Knights of Jerusalem (who met many wicked women on their travels) were wont to say, it was prickly-pears from cactus.

A crash in the forest. Men moved silently, swiftly untying the greased cloth that covered their bows. There was the low rasp of an iron blade being pulled from a scabbard. There was the tiny *click click* of a crossbow being wound.

Cantuar crouched with his sword drawn. Lacy was by Nicolaa, also sword in hand.

The boy, William, had a dagger, and looked wicked.

A call, softly, from the sentry.

Something was moving on the edge of the circle.

Small red eyes in the firelight.

A small pig. An arrow was loosed and caught its leg. It squealed and was gone, crashing back through the forest.

'Shit . . .'

The sergeant delivered a stunning blow to an archer's head, making him howl.

Nicolaa lay back on her fur, which was spread out on couch of bracken, her thoughts seemingly far away.

The archer held his bleeding head and sobbed.

Lacy took William's dagger, leaned forward and cut into the venison. Blood trickled down into the fire.

'Hood's dead,' Nicolaa said. Then, in a rustic peasant voice, 'Cum with me, dear lass, to the greenwood.'

The soldiers grinned.

'Phillip Mark sent Lisle and fifty men to run him down. He was more angered by the songs than by the deer that were being poached. He planned to hang the whole crew from the castle keep and call it *The Jest of the Sheriff of Nottingham*, but Lisle's dogs ran one of the outlaws down, the man's heart stopped and the rest ran off.'

She stared into the fire.

'Was it Hood that died?' said Lacy

'No. He crawled up into Lincolnshire, to Kirklees, in the end, with only Will Stuteley of his *merry men*. He was a greybeard, of course, half starved to death, for it's hard to chew roots with your teeth gone. He begged the nuns to take him in. Joanna de Stainton was his kinswoman seemingly. They say she bled him to death. The nuns of Kirklees are whores, right lads?'

The lads nodded. The priory had a certain reputation.

' "To see the deer draw to the dale," ' Nicolaa sang softly. ' "And leave the hills high. And shadow him in the leaves green . . ." '

She stared into the fire, and finished, ' "Under the greenwood." '

Crok waited for a mocking voice to come from the forest, as it would in a minstrel's story: bold Robin singing, then an arrow through the haunch of venison, and Tuck dropping from the trees above their heads, his black friar's robe all awry, his sword in hand.

But the greenwood slept.

'If Fulk Fitzwarin comes into Lincolnshire,' said Nicolaa, her mind dwelling, seemingly, on famous outlaws, 'I will hang him no matter how many dragons he has slain, or damsels he has rescued.'

Lacy carved slices of venison, then placed them on fronds of fern and presented them to her.

She bit into the meat. The soldiers attacked the carcass with their knives. Crok moved towards the fire, pulling out his dagger. Nicolaa said, 'Stay.'

He slavered. His teeth chattered.

She said, 'Get out your crystal and you shall eat.'

He did not move.

'The necromancer, Meilyr,' she said, 'could see spirits. They appeared in the form of huntsmen, pursuing human souls rather than wild beasts. What can you see, Crok?'

He could see a liar. He could see the demon that exulted and danced on the liar's tongue. He knew that the petty lord of Moulton had been lying when he said the jewels were forever lost.

'Will Louis be King of all England?'

That was a question. A dead king lay in Worcester church. A boy prince was even now in the forests of the Severn.

'It is not a question that should be asked,' said Lacy.

'No?' She turned on him, looked at him thoughtfully. 'But then, your cousin de Mandeville, I think, fights with the French?'

'My cousin was forced to pay King John seven thousand marks relief on coming of age – and his lands had been raped by the crown for two years before that.'

'John needed money.'

'Money? He lusted over my cousin's wife. And when she died he made him marry his own divorced wife, Isabel, and fined him twenty thousand marks for the privilege.'

'There was never,' she said, puzzled, 'money enough. Daubney said it was the silver coming in from Bruges. The more silver that came in, the more, it seemed, that everything cost. Only the wool merchants got fat. You know that John was paying two shillings a day for an archer, instead of the eightpence it was in the time of his father?'

Lacy nodded. Every baron, and every baron's son, knew the cost of hiring archers.

'Anyway,' said Nicolaa, 'the Lady Maud was a whore.'

'The King treated her as one.'

Crok laughed. '*Non mundi quidem Maud juxta falsam et*

frivolam nominis impositionem,' he said, hoping to ingratiate himself, '*sed immundi verius Maud vocata palam et impudenter abutendo.*'

No longer was she called 'the Fair Maud' but instead 'that tart Maud'.

He chuckled again.

There was stillness round the fire.

None of them, it seemed, had much Latin.

Nicolaa stood up suddenly and strode towards him.

'Get him. Get his bag. Get his crystal.'

They grabbed him before he could scuttle into the undergrowth (to be caught and have his teeth pulled out by Much the Miller or Fulk Fitzwarin), but none were willing to put their hand into his loathsome bag.

He opened his hand to show his crystal, which had been there all the time.

The soldiers muttered uneasily, sensing magic.

'Leave him alone,' said Lacy in disgust, or perhaps in terror.

'You are a necromancer,' said Nicolaa. 'What can a necromancer do?'

Deal in forbidden magic. Baptise images. Summon spirits. Invoke unfamiliar names or mix the names of angels and demons. Fumigate the head of a dead person.

What did she want him to do?

'Tell me if Louis,' said Nicolaa, bending down, her eyes sharp as needles, 'will be King.'

It was a matter of some moment, he could see that. Louis had made a French adventurer Eorl of Lincoln. If he won the war, Nicolaa would end up begging for a small manor somewhere: Petty Lord of Moulton Chapel, perhaps, if they ever got the chapel built.

He held up the crystal. It was from the sea, a perfect sphere, dark and dense. He walked to the fire and kicked it to make it blaze. Then he knelt and cupped the ball, and stared into it, saliva running from his mouth, his tongue flickering over the sharp stump of broken tooth.

He could smell the meat, though only a little of it remained on the iron skillet.

She watched him, as she had watched him on many a night in the King's chamber. 'Now listen,' she said ominously. 'I don't want to be told of the Lion of Justice making the island dragons tremble, or the lion's cubs being turned into saltwater fishes.'

She had a terrible tongue.

All wickedness was but little to the wickedness of a woman.

His eye flickering to the skillet, the bone with its shreds of meat, the grey fat congealing.

'Mercury is dim,' he said. 'The helmet of Mars calls to Venus. I see the malice of Saturn pour down like rain. It kills men with a curved sickle. Cancer fights with the sun.'

He wanted his meat. He reached out for it.

A switch, hard across his swollen, bleeding knuckles.

Cicero said: *It may well happen that men commit a sinful deed to gain some personal advantage; but women will commit every crime in the calendar to satisfy a passing whim.*

'There will be a battle that the Earl of Chester and the Marshall will win,' he said, staring deeply into the crystal.

'The Compte de Perché will be killed and Saer de Quenci will be taken captive. The *Norrenses* will return to the north and Louis will try to escape to France. Even now I see the men of Kent slaughtering the French.'

A soldier said, awed, 'It's true. The merchants told us of Willikin killing the French.'

'I see Louis at Winchelsea, with no way to grind corn but to rub it between his royal hands. He eats nothing but beech nuts.'

Nicolaa wasn't listening. She was lying back on her fur, staring up at the night sky.

Lacy pulled his cloak round him. It was cold now at night. One thing he knew: there would be no battles fought this year. The French were snug in London, the rebel barons warm in their castles. It would be a winter of raiding parties, of cattle stealing and attrition.

He said, 'Eat.'

But Crok did not move. The fire had died down but was there a spark of flickering red, deep in his hands. Deep in the black orb.

He cried out.

Soldiers crossed themselves. One said: *Kyrie, eleison*.

Crok cried out again.

Lord have mercy on us.

Black waters bubbled through the sands of Black Buoy. He could see men with lanterns, with ropes and poles. He could see the Petty Lord's daughter, Alison de Pilche, in the light from a lantern, and the lad with fair hair slithering like a snake over straw pallets thrown on the wet, shining mud. The boy was fixing his rope round something beneath the surface. The men were heaving. A box was being pulled from the slime. Yet another lad crawled out across the straw pallets, a rope round his waist, plunging his arms deep into the quicksand. Men heaved the chest up into a cart.

The waters were bubbling in now, through a hundred channels. The lad in the quicksand cried out, then disappeared as the waters rose. Then Crok saw the Roman tower, and the iron chisels hammering at the locks on the chest, and the bright gleam of white gold.

A sword flashed from a jewelled scabbard. The sword of Sir Tristram, who had died of his wounds before Isolde could reach him.

The lad with fair hair, the *Valentine* of Alison de Pilche, had the great crown of England on his head.

23

Wormby Flats, Lincolnshire

They were asking if she was all right, telling her that Felix had been found. A voice said, 'Where's the torch?' and Jude said, 'Pierre, where the fuck have you been?'

'I was checking the birdwatchers' hut.'

'How long did you leave her for?'

'Only a minute.'

'Normandie!'

They shook her. She said, 'Ow!' and opened her eyes.

The man in the hood was very dirty, his skin was mahogany, weathered, his eyes yellow.

'Normandie,' said Pierre. 'Hey, look, I'm sorry.'

Now the man was a million raindrops in the light of the torch.

'Normandie, what is it?' said Jude. 'What happened?'

'Never mind,' said Simon, taking off his yellow waterproof. 'Let's just get her back to the camp.'

They were trying to push her arms into Simon's waterproof. The torch was shining in her face, blinding her. She could see Pierre's white chest, his dripping black hair. He looked like a young merman risen from the deeps. She giggled suddenly.

'No,' she said. 'No, please, I'm all right.'

She looked round for the man in the hood. A shadow rose from the darkness of the dunes. She screamed.

'Oh Christ,' said Jude.

Arms were round her. She hit out. Somebody cried in pain and let her go. She tried to run but they grabbed her again. She struggled and fell to the ground, her face in the wet sand, the sharp smell of crushed gorse in her nostrils. A voice close in her ear said, 'It's all right, it's all right, it's all right.'

Michael.

'She's had a shock of some kind,' said Mr Tymoor into the phone. 'Her friends found her on the sea wall.'

She was in the farm kitchen. Jude, and Simon, and Pierre were standing looking confused. Karen's mother was fussing around her, worrying about her sodden clothes, telling her to take off Pierre's jumper before she caught her death.

She said, 'Where's Michael?'

'He's gone to his caravan,' said Karen, pouring her a mug of tea. 'He said he'll be back in a minute. Are you all right now?'

On the table was bread and cold meat, tomatoes in a dish, a cake. She remembered Michael saying how the Tymoors always ate a proper Lincolnshire supper.

'All we know is that she's been very badly frightened,' said Karen's dad. 'No, no, I don't think it was anything like that.'

Outside the kitchen window was a glassed-in veranda, full of broken television sets and video equipment and lit by an unshaded bulb. Beyond its black panes was the night.

'Here you are.'

She took the mug of tea automatically, then said, 'Oh God,' overwhelmed by terror, even here in the kitchen with its bright, fluorescent light, its row of gymkhana rosettes stuck on the beam over the cold Rayburn stove, its smell of bacon fat and damp dogs. She put down the mug and sobbed.

'She's very upset. She's got a cut on her leg and scratches on her face.'

The Tymoors' Labrador came and put his face in her lap. She leaned down and ran her hands through his coat and put her face against his damp fur. His tail beat softly on the floor.

'I'm sorry.' she said. 'It's all right. I'm OK.'

On a shelf were three small, dusty screens, flickering with fuzzy black-and-white pictures. On one of them a ghostly white figure suddenly appeared, coming towards the camera.

'It's all right,' said Karen. 'It's just Michael.'

The veranda door opened, then the inner door. He crossed the kitchen and said, 'Move over, Bosun.' He knelt down in front of her and held both her hands. The Labrador tried to push his head back into her lap.

'How's she going to drink her tea?' said Mrs Tymoor. 'If you hold both her hands like that?'

'I can drive her in to the surgery if you like,' Mr Tymoor was saying into the phone, 'save you coming out here.'

'Do you want to see a doctor?' Michael asked.

She shook her head.

'She doesn't want to see a doctor,' Mrs Tymoor said loudly to her husband. 'She can stay here for the night and go to the surgery in the morning.'

'I'm sorry,' Normandie said.

'The doctor says he's got to see her if she lost consciousness,' said Mr Tymoor.

'Did you lose consciousness?' asked Michael.

'I think she was just confused,' said Jude. 'She'd had a fright. She was sobbing.'

'Karen, you go in Clive's bed,' said Mrs Tymoor firmly. 'Clive, you sleep on the floor in Darren's room.'

'No problem,' said Clive, who was fourteen and staring fixedly at Normandie's wet, T-shirted bosom.

'It's all right, Mrs Tymoor,' said Michael firmly. 'I'll take care of her.'

The rain had stopped but the long grass was wet and cold against her legs. She clung to him, shivering uncontrollably. Jude, Simon and Pierre stood outside the kitchen, and watched her being carried off.

They went into his caravan and he turned on a gas fire. She said, 'What was it? What happened?'

'It don't know. It could be just part of the mass hysteria.'

'I was on my own!'

'Jude says that two girls from the holiday village have been seeing things.'

'Yes,' she said. 'Yes, I know, but it wasn't that. He was there, Michael. He was there. This man was there with me on the sea wall—'

She started to sob.

'Hush,' he said, 'hush. It's all right.'

'But what was it?'

'Whatever it was, it wasn't real. Whatever you thought, it wasn't real. Did you try to touch it?'

'Christ, no.'

'You couldn't have.'

'If you'd been there—'

'It was most likely thought-transference – some kind of low-level psychokinesis, similar to what happened to the two girls.'

'Michael,' she said, 'I don't care about the treasure any more.'

'The treasure doesn't matter.'

'I don't want to find it. I don't think people should look for it.'

'Take your things off.'

'I think it's evil. You know?'

'Yes, I know.'

He helped her, rubbing her arms and legs vigorously with a towel. He found her a dry shirt. The red light on his computer blinked. There was a low pulsing bleep.

'What's that?'

'It's just the satellite.'

'What, making that noise?'

'Yes.'

'I thought nothing in space made a noise?'

'It doesn't. Here.'

He offered her a pair of his jeans.

'Why can't I just go to bed?'

'Rake's coming.'

'What?'

'Andrew Rake, from the Bohr Unit in Cambridge.'

His phone rang.

'Boulding.'

She heard a voice say, 'I'm just leaving London. I'll be about three hours.'

'Fine.'

Michael put the phone down. They were not great conversationalists, these scientists, not chatterers. She put on the jeans. He knelt and put socks on her feet. She started to sob again. He sat on the bed and hugged her.

'I'm sorry,' she said. 'I'm hysterical.'

'Just be quiet.'

'Is Rake coming to see Felix?'

'Never mind Felix.'

'I don't understand.'

'It doesn't matter,' he said, kissing her gently, her eyes, her forehead, her hair.

'Michael,' she said, after a bit, 'I don't want Rake seeing me like this.'

The police car arrived quietly outside the Dreamboat, without its blue light flashing or its siren sounding, a disappointment to the onlookers. The two policemen got out slowly, looking round them, taking their time.

'So where's this mind-reader, then?' said one of them, a sergeant.

'He's inside,' said Ray grimly.

They went into the club, then into Ray's office. Felix sat, his purple suit streaked black with rain, one hand stroking his jaw.

They stood and stared at him. 'Didn't they like your act then?' said the younger policeman.

'It's not funny,' said Jack Fountain, in the doorway. 'You can talk to the two girls if you want to.'

'All in good time,' said the sergeant.

The phone rang and Ray answered it. He automatically assumed his sunny voice, though it was hardly going to be punters looking for a caravan holiday, not at this time of night. 'You do what you like,' he said curtly, and put the phone down. 'That bugger disc jockey's gone and told the BBC. Radio Lincolnshire wants to send a radio car.'

'So what happened exactly?' said the sergeant.

'Two girls were frightened to bloody death, that's what.'

They looked at Felix.

He smiled, showing bright purple gums.

The sergeant said, 'You don't look too well to me, mate.'

Felix touched his gums with his finger. It came away red with blood.

'Did somebody hit you?'

He shook his head.

'Have you done this mind reading often?'

'He's the Astounding Felix,' Ray said. 'As seen on television with Lesley Crowther. That was in 1972.'

'Well then,' said the sergeant, 'perhaps you ought to be a bit more careful. Have you upset any young girls before?'

Felix said, 'I am ill. A discarnate will latch on to illness. To disease. To unhappiness.'

'A discarnate? What's that?'

'Never mind,' Felix said.

'It's a sort of spirit,' said Ray, who felt he was becoming an authority on matters of the occult. 'From the Other World.'

'Is that right?'

Felix shrugged.

'We've not had many dealings with discarnates round Spalding.'

Felix smiled wearily. Again he showed red, bloody gums.

'You ought to see a dentist. You need that plaque seen to.'

'If he's ill,' said Jack Fountain solicitously, 'perhaps you should take him to hospital.'

'He's not that ill,' said the sergeant.

'What I'm saying is,' said Jack, 'that it would be better all round if he wasn't on the site. We don't want trouble but there are some very angry people out there. Can't you find him a bed-and-breakfast?'

It was August. Most places would be full. The young policeman had a sister-in-law who ran a B&B in Skegness. He half-heartedly offered to phone her up, but even if she had a room free how would Felix get to Skegness?

'We're the only car on call between here and Peterborough,' said the sergeant. 'We can't go buggering off to Skeggy. If we did there'd be an incident on the A16, bet your life on it.'

'It'd be sod's law,' said the young policeman.

They were worried about Radio Lincolnshire, about an attack on police priorities.

'He's got a car,' said Jack. 'Why can't he just drive himself?'

They looked at Felix, at the whisky bottle on the desk, the empty glass.

'How much have you had, then?' said the sergeant.

Felix shook his head and shrugged,

'Can't you put him in the cells?' asked Jack.

'Bloody hell,' said the sergeant, admiringly.

262

'Only for his own good.'

The policemen conferred. They went out into the club and spoke into their radio. Then they came back and the sergeant said to Ray, 'This is your camp site, Mr Monkman. Are you kicking him out?'

'No.'

'Christ!' said Jack, angrily.

'Now listen, chum,' said the sergeant. 'If we took him away because he was being threatened with violence, we'd have to look into who was doing the threatening, you follow what we're saying?'

Jack looked surprised.

'Now, are either of these two girls making a complaint?'

'Of course they're making a complaint! You could have heard them complain in Wisbech.'

'I mean an official complaint.'

'What kind of official complaint?'

'How would I know?' said the sergeant. 'It's not my job to tell people what they ought to complain about. I know what I might complain about and that's people wasting police time. Was it you who made the phone call?'

'No,' said Jack.

'All right then. Now, these girls. Perhaps they ought to see a solicitor.'

'Nobody's talking about solicitors,' said Jack, frightened.

The sergeant spoke again into his radio. The young constable went over to the bar and looked at the fluorescent cocktail recipes. 'Slow Comfortable Screw,' he said in a faraway voice. 'We had those in Crete. Do they go in for nude bathing here as well?'

The policemen left. The holiday-makers who remained outside the club watched them drive away. They drifted back to their caravans.

Two girls had been hysterical – that was the latest opinion.

Felix lay, finally, in the darkness, one hand between his knees, seeking the comfort of the womb, the other massaging his aching jaw. When he had undressed he had found purple blotches on his legs and stomach. He wondered if perhaps he had had some kind of stroke.

He lay in the darkness, breathing softly, tasting blood from his gums on his tongue. He was drifting to sleep when he heard a noise.

A tap at the caravan door.

He said loudly, *'Eradicare et effugare ab hoc plasmate Dei!'*

Depart and vanish from this creature of God

Which would make vengeful holiday-makers draw back, and might even give a discarnate pause for thought.

'Felix?'

He let them in. Michael Boulding. Normandie dressed in baggy clothes a bit like a circus clown. Two strangers, a man in his thirties and a young woman.

'I'm Andrew Rake,' the man said, 'from the Bohr Unit at Cambridge. This is Jennifer Poole, also from the Bohr Unit.'

They examined him. His bleeding gums, the purple stains on his chest. Then they helped him pack his bags.

Outside the humidity had dropped and there was a cooling sea mist drifting down over the wall. They made their way past the caravan where Vicky and Chrissy slept with their foil containers of stolen paella, never having found a party. They went past the caravan where Jude and Simon were in bed, having got back together again just before they found Felix wandering the seashore. They went past the caravan where Shelley Barston was only just now falling into a troubled sleep and the caravan where Jocantha Webster lay awake and terrified, and would have screamed had she known that Felix was passing so close.

They went quietly across the wet sand and tarmac, past Ray's silvery American motor home.

Then they were gone.

For the remainder of the night, Wormby Flats Holiday Village slept peacefully. Undisturbed by discarnates, phantoms, ghosts or spectres.

Part Three

24

Electronic Intelligence (ELINT) Section, National Security Agency, Chicago

It was a long, agonising week before Trudy Pierce even dared to hope that she was in the clear, that her evasion of the AirINTEL security protocols hadn't been detected and that she wasn't going, to see her photo in the *Chicago Tribune*: 'Lake Forest girl jailed for Security offense.' Then, after a further week, she stopped sitting at home every night waiting for the doorbell to ring and her mother to say, 'Two heavily armed gentlemen want to talk to you, Trudy, and the house is surrounded.'

She went swimming and, one Saturday night at the end of August, met a nice boy at a barbecue at her parents' golf club and and started dating him. 'It looks like Trudy's over her wanderlust,' her mother said at a Ladies' Circle coffee morning. But in truth Trudy was still planning her escape from ELINT records, still dreaming of being an agent in the field.

In early September she put in for a CIA survival course in Canada. Meeson, her boss, read her application with a smirk and said, 'Yeah, fine, I'll put this forward.' When she left his office she glanced back through the smoky-glass window to see if he had dropped it in his waste bin, as he had done the last time she applied, but he was staring into space, thinking, she guessed, about his frustrated sex life.

On the first Monday in October she had almost forgotten the query from the CIA jerk in Wilmington. When Meeson called her into his office she thought it was to talk about working rotas – tell her that her Thanksgiving weekend would involve pizza and curly fries in front of her office computer screen.

He had a man with him. He said, 'OK, tell me about an AirINTEL file relating to August 1962.'

The skies fell.

'Why?' she said, her voice sharp with shock, her face, she knew, suffused with guilt.

'Because we're interested. OK?'

Relief flooded through her. Meeson was in a bullying but jocular mood, which meant that a) he was finally dating the Cindy Doll Woman in charge of the drinking-water coolers, and b) the most junior member of his staff was not, at this moment, on the point of being arrested by the military police. Unless, of course, Cindy Doll Woman was giving it to him so good that his staff could go hang themselves.

'We are waiting,' he said, still with his strange, weird good humour.

'I'm sorry. It's a while ago.'

'Forty years.'

'I mean since the query.'

'A small section of aircraft,' he said with an exaggerated sigh. 'With serial markings that we ought to have been able to trace in thirty seconds.'

'There were problems.'

The man with him was aged about thirty she guessed. Thin face, brown hair, looked a bit like an academic. He looked tired. It was typical of Meeson not to introduce him, to keep her guessing. It subtly, or even not so subtly, emphasised her inferior status in the scheme of things.

'Problems, right.' He was getting bored. 'Well, if you could refresh your memory and then give Mr Rake all the help you can?'

'Sure.'

'Mr Rake's from England,' he said after a short pause, an information-hoarder forced to part with a fraction of his wealth. 'He's a physicist with the British Ministry of Defence. They don't like bits of American aircraft falling from the skies over the UK. Let's make this a priority.'

'Fine.'

'We are not normally dilatory,' he said to Rake. 'I guess nobody thought a query about something that maybe fell from a plane forty years ago could be important. You expecting to stay over here long?'

'I hope to fly back tomorrow.'

'Shame,' he said mechanically. 'OK, then, I'll maybe see you both later.'

'I expect so,' said Rake.

Meeson looked alarmed. He had many things to do. 'Miss Pierce will find out everything there is to be found,' he said decisively.

She took him to her desk and borrowed a chair and got them both coffees. She brought up the August query from Wilmington.

There it was, the signal from Maryland jerk, who was, she guessed, a junior copy of Meeson jerk. For a moment she pitied the baby girl who in twenty years' time would find herself saying, 'Yes, sir, straight away, sir,' to this junior jerk in Maryland. The child was out there somewhere. Her card was marked.

'It's got a tag on it,' said the Englishman, staring at the screen.

'That was why it was passed to us. Do you work in America all the time?'

'No, very rarely.'

'You're with MI5?'

She had dealings from time to time with MI5, the organisation in charge of security at Menwith Hill in the UK, where NSA and the British shared a ground segment node for high altitude signals-intelligence sats. Sometimes she worked on stuff flown back to America for secure analysis, the British not being allowed access to US data – though students on her intel wargame induction course believed the British were copying it through a Magnum intercept. Students, particularly male students, thought it was cool to suspect the worst.

'No,' he said. 'I work at Cambridge. I see you pushed it through E-systems in Dallas. What happened?'

On screen was the terse query from E-systems security, and her Pentagon priority-coded reply. It was all coming back to her, her moment of madness. She could hear the boys shouting 'Yes!' as they played their dungeons and dragons games on the other side of the office.

'The gopher got banged inside an intruder trap.'

'Why did you look in SIGINT A Group?'

'In case there was some involvement with former Soviet Bloc targets.'

'OK, that's fine,' he said, more easily satisfied than Trudy was happy with. Rake, she'd decided, was smart.

'Why was the file tagged in the first place?' he mused. He looked at her suddenly. 'It's not still active?'

'Not that I am aware of,' Trudy said and felt herself blush again. 'Can you excuse me for moment?'

She got up and went back to Meeson's office. Through the glass she saw that he was on the phone. She knocked quietly and went in. He looked up irritably, put his hand over the mouthpiece and said, 'Yeah?'

'Last month, I couldn't bring up the Lincolnshire, England, file because it's tagged Most Secret. That means it may be still active. I don't know if it's all right for Mr Rake to know that.'

He said, 'I'll call you back, OK?' then put the phone down. 'Go and take him to lunch.'

'What?'

'Jesus, are you deaf?'

'It's not even twelve.'

He was picking up another phone.

She went back to her desk. She'd been gone three minutes, perhaps four. Her computer screen was unchanged: she looked to see if her mouse had been used, but realised she couldn't remember where she'd left it. She'd make a rotten agent, she thought unhappily; she had so much to learn. Rake was looking out of the window, down at the traffic on North Michigan Avenue.

'Would you care to go to and get something to eat?' she asked, wondering how much they'd let her reclaim, and thinking what a total incompetent her boss was not to have checked things out with her before Rake arrived.

He looked at her, surprised, then said politely, 'Why not?'

She thought she'd take him to the Artists Restaurant, which was a civilised, cultured, British sort of place; but when she described it he said, 'Have this on me, compensation for the trouble I'm causing,' and took her in a cab to Dick's Last Resort at North Pier, where they'd got a famous collection of bras nailed up behind the bar and the staff were notoriously rude and sat at people's tables to insult them, except that nothing like that happened in their case.

He ordered Bloody Marys and buckets of sticky ribs and crab legs, and tried to talk about the CIA signal, but she wasn't having any of that so they talked about Chicago restaurants, which she hardly knew at all, and the Lake Forest suburb where she lived. Keeping the conversation safe – a hard task for he was old and wise, and she was young and naive – involved telling him that the Lake Forest median family income was $182,000 and the suburb had an average of 910 crimes for 10,000 residents, and a most charming Market Square designed by the noted architect Howard Van Doren Shaw.

He thanked her for the information. He sat silent for a minute, then ordered more Bloody Marys. She feared he was going to try to get her drunk. She quickly asked him about his work in Cambridge, and he said he was with the Bohr

Unit, which investigated the theory of human cognition, perception and creativity.

'Yea?' she said, interested. 'My BA was in engineering anomalies.'

He brightened, and asked her what she thought of analytical methodologies for quantitative assessment of precognitive and retrocognitive remote perception data. It would have been a good time, she thought, for one of the infamously rude waiters to come and sit down and join in the conversation.

'The central argument,' he said, his voice raised over the Dixieland music, 'has got to be whether microtubules or neurons form the basic units of the brain. Right?' He was looking at her intently. She wondered if US national security could be compromised by her answer. 'Basically,' he went on, 'it's got to be down to whether quantum physics or classical physics govern the phenomenon of consciousness.'

She risked a nod. He grinned and ordered yet more Bloody Marys. After a while she asked him about MI6, which she knew ran British anti-drugs operations in St Kitts. Somewhere round two-thirty she confided to him her ambition to be a field officer (wondering secretly if he was influential enough to recommend her for an attachment) and if Rake was surprised that this quiet and very small girl from the suburbs saw a future for herself as an armed agent busting South American drugs rackets and personally bringing the wickedest men in the world in handcuffs before the tribunes of international justice, he did nothing to show it.

* * *

When they got back Meeson was prowling the corridor and ushered them both into his office. He said, 'Look, it may take some time to locate this file. Maybe I should get Miss Pierce and a couple of guys to sort it out, and get the details sent to you back in England.'

'We've been asking about this for five weeks, nearly six,' Rake said. 'The CIA has promised full co-operation.'

'We're not CIA.'

'Call Fort Meade, Director of Intel Ops Directorate.'

'I'll come clean. The file is tagged Most Secret.'

'Why?'

'Now how can I possibly tell you that?' Meeson laughed silently, shaking his head from side to side, amused by Rake's wicked ruse.

'A piece of fuselage from a US aircraft,' said Rake crisply, 'fell on the Lincolnshire coast. It's linked through serial numbers to a tagged NSA file dated August 5th 1962. That much we know from our own sources.'

'What sources?' said Meeson, alarmed, looking round as though he suspected British agents lurking behind the arras. Trudy, who had drunk three Bloody Marys at Dick's Last Stand, giggled then coughed.

'The CIA claim they know nothing,' said Rake. 'And according to our own people they do not, on this occasion, speak with forked tongues. The only link we have is here, through ELINT. I have come from London because we have been promised full co-operation.'

'You've got it. But this file was most likely tagged in error. There are five thousand supposedly active files every year closed down by the resource monitors. This one maybe slipped through. It isn't even on our database.'

'Maybe it's too secret to be on your database.'

'It's our file, goddam it.'

'No. It's originally an AirINTEL file.'

'The problem is,' said Trudy, trying to be tactful, 'that the people who were putting archive files on computer record were sometimes careless.'

'Tell me, Mr Rake, purely out of curiosity,' said Meeson, 'why the British Security Services, which are funded, I believe, to protect the security of the United Kingdom, are worrying so much about a very small piece of airplane that fell from the skies in 1962.'

'We want to know what it was. We want to know why we weren't told about it at the time. In particular, we want to know if there was any way it might have involved electromagnetic waves.'

'This has some relevance today?'

'The man who found the pieces of fuselage, who first touched them when the excavators turned them up in the sand, is in hospital with an illness that does not respond to treatment.'

Meeson stared. 'We're thinking about some kind of germ warfare thing?'

'The illness may be epileptic in origin, it may well be totally unrelated. We're not thinking anything till we see the file. Do I get co-operation or not?'

'Sure you get co-operation. I've been ordered to give you *maximum* co-operation,' he went on, impressively, as though the instruction had come down from the President. 'But to trace this file, if it can be traced, and in my view it almost certainly no longer exists, will mean manually accessing, program by program, storage data files from the early Sixties which are currently stored in around fifteen locations. You want to do that – fine. Miss Pierce will help you. No way can it take less than a week.'

'I don't have a week.'

'We'll do what we can when you've gone home. Miss Pierce is a superb operative. If anybody can find it she will.'

Trudy stared at him, knowing that he thought she was a kid who knew nothing.

'I've got twenty-four hours,' said Rake.

'OK. Find it by this time tomorrow, Trudy,' he said, putting some managerial enthusiasm behind the project, 'and you get your secondment to the CIA survival course.'

'Yeah?'

She thought instantly of the gopher she'd sent into AirINTEL HQ, the green referral that had flashed on her screen for a split second before she evaded the electronic cop. 'This Fall?'

'The very next course we can get you on,' he snapped, finally irritated beyond endurance.

Afterwards, she caught him in the corridor. He was on his way to a bar with the woman who had the water-cooler franchise. 'Sir,' Trudy called, and he looked wearily round and said 'Jesus, what now.'

'Sir, can I have a word?'

Cindy Doll said, 'I'll be in Joey's.'

'I'll be right with you.'

'Sir,' Trudy said quietly, 'am I really supposed to find this file?'

'Why would I ask you to find it if I didn't want you to?'

'I don't know,' she said, meaning *I am a stranger finding my path in the ways of deception and low cunning.* 'I thought that maybe you assigned me to it because you didn't think I'd be able to do it.'

'Jesus,' he said again, shaking his head, making off down the corridor.

Later he came back and summoned her into his office. He put a call through to the director in Fort Meade and was told he'd be called back. He sat slumped behind his desk in his overcoat. He said, 'I've been told that without co-operation the British might stop us using Machrinhanish base in Scotland for the Aurora stealth plane, a development which could be very unpleasant for us if the vengeful finger ever pointed toward Chicago, which it surely would. You understand?'

She nodded.

'But I don't like this stuff about a guy in hospital. Maybe we need to play for time.'

His phone flashed. He picked it up and said, 'Hi, Larry,' at the same time pressing a button so that Trudy could hear the conversation: a gesture of trust, his smile said, but Trudy knew he was making sure he had a witness. He outlined his problem. His director said: 'Do we have any reason at all to withhold information on this file?'

'It's tagged top secret.'

'Other than that.'

'Not that he's telling us. He talks about one guy in hospital, but maybe it's a hundred guys.'

'Anything like that and we'd have heard from London. It's the early sixties we're talking about, right?'

'August 5, 1962.'

'Wasn't that the time of the Cuban Crisis?'

'I guess so.'

Meeson had been eight. His director had not even been born. To them both, the Cuban Crisis was an option module in the History of the Cold War.

'The day Marilyn Monroe died,' he added, showing breadth of knowledge.

'You know that clip of her singing "Happy Birthday, Mr President"?'

'Yes.'

'Jesus,' said the director admiringly. 'Those tits.'

Trudy looked blankly at the wall behind Meeson's head.

'OK, then,' the director went on. 'Let's be sensible. It was a long time ago. Let's try to be helpful.'

Meeson put the phone down. He said, 'You heard the man.'

Trudy phoned home and said she'd be working late, maybe all night. Her mother called Eddie, the boy she'd met at the golf-club barbecue, and cancelled a visit that evening to the hockey rink. 'Trudy's tracking down drugs-runners,' she told him. 'She's getting close to Mr Big.' The boy went down to the shore, scuffing his way through the first pine cones of the Fall, worrying about dating a girl who was doing what a guy ought to have been doing, thinking that Claudia MacInvoie, who baked cookies and had a curvaceous figure of which she was justly proud, might be the girl for him after all.

* * *

Rake, in his hotel room, called his assistant, Jennifer.

'Any sign of activity?'

'No.'

He sighed.

She said, 'Maybe it only happens when he's at Wormby.'

'What do the doctors say?'

'They're not happy about another PET scan. There's a new doctor in charge, a woman called Govindan. She think he's got enough problems without us injecting radio-active chemicals into his bloodstream.'

'Yeah, right.'

He stared out of the window. Darkness was falling over Lake Michigan. Coloured lights suddenly illuminated the huge ferris wheel on Navy Pier.

'She's worried by the purpura,' said Jennifer's cool English voice. 'She can't work out what is causing it.'

'Well, what could cause it?'

'Pressure changes associated with the vaginal delivery of a baby.'

'They can exclude that one.'

'Not according to the theories we are pursuing.'

'What, a mother giving birth in a former life?'

'I'm only carrying through the logic. They actually suspect drug-induced platelet dysfunction.'

'He could hardly be getting drugs now.'

'I don't know. The girl calls every day.'

'Ah yes. The Cracker.'

'Yes,' said Jennifer, cooler than cool. 'The Cracker. But it's not only the purpura. There's the deficiency in red blood cells. They say it's caused by inadequate absorption of nutrients from the intestinal tract.'

'Pernicious anaemia. Are they still injecting stuff?'

'B12. The condition retreats, but only temporarily. They can't understand it.'

The ferris wheel was turning. In Dick's Last Resort customers would be gazing out over the dark waters as they ate their crab claws and sticky ribs.

'But he still hasn't experienced clouding of consciousness?' he asked again, pointlessly, hopelessly.

'Not that we can tell. But who knows?'

'This pernicious anaemia. How long might it have been going on for?'

'They say that normally it would be caused by an inherited intrinsic factor deficiency.'

'Speak English, OK?'

'Sorry. Something he was born with.'

'But not necessarily?'

'No.'

'Could it have started back in the early sixties?'

'It's unlikely that he's suffered this condition for the past forty years without somebody noticing.'

'Maybe it was dormant. Maybe it was only triggered recently.'

'By quantum activity in the brain?'

'Christ knows,' he said.

'They've got hold of his medical notes, but there's very little on them apart from irritable bowel syndrome.'

'At this rate,' he said, 'I'll be a fellow-sufferer.'

'How are you getting on over there?'

He wondered about the phone, but there really wasn't any reason for the NSA to be bugging him, even though ELINT were the world's experts and a person using a device as small as a cigarette lighter in the next room could be listening to his every word (not that they'd use a cigarette lighter in Chicago, a place where lighting a cigarette inside a public building was liable to get you banged up in prison for life).

'The file's disappeared,' he said. 'Before it went it was tagged. There's a junior operator who's worried about something.'

He said, 'OK, we're wasting our time.'

It was 4 am. He stood up and stared out at the ribbons of city lights. If the file had been deliberately hidden it had been skilfully done.

Trudy said, 'I'm sorry.'

He nodded and went over to the coffee machine. She stared at her screen. She'd done her best, but there was no way, no legal way, that they were going to trace the file. They weren't going to find it, and she wasn't going to get to go on the Canadian survival course. Not unless she revealed what she had learned when she broke into Kelly Air Force Base.

She fingered the keyboard lightly, then pulled back suddenly, feeling sweat on the palm of her hands.

She didn't *know* that the electronic cop hadn't caught her dabbling her little fingers in the goods. She didn't *know* that this wasn't some kind of patriotism test – that Rake wasn't an American with a fake English accent, that Meeson and a dozen FBI agents weren't watching her on hidden cameras, waiting for her to reveal what she had illegally learned to the agent of a foreign power.

Oh Christ . . .

No, she didn't believe it – they wouldn't go to all this trouble. And if it happened – if they jumped out with guns raised shouting 'Freeze!' – she'd plead inducement.

She tapped the keyboard and brought up a standard NSA depository unit query, deleted the answer and typed in her own words. When Rake came back with two coffees she said, lightly, 'Hey, look at this, but don't ask me how I got there, my brain's in little pieces right now.'

She avoided his eye and tried not to blush.

Rake stared at the screen.

File A-TCAE377.b Aug 5th 1962. Lincolnshire England. Refer 694th Int Grp Archive Witchita.

Meeson arrived at 8 am. They were sitting eating scrambled egg and smoked salmon bagels. Trudy said, 'We got there,' thinking how shagged out he looked.

'Yeah?' he said, stunned.

'Six nine four Intelligence Group,' said Rake. 'An archive in Wichita. The only way to read it, it seems, is to go there.'

'You want to go to Kansas?'

'No, but if Miss Pierce can go, I'd be grateful. You were right. She's terrific.'

She followed Meeson to his office.

'About the CIA survival course,' she said.

'Just find the file first, OK?'

'I've found out where it is.'

'Not good enough. And about Kansas. We've three operators off sick. You can go as soon as we get this place back to minimum staffing levels. The day after tomorrow maybe, but I'm making no promises. Now go home and get some sleep.'

She phoned Rake at his hotel and told him.

He said, 'Just stay where you are.'

An hour later she was called back to Meeson's office. 'You're going to Kansas right now,' he said, yet again looking stunned.

She was sent to Lake Forest in a police car. At her urgent request it used its siren in the Market Square and all the way into the Pinetrees Bay development, and waited with its light flashing while she packed a case. At O'Hara, just after 2 pm, she met Rake again. He bought her a coffee and Danish in the Skyliner Bar, gave her his personal phone and fax numbers, and kissed her on the cheek when he left. She watched his British Airways flight take off and wished that she was going to London herself. At 4 pm she caught a military flight to Wichita and promptly fell into a deep sleep. In Pinetree Bay her mother phoned her new boyfriend, Eddie, and said, 'She's been sent on a mission. She may be gone for some time.'

25

Rutherford Hospital, Cambridge

Felix awoke in the night. A face was peering down at him. The blankets were pulled back gently from his body, his pyjamas unbuttoned: his chest exposed in all its stained, purple glory. He felt sudden irritation as his skin chilled – but a moment later, after a murmured apology, the sheets and blankets were replaced, and the figure was gone.

What were they checking for, hour by hour as he slept?

Silence resumed, but for coughing somewhere in a room down the corridor. Staring up at the ceiling, he could see the faint red dot of the camera's eye.

A distant bell from across the fens, from Grantchester church – or so he liked to believe.

Oh to see the branches stir, across the moon at Grantchester!

He said the words out loud, and far away, in a room above his head, a digital recorder clicked on.

What did Rupert Brooke die of? Septicaemia wasn't it? In a troopship, somewhere off Gibraltar? The poor chap should have been here, in the Rutherford. A dozen top consultants would have fought to purify his poisoned blood and save the nation's favourite poet.

Felix smiled. For he too, after a fashion, was a star. It

was his purpura that was causing the excitement, causing them to check its spread, hour by hour through the night. His *Henoch-Schonlein purpura*. Or, to put it another way, as sometimes the consultants did, his *Anaphylactoid purpura*.

Nonthrombocytopenic, at any rate – they were confident of that. Ecchymoses, spreading out over his belly in dark red petals. The bleeding of blood vessels that ought not to have bled. Haemorrhages on the surface of his body that gave promise of haemorrhages within. Mucous membranes of his mouth, slowly shredding themselves, day by day.

But caused by what?

'Purpura by itself, Mr Shafto,' they said, puzzled, even reproachful, 'is only a sign of other underlying causes of bleeding.'

It was one trick they couldn't fathom.

It was dark now in the mornings when the nurse came in with his tray of tea. There were days when cold rain splattered hard against the window. He knew it was cold because the nurses complained cheerfully, 'Winter's coming.'

And Felix was getting fat. It was more like a hotel than a hospital, this, with a daily menu card featuring smoked salmon, tender, juicy little steaks, and light, tempting puddings. Even at coffee time there was a choice of latte, espresso, or cappuccino. He lay, comfy and comatose, nurturing the purpura and anaemia that kept him prosperous, warm and safe.

Not that they were his only ailments. 'The weakness is acute and no longer localised to his right jaw,' he overheard a young doctor say one morning (his mind was more resilient to drugs than the young doctors realised). 'It could have a neurological cause like trauma. It could be something like diabetes.'

Another voice, a new young female doctor, or *lady doctor* as old-fashioned Felix thought of her: 'For that matter it could be an exacerbation of multiple sclerosis.'

'Do we have his records yet?'

'The practice at Hanger Lane didn't have them. They've been traced to Dulwich.'

Dulwich. He'd almost forgotten about Dulwich. Now that was a place for seances on a wet afternoon . . .

'What's it been now, five weeks?'

'He moved about a lot. They're sending them by courier. They'll be here by lunchtime.'

He smiled privately to himself. A motorcyclist was zooming up the motorway to Cambridge, bearing his medical records. It was star treatment all right. But did they have multiple sclerosis in 1216? It seemed such a modern disease – perhaps because it was so often shortened, in the hurrying modern manner, to MS.

Another voice, another occasion: 'Apart from the pernicious anaemia and the specific weakness of the jaw, there is a general weakness that you might associate with something like infectious mononucleosis. And to cap it all he's got acute inflamation of the gums, gingivitis' – this added for the benefit of the students in their stiff white coats, gathered round his bed – 'and the sort of skin haemorrhages that you'd associate with a lack of vitamin C. What we can't understand is how he got into this state without anybody noticing.'

Felix held up his blotched hand, showed it proudly to his young audience.

'And you're not telling us very much, are you, Mr Shafto?'

He smiled like a trouper. Where would magicians be, if their magic was understood by all?

Andrew Rake came with the neurophysicists. They attached the wires to his head: tiny golden electrodes that linked his brain to the electroencephalograph.

'The brain,' Rake said, as they fiddled about, 'is an amazing thing. A hundred thousand million cells – fatty film dotted with protein molecules – more complex than the world's most advanced computer. Nobody really understands how it all works.'

A nurse held up a hand mirror. Felix looked at his head, covered with sensors. He looked just like Old Mother Riley in her curlers. 'I'm just like Old Mother Riley,' he said, and the nurse replied, 'Who's that then?'

Just a very famous artiste, dear, dead and forgotten.

'What we're doing,' said Rake, 'is checking your brain patterns for intermittent spikes that would denote epilepsy.'

Rake left him a book about the brain, one designed for sixth-form scientists taking their A levels, but Felix's mind was literary rather than scientific. He asked his nurse to bring him an anthology of verse, one with some Rupert Brooke in it.

And, flower-lulled in sleepy grass,
Hear the cool lapse of hours pass,
Until the centuries blend and blur—

'In Grantchester,' he murmured every time the clock struck, 'in Grantchester,' his voice picked up by the tiny microphone over his bed.

The next time Rake came, he had with him a psychiatrist and a neuropsychologist, pleasing Felix, who always gave of his best with an audience. 'Tell us about the summer of 1962,' said Rake. 'And the night you experienced what the doctors thought was an epileptic fit.'

But he remembered very little. The young chanteuse from Bristol. The sudden shock – halfway through his act – of hearing a voice in his head; a voice that did not speak but was in fact his own magnified thoughts – imperious, overwhelming. The next thing he knew he was lying on the splintery stage, and the young chanteuse was bending over him attempting to administer the kiss of life, an occurrence that he was in no position to savour because his bowels were liquid and he was drowning in the brackish, cold water of the fens.

Where is the Sword of Tristram?

Even in London the voice would come to haunt him. Even in Ealing.

Where is the Sword of Tristram?

He had resisted the voice for two years. Then, in the autumn of 1964, after a dismal summer at Minehead where every act in the talent show sang 'Hello Dolly', his agent told him that Butlins would not be requiring his services again. The sixties were starting to swing, and mind-reading had a whiff of the old music halls about it. People were blasé. Easily bored. When they'd seen one bloke catch bullets in his teeth they'd seen them all. Felix's act had been compared – his agent said – to something from *Sunday Night at the London Palladium*.

'Fabulous?' asked Felix, though without hope.

Finished.

It was in that winter, his first chilly winter on Julia's put-u-up, that he had started his long quest in the Hanger Lane lending-library.

Where is the Sword of Tristram?

Buried at Tintagel, a book in the children's section told him, next to Tristan (as the name was now spelt) and the fair Isolde; or else returned to the sea of Lyonesse, of which Tristan was a prince, and which was flooded by Merlin to drown Mordred's knights after the Battle of Camlann.

Rake, the psychiatrist and the neuropsychologist looked at him sombrely.

'You said that this was the great Sword of Tristram,' said Rake, 'when you found it on the beach at Wormby.'

He held something up.

'It is in fact aluminium, and has on it United States Air Force serial numbers.'

He was a clever bastard, Rake.

Nobody pulled the wool over his eyes.

Normandie came.

'Rake's gone to America,' she said.

He'd wondered where the puzzled but confident young man had disappeared to.

'I've been talking to Dr Govindan,' she went on. 'She says they're planning to give you thyroid function tests. They're very worried about your anaemia.' She looked at him fretfully. 'However did you get like this? Did you never eat any oranges? Did you never have any vitamin C at all?'

She was a sweet girl. Not a patch, professionally speaking, on the little chanteuse in that golden summer of long ago, but very good natured and her breasts were similar.

'Now what are you staring at?'

'Nothing,' he said.

'I wish,' she said, looking at him sadly, 'you could explain to me what happened.'

He smiled, his thin blotched hands stroking the coverlet. They sat in silence, both lost in their thoughts.

'Michael's still in Liverpool,' she said eventually. 'They've taken his caravan away but he still has two buoys out in the channel, so he'll have to come back. Do you want to know about Jude and Simon? They're talking about getting married. There's to be a reception at Stoke Poges golf club. It seems that Simon's mum is the Lady Captain. Can you see Jude in Stoke Poges golf club?'

He could see anything, he said.

'Can you really, Felix?'

She looked at him solemnly.

He winked, then closed his eyes.

The veils that obscured the past were being lifted. It was taking a long time, but after eight hundred years there was no hurry. He could wait – spin it out the way the strippers used to spin it out in those northern clubs, where drunken students from the polytechnics whistled and cheered as the girls did their stuff. Bump and grind, knickers waved in the air, then thrown into the audience. All finally revealed in the spotlight – just as Felix's secrets would be revealed.

It was happening even now, as the purpura spread over his stomach and down his legs.

'If he hadn't been under strict observation,' a doctor said, one morning, 'I would still suspect drug-induced platelet dysfunction.'

Sorry, but they didn't do Ecstasy in 1216.

They did everything else, mind you, in the court of Good King John.

'Pump your fingers,' said a nurse, seeking a vein in his arm, 'now clench your fist.' The radio-active injection was made. They forced him to drink four pints of fluid. They laid him out under the huge gamma camera and watched the radio-active stains penetrate his jawbone.

They looked at him in puzzlement.

They asked if he had ever taken medications such as Dilantin, that might have interfered with his absorption of folic acid.

They asked if he had any history of malabsorption diseases.

There was talk of an examination of his bone marrow.

They started feeding him on greens and liver, his least favourite foods.

* * *

Apart from doctors and physicists, Normandie was his only regular visitor. He had refused to see Julia – back from her Mediterranean cruise – and Ray Monkman had come only once, to tell him that life was a real bugger and ask where he ought to be searching now with his metal detector.

The evenings were drawing in. Another month and the clocks would go back. Or had they stopped bothering with that? His mind was growing hazy.

One day Normandie brought him a huge bunch of chrysanthemums. 'Michael's coming tomorrow,' she said. 'He's taking away his buoys and stuff. Then there's only another week and it'll be the end of the season.'

He nodded politely, wondering why she was looking so nervous. 'I'm going back to London,' she said. 'I won't be able to come and see you any more.'

He nodded.

'I might be in panto in York at Christmas. Do you want me to put your name forward? Would you like to play a mind-reading Widow Twanky?'

He laughed politely. He had been there, he said, done that. She should look at the playbill for the Grand Theatre, Bolton, 1957.

'Well?' she said. 'Have you applied then?'

She'd been in touch with Equity, enquiring about retirement homes for thespians, places where weary, broken old theatrical nags could be put out to pasture. She'd given him an application form.

He shook his head.

'Oh Felix,' she said, upset, 'what's going to happen to you? You can't stay here forever.'

But he could. While his red blood cells failed to provide the oxygen to his blood tissues, and the purpura stains proceeded down his legs, and his gums and his internal organs bled.

'Felix,' she said, suddenly, bravely. 'You do realise that when you leave here the social services are going to put you into a bed-and-breakfast?'

But it wouldn't come to that. Before then the veils would be lifted. The crumbling of his body was merely the price that he had to pay. He dreamt, every night now, of jewels. Of sapphires and rubies. Of pregnant pearls, milky white, in clasps of Saxon gold.

She said goodbye in a tight sad voice and left him.

Outside, Andrew Rake was looking out of the corridor window at the rain. She hadn't realised that he was back from America.

'Michael's coming back tonight,' he said.

'Yes,' she said, shortly – she wasn't sure that she liked Rake much. He was conceited and ruthless. She feared that he would open up Felix's head and do experiments on his brain if somebody wasn't there to stop him.

'I'm sorry but I'd like to go over things again. See if there's anything we might have missed. What about dinner in King's Lynn?'

'What,' she said, alarmed, 'me and you?'

'And Michael,' he said, mildly.

She sang 'Autumn Leaves' because she always sang it, and because Felix said she should. 'It's a song for a true chanteuse, sweetie,' he had told her. 'A song for a pro.'

Penguin played on the organ, slowly and sentimentally. Outside the conservatory the leaves were indeed falling from the rowan trees round the car park. ' "I'll love you most of all in September . . ." ' she sang, noticing that Rake had come into the Dreamboat, and was watching her from the bar.

The camp was full of old-age pensioners, members of a northern club called the Autumn Tints. They thought she was singing 'Autumn Leaves' for them and were occasionally given to singing along. 'When Autumn leaves,' they warbled softly, 'begin to fall.'

Next she sang 'Maggie'. She told them that their faces were well-written pages, but that time alone held the pen. They gave a collective sigh of appreciation.

'She's got a good voice,' said Ray, standing next to Rake at the bar, knowing he was Normandie's friend but not sure where he fitted into the scheme of things. 'She's a great kid all round. You know she goes to visit old Spookie? I went myself once but it didn't seem to do any good. You heard all that stuff about King John's lost jewels?'

He looked at Rake with a flicker of hope. He still had the metal detector. He had, in fact, found a surprising amount of money on the pebbly beach and in the sandy dunes.

Rake nodded.

'There's an earth mound,' said Ray, 'where we have the kiddies' castle. I thought perhaps King John's treasure had been buried there, hidden by his knights in a secret chamber, waiting for the King to return. You can smile, but we're not all that far from Sutton Hoo.'

Rake, though, was smiling at Normandie. ' "But to me

you're as fair as you were, Maggie," ' she sang sweetly,
' "When you and I were young." '

' "When you and I were young," ' repeated the Autumn
Tints softly, their gnarled paws reaching out to each other
under the tables, so that Chrissy, standing behind the
complimentary tea and coffee table, blinked away a little
tear.

A policeman, the one who had a sister-in-law in Skegness,
appeared in the doorway. He saw Ray and crept over to ask if
he could have a word.

'What about?' said Ray, knowing that no good could come
of it, whatever it was.

'We're expecting a flood warning.'

'What do you mean, *expecting*?'

'They've been close to issuing one twice. It'd be sod's law
if it came in the middle of the night. This lot won't be easy
to shift in a rush.'

The Autumn Tints moved fast enough, thought Ray, when
it came to breakfast, lunch, or high tea. 'Do you realise,' he
said, 'how much money has been spent reinforcing that sea
wall? Five million Euros. Taxpayers from the Baltic to the
Pyrenees have contributed their little mites to save Wormby
Flats this summer. They even have a sign up *telling* us about
it. And now, *now*, you tell me we're going to be flooded.'

'It's not my fault,' said the policeman.

'What do you say about it?' Ray turned to Rake, but
Rake had moved away down the bar and was waiting for
Normandie to finish singing before carrying her off, Ray
assumed, for a shagging session in her caravan before
Michael got back.

'It was only a friendly word in your shell-like,' said the policeman, injured.

'Environment Agency!' Ray said, in the tone of voice he normally reserved for the Equal Opportunities Commission. 'They ought to have their flaming bollocks shot off.'

'What happened to your seer?' asked the policeman, relieved that Ray was not going to say anything controversial.

'My what?'

'Your seer. Puff the Magic Dragon.'

'He's very ill,' said Ray. 'You remember how his teeth were falling out? Well, now his flesh is crumbling away.'

'Bloody hell.'

Ray nursed a pint. Normandie finished her act, and the wrinklies clapped.

26

Wichita, Kansas

The plane landed at McConnell Air Force base just as the sun fell, a deep red orb over the security fence. Its last, dusty rays showed Air Force One gleaming on the runway next to Air Force One, a sight which made Trudy Pierce blink in astonishment. There were always two Air Force Ones, a young Air Force lieutenant told her, because one of them had to be permanently serviced up and ready to go. 'Same way as we always have a spare President,' he joked, as their truck hummed down the line of B-1 bombers of the National Guard.

She dialled the depository. It was closed. A soothing message advised her to contact Air Force Intelligence duty office. She called Fort Meade, and was told that the depository would open at 9 am the next day.

'There's a guy in England very ill, this is urgent,' she said, but that made them mulish rather than helpful.

She called Chicago, but Meeson had gone home.

Nobody at McConnell knew where she'd been booked in to stay. She called Chicago again and one of the duty guys goodnaturedly looked through the personnel transportation secretary's file, and discovered that she was booked into the Prairie Winds Motel at Tavistock. She felt tears of anger and self-pity prick her eyes, because nobody had cared enough to tell her.

The landscape was bitter and sad and bleak. The taxi to the motel passed a sign saying HITCHHIKERS MAY BE ESCAPED INMATES, which put her in mind of *The Grapes of Wrath*. Tavistock was only a few miles from the Oklahoma border. The Prairie Winds Motel was out of town on the Wichita road. It had a painted sign of tumbleweed blowing past a wagon train drawn up in a circle. She phoned home from her fusty room and told her mother: 'I know how Dorothy felt. Send me a rainbow.'

At nine the next morning she stood outside the depository, waiting for it to open. The staff looked surprised and secretly amused to see her: it was evidently an event in their day. She was taken into the warehouse, where metal stacks held zillions of cardboard boxes and cats prowled the aisles in search of unpatriotic mice. 'Vermin come in from the fields and shred the paper for nests,' said the depository clerk showing her round. 'They think this place is some kind of welfare programme set up for pregnant mice. Poisoning don't work. Cats is the only thing that works.'

The cats were sleek and fat. She asked for the SIGINT files for July/August 1962 and was taken through the green gloom on a golf buggy that had a tourist sticker on it saying *Oklahoma Is Oh So Pretty*, which was palpably untrue.

Back through the years they went, to where two long stacks stretched, it seemed, to infinity.

The buggy hummed away and left her.

* * *

She sat at a metal desk and started on the first of a thousand box files. Faded flimsies from IBM golfball machines, typed by girls who would have looked, she supposed, like Jackie Onassis. Soon she was deep in the secret wars of the early Sixties, leafing through Intel reports from Cuba, from CIA agents in Havana.

She found the text of an intercepted letter from Castro, taken to Moscow by Che Guevara and titled: *Measures to assure mutual defense in the face of possible aggression against the Republic of Cuba.*

There were reports of sightings of MiG-21s and IL-28s over the Caribbean. Photographs taken by spy planes of the Cuban jungle.

There was stuff here on MONGOOSE, the clandestine military operation designed to oust Castro without overt US military involvement. She spent an hour deep in the debate on the morality of an assassination attempt on Castro. One file said: *State assassination of foreign leaders as considered by the British Cabinet Security Committee regarding President Nasser 1956.* 'To assassinate Castro,' said a CIA note in red ink, 'even using Cuban fanatical anti-communist agents and operating through Cuban exile organisations, would mean vastly increased security, over an unquantifiable number of years, to protect the President of the United States from reprisal.'

Ironic words, grey and smudged on the faded yellow paper. ('qv Alleged Assassination Plots Involving Foreign Leaders, 11/20/75' said a two-way reference tag, showing that these files had been active a decade after they had been written.)

But everything of value here had been transferred to disk,

to digital records, to electronic impulses that would exist forever. She sighed miserably. She was sorting through the physical remains of the mouldering corpse, rifling like a ghoul through the bones.

At eleven, as she drank a cup of coffee, a call came from England, passed through the CIA comms net. It was Andrew Rake. He said, 'How are you doing?'

'It's not easy.'

'The files aren't categorised?'

'Only by section and year. This stuff has either been copied or is so low grade it's not worth copying. Most of it would have been incinerated if it hadn't been forgotten about.'

'The file is supposedly marked active.'

'Nothing here is active.'

'So what's the explanation?'

'Maybe nobody thought to close it down.'

'Yes,' he said. 'That's the theory.'

He sounded unconvinced. There was a pause. He said, 'You know what we're concerned about. Some kind of non-nuclear electromagnetic radiation.'

'Yes.'

A man was coming down the corridor between the stacks. She said, 'I'll come back to you as soon as I can. How is he?'

'Who?'

'The guy who's ill.'

'He thinks he's in the days of King John.'

She was hazy about her English history, but had seen *Prince of Thieves* on TV, Kevin Costner being her mum's heart-throb movie star. King John, she knew, was one of the wicked guys.

'That bad, huh?'

'That bad,' said Rake. 'Listen. Something fell from a military craft. They may have thought it fell over the Atlantic. Nobody's blaming anybody.'

Not yet.

She put the phone down. The man said, with faint belligerence, 'I'm Chas Rowlands. You were asking after me.'

He was in his late fifties, early sixties even. A paunch of a belly. Skin bronzed from the golf course, or maybe – Kansas being Kansas – from the farm. Greying temples, a baseball cap on his head. A peevish set to his mouth. Disappointment smouldering away behind his eyes.

'I'm Trudy Pierce. It's great to meet you.'

She'd looked him up in personnel records. In 1962 he had been a graduate intel assistant, an IA as they called them in those days. He'd moved back to Kansas, his home state, in November 1976 which coincidentally (and she had her own interesting theories about coincidence) was the month she had been born in Forest Lake maternity hospital, an autumn child.

'Your initials are on a file I'm trying to track down.' she said, and added, easily, getting into the habit, 'Can we maybe get lunch somewhere?'

They left the depository. The air was clean-smelling but earthy: different from the air that blew in from the Great Lakes, heavier somehow. Tavistock was a small place, twenty miles from the interstate. A small main street with too many of its shops boarded up, an artificial lake, a grain silo and water tower. The wheat harvest was over, and grey stubble stretched to the horizon and beyond. A truck full of livestock passed, heading south to Oklahoma City Cattle Mart. No use looking here for Dick's Last Resort, for a bar with bras suspended from the ceiling, for sophisticated waiters who sat at your table and insulted you.

They crossed the road and went into a diner. 'Scorch the dog,' Chas said to the serving girl, 'and drag it through the garden.' He turned to Trudy. 'How about you?'

'Yeah,' she said, brightly, 'why not?'

The girl brought them grilled frankfurters with salad.

Chas said, 'You're an IA?'

'That's right.'

'Is the section still run by ass-licking bastards?'

'Yep,' she said, thinking how easy it had been to find a common bond.

He drank his coffee and looked at her calculatingly. She waited for it.

'In my day,' he said, 'the only females in ELINT were secretaries.'

'Well, there you go. The file I'm looking for is dated August 5th 1962 and it relates to some kind of incident that took place off the coast of Lincolnshire, England.'

'I was in Chicago seventeen years. I must have processed twenty, thirty files a day.'

'The file's tagged. It's most secret and it's still active. It was the day Marilyn Monroe died.'

He shook his head, though whether he was sad over Marilyn's demise or his lack of memory she could not tell. 'Boy,' he said, unconvincingly, 'was I glad to get out of that place.'

They ate their frankfurters and she sympathised while he complained about the ways of the world and the knives that had been stuck into him because he was a man of principle. He had returned to Kansas, it transpired, after his fourth failure to secure promotion. He had married a girl he knew at high school and had worked as a civilian debriefing expert at McConnell, taking early retirement at fifty. He still worked part-time at the depository.

'Can you remember anything about the summer of 1962? The time of the Cuban Crisis?'

He paused for a long time. She wondered if she ought to play some Bob Dylan on the juke box.

He said, eventually, 'It was my first year. I can remember sitting on the fire escape at nights as things developed. Do folk still sit out on the fire escape?'

'Bad people do,' she said. 'For a cigarette.'

'I remember the signals coming in. The pictures from Cuba, taken by the spy planes. The reports from the Baltic of the cargo ships being loaded with missiles. MRBMs. I was just about your age, new to the job, shit scared.'

'I'll bet.'

'The public knew nothing. It was weeks before McCone went to the President. Weeks before anybody in the public knew what was going on.'

'Yeah, right . . .'

She half listened, letting him talk.

'We were heading for war – don't let them tell you any different. The stuff that's come out under the Public Information Act is nothing. We were halfway into war with Russia before Kennedy even knew he had a crisis. You heard the military wouldn't let McCone tell the President because there was no hard evidence? Crap. The generals wouldn't let him speak because they weren't quite ready.'

'What for, a nuclear response?' she said, startled even though she was talking to a man who believed in conspiracy theories, who believed, in all probability, that there had been a Fort Meade conspiracy to block his career.

'No,' he said, surprisingly.

Two truckers had come into the café. One of them turned on the juke box and selected 'Twenty-Four Hours From Tulsa'.

'I guess this is my favourite song,' said Chas,

'Yeah?'

If it hadn't been that, thought Trudy, it would have been 'Wichita Lineman' or 'Route 66'. He was looking out through the window at the vastness of Kansas. Nothing had stopped him getting home to Tulsa: no girl had stopped him, in the nick of time, from returning to his homely sweetheart.

'OK. So the military was ready for war,' she said, bringing him back to business. 'Stuff we still don't know about.'

'There was a major war-games session in the Pentagon. They concluded that there'd be a nuclear stand-off in the Caribbean and a limited conventional war in Western Europe. The Reds wouldn't get Cuba, but they'd get Berlin in around fourteen seconds. The response would be an American push eastward across the North German Plain.'

'Is this anything to do with what might have happened off the coast of Lincolnshire, England?'

He shrugged and signalled to the girl. She brought them

both cherry pie and whipped cream.

'I'm trying to explain that stuff was moving all over the place. It was all very...' he paused, choosing his word, licking at the cone of soft cream, '...chaotic. Materials and men were being ferried into Europe at the same time as stuff we couldn't afford to let the Reds get hold of was coming out. Top secret stuff, a lot of it. I remember the files from Army Group Hanover were moved to England – we even had an ELINT unit attached to Third Army. Did Wally Speyer get the director job in the end?'

'No. He retired last year, just when I was joining.'

'Shit,' he said, pleased. 'Poor Wally.'

'The director's Dick Meeson.'

'Never heard of him.'

He finished his pie, a look of contentment on his face.

She went wearily back to the depot and sat in the green gloom at her metal desk. She dialled Rake's mobile. She told him what she had learned. Then she phoned home and spoke to her mother and said, 'I'm still in Kansas,' and her mother said 'Yes honey,' knowing that she was really in St Kitts or Nicaragua doing dangerous things.

'Did Eddie phone?'

'No,' said her mother guiltily, knowing that Eddie was now going out with Claudia MacInvoie.

'I guess I'll be here another day or so,' she said. 'If he calls, tell him I'll be in touch as soon as I can and I love him. OK?'

'Yes, honey,' said her mother.

* * *

That night she lay in bed in the Prairie Winds Motel, Tavistock, listening to the silence of the Kansas night, then to the distinctive drone of a KC-135 tanker coming in to land at McConnell.

She knew she was being set up.

The file *A-TCAE*377.b might be in Wichita, assuming nobody had moved it. But more likely it was someplace else.

No way was it lost, as in lost in a haystack.

Somebody, somewhere, knew where it was.

27

Wormby Flats, Lincolnshire

Normandie stopped suddenly when they reached the place where the path climbed through the dunes to the sea wall.

'I'm sorry,' she said. 'I'm frightened.'

'It's OK,' said Rake. 'Don't worry.'

'I've kept away from here after dark. I know it's stupid but I can't help it.'

He held out his hand. After a moment, feeling ashamed, she took it. They went on, up the path to the top of the sea wall.

Darkness out in the vast bay, but for the distant lights on the Norfolk coast.

'I want you to show me where exactly it happened,' he said, still holding her hand. She turned eastwards and her heart suddenly pounded, blood rushing through her brain, for a figure was standing, motionless, staring out to sea.

'Was it near here?'

The figure turned towards them. Her fingers tightened round Rake's.

'What's the matter? What is it?'

'There's some real weather coming,' said a cheerful voice.

It was a man with night-binoculars round his neck. A twitcher, on the look-out for wrynecks and ospreys.

'According to the Met Office,' he went on, 'we'll have geese coming down from the north like a snowstorm.' His personal radio crackled. He said, 'Wilco. Roger and out,' and went, jogging rapidly off through the dunes.

Rake had his arm round her. She leaned against him for a moment, then recollected herself and pulled away.

'It's along here,' she said.

She led him along the ridge. Ahead of her, after a short while, was the blackness of the dip. She remembered Pierre standing here, giving her his jumper: she remembered his smile, his smooth chest with the warm rain coursing down it.

'Are you all right?'

'Yes,' she said. 'I'm fine.'

Again she took his hand. They went down the path, then slowly up the other side and along the wall.

She stopped.

'Here,' she said, drawing with her foot in the sands of time.

Darkness. There was no horizon out over the sea, no line between water and sky. She could feel the wind, clean and pure, flowing up from the salt flats.

'He just stared at you,' Rake said, 'without saying anything?'

'I'd have died if he'd said anything.'

'You didn't try to touch him?'

That had been Michael's question. She shook her head.

'The American fuselage was found, what, about two hundred metres to the south of here?'

'I suppose so. Near enough.'

He was looking back towards the caravan park, then out

over the dark waters to the north, towards Boston and the Haven: the old Fosdyke shore.

'What do you think happened to me?' she said.

For a moment he did not reply. Then he said, 'Have you ever wondered why the sky's so dark?'

'I suppose we wouldn't be able to sleep very well if it wasn't.'

'No, we'd just have evolved differently. The sky at night shouldn't, actually, be dark at all. There is an infinite number of stars in the universe, and however far off they are, however faint, they ought to make the night sky as bright as day.'

She looked up. The clouds were clearing, the weather front from the North Sea pushing them to the west. She could see the outline of the Plough.

'So why don't they?'

'Because of time.'

'Time?'

'When the stars were together was the past. When they are apart is the future. When you look at the gaps, you are looking at time that has gone. Time flows, and the sky is dark because it is flowing.'

She stared up at the blackness between the faint blue specks of light.

'Is this relevant to what happened to me? To what happened to Felix?'

'There is nothing in the laws of physics to say that time should always flow in the same direction.'

She was lost. 'Michael said you thought it was to do with quantum activity in the brain.'

'Perhaps.'

'Is that the same as time flowing?'

'It's connected.'

'I have to tell you that Michael isn't convinced that it actually occurs.'

'Quantum activity in the brain? It's controversial but it must be happening at an underlying level. The chemical forces that control the interactions of atoms and molecules, the action potentials that physically control nerve-signal transmission – the chemical actions that govern the behaviour of the neurotransmitter substances that transfer signals from one neuron to another across synaptic clefts. Don't ask me to go deeper.'

'I wasn't going to,' said Normandie honestly.

'Normally there's got to be a protection. OK, quantum effects have their role to play at underlying levels, but the large-scale implications conform to classical interpretations. The quantum effects are somehow *contained*.'

'What happens if they're not contained?'

'In theory you start to live in the quantum world.'

'Which means?'

He paused for a moment, then said, 'It's complicated. Let's go and get a drink.'

They went to King's Lynn, parked, and found the Indian restaurant where they were to meet Michael. Rake ordered beer and poppadums. He looked tired and seedy, she thought, in need of a hot shower and a clean shirt.

'What time did your plane land?'

'Just before midnight. But I didn't sleep at all the night before.'

'Chicago, Chicago, eh?'

'Something like that.'

'Can you tell me about the quantum world now?'

Meaning: can you tell me what happened to me? What's happening, still, to Felix?

'What do you know about quantum mechanics?'

'Nothing.'

'Right. OK. Well, first of all it isn't just some weird theoretical game that physicists play. We've known for nearly a century that quantum physics operates at sub-microscopic levels. We've used it to understand nuclear structure – the electrical and thermal properties of solids – super-conductivity – predictions of anti-matter. In practical terms it's led us to the electron microscope, the laser, the transistor. The quantum world is a real world. Our world. No known experiment has contradicted it. OK?'

'Yes, but I still don't know what it actually is.'

'Basically, it's crazy.'

He broke a poppadum into pieces. 'Imagine you see a skier going down a hillside. He reaches a tree.'

One bit of poppadum was the tree, and another bit was the skier.

'Before your eyes, the skier splits himself into two people, and goes round either side of the tree.'

He broke the bit of poppadum that was the skier, and moved the pieces round either side of the poppadum tree.

'You examine the snow and you see that the ski tracks indeed divide. But an examination of the skier *scientifically proves* that he did not divide at all.'

He tried to put the bits of skier back together, but they crumbled.

'Your poppadum man's broken.'

'Yes, because we live in a framework of classical physics. A world of objective reality. In the quantum world, though, this poppadum is as whole as the moment it was made.'

'It doesn't make sense.'

'No, it doesn't, does it? You have to imagine a world where nothing makes sense. A world where creatures can be simultaneously alive and dead. Where there are certainly twelve, and possibly twenty-six, dimensions. A place where time ceases to flow in a predictable manner, or indeed ceases to flow at all. A place where the past and the present can be as one.'

She was back there, on the wall, with the rain on her face and the man staring out to sea from under a dark, thick hood.

'You think that that's what happened to me? That I was taken back through time?'

'For a moment. Possibly. Mentally, you understand, not physically, although in quantum terms the one is perhaps no different from the other.'

'Oh God.'

'You were taken back into the past, or the past was brought forward. Quantum activity – normally trapped within its classical framework – somehow escaping. Perhaps it's always happened to some extent. On a low, non-threatening level it could account for ESP, poltergeists, telekinesis, ghosts – all the parapsychological baggage that goes with seers and mind-readers and mediums making fifty quid from a seance. Perhaps clairvoyants just have a knack of utilising, in a very small way, the quantum actions of the brain. Perhaps they have some ability the rest of us don't have.'

'They have guides.'

'Yes, Felix has told us about his guides. I was actually thinking more of neurons in the brain acting as quantum detection devices.'

He was suddenly irritable. Tired and irritable.

'Yeah, right.'

'But we can, if you prefer, describe the totality of microtubules in the cytoskeletons of a large family of neurons as "Bright Running Water".'

'Piss off, Andrew,' she said, feeling tired herself.

He looked at her, surprised. The restaurant door opened; people came in. There was a rush of wind that shivered across the tablecloths. The storm was coming. ' "What danger lowers by land or sea?" ' said Rake, softly, ' "They ring the tune of Enderby?" '

'Don't.'

'Sorry.'

He drank his lager.

Normandie said, 'Felix's mind. The things that happened to him. Do you think it's connected to the bits of that American aircraft?'

He nodded.

'There's been talk about nerve gas, or anthrax.'

'No, it's nothing like that.'

'Well then?'

'Electromagnetic waves. Electromagnetic waves in a foamlike, microscopic structure – the structure of space-time. There is, or was, a file.'

'Saying what?'

'We don't know. It's lost in an American archive. But it relates to some kind of incident on the Lincolnshire coast – and it's dated August 1962.'

'The time when Felix was first summoned by the past?'

'The time when he experienced something regarded as being an epileptic fit, yes. It was logged through a National Security Agency organisation called ELINT that deals with electromagnetic radiations emanating from sources other than atomic detonation or radiation.'

She sat, hopelessly, not really understanding, thinking of Felix lying in his bed, his gums bleeding. She said, 'Can they track this file down for you?'

'There's a young operative,' said Rake as the door opened and Michael came in, 'who's doing her best.'

His phone buzzed softly. He answered it as Michael took off his coat, said how bad the roads had been from Liverpool.

'You're with the Cracker?' said his assistant, Jennifer.

'Yes.' he said, watching Normandie and Michael kiss.

'You ought to be here. He's very agitated. Mike Lean thinks we're getting something. I'm playing the recording now. OK?'

'OK.'

Down the phone, after a moment, came the deep breathing of a person who was running – then there was a whimper, a tiny howl almost.

A small cry of pain and affront.

28

Gloucester, AD 1216

Crok was lying asleep in his lodgings in a hovel on the west bank of the Severn, when soldiers dug him out from his straw and frog-marched him to the castle.

'Easy, lads, I'm but a little fellow,' he said, his little legs racing as comically as he could manage, but they were strangers, crossbow-men with blue tunics, humourless men of the west. They crossed the bridge, a bright sharp moon glinting on the river, shining on the eel-fishers with their nets. Once inside the castle he was taken through the inner bailey and into the hall where the army commissariat toiled, then up the privy stairs to the keep and into a chamber high up over the chapel.

A fire burned in an iron brazier and the louvre clacked as it drew up the smoke. Behind the *chancele* screen the clerks busied themselves, just as if the King's corpse were not lying cold in Worcester church.

'This one knows,' said Nicolaa, standing by a window and staring out over the rooftops, 'if anyone does.'

'The great crown,' said the King's admiral, Daubney. 'Was it in pawn?'

Two other barons were in the room. William Brewer from the west, and Sandford, the Castellan of Devizes. A clerk stood by a table that was covered in parchment rolls.

'It was in pawn once,' said Crok cautiously, anxious to please.

'When?'

The fourth, fifth year maybe. Soon after he had joined the royal service.

The clerk said, 'It was the King's fifth year.'

He shuffled through parchments. 'The great crown of England,' he said, reading from an exchequer roll, 'the gilt sword, surcoat, tunick and dalmatick of Edward the Confessor, with his girdle, sandals, gloves and spurs, were sent by hand of John de Ufford to the Knights Hospitallers.'

'So, is it still with the knights?' asked Daubney.

The clerk shook his head. 'It was delivered up last year, at the feast of St Thomas.'

Daubney turned to Crok.

'You know what was lost in the sea?'

'The chapel.'

'Yes, we know of the chapel.'

'Sumpter horses.'

'Bearing the King's treasure?'

'The treasure chests were carried in a carette,' said Nicolaa. 'It was lost in the quicksands.'

'Everything was lost?'

'Everything,' said Nicolaa.

Crok felt the purse of little gems, throbbing over his heart.

'The Lady Maud's regalia?' Daubney said. 'The great crown from Germany? The great sceptre? The golden wand? The Sword of Tristram?'

'All lost,' said Nicolaa, still staring out of the window, the moonlight catching the gold of her crespine.

Daubney looked shocked. He turned to the clerk. 'What else did he have, to our certain knowledge?'

The clerk had prepared a list.

'*Teste* 4th July at Marlborough,' he read. 'Know that we received in our chamber at Marlborough, on the Saturday next after the feast of the Apostles Peter and Paul, one staff ornamented with nineteen sapphires, and another with ten. *Teste* 5th July at Devizes. Know that we received at Devizes, on the Sunday next after the feast of the Apostles Peter and Paul, a golden cabinet set with stones. *Teste* 6th July at Devizes. Know that we received at Devizes, on Monday the octaves of Peter and Paul the apostles, sixty-six sacks of money.'

'How many?' said Sandford, startled.

'Sixty-six,' said Brewer. 'Each containing a hundred marks.'

'Little more than a week's pay for the army,' said Nicolaa.

'*Teste* 10th July at Ludgershall. Know that on the Thursday next after the octaves of Peter and Paul the Apostles, we received at Ludgershall Gilbert, the son and hostage of Walter de Lacy and fifteen sacks of money.'

Silence in the chamber.

Crok could hear the sound of horns and fiddles from the inn, the Gloucester Tuns, under the castle walls.

From over the river dogs barked.

'Always hostages,' said Daubney wearily.

'If he trusted no one, my lord,' said Nicolaa, 'it was because he had been so often betrayed.'

'Trust begets trust, dame,' said Brewer.

Nicolaa's eyes rolled. If she called Brewer a fart there would be trouble, thought Crok. They'd see the sparks fly if that happened.

'You are telling me that the treasure of the entire kingdom,' said Daubney, turning to Crok, 'was lost in the *Vēlandi*? In the Welstreme?'

The names of rivers meant nothing to Crok.

'They were lost,' he said, 'in the sand called quick. *Et sabulo*,' he added, '*qui vivus dicitur*.' He waited for them to start in surprise, for Brewer to say 'A troubadour who knows his Latin?' and Nicolaa to say, 'John loved Master Crok for his singing, his wisdom and his wit.'

Nicolaa stared out of the window. She was angry with Daubney.

'What's all this,' said Daubney, turning to the clerks, 'about ships being hired at Wisbeche?'

The clerk said, 'The King issued a safe conduct for eight days from Friday after the feast of St Denis. Five ships of Lenne were to take goods and merchandise to Grimsby.'

'The treasury?'

'Cattle,' said Nicolaa. 'Swine. Sheep. The army raided from Crowland to Bury. Two busses with corn from the abbey granaries at Ely.'

'Did the ships sail?'

'Ask de Mauléon. What does it matter?'

'What matters is that we know for certain that the crown is truly lost.'

'And is not with the Jews,' said Sandford, 'or with the mercenaries of Poiteu, who doubtless were unpaid.'

'The army was paid,' said Nicolaa.

'There is a monk who went to Newark to sing a mass for the King,' said Brewer, 'who says the road was filled with soldiers carrying away treasures. What treasures were these if all was lost in the sea?'

Crok sat in his fur pelisse, still as still.

A bell tolled.

Daubney's eyes were on Crok.

'You were at Newark when the King died?'

Crok nodded.

'What happened?'

'A whirlwind came,' said Crok, 'in the middle of the night. It was in that hour of elemental disturbance and human terror, that the King's soul was taken.'

His bowels water, his head burning, but mercifully quiet at the last.

'I told you,' said Nicolaa, 'that Crok was with John always. I told you he was with him to the end.'

There was an expression on her face that he did not at first recognise: it was a kind of softness.

'And what was he like,' asked Sandford, coolly, 'at the end?'

Crok thought of John as the medicant monks tried to free his throat from grey pus.

'He was like a boar growling,' he said, moved. 'Or a lion attacking, so raged his ferocity against his foes. Alas for the glory of battles! Alas for the shield of knights, the splendour of arms! Alas for the arm of prowess, the hand of generosity!'

He stopped, overcome by tears.

'Generous?' said Sandford.

'When he lost at dice he payed his dues, my lord,' said Nicolaa sharply, 'which is more than Richard ever did. Generous? He feasted a hundred paupers, as I recall, to atone for you having eaten meat on a saint's day.'

'The eye of reason, the light of worthiness,' cried Crok, encouraged. 'A Tydeus for doughtiness, a Solomon for wisdom, and a Nestor for gentleness was my master!'

'Be quiet,' said Daubney.

He was very like Nicolaa.

There was silence in the chamber.

'And the crown of England?' asked Daubney, grimly, refusing to let go.

'The crown and the treasury were lost,' said Nicolaa. 'I was at Newark the day after he died. There was nothing. I went down to the sea with Walter Lacy's son and there was nothing.'

Nothing but Crok, scampering around in his fur pelisse, which was his own special booty, his particular loot.

'We have half a king and half a kingdom,' Daubney said. 'It would have helped to have a crown.'

The door opened. A council was called, the legate presiding.

The barons went, the clerks following them.

Crok and Nicolaa were left in the chamber.

'The Council awaits Ranulf of Chester,' said Nicolaa, staring into the brazier. 'The grandson of Ranulf les Gernons, who claims hereditary right to Lincoln Castle.'

She kicked the fire and watched the sparks fly upwards to the ceiling vent.

'I'll tell you what,' she said, 'between the false Earl Gant and this Ranulf I will find it hard to hold on to my own.'

Then she, too, was gone.

Crok was alone in the high chamber. He went to the arched window and looked out at the moon and stars. He could hear the pipes and fiddles from the Gloucester Tuns that nestled under the castle walls.

The Angevin Kings had worn the crown once a year at Gloucester. He, Crok, had seen the treasure chests opened here in this castle – he had seen John sitting by the brazier in his chamber, examining them. The rings and the white-gold cups.

He crept back to the fire and held out his hands. He felt the heat on his throbbing jaw, and was comforted. If they would leave him here all night, he thought, he would curl within the *chancele* screen and sleep. For a few hours he would be dead to worldly sorrow, to man's sad destiny.

He sat and dozed. In time, in his head, he heard the horn sing its battle song.

He woke suddenly, sweating with fear. He had been on windswept wolf-slopes, alone and frightened.

Where would he sell the tiny, precious jewels he had found on the beach? It would have to be Bristol or Lincoln, for they were the only places – apart from London – with Jews who bought and sold such things. But it was a dangerous business; the Jews cheated and so much could go wrong.

Would the Lady Nicolaa grant him her good lordship and find him a small place in her retinue? But what if Louis of France won the Kingdom and the false Earl Gant expelled her from Lincoln Castle? Or what if the new King's men gave Lincoln Castle to Ranulf of Chester, the most powerful baron in the land?

What would happen to Crok then?

It seemed so little that he wanted of the world: to sit on clean rushes by a warm fire and toast his toes.

29

Rutherford Hospital, Cambridge

Rake stared for a moment at the screen: Felix lying on his back, asleep, his ghostly outline bathed in infrared light.

He sat at the desk. He put a call through to Kansas but there was no reply. He looked at his watch: 1.30 am, which meant that it was just after 7 pm in Tavistock.

He stared again at the screen. Then he started to read, yet again, through the dossier that was building up on Felix's brain.

The CAT scan showed that his head was on the large side, with more than two inches of brain tissue between the ventricles and the cortical surface, but displayed no abnormalities.

The PET scan of his cerebral cortex – the injection of radio-active glucose into his bloodstream to measure blood flow to his brain cells – showed that he was using different parts of his brain for verbal and nonverbal memory tasks.

Working just like any other brain, in fact.

Was the brain just an electrochemical machine? Complicated but subject to the classical laws of physics? And if so, then who was operating it? All machines needed to be operated – sewing machines needed people in order to sew; computers needed programmers. Who – or what – was now running Felix's electrochemical machine, with its 10^{11} neurons?

He rubbed his eyes. His own brain was fuzzy with tiredness. He'd been over all this in his first year at university. *Only quantum theory allows for free will.* Only quantum theory allows for the existence of God – proves, some said, the existence of God. OK, perhaps that was going too far, but quantum physics underpinned all physics; and it was not, in any way, compatible with the naive image of reality.

He looked at the screen, at Felix, lying still and silent, his head covered by a net of silver nodules.

Was he a fraud? A skilled magician playing to his last audience? A Houdini intent on pulling off his most difficult trick?

Or had a quantum-engineered device – an American prototype, abandoned in the early sixties for reasons not yet known – finally allowed the horrors, and wonders, of the quantum world to invade the human brain?

The door opened. Jennifer came in with coffee.

'Oh, you're back,' she said. 'How was Krakatau?'

'Cracking as ever. She sang a song all about loving me when the leaves began to fall.'

'You poor sap.'

'Yeah, right. What have you got?'

'Just what you heard.'

She pressed a pad.

'We were getting alpha waves but he wasn't dreaming. At least he wasn't dreaming the way other people dream.'

On the screen now, a living blueprint of Felix's brain, the

computer-enhanced image showing red blood vessels against grey glistening matter. In the corner of the screen a clock ran: time passing.

Tiny lines sprang to life, showing the brain's activities.

'Is he accessing memories?'

'What, those loops of electrical current in the tissue? Not according to Mick Lean.'

'Well then?'

'Something from the outside? Morphic resonance?'

The sensors on Felix's head were dragging at the nuclei of the atoms in his brain, controlling them with a strong magnetic field, then exciting them with a beam of radio waves so that they spun back, emitting radio signals that the machine picked up, quantified, and analysed.

Rake realised that the machine had coloured the flickering traces green: the colour normally used to outline a tumour. On what basis had the machine made its choice?

He watched as the green worms wriggled and died.

The screen went blank.

'Sorry,' said Jennifer. 'That's all there was.'

'But it was definitely not dreams? Not memories being accessed?'

'Mike says not.'

In the quiet, the wind slammed against the window.

Normandie woke to its whine, high-pitched like a swarm of wasps. She looked out of the window and saw Autumn Tints being blown like leaves in a storm, all the way to the conservatory for their full English breakfast.

It was nine o'clock. She remembered that Michael was

planning to gather in his buoys from the sea. She dressed and swallowed a mug of coffee, then went outside and fought her way along the heritage path and up to the sea wall. The tide was in, white caps covering the grey waters, waves smashing against the new sea defences. Michael's boat was safe enough, high on the Environment Agency's concrete jetty, but it would not be launched in this sea, she thought, not on this tide.

One buoy had vanished. The other, pulled from its anchor, was bobbing in the surf. Michael was standing watching its anchor line curling and writhing in the waves. She ran down to him. He grinned in a piratical way as he waded out into the retreating surf, and she went behind him holding his hand. He tried to grab the line. A wave broke over his chest, and he stumbled and almost pulled her down. They both crawled back to the beach, coughing and sodden.

They tried again, following the wave out, waiting for the blue line to snake towards them. At their third attempt, their third soaking, they caught it.

They pulled the buoy up the beach to the edge of the dunes and lay fighting for breath. Normandie said, bitterly, that a plastic buoy could never be worth such peril to two young lives. They crawled to each other and held each other tight, wet and cold and shivering, and watched mesmerised as the tide ripped in, the waves smashing against the granite boulders then rising up the defence wall in a mass of foam.

A twitcher came towards them, running, bent double. The sand whipped up from under his feet and flew, stinging, into their eyes. It was the man from the previous night, the man she had met when she was here with Rake.

She remembered, as she huddled up to Michael, how Rake had put his arms round her.

The twitcher had a tent in the dunes. It was half buried under sand. What could he be looking for? No bird, surely, could fly in this?

Then they saw them: geese of some kind, long bodies, necks extended, wings flapping slowly, almost lazily, but moving across the sky at tremendous speed.

'From Siberia,' the twitcher shouted, shivering with excitement or cold. 'They must be travelling at a hundred miles an hour.'

He ran back to his camera.

'It's still two days to the spring tide,' said Michael, his mouth close to her ear.

'You mean it's going to get worse?'

'All we need is for the wind to veer, followed by a gale in the North Sea.'

'A gale? What's this if it isn't a gale?'

He laughed.

'What will happen,' she asked, 'if the wind does veer?'

He laughed again and pulled her up. She saw in his eyes that he wanted to take her back to his caravan, help her to take off her wet jeans as he had once before.

A voice, shouting.

It was the mad twitcher. He was crouched under the old Victorian sea wall of earth and stones, looking at something revealed by the night's tide. He was scraping away the sand.

He turned and waved to them urgently, calling them over.

Normandie had a feeling of *déjà vu*.

Yes, she had definitely been here before.

* * *

'Sorry about having to wake you,' said Mike Lean, 'but I found this on the tape when I came in.'

He pressed a button.

Felix's voice. Faint, indistinct.

Rake said, 'Can we make out anything of it?'

'There's something about a chapel of roses for de-man-all,' said Jennifer, who looked fresh and neat and who seemingly never slept. 'We thought it might be "demons all". Whatever it is, it made him angry.'

'And ten minutes ago,' said Lean, 'we recorded this.'

Again Felix's voice.

'What he seems to be saying is "fuck the Sheriff's servant",' said Jennifer.

'Have you got anybody on to it?'

'The British Library electronic archive. I've also a call through to Fisher at Balliol.'

Rake looked at the close-circuit screen. He pressed a switch. The camera over Felix's bed zoomed gently down.

'What's he doing?' he asked, a moment later.

'Oh, he always does that,' said Mike Lean.

Felix, his eyes closed, still only halfway home from Dreamland, heard the gentle whirl of the camera motor. He raised his hand, blotched purple as it was, from the coverlet, and moved the fingers in a little wave.

Apart from his solitary appearance on *The Golden Shot*, catching bullets in his teeth for Bob Monkhouse, he had never had much luck with the world of television.

But all things come to he who waits.

He drifted back to sleep.

'OK,' said Mike Lean, a few minutes later, 'something's happening.'

A screen next to the EEG unit had sprung to life. On it was a distorted spider's web of pulsating blue lines, the electric cables of the neurons.

'Nerve cell discharges,' said Lean, his voice tense. 'Excessive and synchronous.'

Now the EEG machine itself was active.

'Deltas with intermittent spikes. This may be it. This may be the big one.'

'The alarm will have sounded,' said Jennifer. 'The doctors will be with him in another thirty seconds.'

A computer bleeped. She turned to the screen. She said: 'The archive search on sheriff and "de-man-all" is coming up with the name de Meinnel, servant to the Sheriff of Nottingham in AD 1214.'

'He's trying to say something,' said Rake.

Lean punched the sound-recorder.

'What's that?' said Rake. 'What did he say?'

'The priests will have him?' said Jennifer.

Felix's mouth was moving again.

'The priests won't let this one go . . . Isabel was that? Isabel . . . fair Isabel . . .'

A shadow passed over the bed: a nurse.

'They'll give him epilim,' said Lean, 'or something like it.'

The phone rang. Jennifer picked it up.

Rake turned to the other screen, to the blue lines chasing round Felix's brain.

'It's for you,' Jennifer said. 'Michael Boulding. They've found something on the beach. Another piece of aluminium.'

'We really need to take him away,' said Mike Lean, watching as the needle went into Felix's arm. 'Some place where they don't have doctors and nurses. Some place where we can open him up.'

30

Gloucester, the Feast of St Simon
and St Jude, 1216

*Will you all the days of your life maintain the honour, peace,
and reverence due to God, His Church, and His ordained
ministers?*

They'd asked John the same question, of course. Yes,
indeed, sir priest and kiss your arse, John had humbly replied.

Then he had brought a papal excommunication crashing
about their ears.

Crok cackled.

'I will. So help me God.'

The boy spoke loudly, as no doubt he had been taught. A
little sigh went up from the good dames of Gloucester.

*Will you render right and justice to the people committed
to you? Will you abolish bad laws and evil custom, if any
such are in the realm?'*

'I will. So help me God.'

Crok's eyes found Nicolaa de la Haye, standing next to
Daubney. Her face was carved from stone. Was she thinking
of John, and his queer, obsessive passion for the law?
'Our Peace,' he had said once, in a voice as cold as Satan's
breath, while sentencing Jew-baiters to be hanged, 'shall be
inviolably preserved even if it were granted only to a dog.'

*Will you observe good laws and customs, and cause them
to be observed by all men?*

Which meant, of course, the charters, Forest and Magna,
signed at Runnymede. The Pope might not like it but the
world had moved on and his legate – now kneeling before
the altar in gold-encrusted robes – had accepted that the
charters must be reaffirmed.

Again Crok looked at Nicolaa. Would she say 'Fuck the
charters' here in Gloucester's cathedral church?

The legate had risen. He moved forward and stood by
Peter des Roches, Bishop of Winchester.

I, Henry, by the grace of God.

'I, Henry, by the grace of God,' repeated the kneeling boy.

King of England and Lord of Ireland.

'King of England and Lord of Ireland.'

*From this hour forth will be faithful to God and St Peter
and the Roman church and my lord Pope Innocent and his
Successors . . .*

And the Lord Pope shall receive a thousand marks sterling
a year, Crok told himself. Five hundred marks at the feast of
St Michael and five hundred at Easter. Peter's Pence with a
vengeance – John's rage, when forced to sign the deed, had
been awful to behold.

Crok looked at the barons, each man standing with his
squire and standard bearer. The Marshal – ancient but with a
beady eye. 'For God's sake, beg Guillaume le Maréchal to
forgive me all the wrongs I have done him,' John was
supposed to have said on his death bed at Newark, 'and grant
unto him the guardianship of my son, who will never manage
to hold the land except with his help.'

That was the story but it was all nonsense – all spread by the Marshal's men. Crok had been in the royal chamber when the wind rattled the roof tiles of Newark and messengers galloped with their fell news across the hundreds of Lindsay. The King's last words had been to Sire Rogier and none knew what he said, least of all Sire Rogier, who was deaf. Besides, the King's mind had been wandering. He had not known Crok, or William, in that final hour. He would not have known Nicolaa, had she arrived before the end.

The legate stepped back. The Bishop of Winchester took his place. The boy was to be crowned by an Englishman after all.

Isabelle of Angoulême rose to her feet.

Slender, pale, a witch that John had kidnapped from her vine-covered castle of Lusignan, she took a chaplet of gold from her hair. She passed it to the legate, who gave it to Peter of Winchester.

He placed it on the Boy Prince's head.

Henry, by the grace of God, King of England, Lord of Ireland, Duke of Normandy and Aquitaine, Count of Anju!

The trumpets blared.

God Save The King!

God Save The King!

Daubney held the boy high in his arms for the people to see.

John's boy. Henry the Third, *Anglorum Rex*, by the grace of God.

God Save The King!

Crok looked at Nicolaa and thought she looked old and of another age.

* * *

Outside he saw proud Ferling and squirmed towards him through the crowd, and asked after Thomas de Porkericiis and his hounds, but Ferling had not seen de Porkericiis since Newark, and knew nothing of Florence or William (they could both be starving in a wood for all he cared, he being already in service with the Earl of Pembroke) so Crok said, 'May you rot in hell, proud Ferling,' and would have said more, but they were swept apart by knights and men-at-arms, for the Boy King and his mother were being led out.

Isabelle of Angoulême leaned over her son and kissed him, her fingers running over the gold chaplet she had given him for his crown. He had last seen her on the walls of Corfe, on that summer's day when the army marched north. Pale, fair Isabelle! Soon she would go back to Angoulême, back to her lover, Hugh de Bruin, the man from whom John had kidnapped her in a fit of passion all those years ago, a business the Archbishop of Canterbury had had such a terrible job justifying to the Pope (let alone to God), Isabelle being but a maid of twelve.

She straightened. Daubney again took the young King in his arms, held him high, and carried him towards the castle.

Isabelle stood and watched for a moment, then slowly followed.

The barons stood in groups. After awhile they drifted towards the castle hall, where the coronation banquet was spread. Crok bowed low to Nicolaa as she passed, but she affected not to see him.

* * *

That night he was drunk on free ale in the Gloucester Tuns. For a hot pie he sang his packman's song, his song of the rover. He found he had twopence and bought himself a whore, teasing his choice out between Beatrice Bodik, Ellen Turs and Hawise Cundy, telling them what a shame it was to charge fees on the day of the King's coronation; enjoying the conversation, really, for he hated nothing so much as loneliness. He chose Hawise in the end, her keeper being a smiling young Poivetian who helped her support Crok as they crawled back over Severnside to the hovel where stable boys were singing of the knight with no prick – a lewd ditty about King John that had come over with Louis's soldiers and had been spread through the land by the minstrels.

Crok lay in the straw and mumbled. The days of the troubadours were over, he told first himself, then Hawise Cundy, and then her keeper. The days were gone when songs were songs . . .

He woke to find himself alone. He lay and trembled with cold, though sweat ran down inside his tunic. He fell again into a hoggish slumber, only to be kicked awake, his straw and shelter requisitioned by the commissariat. He stumbled through the door, out into the mud of Severnside. Riding down the road from Tewkesbury came the knights and men at arms of the Earl of Chester, each man's shield painted azure and decorated with three golden wheat sheaves. Behind the knights marched crossbow-men, archers and pikesmen.

The bridge, city walls and castle keep were lit by torches. The cavalcade went in through the town gates, through the cheering crowds that came pouring from the taverns.

Crok cheered with the rest.

At dawn he hunted through the town for the Lady Nicolaa. But already she was gone, back to the north.

Crok hurried to the stables where he had cunningly placed his rouncy among the horses of the commissariat. It was also gone: sent back to Nottingham, the ostlers told him, after many urgent demands from Phillip Mark, the Sheriff.

He stood at the castle gates, his bag slung over his back. Should he go to Bristol, and sell his little hoard of jewels to the Jews? He slipped a hand under his pelisse and fingered the velvet pouch at his chest.

Something was wrong.

He pulled out the bag, turning, as he did so, into a ginnel between the Gloucester Tuns and the castle, a place dark and sour and green with piss. His fingers fumbled for the tiny sapphires and diamonds. His heart lurched at their touch. He turned them out into his hand.

Pebbles and dirt.

He heard laughter through the thin, rat-eaten walls of the Gloucester Tuns, in the room where he had sung for his supper.

'*Whores* of Charing and *Scarlet* of Lincoln,' he had sung. '*Soap* of Coventry and of Gloucester *thieves . . .*'

It had been Hawise Cundy. Her and her keeper between them.

'*Asets iad des uiles,*' the Poivetian had sung in return, as they helped him unlace his hose while Hawise raised her skirts, '*Mes trop iad des g'les . . .*'

There's plenty of places,
And too much to drink.
And much more to say
But my wits are away.

Crok remembered how he had laughed as they lowered him down in the straw.

31

Wichita, Kansas

Trudy was on her way out of the Prairie Winds Motel when the girl on reception called her back. Tonight was Panhandle Country Hog Roast, the high spot of the Tavistock Social Year, and her room was pre-booked. If she wanted to stay on at the motel they'd have to move her into Elvis's room.

That Elvis lived, Trudy knew, and where else but in a two-star motel in Kansas? 'But surely he's not going to be away from Tavistock on Hog Roast night?' she joked.

Reception smiled tightly. Elvis had stayed many times at the Prairie Winds in his early touring days. His suite cost seventy dollars a night instead of the usual thirty-five, but was decorated in authentic Fifties style and redolent with memories of Route 66.

Trudy said, 'I'll take it.'

She went to the depository. She called Chicago, but Meeson wasn't yet in. She told personnel about the room change.

She pulled out a box marked *UK 1962* and flicked through the papers it contained – an intelligence summary of British cabinet changes made by Premier Macmillan; a Senate Arms Technology committee report on a British invention called a 'hover-craft'; and an MI6 political assessment of France following an assassination attempt on president De Gaulle.

The date on this last file was August 22, 1962.

She was past the time of the incident in Lincolnshire.

She put the file back in its box, and the box back with the other boxes that stretched into the dusty green distance.

She sat down again at her desk. It was pointless looking further. She was being set up. Left to sit at a metal table in a Wichita depository till the end of time.

She got herself some coffee. Then she called Eddie's number in Pinetrees Bay. His mother answered the phone. She sounded embarrassed, as if she was having to dredge back through her mind to remember who Trudy was.

Perhaps Trudy had been in Kansas longer than she thought. Perhaps Kansas time was different to everywhere else, or she'd been fed some kind of drug.

Eddie's mum said she'd certainly tell her boy that Trudy had called. He was spending most evenings out on the water, she said, in a false warm voice.

'Sailing by himself?'

'Sometimes.' A pause. 'Sometimes with his friends, you know?'

She feared she did. She left her number at the Prairie Winds Motel and, because she had nothing else to do, went back to the files.

In one box – caught between various MONGOOSE proposals – she found a programme for a 1962 Bob Dylan concert in Wichita. Had some bored operative been reading it, and stuffed it into a file when a supervisor came prowling down the aisle?

The phone rang. It was Meeson in Chicago.

'Personnel say you're moving to a fancy hotel.'

'I'm not moving anywhere,' she said with feeling. 'They're just switching me to a different room.'

'Why?'

'Because it's Panhandle Country Hog Roast Night and the room I'm in is booked. Listen, I believe I'm wasting my time. I think this Wichita thing is a cover.'

'For what?'

'How would I know? Maybe there's some kind of conspiracy going on.'

'You think this lost file has an X prefix?' he said, humorously.

She closed her eyes. She said, calmly, 'The British say this is urgent, right? There's a guy very sick?'

'They've found another small section of fuselage. At this rate we're gonna end up with a Boeing 747.'

He was in cracking good form.

'I don't believe the file is in Wichita.'

'You wanted to go there. You got *special priority* to go there. It's out of my hands. Enjoy the hog roast.'

He put the phone down.

She sat and thought for a long moment.

She went to the security office. She said, 'I need a computer.'

The man found her a room with a terminal. Through the window, down beyond the business park and the tyre warehouse, was Tavistock's artificial lake. There were fairy lights in the trees, reflecting on the water. Smoke rose from the lakeside barbecue.

She stared at the computer, like a junkie over his hypodermic.

She hesitated.

After a moment she picked up the phone and called Chas Rowlands. 'I wondered if anything might have stirred in your memory? Anything about that night in August 1962?'

He was surprised that she was still in Tavistock. 'Listen,' he said, 'if a file is tagged then somebody, some place, knows where it is.'

'It was copied to CIA and NSA from AirINTEL,' she said. 'It was their baby.'

'OK. So maybe the airforce is hiding something.'

'Is or was?'

'From your point of view, does it matter?'

He sounded brighter, more alive. She was fighting the system and she was asking for his help. 'You could push a query through Kelly Air Base,' he said, 'something innocent that might fool them.'

She spent two hours trying the legal options, making the legitimate requests, sending innocent gophers into the Cray C916/16515 machines in Dallas, and letting herself be carried along the logic paths like flotsam on the Mississippi.

Now it was there: on her screen.

AIR INTELLIGENCE AGENCY

Rapid Radio Relay, Secure Communications and Command.

A logo. A mission statement.

Again she was back in that summer afternoon in Chicago, with the duty guys playing Dungeons and Dragons. She could feel the humidity, the sweat on her palms.

Suddenly her fingers were stroking the keys, finding her way intuitively round the defence protocols.

How long had she managed access last time? Five seconds?
A query on screen. She typed in an NSA general code.

Another query, more urgent. She typed in K Group,
cryptologic research, and a definition code that would cause
some puzzlement, she thought, to an electronic brain in Texas.

ACCESS DENIED

She smiled. Already she was feeling her way round the
edges, nudging the parameters, lost in a world of her own,
oblivious to the faint sounds of country music now coming
from across the lake.

The screen cleared.

The logic gates were open. She was inside the net.

How long had she got before the electronic cops realised
there was a prowler in the system? Ten seconds? Twenty?
She keyed in the NSA tag number and the serial numbers on
the aluminium strip. She was directed to 694th Int Grp
Archive Witchita.

This was as far as she had got last time. At this point she
had pulled the plug, just a nanosecond before the trap shut.

She entered a search code and keyed 'submit'. A code
came up that belonged to 704th MI Brigade at Fort Meade,
which meant that the missing file was in the system, that
everything she'd been told to date was fucking lies.

She was being transferred to 704th MI database. It came
on screen suddenly, taking her by surprise:

Field report on loss of Ryan RPV with two experimental 1K low-frequency electromagnetic radiation devices East Anglia UK August 4th 1962

Time to get out. Her finger moved to press 'cancel', but a black curtain was dropping swiftly down the screen. Her status was frozen. A message asked for her password and authority. When the electronic cops sprang security traps like this in Chicago she abused them foully and keyed in the release numbers. This time she had no release numbers. Her gopher was trapped and her fingerprints were all over it.

After twenty seconds the screen went blank.

By now some human cybercop knew the terminal she was working from.

She heard the sound of country music, faintly on the wind. Through the window she saw smoke billow from the lakeside barbecue, where the hogs turned slowly on the spit.

A telephone rang in the distance, then stopped as it was answered by the depository's security guard. She quickly picked up the phone and dialled her mother. It was ringing out as she heard footsteps coming down the corridor.

'Mom? Is that you?'

'Trudy?'

'Oh Mom . . .' she cried.

The line went dead.

Now, she thought, listening to the security guard's urgent footsteps, her mother would think she was phoning in desperation from a drugs den in Caracas.

32

Fort Meade, Maryland

They took her back to the Prairie Winds and collected her bag from the Elvis suite she would never sleep in. Then they drove her north through the darkness to McConnell and found her a place on a Learjet that was taking a general to Washington. The general looked at her with evident signs of amusement. When he was given coffee and cookies he delicately indicated to the steward that she should be offered some. She shook her head: she didn't want to be sick over a general's Learjet.

At Washington military airport she was taken to the office of the Air Police. Nobody asked what she had done. Soon after 3 am she was driven out to Fort George G. Meade and allocated a room in the duty officers' hostel. She surprised herself by sleeping instantly and soundly, and having to be shaken before she woke up. She was taken to the office of the Deputy Chief, Central Security Service.

Meeson was already there. He'd flown down from Chicago in the pre-dawn and looked shattered. He stared at her, his expression one of horror and reproach. The Deputy Chief said curtly, 'Go outside and phone your mother.'

She went to the outer office and phoned home. Her mother was tearful, still on the verge of hysterics, only reluctantly convinced that her daughter was not dead or kidnapped. Trudy calmed her. She went back into the Deputy Chief's office.

He said, 'You know the penalty for busting security codes?'

'I was told to trace a file.'

Meeson's eyes widened. 'Oh Jesus,' he said in disbelief.

The Deputy Chief had a slender file on the desk in front of him. She could read its title: **Field report on loss of Ryan RPV, East Anglia UK August 4th 1962**.

So this was it, *A-TCAE*377.b, the file she had sought for so long.

The Deputy Chief started reading it. His phone bleeped softly. He picked it up and said, 'Send him in.'

It was a young man, around her own age, who smiled and said 'Hiya,' as if they had met before.

'We spoke on the phone a few times?' he said. 'Back in August?'

It was the jerk from the CIA. She said – bitterly, for here, before her eyes, was the wrecker of her promising career – 'Did you have a good lunch at the Epicure Grill that day?'

'L'Epicure? I guess so,' he said, looking puzzled.

The Deputy Chief said, 'Tell me about this drone, this RPV.'

'They were designed for use in Eastern and Central Europe in the event of non-nuclear war,' said the young CIA operative. 'As you know RPVs are small, so their signatures – RCS, visual, IR and noise – are also small. A whole range came in after 1945, mostly made by Ryan. They started as target drones called firebees, but gradually became a diverse family including versions for attack and reconnaissance that persisted through to the Vietnam War. The particular drone we're talking about here was a USD-9B – the B being for "baby". It was driven by a miniature turbojet and launched accidentally from its mother aircraft, an A-12, in the early hours of August 4, 1962. It had four small wings round its sixteen-foot six-inch body – two sections of the wings have now been found on the beach near Wormby in Lincolnshire. Normally the drone would have carried an IRLS – that's infra-red linescan—'

'I know what IRLS means.'

'Sorry, and a Carl Zeiss 3-lens reconnaissance camera, but in this case it carried two prototype electromagnetic devices. Dr Powell should be here shortly, he's the expert on acoustic and electromagnetic weaponry. The drone also carried a quantity of conventional high explosives.'

'High explosives?'

The CIA boy nodded.

'That could still detonate?'

'Almost certainly.'

The Deputy Chief went wearily through the specification sheets, his body language saying that this was something he did not need.

He put the file down. He stared at Trudy thoughtfully. 'Nobody's supposed to be able to get through the logic gates on the AirINTEL computer.'

Silence. Something was expected of her.

'I'm sorry.'

'A billion dollars or so's been spent to stop that from happening.'

'I was told to locate the file. I was told it was urgent.'

Meeson was staring at her: at the viperess he had nurtured in his Chicago nest.

A secretary brought in a signal.

The Deputy Chief said, 'Let me read this.'

They sat and waited. A man came in and quietly introduced himself as Powell, a physicist from ELINT HQ. He sat down and read studiously from his own hard copy of the file.

The Deputy Chief said, 'The guy who found the serial plate on the beach is now said to be seriously ill. Symptoms include purpura and gingivitis – gums bleeding, that sort of stuff. There's evidence of an aura. Clouding of consciousness.'

He looked at the physicist. 'If one of the electromagnetic devices exploded in 1962, could the soil have stayed contaminated over what, forty years?'

'No way. And it didn't happen – if it had, it would have affected electromagnetic systems within a five kilometre radius. We'd have known about it.'

'Some kind of seepage then? The device no longer stable?'

'I'd have said it wasn't possible for a human to be affected,' the physicist said, sounding puzzled, confounded by the evidence of purpura and bleeding gums.

'If we stay quiet,' said Meeson toughly, 'what are the chances that the British will never find the body of the drone at all?'

'Don't even think about it,' said the young CIA agent curtly.

Meeson stared at him, shocked.

Trudy decided she might have misjudged the CIA boy, whose name, she remembered now, was Rob Marguerie. He clearly wasn't a jerk at all. He was, in fact, highly intelligent and possessed of sound judgement.

'I agree,' said the physicist, 'particularly if the device is damaged and unstable.'

Meeson was slowly turning red.

'We don't know that,' he said.

'Jesus,' said the intelligent Rob Marguerie, 'how many people do you want in hospital with the molecular structure of their stomach lining destroyed? How many children do we get to see on television with their teeth falling out?'

'Now wait a minute,' said Powell, alarmed, 'nothing like that is supposed to happen.'

'Denial is not an option,' said the Deputy Chief. 'According to this signal the drone was located at eight forty am GMT, that is just over five hours ago.'

There was a moment's silence.

'It is buried in a sea-defence wall,' he went on, reading from the signal, 'about a hundred metres from where the pieces of wing fuselage were found. The British military are evacuating the area.'

The phone rang. He picked it up. He turned to them and said, 'Wait outside please.'

They waited outside. Trudy kept away from Meeson, wary that he might brutally assault her, even if, for the present, only verbally. She stood close to Rob Marguerie who said conspiratorially, 'I don't suppose we can risk getting some coffee?'

'I'm not risking anything.'

He grinned and went away. Meeson stared out of the window at the rain and ignored her. Perhaps he disowned her. Perhaps he would call together the staff in Chicago and tell them her name must never be mentioned in his presence ever again.

Rob Marguerie came back with two plastic cups of coffee, just as she was getting anxious about him missing the meeting.

They were called back into the Deputy Chief's office. His head was deep in the file. 'That, gentlemen, was the State Department,' he said heavily.

He looked up.

'I am being asked why our only response to this extremely serious issue was to send a junior operative from ELINT to search manually through a depository in Kansas.'

Meeson looked stunned. 'Now wait,' he said. 'Just wait a minute—'

'Later, Frank, you can explain later. For now we are to give the British all the information we usefully can, as soon as we can. You, young lady . . .' He turned to Trudy, who had been sitting as quiet and small as a mouse in the hope that they were going to forget all about putting her in jail for twenty-five years. 'You already have liaison with this British physicist, Andrew Rake?'

She nodded.

'Get together everything you can about the drone, its electromagnetic devices, and on the medical consequence, if any, of electromagnetic radiation leakage. DIA scientists are on their way from Fort Worth to tell you anything that's secret but not relevant and can therefore be withheld. ELINT will give you all the help you need, right?'

He turned back to Meeson.

'Right,' said Meeson.

He turned back to Trudy. 'You're going to England,' he said, 'sometime this afternoon.'

* * *

In the outer office she said to Meeson: 'Can Kate Garland get stuff on the drone from Ryan, the full specification with blueprints? And either Dwight B or Dwight J chase up the type of high explosive they used? Also I need to know of everything, meaning everything, OK, on the electromagnetic units, including the anti-tampering devices.'

'Where will you be?' Meeson asked, in a dazed, drugged voice, deep in the nightmare that had started when his bleeper had bleeped as he lay warmly next to Sharon Diefenbaker.

'It's OK,' said Rob Marguerie. 'I'll find her somewhere to work from. We'll be in touch.'

He took her to his desk in the CIA building. 'Have a seat. Use my computer. Use anything you like.'

He went away.

She slid open a drawer and looked, automatically, for a photo of his girlfriend, but shut it again hastily as a man from Security came towards her and said, 'Miss Pierce?'

He gave her a password to priority-access the NSA and CIA Intelligence and Security command systems. 'The password's just to save you wasting thirty seconds hacking in,' he said sourly.

She called Chicago. The awed voice of Kate Garland said: 'The boss says we're to drop everything and do whatever you want.'

'Send Homer for some bagels,' she said joyfully but then regretted it, for her mother always said that hubris was swiftly followed by nemesis.

Rob Marguerie brought her more coffee and a chicken sandwich. 'I'm your gopher,' he said. 'It's official. How are you fixed for clothes to take to England?'

He offered to send a secretary to buy her underwear and stuff if she'd tell him her bra size. She was OK for bras, she said sweetly, but told him her size anyway, reflecting that Eddie in Forrest Lake would never know.

He brought her lunch on a tray. He fixed up State Department travel documents, her passport being in Chicago. He fixed a helicopter that took her to Washington Military Airport and went along with her, which was not strictly necessary but – as he said – he had a responsibility here.

At Washington he smoothed her way past the Redcaps and an appreciative squad of GIs heading out to the Sierra Leone embassy. He used his CIA pass to get her into the senior officers' transit mess. He gave her a brand new travel-bag and said, 'The secretaries were all busy, so I had to get the stuff myself.'

He said, in a deeply serious voice, that he would need to see her in Chicago on her return, in order to complete his report.

Half an hour out over the Atlantic, leaving the American afternoon and heading towards the English night, she opened the bag and looked at the underwear and very short nightie he had chosen. Then she stared out of the window, down at a tiny ship on a painted ocean.

Soon weariness caught up with her and she slept, smiling gently.

Three hours later she woke to hear the captain's voice over the tannoy. They were over Belfast. There were gale force winds from the north east, he said, and they could expect severe turbulence on their approach to Heathrow.

33

Cambridge

'The King to his beloved sister Berengeria, formerly Queen of England . . .'

John was at Feckenham. It was summer, with cool green leaves crowding the windows of the hunting lodge.

'Greetings, with sincere and affectionate love.'

Nicolaa laughed.

'Sincere,' said John, his eyes bulging with mock rage, 'and affectionate love! Whereas by the machinations of the enemy of mankind . . .'

'Oh the enemy of mankind! It's the devil's work then, is it?'

'The enemy of mankind, and the agency of our barons whom he has prompted to rebel against us, much disturbance has, for a long time, been wrought in our realm of England . . .' – he paced the floor while the clerks scribbled, scribbled – 'and is now more than ever inflamed by the arrival of Louis, eldest son of the King of France, who, regardless of offending either God or the church, is striving to dispossess us of our kingdom—'

'Why not,' said Nicolaa, lolling by the window, 'just pay her her pension?'

'And because we have spent,' said John loudly, 'and are

daily more and more compelled to spend, the greater part of the sums we had destined for the recovery of the Holy Land from the hands of the enemies of the cross—'

'Oh for shame!'

'I would go to Jerusalem, madam.'

'Would you take me with you?'

'Aye.'

Nicolaa laughed. She held up her wine cup. A servant poured into it the cool white wine of the Loire, from the vineyards of Chateau Galliard. Her eyes were on the King: her eyes were everywhere.

'Crok,' she said.

He stood by the door, where he had been a-peeping, as still as a statue.

'Come here, Crok. Come here, William.'

A gust of icy wind thudded against windows, the branches of the cherry hitting against the panes.

'Read for us in your crystal. Tell us what will happen, *William.*'

'Quantum particles do not have well-defined paths in space or in time.'

Felix opened his eyes. Rake was by his bed. Claudia, his favourite nurse, was in the doorway, looking anxious.

'Is that the key to all this?'

Was Rake looking to him for answers? Too late if he was.

'The Americans,' Rake said, 'dropped an electromagnetic anti-personnel explosive device at Wormby in 1962. It was not designed to affect the human brain, beyond a temporary and mild distortion of the particle structure of nerve signals as they travel out from the central bulb of the neuron. It could however – though nobody thought of it at the time – affect quantum activities that govern the behaviour of neurotransmitter substances transferring signals across synaptic clefts. If quantum activity is not hostile to actions at a distance it will as happily transfer signals originating in 1216 as in the present day. It will in theory transfer molecular structure – matter. Is that what this is all about?'

Rake was a dog quartering the ground in search of a scent.

'How did you get in this condition? General weakness. Anaemia. Skin haemorrhages. How does a well-nourished man get what you've got, in this day and age?'

He wasn't sure about well-nourished. He had lived mainly on sweet biscuits and toast in Ealing.

'But we're not in this day and age are we?' said Rake.

The answers, it seemed, were coming together. But it was all too late. *The feet had hardly time to flee, before it brake against the knee—*

And all the world was in the sea.

Rake said softly, 'Who are you?'

Nurse Claudia said, 'I'm going to call the doctor.'

'What,' said Rake, 'is your name?'

The wind slapping against the windows, the cherry branches tapped like pebbles.

'Two shillings to a servant of the Sheriff of Nottingham,' said Rake, 'for carrying a chaplet of roses? Why did that anger you?'

Why? Because his servant, Adam, had been given only a royal shilling for the head of a Welshmen, despite all the trouble Crok had had in killing the bastard first.

But his ire against the King had been unjust. There had been six Welsh heads at Rochester, which meant the King had paid six shillings at a time when he was sorely pressed for coin, a time when the mercenaries were demanding their wages and his brother Richard's widow was, as ever, demanding her pension. Also they had charged John dearly that day for forty fat pigs he had stuffed into the mineworkings under the castle walls, setting them ablaze so that their melting fat brought down the timbers.

The walls had cracked and tumbled down to the glorious smells of roasting pig!

That was John in his glory.

'Were you jealous of the Sheriff's servant?'

Jealous of de Meinnel? The prancing, pretty groom of the Sheriff of Nottingham? The mincing lad who gathered pink roses in a garden at Ditton, when true men were busy chopping the heads off Welshmen?

Yes, it had been de Meinnel who had roused his anger.

He remembered the roses, a froth of pink and white, bound with green ferns, presented to the King's mistress, though which mistress he was unsure: the Abbott of Swinehead's little sister, perhaps, or the daughter of Ferling the huntsman. De Meinnel had followed the court from Ditton to Carlisle to get his two shillings reward – sent north by Phillip Mark, his fey, indulgent master. If they had men in Nottingham Castle who knew how to catch Welshmen, instead of men who could fashion a chaplet of roses, the heads of Much the Miller and Hood would long since have been cold kissing over the town gate!

So, at least, Thomas de Porkericiis had said as they sat by a moorland fire a day's march from Grimsby. Where was Thomas the houndsman now? Where were the king's hounds?

'We can do a great deal in the Bohr Unit,' said Rake softly. 'We can build theoretical models that describe the interaction of consciousness with its environment. We can represent consciousness by quantum mechanical wave functions, and its physical environment by potential energy profiles. We can use Schrödinger wave mechanics to indicate psychological and physical experience.

'But in our understanding of the quantum world we are still blindfolded, ignorant men on a seashore, listening to the waves, and trying to extrapolate from their sound the magnitude and nature of the ocean.'

'What's happening here?'

It was Dr Govindan, her voice like a razor.

'You could illuminate the world,' said Rake, staring down at him.

'No,' said Felix. 'No, not me. I don't understand anything.'

He said it truly enough to bring a tear to Nurse Claudia's eye, though it did not fool Rake.

'Who are you?' he asked again.

'Have you any idea what time it is?' said the doctor.

'Around nine pm in Maryland. The Americans think he's been dosed on electromagnetic radiation from a device they dropped more than forty years ago off the coast at Wormby. They think that's what's caused the purpura, the hemolytic anaemia, the bleeding gums. They're asking how many people live within five kilometres of Wormby Flats and wondering how much compensation they're going to have to pay out.'

She stared at him, shocked. 'Are you telling me he's got some kind of radiation sickness?'

Felix tried to ignore his aching jaw. He thought of the cold outside his room, and the warmth of the radiator by his bed. The lovely warmth that soaked into his bloodied, wounded, filthy limbs.

'Actually,' Rake said, 'as a secondary disease, I believe he's got scurvy.'

Silence.

'That's ridiculous. If it was scurvy it would have cleared up. Scurvy is simply a lack of Vitamin C.'

'It would have cleared up,' said Rake, 'if you had been treating the right patient.'

'You're not making sense.'

'This scurvy, doctor, was contracted eight hundred years ago.'

Silence again.

'As was his other, and more serious, disease.'

A distant bell of Grantchester carried by the wild wind. The cherry trees clattered against the window.

Felix moaned softly.

Rake leaned over him.

'Who are you?' he said again.

The pain was in his jaw, his teeth. You cured toothache by taking a candle of mutton fat, mixed with seed of sea holly, and burning it by the offending tooth. You held a basin of cold water beneath so that the worms that gnawed the tooth would fall into the water to escape the flame.

He could feel the worms itching and digging and boring . . .

He cried out.

Nurse Claudia was by his side, pushing Rake out of the way. He felt the heat of her bosom as she leaned over him, raising his old head.

'An eagre,' he said loudly.

'What?' said Rake.

Felix could see the tide running in through Black Buoy and the Boston Deeps. He could see it, by the glimmering light of a long-dead moon.

He held his jaw and moaned.

He said, 'Help me.'

Dr Govindan said, 'What's he on?'

Nurse Fairbairn reached for his notes. 'Stemetil and diazepam. Pethidine.'

'Not pethidine.'

Rake said again, 'Who are you? What is your name?'

'Get out,' said Dr Govindan, looking in the drugs cabinet, 'or I'll have you thrown out.'

'Is it the treasure? Is it *still* the treasure?'

Still? What else would bring him snaking through the centuries of space?

A syringe was held up against the bright light. Ten milligrams of diamorphine hydrochloride.

Heroin.

He sighed gently as the needle went in and the air was expelled from his lungs.

'He mustn't be left alone,' said Rake. 'He is infectious and might be dangerous.'

'No. No, actually, I think you are the dangerous one,' said Dr Govindan.

'I shall not commit the fashionable error,' said Rake, 'of regarding everything I cannot explain as a fraud. Have you read any Jung, doctor?'

'Go away, please.'

'He may have the ability to transmit thought forms – pictures, God, I can't explain it in layman's words. There's a paracrystalline hexagonal lattice in the brain's pyramidal cells that acts as a quantum site, and the American device has somehow triggered it. The superpositions of quantum theory with complex-number weighting factors is not supposed to operate on lager scales, but somehow it is happening.'

Jennifer was in the doorway.

'Army bomb disposal are at Wormby. They want to talk to you. And Mike says he's going again – a hell of a lot of activity, deltas with spikes.'

Rake turned to look at Felix, whose eyes were closed, whose face was grey, his skin flaccid.

Suddenly he shivered violently then cried out.

'Maybe it's the heroin,' said Dr Govindan.

Rake shook his head.

It wasn't the heroin – even though Felix was, perhaps, the first man of the Medieval world to take the stuff.

34

December to January, 1217

Crok was back, yet again, in the hunting lodge at Feckenham. It was a winter's day during that still, frozen time when the Lord Pope had placed all England under a pall of excommunication. The clergy had been idle and the people had been barred from the churchyards, forced to bury their dead in woods or roadside ditches.

How popular John had been in those days! Trouble had come only when the excommunication was lifted and the parish priests had been hauled out of the alehouses and forced back to their duty (with great difficulty, the bishops complained), and the people had to pay, once again, to bury their dead.

In his dream, he was in the royal chamber. Nicolaa and the King were lying like Romans on the thick-wove tapestry that covered the floor (a strange custom, this laying of tapestry on floors, brought from France by John's mother, Eleanor: it puzzled the dogs who could find no rushes to hide their bones).

They had the treasure chests open before the fire. John was running the gold regalia comb, that was adorned with stones and used for arranging the royal hair after the anointing, through Nicolaa's long dark hair. The air was filled with the scent of frankincense. Jewels flowing through their warm fingers, flashing in the light of the brazier, of the wax candles.

The two of them, lying side by side in the warmth, in a room with glazed windows.

Crok in the corner, peeping inquisitively from behind the *chancele* screen.

He awoke cold and hungry, in some hovel on a nameless road.

Through December he moved north by Severnside. He begged his food from the monks and bought his nightly bed by pulling the teeth of Welshmen – reflecting as he did so on the days when he had taken more from a Welshman's body than a tooth. Welsh folk were particular, he found, about their ivories. They cleaned them every day with green hazel shoots, and sought to protect them by not eating hot food: but Welsh teeth decayed as all things decayed and Crok pulled them out by the score, though he was unwilling for his own broken, aching tooth to be drawn.

At Tewkesbury he wandered round the castle walls and was overcome by melancholy. The King had kept Christmas here in the seventh, or perhaps the eighth, year of his reign. He sat with his back to the cold stone and remembered how the wagons of wine had come trundling up the frozen road from Southampton. How de Porkericiis and his hounds had run through the frozen water meadows, and Florence had stirred her cauldron of washing in the castle yard. His nose twitched to catch the scents of the capons, the fat geese, the smoking sides of beef that were being prepared for the Christmas feast.

Had there been sugar pies at Tewkesbury? He tried to remember when sugar had come into England. The year six or seven, perhaps – he knew it had cost two shillings a pound.

He wandered to the abbey and sat in the cold porch, and thought of larded boar's head, and of minced onions steeped in broth of blood and vinegar. His mouth salivated and he dribbled spit that froze into icicles. He yearned for a gingerbread soldier oozing warm honey (he'd bite off its head, he told himself, as though it were a Welshman) or a dish of rice in almond milk.

Troubadours were luxurious by nature. He had a stomach (as the wicked Sergeant Holbrook said) grown proud. He could no longer eat rancid porridge, or drink wine that was sour and greasy and smacked of pitch.

By the Feast of St John the Evangelist he was in Worcester. He went into Wulstan's church and looked where his master's body lay. Dead bones, he thought, stripped bare: the monks would have stolen the rings from his fingers, worms would be at the flesh. He sat awhile and mused, pleasantly, on mutability.

There was already a trade starting in pilgrims. Wulstan – canonised at John's insistence – was the English saint, and throughout the West there was a cult for all things English.

Crok sniggered.

Wulstan, it was said, had the power to bring the dead back to life. Perhaps that was why John had wanted to be buried here.

* * *

He took the road east through the valley of the Avon. He tried to earn his daily pence as a troubadour, but fashions had changed and he did not know the latest songs from France. He tried to sing his song of the packmen and they called it rusty old stuff and him a rusty old bard, and kicked him out of the tavern without giving him any dinner.

He pulled teeth, and when there were no teeth left to pull he peered into his fisherman's ball and told maids when they would find husbands. When there were no old maids, he peddled his favourite patent remedies for the ills of the flesh. 'Take a fat cat,' he would say (a favourite remedy, this), 'and skin it and draw out the gut. Stuff it with fenugreek and sage, and roast it, and anoint your ailment with the grease.'

When there were no cats available he wrote *In nomine Patris+et Filii+et Spiritus Sancti+Amen* on a scrap of parchment, and told patients to keep it in the pocket of their smock.

He had a variety of other remedies.

A verse from the gospels will protect against calamity.

The touch of the church-door key will cure rabies.

When all else fails, splints of the martyrs' bones will remedy the very worst of ills – and he had a box of splints from martyrs' bones, conveniently for sale.

In February, on the feat of the purification of Mary the Blessed Virgin, he was in Northampton, the most easterly stronghold of the English forces. It was a place that thrived on rumours of war, where messengers came clattering over on the cobblestones at all hours, and the alehouses were full of adventurers who talked of battle with the French, and of capturing themselves a Burgundian count and buying their knightly manor with his ransom.

It was in such an alehouse that Crok found Obb Corfe, the essoiner who had followed the King's court in the days before the war, and who was now teaching law at the university. Obb remembered Crok's skills as a physician and, for the sake of old times, secured him three pence to speak to the medical students.

'The first and most vital task, my masters,' he told them, with a wink and a leer, 'is to decide whether or not your patient is to live or die.'

The clerks – a thin, raggedy, philosophical bunch – told him rudely that all men died; that death for every man broke the wheel of Fate. Crok was shocked by the naivety of youth. 'You must know whether they are to live or die, in order to know whether you need to demand payment *before* or *after* treatment,' he spelt out. 'For no relative will pay your fee when the corpse is cold.'

They should collect cinquefoil, he told them, and boil it in a jar of water while saying a Paternoster for their patient's soul. If the water stayed green the patient would survive his treatment, if it turned red then he would die. 'This is an infallible method of prognostication,' he said solemnly, as they started to scribble on their slates.

But they were a poor lot at Northampton. The university was once the Kingdom's pride for learning, but it was now in decline, a place notorious for students who kept ferrets and weasels in their rooms, and went around the town baptising cats. Oxford – it was whispered – was the coming place.

Oxford professors were cunning and corrupt, and were scheming to have the university at Northampton abolished – they waited only the outcome of the war to know which king to bribe.

On a wet misty February morning Crok lay in the undergrowth by Ermine Street. The road ran northwards through dangerous woodland, though the brush had been cut back to give at least a few moments' warning of outlaws. To the east lay the lands controlled by the French, the *Norrenses*, and the rebel English earls. Behind him lay the English west, where the writ of King Henry ran.

He lay and watched and listened, the wet seeping into his boots, his bones.

How many days through a dangerous land was it to Woken's Eye? To the King's treasure, that he knew had been pulled from the sea?

He lay and thought of jewels, glinting in rock pools in the moonlight.

His eyes flitted up and down the misty road.

Nothing moved. Even merchants with their packhorses were scarce this winter, for the French grip on England had tightened. Berkhampstead had been taken. Norwich had been taken. Oxford had been taken. King Louis himself had travelled north and the grim, grey legions of the *Norrenses* had come south to join him.

In all of Eastern Britain, now only beleaguered, starving Lincoln Castle still flew the English flag.

Was Florence at Lincoln? Was she rub-a-dub-dubbing at her cauldron in the castle yard while William the *Aquarius* prepared tubs of hot water, scented with rose-leaves, for Nicolaa de la Haye? It was as likely as not – King John's bathing tub had been at Newark and the army captain now holding the castle would have no use for it (it was likely, indeed, that he would be unaware of its purpose, having never had a bath in his life). Perhaps William and Florence and Thomas de Porkericiis still messed together, and sometimes as they sat round the cooking pot said, 'What can have happened to Crok the troubadour?'

His eyes moistened.

Should he return to the sea, to the jewels?

Or should he go to Lincoln? Seek Nicolaa's good lordship?

He crouched in the wet, dead bracken and hesitated. King Louis had gone back south, they said – gone to save his army in Sussex, where Willikin of the Weald was chopping French heads like beanstalks. He thought, for a moment, about French heads being chopped: he shuddered, either with delight or with cold.

He looked cautiously to north and to south, then slipped across the highway, his heart thudding.

He was in the realm of King Louis.

He disappeared into the undergrowth. It was as wet and cold as that of King Henry.

35

Wormby Flats, Lincolnshire

Someone was banging on the caravan. It penetrated Normandie's dreams: that and the sound of Jude tumbling to the floor with a little scream and a muttered obscenity. She opened her eyes and saw a blue disco light flashed rhythmically across the roof. One moment she could see Jude crawling around, looking for a lost earring – a lost drink, a lost dance partner – the next moment everything was black. The knocking stopped. There was a sudden slam as if the caravan had been rolled into by a car – hooligan children, her brain told her, up to tricks.

It was the wind. Suddenly she could hear it, an angry, high-pitched whine.

'Shit . . .' said Jude thickly, blanched of colour by the disco light that appeared then disappeared, looking like the flickering heroine of an old, silent movie.

More banging on the side of the caravan. Normandie rolled out of bed and opened the door. It was Ray, an anorak over his pyjamas. 'Why isn't your fucking mobile switched on? Come over as soon as you can.'

He turned and scurried away, the gale, behind him, propelling him down the avenue of caravans like a motorised goblin. The blue disco light was from a police car parked outside the club.

They pulled on jeans and sweaters and went outside. Above the sound of the wind there was a deep rumbling noise that Normandie had never heard before, at least not at Wormby: the sound of a huge sea crashing down on a pebbly shore. By the police car's blue flickering light she could see wraiths of mist curling slowly down over the defence wall, which didn't make sense with such a gale blowing.

She felt her face suddenly wet: it wasn't mist, she realised, but spray.

Jude said, 'Shit, oh shit,' and reeled about theatrically in the wind, like Mary Poppins trying to take off. Then she knocked on the boys' caravan, and made Pierre let her in. Normandie made her way towards the club. Some of the caravans had lights on but most were in darkness, their occupants wedged grimly in their narrow beds, waiting for the storm to pass, as all things passed.

Ray was pouring himself a whisky. A policeman wearing a shiny yellow coat was talking into his mobile.

'Ah, there you are, petal,' Ray said. 'The new sea-defence wall is fucking useless. Seven million euros it cost and soon it will be as one with Nineveh and Tyre. Where's your chum, what's he got to say?'

'I don't know,' she said, reaching for the phone.

'Henceforth,' he said, taking a refreshing gulp, 'Wormby Flats will be known as Fantasy Island New Atlantis.'

He was, she thought, on surprisingly fine form. Perhaps he had always yearned for excitement. Perhaps that was what all those trips to Norwich, to demonstrate against the euro, had been all about.

'It means a new bloody sign, of course, and a different ad in the Lincolnshire Holiday Guide. "Underwater novelty resort. Mermaids Welcome".'

The policeman said loudly, 'This place must be evacuated in the next hour,' then went back to his mobile.

'All right,' said Ray, 'there's only us here, we're not deaf.'

Michael's voice: 'Boulding.'

'It's me.'

'I've been trying to get you for an hour. Why isn't your mobile switched on?'

'I really couldn't say. Why are we being evacuated?'

'The American fuselage on the beach was part of a plane that crashed.'

'A plane?' she said, amazed, thinking of jumbo jets.

'Actually a drone. Something called an RPV – a reconnaissance pilotless vehicle. Very small, anyway, that's why it didn't show up when the police searched the shore earlier.'

'Is it still there?'

'Yes, but don't say anything, I don't know if it's public knowledge. I'm meeting an army bomb-disposal team. There's also a flood warning. Get everybody out of the camp as fast as you can, OK?'

'Yes. Take care.'

'Right,' said the policeman. 'There's a reception centre being opened at Spalding. If anybody hasn't got transport there's a bus being laid on.'

The phone behind the desk rang. Normandie picked it up. Ray said, in a parrot voice, 'Wormby Flats, your sunshine resort on the eastern coast, how may I help you? Those were the days,' he went on in his normal voice. 'Tell them not to forget their snorkels.'

'It's Anglia Television,' said Normandie.

Ray was pouring another drink. 'I don't think that's a good idea, do you, sir?' said the policeman, making 'sir' sound frightening, the way he did when dealing with drunks at Skegness.

'Piss off,' said Ray.

'It's their newsroom. They say, do we know there's a four-hour flood warning?'

'It's not four hours, it's three,' said the policeman in a tight voice. 'I want everybody up and ready to move on that bus in ten minutes.'

'They say, is it worth sending a camera crew?'

'What for?' said Ray. 'To see a man's lifework being destroyed?'

'I'm not asking you,' said the policeman, 'I'm telling you. Is that clear? Sir?'

A slam of wind like a bomb blast. The crash of breaking glass from the dark Conservatory Restaurant.

'Jesus,' said Ray, surprised and startled.

'No,' said Felix, 'no,' his voice activating the distant recorders.

He shivered under the thermal blankets while the wind slammed against the windows, and the branches of the cherry tree tapped and beckoned. He wanted the warmth. He craved the comfort.

'No . . .'

The pain in his jaw intensified. He raised a hand and gently stroked his face. Tears welled up in his eyes.

The pain throbbed, focused, pinched the nerves.

'No . . .'

But after all, what had he come here for? He was nearing the end of his journey – the last mile is the longest mile, his old dad used to say. And what a long journey it had been!

He closed his eyes, and thought of those rainy winter afternoons in the Hanger Lane library, sitting under the Victorian lamps, under the homily painted on the wall: *READING MAKETH THE FULL MAN*. Once, a tramp had sneaked past the assistants, sat next to Felix and pretended to read an Enid Blyton book. He had whispered, 'Chips, they mean. Chips is what maketh the full man.'

How many afternoons had he passed, smelling the warm smell of ancient radiators and institutional floor polish, reading the story of John, *Rex Anglorum*, and the lost treasures of The Wash?

Nine great necklaces set with many precious stones . . .
A monile set in the middle with diamonds and
    surrounded by rubies and emeralds . . .
A pair of gloves decorated with flowers of gold . . .

Around four o'clock, schoolchildren used to come in, banging and clattering and bating the assistants. At five he went, as a rule, to Ealing Broadway, to a café where he had a cup of tea and looked through the work he had done. Even then, there had been the shadow of an ache in his jaw. What had Rake said? Quantum physics is not hostile to actions at a distance?

How far was it from Woken's Eye to Ealing Broadway? Four score years and ten?

And a good bit more, he told himself, opening his eyes and staring up at the ceiling, at the little red light of the camera. And you needed more than a candle to light your way.

Pain shot through him. He groaned softly and again the recorders were activated, the sound logged.

This time his legs moved – reluctantly but they moved.

He was shaky on his feet at first and his head swam. But his reward was instant – the pain in his jaw lessened. He found his clothes in a cupboard and slowly dressed. He could hear a trolley rattling and wondered, as he had wondered before, what they needed to trolley around the carpeted corridors in the middle of the night (the bodies of the dead, he had concluded).

He evaded the nursing station and was down the corridor and stairs before a nurse appeared from an office and said, 'What's this? Where are you off to, Mr Shafto?' in a normal, chatty voice that did not quite disguise her alarm.

'I'm discharging myself.'

'Don't you think you ought to speak to the doctor first?' she said, reaching for her little bleeper. But he was already past her, heading for the main entrance, checking through his wallet to see how much money he had, searching in vain for his car keys.

She ran after him. He could not discharge himself, she said, without signing a form to absolve the hospital from the possible consequences. He turned, so that she stopped, startled. He held up his blotched hand and absolved her from all blame and all sin, for the past and forever. '*Et in saecula saeculorum*,' he added, in the manner of the monks of Peterborough at Compline.

World without end.

'Not me personally, you don't have to absolve *me*,' she tried to explain. 'Wait just a moment for the doctor. Please Mr Shafto. She's on her way.'

She was looking round for a porter, but already Felix had pressed the switch to open the plate-glass door.

'Mr Shafto! Come back! At least tell me where you're going!'

The phone on the desk rang. She picked it up. 'Dr Govindan, it's Mr Shafto, he's insisting on discharging himself—'

A porter came clattering down the stairs.

Felix had gone.

'I am aware of that, but we have no authority to hold people against their will, it is actually an offence. Yes, we'll try to persuade him . . .'

They went out into the courtyard. Their movement instantly triggered the security lights which threw fantastic, moving shadows as the wind bent the trees.

But why hadn't the lights been triggered by Felix?

The nurse stood and puzzled and shivered in the cold. The porter went round a gravelled path to the car park, but then came back shaking his head.

Felix had disappeared: vanished into the Cambridge night.

Part Four

36

Lincoln, AD 1217

Crok was on the wall of the great keep of Lincoln Castle, swinging his axe and howling 'Fuck the Scotch and Fuck the French' – the battle cry of the old varward division – as the English army appeared on the high ground of Kirton Cliff, the gold-and-azure shields of the Earl of Chester's knights flashing in the sun.

Then the French in Lincoln town were clattering their alarm – *Guardé! Guardé!* – and the bells of St Botolph, and St Peter at Gowts, and St Mary le Wigford, were added to the Frenchmen's din, though listeners on the castle walls noted that St Faith's bell was silent – either in mute support of the English King, or because it lay outside the town's walls and was in the path of his army.

Nicolaa was out of her chamber. She went to the battlement's edge and peered uncertainly towards Kirton, her sight not as good as it once had been. Serland, her captain, pointed to the mounted English scouts that had been thrown in a screen to the south of Ermine Street, to warn of a breakout by the town's defenders. *Guardé! Guardé! Guardé!* rang out the Lincoln bells, as the French stumbled from their lodgings. 'De Breauté!' voices on the battlements cried, as a force of English crossbow-men were suddenly seen moving down the hill ahead of the four main *battels*. There was a ragged cheer, for many of the castle's defenders had served, at one time or another, with the rapacious Norman adventurer.

De Breauté's men disappeared into the great monastery orchards beyond the Newport Gate. Soon there was the flash of armour among the white, blossom-loaded trees. There was silence now on the castle walls. All eyes were on the approaching army, the army of England that for so long had been but a rumour, a flickering candle of hope in the dark of winter.

It had been called into being at Northampton, on the eve of Pentecost. Within a day the Marshal's great speech had been carried into Lincoln Castle and read to the garrison by Crok, always a man to make himself useful. 'Would we not be soft if we did not take vengeance on those who have come from France and who desire our destruction?' Crok had roared on the Marshal's behalf, standing on a wooden stage as a sharp spring wind, a ploughman's wind, blew through his starved bones, his filthy pelisse. 'On those,' he had cried, 'who come to England to destroy our lineage?'

Few of the garrison had much lineage to speak of, other than Nicolaa de la Haye, great-granddaughter of Coleswegan. But the Marshal in Northampton had been addressing the English barons – reminding them, subtly, of how Edgar the Atheling had been forced to flee his country and had spent his days as a poor landless knight of Constantinople, fighting the Turk. 'They are ours, if heart and spirit do not fail us!' Crok had cried, referring to the impudence, nay the *impru-dence* of the French in venturing north from Mountsorrel.

'Yet if we die in this enterprise, God knows well how to distinguish the good! Yes, and he will place us in his paradise!'

The soldiery had stared up at Crok, an adventurer with a blood-stained sack of loot, perhaps on his way to paradise. 'For the peace of our church, which our enemies have broken,' Crok had concluded, making the sign of the cross, 'to be pardoned our sins. Amen.'

'The Earl of Chester!' voices cried. 'The Earl leads the avant guard!'

The English army was down on St Faith's great field and Chester's men were moving to the right, to the place of honour, while the standard of William Longsword, Earl of Salisbury, was rising over the third division, and that of the Bishop of Winchester over the rearward.

'Yet it is the Marshal and his sons that lead the main division,' said Nicolaa's captain, Serland, who knew her secret fears.

She nodded grimly.

A spy from the town came running up to the battlement, stuttering his news. Saer de Quincy had wanted to sally out from the town and fight the English – but the Compte de Perché had taken the English baggage train for a fifth *battel*, and thought the venture too dangerous.

Nicolaa's sergeants roared. Why, it was better than having breakfast (the castle starved). Crok swung his axe and howled.

Nicolaa said, 'Be still.'

Crok was still, though his limbs twitched, and the

crossbow-men on the battlement winked and told each other that his teeth chattered as a cat's teeth did at the sight of a little wounded wren. They would gladly eat a little wren, but no bird was foolish enough to alight on Lincoln's castle walls, not this season.

A mounted knight was leaving the main battle division. The men on the battlements shouted encouragement as he passed in front of Fawkes de Breauté's crossbow-men, circled St Nicholas's church and dashed across the great field towards the castle's postern gate, outpacing the French knights that sallied out from the town to stop him.

Nicolaa said, 'Come,' to Crok, and went up the steps to her chamber.

She poured herself wine, a chivalrous gift from the Compte de Perché. 'If you have a Scotchman's head in your sack,' she said, 'I might well eat it.'

From outside came the roar of the *perrier* engine. In the weeks that had gone, they had all learned to distinguish the different sounds of the *perrier*, *mangonel*, and *trebuchet*.

A dull thud as the missile hit the curtain wall, close to the keep. Plaster fell from a window arch. The wall was moving now with every hit. Dust rose and Nicolaa coughed. 'Another week and the wall will be breached. At least we can all run out *per posterulam*.'

She looked at him covertly. She liked to pretend that she spoke Latin: it was her vanity. Crok nodded and grinned.

'Then we can fall on our knees and cry succour to the Earl of Chester,' she went on, bitterly, drinking deep. Crok's eyes were on the flask. It would be sour and greasy, this wine, having rattled and rolled its way by barrel from Anjou at least four years since, and been carried to Mountsorrel and endured the English siege, and then been rolled north up the Fosse to Lincoln town with an army of French adventurers. But if she was called back to the walls he would steal it. He could feel it already, burning his stomach with heat, taking away the pain.

'His forefathers won Lincoln Castle by a trick,' she said, 'in the time of King Stephen. You know the story?'

Crok nodded, but she went on regardless.

'It was in the midst of a hard, frozen winter, when the men guarding the tower were out in the meadows at their Christmas sports.'

Crok nodded again. He had seen these sorts of Englishmen – running round with their pig bladder, kicking each other's shins till the snow ran bloody. Frenchmen sat in their chambers and sneered, and would not venture out unless it was a wolf hunt, or a winter tourney.

'Then this cunning Earl,' said Nicolaa, 'together with the vile Earl William of Roumare – they were in the town and holding the castle under siege, you understand, as the French do now – both sent their countesses to visit the citadel – to chatter peaceably to the wife and daughters of the Castellan.'

Which English Castellan was, thought Crok, busy kicking a pig's bladder over the frozen river and shouting 'ha, ha!' whenever a leg or arm was broken.

'And while the countesses thus chattered to the Castellan's wife,' Nicolaa cried, with sudden passion, almost spitting out her wine, 'the Earl of Chester came across the snow smiling and whistling a carol like Wenceslaus on the Eve of

Stephen.' (She was romancing, building up her woes: it came from so many months brooding on her injuries.) 'Just strolling, he came into the tower on a day of peace as if to fetch his wife away. And then three of his knights came wandering after him – to see him safe, and the countesses safe – and d'you know what?' (Crok knew what. He sighed for the wickedness of the world.) 'They had arms hidden under their cloaks and in an instant they subdued the tower guard and threw out the Castellan's wife and daughters!'

Who must all have had a hard time of it, thought Crok, when the sport-loving Castellan discovered that his castle was lost and that other men would dine on the hog that turned on the castle spit.

'*Cara Stephani regis Anglie,*' said Nicolaa. '*Per quam dedit et concessit Rannulfo comiti Cestrie castellum Lincoln.*' She had picked up a parchment from her desk, and was reading it. She passed it to him: she had reached words that she did not understand. 'My eyes grow feeble,' she said.

'*Et ciuitatem donec idem rex fecerit ei terram suam Normannie,*' said Crok, '*et omnia castella sua—*'

'Well?'

'King Stephen gave Ranulf, Earl of Chester, the castle and city of Lincoln as a pledge until he should restore to him his lands and castles in Normandy.'

'Normandy!'

'But, dame, this was in the time of Stephen, in the days of the grandfather of the present Earl—'

'He wants my castle! He is here to take it! Cast for me.'

He hesitated, then slowly took out from his bag his sea crystal, his fisherman's ball.

'Tell me,' she said, 'why Ranulf of Chester has been given the avant guard?'

'Because, dame, he has four hundred knights in his service?' Crok hazarded, not needing his ball for this.

'Tell me,' she said, staring at him, her eyes sunken in her gaunt face, 'who will be Castellan of Lincoln when this war is done?'

It was the question she had asked the first night, when he had crept in through the postern having axed two French sentries by the Newport Gate. 'Crok, you are a man without a master,' she had told him, standing at the top of the postern stairs in the light of a feeble taper (the castle had long since burned all its wood) and staring at him: an opportuning, grovelling cat with a present of two fat mice. 'And neither, now, have I,' she had added, turning away.

You would have thought that King John had been her husband.

Later she had called him to her chamber, where she sat over the castle's only fire. She was filthy, like everybody else, her skin grey with dirt, her clothes unwashed. Her gold *crespine* was long since sold for food.

Crok had looked at her mournfully. Only the silver in her hair now shone.

'Well? What moves in the world?'

'King Louis rules in Winchelsea, but King Willikin rules all Kent.'

'Who is this Willikin?'

'Why, Sir William Cassingham—'

'But who *is* he?'

'A gentleman.'

'He was never heard of until these times.'

Crok had nothing to say to this. After a moment, he ventured, laughing: 'They say the French army starves.'

She turned to him, her gaunt head with its sunken eyes.

'There is corn in Winchelsea,' he went on, chortling over his tale, 'but they cannot get to the mill and can only grind it by rubbing it in their hands, and are so desperate that they eat the husks. They live on a kind of large nut they have found in store, but are so hungry that the Viscount of Mulun could not find four knights to keep the night watch, and Lord Daubney sent boats in from Rye and stole away a great ship on which the Monk Eustace was building a tower. They say that King Louis himself now starves.'

Crok laughed again. He had yet to feel the gnawing of his own bowels. 'These are great days, dame.'

'And what, in these great days, do you see in your ball?'

He took out his ball. He moved to the fire. He peered into it.

'Will my son be Castellan of Lincoln?'

Crok said nothing. He knew that Sir Richard would not live long: a month at most.

'Well then, what *do* you see?'

Gold, shining in the void.

'I see the King's great crown,' he said, his voice thick.

She stared at him, then turned and peered into the smoke from the damp, smouldering wood. She blew gently until a small cold flame appeared. 'Let Edward's crown lie in the sands of the sea. There will be no more kings in England. We have served the last, you and I. Now go.'

He did not move. She threw her goblet at him. Wine splattered over his fisherman's ball.

He crept away then, in search of Florence and William, but neither was in the castle: only wicked Sergeant Holbeck who said, 'Bugger me, lads, we'll have to make sure we have our heads on our shoulders when we wake up from now on.'

'Who will be Castellan of Lincoln when this war is done?'

Again the whine of the siege engine, this the *trebuchet*, the thud of rock smashing against the castle's curtain wall.

Again a cloud of dust from the mortar of the keep.

Tiny stones fell with a clatter.

The curtain wall was about to crumble and fall.

'Well?' said Nicolaa. 'Will I hold my own?'

She would be betrayed. He did not read it in the fisherman's ball, but in the mist that clung about her.

She read his face. 'What will happen to Idonea?'

Her granddaughter. Her son Richard's child. Richard was dead, just as the crystal had foretold. He had been buried in St Bartholomew's church, by courtesy of the French who had sent twelve knights to do him honour. All her hopes now lay with this Idonea, a dark-haired child of six or seven.

'Crok?' she said, her voice urgent, almost pleading.

In the ball, when he looked, were flashes of red, amber, and brilliant blue.

He could not lie.

'I see only the King's jewels.'

A long sigh. Silence.

She turned away and drank her wine. 'I told you to leave

all that.' She paused. 'But I daresay a necromancer will seek treasure as a sergeant seeks a whore.'

Again the high whine of the *trebuchet*.

A crash and a cloud of dust. The crystal was dark, impenetrable.

A clatter on the stone stairs.

Lacy in the doorway.

He said, 'Lady,' and bowed low, just as he had when they met on the sea wall by the Roman tower. He was full of chivalry, having ridden boldly and swiftly and outpaced the French knights.

'Have you bought anything to eat?'

He looked startled.

'Have we your horse?'

Crok salivated.

'There will be food soon enough,' he said, shocked.

He was looking at her: her grey face, her hair matted. It had been a long winter. Her son had died. Hunger stretched the skin over her bones. When she opened her mouth she was near toothless.

She was old.

'Why does Ranulf of Chester lead the avant guard?' she asked, as though it was the only question in the world.

'Because, dame, he said that if he did not then he would not march. There was a great dispute by the Kirton windmills – the Normans said it was their ancient right to strike the first blow in every battle, but the Earl said they could eat their ancient rights.'

Crok would eat anything.

'Lacy, you know the secrets of the Council,' she said.

'Do I remain Castellan of Lincoln?'

'I do not know of any man,' he said, gallantly, 'who could take it from you.'

He bowed low. He had been reading the history of Britain, thought Crok. Everyone in Northampton had been reading it. He thought he was Sir Lancelot *du Lac* and Nicolaa was Guinevere.

'I'll tell you what,' she said, this Guinevere. 'I'll piss on the Earl of Chester if he tries to take it from me. Where's Fawkes de Breauté?'

'Bringing in his men through the postern.'

'And the Marshal?'

'He seeks to breach the Newport gate. He wants to know the strength of the French in the town.'

'Six hundred knights, a thousand sergeants and crossbowmen, near enough. What if they sally out to meet you?'

'Winchester has prepared two hundred sergeants to slaughter their horses for a barrier. He talks also of an ancient door in the castle wall, blocked up in former days and forgotten long in the memory of man.'

'It's by the west gate. It's used by the spies.'

A knight was in the doorway.

'The Marshal,' he cried, 'is through to St Paul's.'

'Jesu's blood,' Nicolaa said, startled. She strode across the chamber, Lacy behind her.

Crok was left, still hunched over the table. The crystal rocked gently as another massive stone hit the castle walls. It clouded then cleared.

He forgot the wine still in the flask, the ache in his jaws, the fact that he could no longer feel anything in his fingers, and could stick a knife's point into the flesh of his arm without pain.

The roar of the *trebuchet* was the roar of the sea on shingle.

He was on the shore at Woken's Eye.

He saw silver pennies flashing in the surf.

A gold crown, caught in a net of green samphire.

Tiny figures danced: the girl, Alison, her cloak sodden, her hair wet with the spray, her pinched, anxious face with huge eyes. Her voice calling, 'Ware, ware!' as she turned her head to him, in fear and loathing.

37

Cambridge

There would be no trains to King's Lynn for two hours, said the man in the parcels office, and perhaps not then because the Great Ouse was overflowing its banks. 'Come back for the seven nineteen, but don't shout at me if it's cancelled. Phone up first, or else have a look on the Internet,' he called after Felix – surmising that he was a mature student at one of the trendier colleges.

Outside the station was a solitary taxi. He negotiated a price to King's Lynn. As they drove north, water sheeted across the roads but after a while it eased. They passed a dark, unlit café on the bypass (how Felix yearned for a cup of coffee) and turned eastwards. Daybreak was a brief yellow rent on the flat, murky horizon: then the blackness rolled down again from the north and with it came more driving rain. Huddled over the passenger heater-outlet Felix dozed, and was only jerked back to wakefulness when the taxi stopped.

They were in Ely, by the cathedral. The driver was talking, saying that he couldn't go any further. Local radio was carrying reports of dykes overflowing, trees blocking the roads.

For, lo! along the river's bed a mighty eagre reared his crest . . .

The driver was advising him to return to Cambridge.

And up the Lindis raging sped.

He closed his eyes. The taxi's engine was still on, the heater blowing warm air over his hands, his face. He wanted to rest, but the driver was urging him to contact his friends in King's Lynn – offering him the use of a phone. He took his hands away from the heating duct and took out his wallet. He paid what was asked and got out of the car, out into the biting cold. The trees in the cathedral close tossed and swayed, their leaves flying upwards into the blackness.

'Don't be stupid,' said the taxi-driver, angry and upset. 'Come on. Get back inside.'

Satan offering him the world. Shivering, he looked down into the warm, metallic womb, the friendly yellow light of the radio that was playing the easy-listening sounds of *Wake Up East Anglia*. He hesitated. A pain shot through his jaw and his stomach was caught in a vice. He gasped and turned away. The taxi-driver watched him walk over the sodden grass of the cathedral close and disappear under the deep darkness of the tower.

A dirty, tired daylight found him out on the Wisbech road. He was picked up by an early-shift market-gardener, who offered to take him to Crowland.

Ely to Crowland. Past March on its island in the fens. He was following the old roads and paths of the Angevins. He looked back and thought he saw Peterborough's tall spire to the west, across the forests, but that had been in another time, on another journey.

They were over the Cat Water now. Heading into

Crowland, with its abbey church, the place where rebels had been found, and killed, in the King's last days.

The market-gardener dropped him next to a pub. He walked east, and after only a few minutes an electricity-company van pulled up. The driver was heading towards a generator sub-station at Long Sutton – he had been called in from another area because of the emergency, he said, but wasn't sure of his way. As he carried Felix eastwards he phoned his operations room and said, 'You can't lose me in Northants, love, but this is alien territory. Hang on, there's a bloke with me who might know.'

Then turning to Felix: 'Have we crossed the South Holland Main Drain?'

How would Felix know? They were in country impenetrable to any but the sokesmen, a place where the only road was a causey of faggots, maintained with infinite labour and able to support no more than a train of packhorses. This land would not be drained for another four hundred years. Why else had the army been sent north across the Welland estuary?

'Have you any idea where we are, mate?' the electrician appealed.

North of the old Roman *vallum*, perhaps; but it was all in a mist.

The fens on either side were brimming with brown water that bubbled out across the road. 'I think I'm in trouble here,' the driver said into his mobile.

The van stopped.

Before them the road was a river: the North Level Main Drain, burst from its banks. Over the fields was a church spire.

Felix pointed. He said, 'Tydd St Giles.'

'That right?'

They looked at the map. Then they went back, took a right-hand turning. 'Thank Christ,' said the electrician five minutes later as they came across the first bungalows of Tydd St Giles, then soon afterwards, Tydd St Mary.

People stared out of the windows of their houses. A tractor struggled through mud and water with bales of hay. They drove east towards the Walpoles and the Wingland Marsh. Just before Sutton Bridge they found two Eastern Electricity vans parked next to a sub-station.

Felix accepted a cup of coffee from a flask, and swallowed four tablets of pain-killers, a double dose but then these pills had a lot to cope with. The rain had stopped and he could see the houses of Sutton Bridge across the fields. He made his way on foot along the lane to the A17. There was a road block – police cars with flashing lights, policemen in yellow coats warning motorists to stick to the main road. He walked past them warily, crossed the bridge over the foaming waters of the Nene, and turned down a lane towards Guy's Head. He trudged along a path of wet grass round fields of onions that were, a sign said, the result of a partnership in farming between supermarket and grower.

He crossed the Lutton Marsh and stopped. He was finished. He could go no further. Not for all the goading in his jaws, the spurs that raked the soft tissue of his stomach. He leaned on the fence, and closed his eyes.

In time – five, ten, fifteen minutes perhaps – a Land Rover pulled up beside him. A woman shouted – asked if he was all right. He lifted his head and asked for a lift to Whaplode Marsh, to the field path to Wormby Flats.

'You won't find anybody left at the holiday camp,' said the woman, as he climbed in beside her. 'They evacuated it first thing this morning. A coach was sent to collect the Senior Citizens. It was on the television news – they had pictures taken from a helicopter.'

She thought he was an OAP who had wandered away from Wormby Flats, possibly looking for entertainment. At Whaplode Marsh she pulled up and said, 'Why don't you let me drop you in Fosdyke, at the café?'

He thanked her, but climbed out of the Land Rover.

'Your friends will be in a real panic, wondering where you've got to,' she called, as he turned towards the field path. She sat for a minute and watched him. His purple suit was turning to black, soaked by rain that only a moment ago had been a few scattered drops, but was now sheeting down in a solid wall of water.

She hesitated. What if he turned from being an awkward OAP into being a flood-victim corpse? Did she want that on her conscience for the rest of her life?

But she had three cats and two cocker spaniels in the back of her vehicle, and upwards of fifty hens in makeshift crates, and what would happen if they all got stuck in the floods?

She let out the clutch and drove to the main road. She decided that she would have a word with the police at Boston. But the A17 was flooded, blocked with abandoned cars, and it took her two hours to find a way through scattered villages and across the Welland at Spalding, by which time the dogs were whining without pause, and the hens were hysterical enough to go off lay for six months, and she had forgotten all about Felix.

Whaplode, and the swollen estuary. The ancient sea bank. The road to Sutterton and Wigtoft, and – at the end of the short October day – the abbey of Swinehead and the blazing fire in the Abbot's chamber.

The wind was rising again: the old wind, he thought, in the old anger, though in those days it threshed another shore. Herons rose before him and were blown westwards like dead leaves. Crane and spoonbill soared from the sludgy, distressed waters of the meres, and headed inland towards Ely's vast and uninhabited fenlands, and the little town of Peterborough where the monks toiled on their tiny hill.

How the twitchers would have stared in disbelief!

He scanned the sky for the farmer woman's helicopter. But no helicopter, he realised with satisfaction, could fly in this wind.

Now the great sea birds were back. Grey-lag geese, a cloud of them, speeding like arrows across the estuary. He watched them rise over the black tower on the ramparts of the Saxon shore.

The army drums throbbed through his brain and into his blood.

38

Woken's Eye, AD 1217

And he saw again the windmill over the priory at Spaldynge, and in his ears were the plaintive songs of the Poetevin mercenaries.

He was bent with weariness, his sack heavy on his back, his axe trailing the ground behind him. He reached the banks of the Asendyke and slowly followed its watercourse seaward past the sluices. He came to Moulton Chapel, and then to the sparse, muddy huts of Moulton Second. He came to the causey that ran out into the estuary. A ship was under sail, heading into Buttolphston, the tiny port that lazy-tongued locals now called Boston, which they would not have done in Buttolph's day.

A late May wind blew from the sea, cold and salty, but the sun warmed him. He rested for a while, sheltering on a bank of marigolds.

He was near dead with hunger. The gorging of Lincoln was less than a memory – the meat, half-cooked, torn from the spit and stuffed down into his belly, the loaves they had found when they smashed their way into the Bishop's house ('Save for me the Bishop's house,' cried Peter des Roches, the fighting Bishop of Winchester, but nobody took heed).

He lay in the marigolds, looking up at the blue sky, listening to the larks.

Lincoln Fight. Lincoln *Fair* as already it was being called, because of the ease with which the French had been killed, the vastness of the plunder. He recalled how the cathedral plate and treasure had been gathered in the castle bailey, piled in a heap by the light of a great bonfire. He recalled Nicolaa de la Haye's face when the Earl of Salisbury – *Salisbury!* – was made Castellan of Lincoln.

She had feared Ranulf, Earl of Chester, without cause.

Salisbury had been gracious. There was no hurry, he said, about her moving to one of her manors, or to a nunnery even, if she so desired.

He forced himself up and tramped again along the dyke. Soon he was out on the causey, with its little islands, each bearing an oak cross in honour of Our Lord. One island, he saw, now bore a gallows tree.

Woken's Eye. The end of the World.

Who had called it that? The young knight, Walter Lacy? Cantuar?

Men were at work in the three great fields. They were tilling the black soil between the dykes, breaking the crust of drying mud. But there were not as many men as there once had been. Some had been to Lincoln Fair, perhaps, and been so bemused and dazzled as to have *lost their heads!*

He snickered and slipped into a hovel and stole barley-chaff bread; vile stuff that hurt his teeth. Then he climbed up on the Roman Wall and made his way towards the watch-tower. In a boggy dip he found a patch of samphire and chewed it raw. His mouth burned; the salt stung in his broken tooth and his torn gums. He dug a hole in the sand and covered it in branches and clods of earth, and lined it with smooth, spiky marsh grass.

That night he lay listening to the wind moan and the sea surge, back and forth, in and out, running over the Black Buoy, over the King's treasure chests.

How much had been recovered by the cunning sokesmen?

He looked into his sea crystal. It shone with blue lustre, it being so close to its native environment. But his eyes were too rheumy, or the future too dark, for him to see.

'Cusha! Cusha!'

Her cry woke him. He crawled out of his hidey-hole and looked over the fields. She was taking out the cattle, calling them from their byre. He crept through the dunes and slithered down the bank ahead of her.

She stared at him, wide-eyed with shock.

'Where are the King's jewels?'

She looked round but nobody was close by.

'Are they sold? Are they hidden?'

That frightened her.

'They are lost.'

'And found.'

'Lost in the sea.'

He saw the devils dance on her tongue. If he were to place a sliver of holy wood – say from Christ's crown of thorns, or a true splinter from the Cross – on her lips, the devils would retreat down into the back of her throat, and choke her as likely as not.

'Do you know what happens,' he said, 'to those who lie?'

He burrowed in his sack. She tried to say, '*Eradicare, et effugare ab hoc plasmate Dei!*' (though she muddled it, and anyway Crok was not going to depart or vanish anywhere). She cried '*Kyrie, eleison!*'

'Indeed, may the Lord have mercy on us all,' said Crok, pulling out a psalter. 'Hold this,' he said, moving towards her.

She backed away.

'Hold this in your hand, and tell me *then* that the King's jewels are still in the sea. Think carefully though, before you do it. A cellerer at Winchcombe lied about his fornications, and the psalter stuck to his flesh—'

She put her hands behind her back.

'Take it, take it.'

She was breathing deeply. For a moment he half forgot what he was about, and went into a little dream. She saw his expression and hastily put one hand over her breast.

'The murderess Quendrada,' he said, 'lied about killing her brother and do you know what happened the next time her eyes fell on a psalter?'

She stared at him blankly. Then she shook her head.

'They were torn from her flesh and fell – plop – on the open book. I can take you to Coventry and show you the stain of blood. Now, look on this psalter and tell me that the holy relics are still in the sea, but have a care for your eyes, lady, have a care they do not leave your head *never to return*.'

She turned and ran, calling out to Nicolas, whoever he was – perhaps her butter-haired boy. Crok was shocked, for she was a wench still living under her father's roof, and it was a grave discourtesy not to seek his protection rather than that of her lover.

The world was all awry, my sweet lords, as the Lady Nicolaa said.

Or perhaps her father was dead in Lincoln.

There was an alehouse in Holbeche. He sat and listened for gossip, but the talk was all of new-built dykes, Lord's dyke and Asgar, and the decision to split new land between the sokesmen rather than hold it in common, and how the monks of Spaldynge were laying claim to Whaplode Grove, land now rising from the sea, although they had never worked a day at winning the soil.

He cast himself as a soldier, swearing 'Fuck all foreigners, especially the Scotch,' with every breath, and telling them how he had marched with a varward echelon, and carried his axe the length of Ermine Street and Fosse. He tried, subtly, to discover if anything was known about the King's treasure. 'Some say the sea yields a strange harvest,' he whispered one night, giving a rural wink of his eye, waiting for some drunken sot to wink back and produce a gold ring set with rubies and engraved with *King John Had Me Made* for Crok to look at.

But the sots looked at him blankly, and talked of fish, and of the *rhynes* that had to be dug across the new lands, and the better fertility of clay soils over peat.

The village brewster was a woman, as they mostly were. She charged a half-penny a gallon for her beer, although the last Assize of ale, in John's day, had fixed the price at a farthing. Crok had no pennies nor farthings. He earned a bowl of ale-slops by telling them of Lincoln Fair, and the part he had played, and about the torrent of blood that had gushed down Steep Street, and the amazing length and blueness of Frenchmen's entrails, pulled from the corpses in the Square and fought over by the dogs. He made the rustics chortle with his story of the French chief engineer, still busy with his stone-caster – in the act of placing a stone in his *trebuchet* and giving the signal for its firing! – when an English knight struck off his head.

He told them of Bloet, the standard-bearer who rode his horse off the bridge and into the river, all in the impetuosity of youth. He told of the Compte de Perché, dead of a lance through the eye-hole of his helm which pierced his brain, though, curiously, he delivered three terrible sword blows at the Marshal after that, in the manner of a headless chicken. It had been a sad moment, he told them, when the young Compte de Perché fell. The Marshal had thought him merely unconscious and had cleared a space round him and taken off his helm to help him breathe. Everyone had been astonished when blood and brains gushed forth.

The woman brewer of Holbeche was full of avarice but she was not without a heart. She wept when he told her of Sir Richard Samford who – having been robbed of his lands by King John – had angrily thrown in his lot with the French. When the battle was lost the unfortunate knight had taken his young wife up on his saddle in front of him, to save her from being raped by the sergeants. 'Leave her, you cannot take her!' a Norman knight had cried, prepared no doubt to stop for a moment's rape himself on this fine May morning. Sir Richard had put his young wife gently to the ground, turned on the libidinous Norman, and unseated him with a blow of his lance in the chest. Then he had gently taken her up once more, and so saved her.

The story, which was true, earned Crok a mug of ale.

Word came to the Holbeche hovel of another French invasion. The black monk Eustace was planning to bring an army to Winchelsea, to rescue King Louis who was still living on nuts, and then to truly conquer the English. The feudal levy was called to arms (this was fair enough, the sokesmen decided: let the earls, barons, knights, and sergeants earn their fees) but then, swiftly, came word that burgesses and rustics were also to be mobilised: all Englishmen in fact – *whoever they are and from whomsoever they hold, provided they ought to, or are capable of, bearing arms*.

This made the rustics mutter and complain, and wonder if they might not slither away into the watery fenland for a season.

Fast on the summons to arms, though, came word that the Lord Daubney had led the English fleet out from Rye on St Bartholomew's Day, and had manoeuvred to windward of the French and thrown powdered lime into the wind, which lime had stung the Frenchmen's eyes and driven them mad. And Eustace the monk's ship had been boarded by Daubney in person, and Eustace had been found below, and had been dragged to the deck and straightway beheaded.

And so the feudal levy was not called and the rustics of Holbeche were left in peace.

* * *

Crok lay in his hole in the sand. On Severnside they said, *Dychaun Dyu da dy unic*, which meant *God provides for the lonely man*.

But nobody provided for Crok.

He munched on samphire and on what he could steal.

The salt from the sea burned his arms and legs. When he looked at his stomach it was raw. He had little feeling, now, in his fingers.

'Cusha, cusha!'

The cows heard her call and came homeward across the late spring pasture, through the dandelion flowers. Each cow had a name and a place in the byre.

The girl's father, Crok had learned, was dead. He'd been called to the array by Henry de Bohun and fallen, ignobly no doubt, somewhere between Mountsorrel and Lincoln. Such was the price paid, Crok told the rustics of Holbeche, for a Petty Lordship over three fields of shit.

The butter-headed boy, the boy she called Valentine, was a sailor, voyaging away up the coast in a ship of Peter the German. She was alone but for her villeins and her reeve, Nicolas, who was a poor feeble creature.

One day Crok crept into the byre behind her, his axe in his hands. She turned from her milking and caught him with his face in the pail, creamy foam round his chops.

'Remember the whore of the priest of Howcen,' he mumbled, still drinking the milk. 'His whore, his *belle amie*, his hearth girl. The slut, if you like, who kindled his fire but extinguished his virtue.'

She was looking past him, out of the byre: uselessly, there

was nobody within a field's distance.

'The whore of the priest of Howcen sat on the wooden tomb of Saint Osana, sister of King Osred,' he went on, invigorated by the sweet warm milk. 'And her backside stuck fast to the wood because of the lies she had told. And they cut away her smock till she was naked, and beat her with lashes till the blood ran. And only when she confessed herself to be a grievous liar was her arse released from the saint's tomb. Where are the holy vessels of the King's chapel? Where is the true splinter from the Cross of Calvary?'

She said, '*Christe eleison.*'

'Christ will not have mercy on a liar. Think of the knight, Gilbert Hargurnell, who after three years of unremitted anguish gave birth to a calf.'

'It was a portent of a great calamity,' she said bravely. 'Everyone knows it.'

'It was a punishment for lies. Where is the treasure?'

'It was taken by the eagre.'

But the devils danced still on her tongue.

'For the eternal soul of your father,' he said, 'tell me where the treasure is hidden.'

'You are mad,' she said.

And this time the devils did not dance.

One day he broke through the door with his axe and scattered the fire from the hearth, and dug through the ashes beneath, which was the usual hiding place for peasants' pennies. He pulled apart the bed and scattered the straw.

A horn blew. Men were running back from the fields. He stood in the doorway and they saw him with his axe and stopped and crossed themselves. He went back into the hall and searched again through the compacted soil and prodded the wattle from the walls. Clods of earth fell from the roof. Then the roof itself fell in on him, and the dust in his eyes filled him with pain and rage.

Outside, the girl was calling, 'Ware, ware!' as she had called when her lad, her Valentine, was sucked into the sands.

Crok slipped out of the back of the hall and into the undergrowth.

Nobody followed.

He lay in his hole on the sea wall. His nose was stuffed up. The ends of the fingers on his right hand were turning black. The nails fell away at his touch.

When he scrambled down to the byre she was ready for him.

'Go,' she said, 'or they will kill you.'

'Remember the woman of St Edmunds, who pretended to kiss the saint's shrine in order to steal the silver pennies left by pilgrims. She tried to suck them into her mouth but her lips stuck fast to the altar.'

'The treasure was lost. There was an eagre.'

'Remember the little jewels you hid in the pool.'

She stared at him, shocked.

'Remember the man who tried to steal the gold torque of Saint Cynog and whose eyes fell out,' he said, smoothly, coming close. 'Remember the boy who tried to steal young pigeons from a nest in St David's church in Llanfaes, and whose hand stuck to the stone and was not released until his parents had offered vigils, fasts, and prayers for three days.

Who have you, in the whole world, to offer prayers for your soul?'

She was crying. Her face was drawn, the skin tight over the bones. How old was she? Sixteen? Seventeen? Her parents and her siblings were all dead. She needed a husband, a father. The Abbot of Peterborough had been her father's overlord, and the monks would be settling her affairs. The new-won land of Woken's Eye was fertile: the people fat on fish and waterfowl. Nobody starved in the fens, it was said, even if men did live half their lives in water. The manor would fetch a good price: it might pay her dowry to a nunnery, if the monks did not cheat her which assuredly they would, though not so much as the officers of chancellery if she was put to be a ward of the King.

Or she might be found a husband, for she was good with the cattle, a good hus-wife. Perhaps her sailor lad would return from the sea.

Perhaps Crok could marry her himself.

'Where is the great crown?' he said softly, wheedling, knowing that she was burdened, that she longed to tell him. 'Where are the King's jewels?'

'Go,' she said, 'or they will kill you.'

But nobody stirred to help her. He was a necromancer, a gobbler of souls. He was still living in his hole in the sand, scouring the rock pools by moonlight, when men came down from the north – French adventurers, *Norrenses*, lordless rebels. They were roaming the country in hungry packs. To the east, Fawkes de Breauté was hunting them down like wolves; to the north, Salisbury was sweeping them clear of

Lindsay; while in Sherwood, Phillip Mark was seizing the chance to clear the forests of infestation, to settle old scores.

Crok woke at midnight to the smell of burning thatch. He slithered out of his hole and scurried to the top of the sea wall. Horns were echoing from Moulton, from Holbeche and Spaldynge – the hue and cry was being raised, though most men, as ever, would be quietly hustling their wives, daughters and pigs to safety in the woods.

The byre blazed. They had fired it to warm their hands. Where was Alison de Pilche? Where was her reeve, Nicolas, that tottery old man?

A woman's scream. Men laughing.

Not many men, though. Perhaps only two or three.

Suddenly the byre's timbers collapsed. Huge flames shot up into the sky. Crok slithered down the bank, crept round the circle of light and slipped into the hall. He felled one man as he tried to mount her and sliced through a second man's arm; the man stared wide-eyed as blood spurted like a fountain, then moaned and fell, dying of no good cause, a peculiar thing that Crok had seen once or twice before.

The other adventurer scuttled through the door and vanished into the summer night.

They were poor things, the scum of Lincoln Fair: half-starved and weak in the head.

She brought him a bowl of milk, and left it outside his pit. Later he watched her go along the causey to Moulton and wondered if perhaps she had been summoned to see the priest. At dusk he waited under the gallows that Bohun had made when he came from Lenne, following in the path of

John's army. Two skeletons still embraced, clacketty clack, as the winds blew.

She found him squatting, a black toad in her path.

Her eyes widened then flickered up to the gallows.

He watched her, puzzled.

'They have sent to Peterborough,' she said, her eyes still on the gallows.

'No,' he said, judiciously, shaking his head. No, he would not end his time swinging from the kissing tree. If that were to be his fate he would not have been able to pass under it without feeling the hand of death.

'You must learn the lesson of the beaver,' he said. 'Who, when pursued, castrates itself, and throws its testicles down for the hunter to eat.'

It was a true tale, that had been told him at Tewkesbury.

She stared at him in astonishment. Then she giggled.

'It is because of this act of self-castration,' he said loudly, irritated by her disbelief, 'that the beaver is called *castor* in Latin, from the Latin verb *castrare* and not, as certain supposedly learned teachers at Northampton University will tell you, from the Hebrew word for musk. Note the wise words of Saint Bernard: *the beaver saves his life by offering at full speed, those vital organs which the lustful hunters need*. The beaver saves itself, lady, by giving its pursuer what it wants. Where are the treasures hidden?'

Again her eyes flitted to the gallows, to the swinging bones.

'Where are the holy relics?'

He reached out to her.

She opened her mouth to scream.

It was his hand that she was afraid of.

His fingers. His stumps.

'Tell me,' he said, 'or I will touch you.'

Her scream was a low hissing noise.

'Tell me,' he said, touching her face, her lips, 'or your flesh will rot.'

She spat.

Then she collapsed. He grabbed her as she fell. 'What? What?' he said, as her weight pulled him down to the ground.

She said, 'The church.'

Well, where else?

It was a long, low room, mud-and-wattle walls, a roof of straw. His axe smashed into the wood of the dais. Behind it, under the crude stones that supported the altar, was a chest. Its locks were broken open. Everything gone but for the crown, dear Jesu, the crown, which meant that Nicolaa de la Haye, Sheriff of Lincoln, had sat on top it, on top of the great crown of King Edward, while Lacy had fretted over the tides and the sokesmen had nodded and winked and cracked pignuts.

For the last time in his life, he laughed. How much had they taken away, melted down, sold in Lenne, buried in little private hoards in their hovels? How much did Alison de Pilche *still* have hidden? By Christ, if the lads from the varward division were here now! They'd raze every building before you could cry Jesu Mercy.

The blast of a horn. Men shouting.

He pushed the crown into his bag. He went out through the door at a run. They were terrified of his necromancy and wore animal heads – deer's horns and wolf skins – which made them clumsy. One sweep of his axe and a man fell.

Alison de Pilche had been dragged to the church with them. She lay on the ground, a red wheal across her face, a swollen eye weeping and almost closed. For a second, Crok stared in amazement – this was shocking treatment for a daughter of the Lord. Fawkes de Breauté, if he knew of it, would hang the whole village.

He leapt in the air as a stag's head came lunging, a vicious dagger beneath it. Again he swung his axe; the miller from Quaplode was revealed, his mask falling away as he died.

Crok ran. The blood pounded through his brain. His head spun. His flesh was wasted and corrupt, and besides he had not eaten for two, or perhaps three, days. He rolled down into the deep undergrowth by the great field, then stumbled again to his feet.

A beaver that has lost its testicles and is hunted a second time, needs only to rush to the top of a hillock and cock up its hind-leg, to show the hunter that the desired organ is gone.

Wisdom from a Welshman, culled in the alehouse at Tewkesbury. He reached for his bag – to throw it behind him and so to feed the hunter – but there was no point, for they would kill him anyway.

The horn again, now closer. The cry of greyhounds. The crash of men through the reeds.

He fell. He could run no further. He rolled on to his back and reached for his dagger.

Birds were rising from the fen, filling the sky. Geese skating across the water with their wings flapping, crying in alarm.

In his mind, suddenly, he saw the kissing tree and the corpses swinging. And he knew where Alison and her yellow-haired boy had hidden their treasure.

The hounds and their keepers passed.

He crawled down into the mud, pulling his bag behind him.

39

Wormby Flats, Lincolnshire

'. . . *two hours before the tide is at the full, and the Met Office has warned of gale force winds sweeping in from the North Sea. To add to the general misery, MoD personnel are investigating reports of a wartime bomb on the beach at Wormby. During the night old-age pensioners enjoying a late holiday at a caravan park were taken to an emergency reception centre at Spalding—*'

Rake reached forward to cut the radio. 'We're calling it a wartime bomb to simplify things,' he said, his voice coming through Trudy Pierce's headphones. 'Have you heard of an eagre?'

Perhaps it was the British way of saying eagle. She hesitantly shook her head.

'A tidal wave in a narrowing estuary.'

He pointed down, through the rain-washed plastic. 'Men say it was a stolen tide. The Lord that sent it, He knows all.'

Poetry, inside her head. 'Right,' she said, nodding, thinking it was some kind of literary allusion, maybe a reading from the Prayer Book.

The helicopter rose suddenly, its engines screaming.

The pilot's voice, also inside her head: 'I'm turning now.'

They wheeled and the sky spun.

Rake reached across her and pointed down. 'Gibraltar Point, OK? You see the dunes going south? That's Wrangle Flats.'

She peered down at the grey coast with its line of white surf.

'That town you can see is Boston. Lincs rather than Massachusetts. The river you can see is the Welland.'

It looked more like a canal, running in a straight line to the coast.

'Was that where King John's army crossed?'

'Somewhere down there, yes. The estuary was much wider then and the shore was at the Fosdyke. You see the modern sea wall? Look behind it and you can just make out the line of another, ancient wall. That was the coastline in the thirteenth century.'

She looked carefully for anything that might have existed since the thirteenth century.

Shadowy lines ran across fields.

'By the white house?'

'No,' he said, following her gaze. 'No, that's the course of an oil pipeline.'

'Where's Wormby Flats?'

He tried to show her but the helicopter banked and his hand was suddenly pointing upwards to the sky. When the horizon righted itself she looked down at grey, moving waters. He touched her arm and pointed. A headland. What looked to be sand dunes with a vast stretch of water behind them – flooded fields, occasional hedges and trees standing clear. A wall of earth with tiny yellow machines moving back and forth. As she watched one of them turned inland, along a track that bisected the flooded farmland. A moment later, the others began to follow.

Rake touched her arm again. She followed the direction of his pointing finger and saw toy caravans, laid out in neat rows.

'Somewhere down there – that's where your drone came down.'

Forty years ago, while Soviet ships in the Baltic were being loaded with MRBMs and Marilyn Monroe lay dying alone in California.

A light flashed. Rake fumbled with his seat comms console.

She stared down at the caravans. Had anyone heard anything, she wondered, on that summer's night when the USAF bomber from Berlin inadvertently released its load? When the drone had come skimming down over the sea and buried itself in the mud?

Rake was speaking soundlessly into his microphone. She twiddled her comms dial until she found him: 'Surely it was not beyond the capabilities of the medical profession,' he was saying rapidly, with irritation, 'to keep a seventy-year-old man suffering from acute weakness, scurvy and pernicious anaemia in his bed? No, I have no idea where he might be – but I have told you that he is a danger, certainly to himself and possibly to others. Call it dementia if you want to but find him.'

He cut the link.

For a moment he sat lost in thought, then he said: 'Wormby – Woken's Eye as he's started to call it. He'll try to come back.'

He started to punch numbers into his comms pad.

The pilot's voice. 'The army wants to talk to you.'

The helicopter had turned northwards into the wind, lower than before, following the line of the wall. Below, Trudy saw two army vehicles, about a dozen men.

'OK,' said Rake, cancelling his call.

Through her headphones, a moment later, she heard the sea pounding, the whine of the wind. A voice said, 'OC B Company to helicopter. Do you have the data for us?'

'Yes, we have it,' said Rake, his voice still grim.

It was in Trudy's briefcase which was clutched in her arms. If the chopper crashed she would try to throw it clear of the flames, and her life would not have been sacrificed in vain. She pictured the memorial service in the white clapperboard church in Lake Forest. She saw her mother in a deep mauve coat and hat with matching gloves. Eddie and Rob Marguerie stood by her coffin in sober suits.

Rake said, 'Can we land?'

The pilot's voice. 'Not unless you want to end up arse over tits.'

Trudy didn't want to end up arse over tits. She hoped that Rake didn't either.

The voice from the beach. 'You may be able to land in the caravan-site car park.'

The helicopter wheeled again. She looked at the line of surf racing through the dunes, foaming over a line of fence posts, tumbling down the other side. They skimmed down towards a building that had an illuminated blue neon sign that said *DREAMBOAT*. By it was a little patch of fairy lights that reminded her of the lakeside trees at Tavistock.

A car park, with a car turning into it. The machine swooped down low then rose again, its engine screaming. Two white, startled faces looking up at them.

The pilot said tensely, 'No can do. There's too much turbulence.'

The car, Trudy saw, had driven into water deep enough to cover its wheels.

'Take us back over the wall. Patch me through to the beach.'

They wheeled back towards the sea.

'OC B company – over,' said a voice.

'Helicopter to officer commanding B company,' said Rake. 'Can we talk you through it?'

Trudy unfastened her briefcase. Her hands were trembling.

A different voice.

'Rake, it's Boulding here. It's no use. The drone will be under water in a matter of minutes. The army are cordoning off the path along the sea wall, then we're pulling out. Have you any information on what happens if it goes off?'

Rake said, 'The intention was interference to electro-magnetic equipment within a five-kilometre radius of detonation. By equipment read battle tanks, radios, aircraft and field guns. The risk to human electro-magnetic systems was not, at the time, considered significant.'

'OK, but bomb disposal are getting some odd readings on their equipment. There's a very low level leakage they think has been here for a long time. There's also something else that's started perhaps even within the last few minutes. It may have been caused by a small rock fall as we dug into the bank.'

Trudy said, 'Don't let them mess about. There's a charge of high explosives.'

'There's a charge of high explosives,' said Rake.

'Yes, they know that. Can they make it safe?'

Trudy looked helplessly at her data. She felt sick, her brain slow and unresponsive. She hadn't slept for more than an hour since she'd been awakened in the Fort Meade hostel. She hadn't had a full night's sleep since she was at the Prairie Winds Motel, and that seemed a lifetime ago.

'OK,' she said. 'They have to find an access panel under the vane marked with yellow, repeat yellow—'

The wind caught the helicopter, jerked them up and then dropped them sickeningly.

'I can't hold this position,' said the pilot crisply. 'Sorry, but it's time for home sweet home.'

The helicopter rose. It wheeled out over the water, then turned westward, passing back over the wall. Looking out, Trudy saw soldiers hammering stakes into the sand, and running wire across the dunes. Then a massive wave broke over an outer line of granite boulders and surged towards them, and they scurried to safety.

Rake was speaking into his phone. 'I don't care how many acres of Lincolnshire are under water, the police have got to find him. Get Tom to speak to Biggin in the Cabinet Office. He's to tell him that Shafto's gone missing and is likely to be trying to get to Wormby Flats. Tell him also that the device is leaking enough to show on the field monitors. The Americans say it shouldn't affect the human brain but we know it already has done. I'm trying to do the maths now. Put me on to Mike Lean.'

He paused. On a pad on his knee he had scribbled $5 \times 10^{10}Hz?$

'Mike? OK, basically we're talking about effects in the micro-tubular cellular automata. No, I know we can't measure quantum oscillations on a beach in a bloody great storm with Second World War bomb-disposal equipment, but we know the frequency region, and we know that something is causing quantum entanglement. We've no reason to belief that Felix Shafto is unique in being affected by the oscillations, it could easily be happening to others – a radius of five k, perhaps further, who knows?'

The helicopter was crossing low over the caravans and over the concrete block building, its little garden still lit up with fairy lights, its blue illuminated *DREAMBOAT* still shining brightly.

Trudy wondered what a Dreamboat was doing in a place like this.

Ray was in denial. He sat at the bar drinking a Screaming Orgasm (Baileys, Cointreau, Tia Maria and cream) while music filled the clubhouse and drowned the wind and even the roar of the helicopter. 'Take me home, country roads,' sang Olivia Newton-John, and he reflected, as he crooned along, that nothing after Olivia Newton-John had been truly real. The eighties and nineties had never happened; his brief flirtation with the modern – in the shape of Baby Spice – was finished. He was going home, home with Olivia, to the place where he belonged. After a bit he got down and started to stack bottles of spirits into crates. In time the Fab Four told him that Strawberry Fields would be for ever.

'You know there's a bomb that might go off any minute?'

Normandie stood in the doorway, hands on hips, looking a bit like Mrs Peel from the days when television was black and white, and Watneys Red Barrel cost 1s 11d a pint.

'All the lonely people,' Ray sang nasally. 'Don't you worry, petal.'

'Has Michael called?'

'Afraid not.'

He went back to collecting armfuls of bottles from behind the bar. He'd told the staff to do it and they'd told him he was insane and then buggered off with the old-age pensioners. 'What kind of bartender is it,' he asked Normandie now, 'that refuses to go down with his sherry?'

He laughed and shook his head from side to side, then, because she wasn't chuckling, said again: 'I said, what kind of bartender is it—'

Jude came in. 'Hullo, Ray,' she said.

'He's drunk,' said Normandie. 'Have you got the car to start?'

'No way.'

'Shit,' said Normandie. She picked up the phone.

He went back to putting the bottles into a cardboard box. It had all been very different on the *Titanic*. Bartenders on the Ship of Doom had served Scotch on the rocks for Kate Winslett when the rocks could be scooped up off a passing iceberg. The English were a different breed in those days, of course. And – he added to himself, in justice – the bartenders on the *Titanic* didn't have a coach to take them to Spalding.

It had not been a pretty sight at Wormby Flats in the early

hours before the dawn: two beefy chefs and four kitchen lads jostling the Autumn Tints out of the way as they scrambled up the steps of the coach.

'Ray?' said Jude, leaning over the bar, peering down at him. 'Sunshine?'

'Fuck off.'

'Yeah, right.'

She sat herself on a bar stool and ordered an Exotic Sex 'n' Sun cocktail, which witticism he ignored. 'Did you see that helicopter?' she said. 'It's probably Customs and Excise. They're on to your little tricks, Ray babe.'

God he disliked her. She was on drugs, of course.

'I'm finished,' he said, abandoning his box and sitting down heavily on the beer-sticky floor, his back to the shelf of brown ales. 'I'm done for.'

'Never say die. Think of the insurance.'

But it was three years since they had refused him insurance on the caravans, or on the clubhouse.

'Why not open a bar in Spain?' she said, crossing her long, still suntanned legs. 'I'll come and run it for you.'

He shuddered.

'Ray, we've got to go,' said Normandie, putting the phone down. 'I can't get through to Michael. Have you got room for us in your Discovery?'

Were they mad? His ancient, though still classy, Land Rover was all he had to carry himself and his possessions to another world.

'Can't you get a taxi?' he said.

Jude laughed. She slithered off her bar stool and went outside, into the rain.

Normandie stared down at him. 'Ray, get up. Please get up.'

He slowly got to his feet. What time was it? The bar clock, its face cleverly disguised as a little ship's wheel, said it was just gone 10 am. He wondered why it was so dark and gloomy.

'How about a cup of coffee?' he said brightly.

'Oh God. Are you really pissed? Look, let me help you with that stuff. We'll take the one case and go, OK? Nobody's going to come and pinch anything.'

Shadows were moving.

They were moving through the dark conservatory with its broken window, its tables still laid with sodden paper serviettes and salt-and-pepper cruets and bottles of ketchup. (Had he time to collect them up? They'd last him for years and years.)

Shadows.

Will o' the wisps. Hooded heads. Nut-brown faces.

Normandie said, 'What's the matter?'

'Can't you see them?' he said, surprised.

A wall light crashed to the floor. 'It's Poltergeist Time at the Dreamboat,' he told himself with a laugh. Which was something they hadn't managed yet at Fantasy Island.

'See what? What are you talking about?'

Christ, he though, as a stench hit his nose.

'I've chucked four gnomes out of the Land Rover,' said Jude in the doorway. 'They pleaded for their lives but I told them it was women and children first. The keys are in the ignition. Do we take him or what?'

Ray said, confused but incensed: 'Him? Who's him? The

dog's dinner? I'll not fucking take you anywhere if you don't watch it.'

They stared at him. Then they went outside. Ray saw, in the wreckage of the conservatory, a group of men huddled together against the wind. They had cloaks wrapped round them. They looked brown and clayish and muddy.

He closed his eyes, then opened them.

The figures had gone.

It was the last Screaming Orgasm he'd have in a hurry.

A distant thud from somewhere outside: more windows in the conservatory smashed, glass showering down over the tables. The lights behind the bar went out, then came back on again. Through the broken windows he could see the Magic Garden, its lights twinkling away: blue and green along the secret paths and glades, a red glow from the treasure caverns, sparkling white fireflies in the lavender hedge.

Jude cried out in the doorway. She peered back in. 'Ray, come here. Now!'

He got up and went to the door.

The sea wall – just visible over the far row of staff caravans – was moving.

He blinked, then focused his eyes again.

It was still moving – writhing almost. Sand and stones slithering about.

The staff caravans suddenly vanished under a deluge of water.

'Can we get on the roof?' said Normandie.

He ran out into the rain, round to the back of the clubhouse, and grabbed a ladder that was generally used to replace the

Gnome King on his summit of Gnome Kingdom after the lads had knocked him off with stones. Jude and Normandie followed him. The water surged round their knees in a foam that looked like brown ale. He placed the ladder against the wall and helped the girls up it. He held it until they were on the roof, then he sloshed his way back into the club.

Tables were overturned in the conservatory, some of them floating like rafts. He tried to get on one, thinking they could all float away across the fields to Holbeach, but it immediately sank under his weight. He waded round the bar and picked up the phone and dialled 999, but the line was dead. He got his coat – waterproof on the outside, fleecy lined within – from a hook and stuffed its pockets with packets of crisps and nuts. He grabbed a plastic tablecloth and an armful of cellophane-wrapped Wormby Flats Holiday Village sweatshirts. Then he waded back outside, holding his coat and the sweatshirts over his head to keep them dry. With his one available hand he could hardly grasp hold of the cold wet sides of the ladder, but he finally managed to clamber up to the roof.

They sent him straight back down for his mobile phone, which was on a shelf behind the bar. This time the water, icy cold, soaked him to his crotch.

Back on the flat roof he gave them his coat to share and a sweatshirt each. He said, 'Those buggers down there won't like it,' and laughed.

They stared at him.

He chuckled again, thinking of the shadows. The faces. A physicist would explain to him, in due course, the effect of alcohol on the microtubular structure of the brain, on the neurotransmitter substances that governed thoughts and perceptions: tell him that the inveterate drunk who saw proverbial pink elephants was not necessarily deluded. For the moment, though, he assumed that he was mad – but it didn't matter because the world was mad. It would not become sane again, he decided, until he was standing at the bar of a particular hostelry in Wapping, with other old-mucker production workers from the *Daily Star*, drinking a pint and eating pickled eggs.

'Are you all right, Ray?' asked the girls.

He nodded and wrapped the plastic tablecloth round his shoulders. The wind tried to pluck it away. Looking up, he saw clouds hurl across the sky like a speeded-up nature film on television. Perhaps he would whirl up himself, like Dorothy in *The Wizard of Oz*.

The girls huddled inside his coat. After a bit they offered it back to him, but he shook his head.

They all watched the sea wall.

At first the water had come through the breech in occasional bursts. Now every wave brought a huge green ocean that crashed down over the caravans.

Normandie was speaking into the mobile phone.

'There was a noise like some kind of explosion. No, I'm not nauseous, why should I be nauseous? I feel fine, so does Jude. Ray?'

She was looking at him doubtfully.

'Yes,' she said after a moment, 'I think he's all right.'

He put his hand covertly over his balls to stop them freezing.

'It's about fifty metres across,' she said, turning to look at the sea wall. 'But it's getting wider all the time. Yes. Yes, OK.'

She closed the phone. 'They can't send a helicopter yet because of the wind.'

And the wind was rising.

And the sea was rising.

And all around them was water.

40

Tymoor's Farm

Felix sat with his back against the farmhouse wall, his cold hands on the stone that ran under the Victorian brick, stone that was from the old tower, first quarried and dressed by a Roman auxiliary. There was a high-pitched whine from a loose cable that snaked up to a satellite dish on the roof. He shivered in spasms. His hands and feet were frozen, but his head burned. He could hear a voice, dim and distant.

He closed his eyes.

Cusha! Cusha!

Faintly still – but stronger than before. The taste of samphire in his mouth.

'Are you OK?'

He opened his eyes.

She was wearing a yellow storm-jacket but her head was uncovered. Rain beaded her brown hair and ran down her face.

'I came back for my pony. I was going to ride him to safety but Dad must have come back. He'll fucking kill me when he finds out.'

Felix pursed his lips. He had always disapproved of the young girl dancers swearing. Year after year they came into the troupe as shy, sweet little things, but after a season at the seaside they were effing and blinding like sailors.

'I only just managed to get here. I don't think I can get out, not now. The water was coming up over the car wheels at the crossing.'

No flicker of memory. Julia would have regressed her, rifled through her past lives, sorted her out.

She was staring at him, puzzled, a wary expression in her eyes.

'Were you going back to the holiday village?'

He pondered for a moment, then nodded.

'It wouldn't have been any use. There's nobody there. They were all taken away in a coach during the night. I don't know what to do about the cows. If I let them out they might panic and get caught in the mud. Cows are always doing that, and then people have to call the fire brigade. I don't think they can swim. Have you ever seen a cow swim?'

Felix shook his head.

'But what if they drown in the shed? I'll try to get them into the kitchen if it really gets bad. The kitchen is higher than the shed. You'll have to help me.'

It was raining hard again: scything down in sheets, driven by the wind. He closed his eyes.

'Are you sure you're all right? Don't you want to come inside?'

Silence, but for the whine of the wind.

When he looked, she had gone.

A heron came sweeping low over the roof. How long had the storm raged, that it should be hungry enough to try to hunt in this weather? Surely fish would be lying deep in their pools? Perhaps herrings were being tossed over the wall, he thought, to flounder in the shallows.

Water surged against the mud and gravel of the path, and left tiny bubbles as it receded. Each time it returned it came a little higher.

She came out of the house, a mug in her hand. 'The electricity's off but I used the camper stove.'

'Thank you,' he said.

He drank the coffee. Warmth flooding his stomach.

'Were you coming back looking for work? It wouldn't have been any use. It's the last week of the season, he wouldn't have taken you on.'

He looked again for a flicker of recognition.

Nothing.

Yet he had killed a man for her. In truth this meant little – for he had killed a great many men. But he had killed for her all the same.

How? How had he killed for her?

He tried to think. Somehow he had been betrayed. Betrayed by this girl.

'I don't think it's rising as fast now, do you?'

She was trying to sound brave. She was seventeen but young, he thought, for her age.

'No.' he said. 'Nothing like as fast.'

She hesitated. 'Why don't you come into the kitchen? It's still quite warm in there.'

Burning pain sliced through his jaw. He shook his head. She looked at him for a moment, still puzzled, then turned and went back into the house.

The water was still rising. Rubbish floated in a circle. Stuff from the bins. Bits of ancient, discarded plywood kitchen units, covered in blue-and-tangerine plastic. Bottles that would at some point be carried away, to bob messageless on the flood.

She was standing at the window, speaking into a mobile phone, looking out at him. He imagined the kitchen, with its warm stove.

There was another sudden pain in his jaw.

He staggered to his feet. Immediately, the pain eased.

He leaned against the wall to gather his strength, then slowly made his way round the side of the house. Water lapped against the door of the cowshed and he could hear the animals moving fretfully inside it, moaning their fear. He found a spade. He went back to the front of the house, sloshing his way through a foot of icy water.

She was standing in the porch.

'The police say you've to come inside,' she called. 'They've been looking for you everywhere.'

He waved in acknowledgement, then turned away from the house and into the wind. The rain beat against his face. He could hear the roar of the sea and the wild cry of herons and bitterns.

Cusha! Cusha!

He closed his red, stinging eyes.

What was it that Rake had said while he slept, or they thought that he slept?

We know that in quantum physics it is theoretically possible to superpose reasonable space-time geometries next to unreasonable space-times in which there are Closed Timelike Lines. In theory, under such circumstances, an observer would, after a finite passage of his own perceived time, find himself back in his own past . . .

His own past . . .

He opened his eyes.

The Roman tower was sharp and clear. Beyond the sea wall was the estuary and beyond that, on the far Lindsay shore, was the start of the King's road to Swinehead and the north. Before him stretched the reclaimed lands of the wapentake of Elloe, and the new-dug groines that collected the silt from the Welande, and the sluices that he had watched the dyke-reeves dig during that terrible springtime.

A flame flashed yellow from the Tower – a warning to the guides that the tide was on the turn.

He turned and looked along the black spine of the causeway to the little islands, each with a cross, one with a gibbet. He set out towards it.

'Where are you going? The road's under two metres of water.'

She was behind him.

'Listen, it's going to be OK. They're sending a boat for us.'

For a moment he faltered, his head burning, his limbs like lead.

'Please,' she called. 'Please come back. You're ill. You shouldn't have left the hospital.'

He was out on the causey. He could see the gibbet clearly now – see the bodies swinging.

Her voice faded and was lost.

The Lord sent the floods as a scourge to the earth and to fulfil the threat that was made in the gospel: There shall be upon the earth distress of nations, with perplexity; the sea and the waves roaring.

The *thump, thump, thump* of the drum echoed the beat of his heart.

A noise behind him – somebody crying out. He looked back.

Alison de Pilche was following him, jumping from tuft to tuft of marsh grass. Nothing in this world changed.

41

Wormby Flats

'Felix is at the Tymoors' farm,' said Normandie, startled, 'the police have had a call from Karen.'

She shut the phone. 'I don't understand. Felix wasn't fit to travel.'

'What did they say about us?' asked Jude, shivering.

'Just to sit tight.'

'Oh great.'

They had Ray's fleecy coat gripped tightly round their shoulders, but the wind was steady from the sea, penetrating and bitingly cold.

'Michael says we're not to worry.'

'Hear that, Ray? Michael says we're not to worry.'

Ray sat with his plastic tablecloth wrapped round him. He seemed far away.

'Oi, Ray,' said Jude. 'Are you all right?'

'Yes, flower.'

Jude and Normandie looked at each other.

'No, Ray,' said Jude. 'She's flower. I'm bitchwoman-fromhell. Remember?'

Ray wasn't listening. He was watching the water pour through the sea wall. Already the caravans by the dyke were half submerged. His hopes, his dreams, drowned like kittens in a well. He began to hum the *Dambusters* theme tune.

'Do either of your remember Richard Todd?' he asked.

Normandie and Jude exchanged glances again.

'There's a boat at Holbeach picking up elderly people who're stranded, Ray,' said Normandie in a false, kindly voice. 'It'll go there first then come for us.'

He nodded.

She stared at him for a moment, then opened the phone again.

'I want the number of some people called Tymoor who have a farm at Wormby Flats. No, I don't know the initial.'

Southern Breeze began to tilt over, a bit like a cargo ship hit by a U-boat. Ray made ack-ack-ack noises, imagining the Huns machine-gunning poor English sailors.

'Ray?' said Jude. 'Ray, baby?'

He froze into silence. He heard her whisper, 'He was having a fit just then.'

What would happen now to Jack Fountain and his lady wife? To the other stalwarts of the Owners' Club? What about those little girls in places like Barnsley and Rotherham – thirteen- and fourteen-year-olds trembling on the verge of womanhood – whose burning ambition since they were toddlers had been to enter the Miss Wormby Flats beauty contest? They'd have to be told the sad news (and watched carefully to make sure they didn't top themselves).

Then there were the young couples – sons and daughters of the stalwarts – who were even now planning a Wormby Flats honeymoon. They'd have to reconsider both their wedding date and their budget, for not many dream honeymoons cost only a hundred quid, even in February.

'We'll have to do a new honeymoon brochure,' he said.

'Yes, Ray,' said Jude, after a moment.

The brochure compared itself, advantageously, to the Carribbean. OK (it said with disarming honesty) Montego Bay had sunshine and in St Lucia the bougainvillea wasn't plastic. But did you get a full English bridal breakfast? Did you get two large complimentary Screaming Orgasm cocktails, personally served in your caravan by *le patron*?

'Line out of order,' said Normandie.

They sat for a bit, the girls huddled together, Ray huddled by himself.

The wind moaned.

It started to rain again.

'Another metre,' said Jude, watching the waters rise, 'and we're swimming with the fishes. Shouldn't we tell them that?'

Normandie dialled. She said brightly, 'Hi, Michael. Look, sorry to bother you again. The thing is, another metre and we'll be swimming with the fishes.'

She listened. She said, 'Yes, yes we appreciate that. Look, just don't bother about us, OK?'

She closed the phone. 'The boat can't leave Holbeach and the wind's too strong for helicopters to take off. We've got to wait for the army to fly in inflatables.'

Ray pondered. Then he tittered. He'd come out with that the next time he stood at the bar in Spalding Conservative Club. They'd be asking him how he survived his terror ordeal, and he'd say, *We got a message that the army were flying in inflatables and I said, 'Tell the buggers to fly in aeroplanes like everybody else'* (roar of laughter) *'and tell them to bring*

me a bottle of Scotch while they're at it!' (Good old Ray!
Give the man a drink!)

He snorted.

The girls were looking at him beadily.

'Something funny, Ray?'

'Not really, flower.'

His trousers were sodden. His feet were like ice.

'They just weren't prepared, were they?' said Jude. 'It's
always the fucking same.'

'It wasn't Michael's fault. He's in a terrible state about
me.'

'Yeah, right,' said Jude.

'And about you,' said Normandie hastily. 'He's going
berserk about both of us.'

'He's not the only one going berserk,' said Jude meaningfully.

Ray's balls were numb. He turned furtively away to give
them a rub.

'Ray?' said Normandie. 'What are you doing?'

'Nothing, flower.'

The wind howled with new vigour: a North Sea wind, full
of ice shards, or so it seemed. He huddled up on the edge of
the roof and looked down at the Magic Garden.

The electricity, amazingly, was still on. The garden was
transmogrifying itself, even as he looked, into a Magic
Island, glowing green and red, lapped by illuminated seas.
Butlins had once had a similar special-effects display in
the Beachcomber Bar at Minehead, he recalled – but their
effort had been pathetic by comparison and had lacked
gnomes.

He stared down in admiration, thinking what a pity it was that there weren't any punters here to see it.

Then the lights went out in Fairyland.

'God,' said Jude, 'I'm cold and I'm wet and I'm hungry. Do you think it's stopped rising?'

'No,' said Normandie.

They ate crisps and nuts with wet, frozen fingers.

Ray still peered over the edge of the roof, watching the water as it began to cover the *DREAMBOAT* sign, which was still illuminated. Soon it was almost submerged, a blue neon message beaming down into the bosomy ocean. It would become a late-night rendezvous, he told himself, for the younger, livelier plaice and haddock.

It flickered and died.

'Don't touch the water,' said Ray, 'or you'll electrocute yourself.'

He spoke flatly, without much interest or emotion. The girls looked at him anxiously. He had been like this – calm, resigned, peculiar – since the waters had risen in the car park and his Land Rover – after floating for a few moments in a triumph of British engineering or, at least, of British door seals – had sunk, like all else, beneath the brine.

He wondered what they were whispering about. They were looking at his plastic tablecloth. Perhaps they were going to attack him and steal it.

Jude said, 'OK, this is it, Ray, your dreams are coming true.'

'Pardon?'

'Come and sit between us,' said Normandie. 'It's stupid not to.'

They waited for him to brighten up, to slither clammily in between them.

Nothing.

'Ray?' said Normandie. 'Come on, under the coat.'

'It won't stretch over three of us.'

'You don't want to get hypothermia, Ray.'

But hypothermia might well be the answer to his problems. Certainly he couldn't think of a better answer, other than applying to be a deckchair attendant at Skegness, where numerous of his old *Daily Star* muckers would discover him and have a laugh.

'Come on, Ray,' said Normandie gently.

Eventually the girls got up and sat on either side of him. 'This is just for body warmth, remember?' said Jude. 'I don't want to find your fingers wandering.'

'My fingers are frozen,' he said, as they put his fleecy-lined coat round him and then tried to snuggle under it themselves, pulling the tablecloth round the three of them.

'All the more reason,' said Jude, 'why I don't want them fondling my tits.'

'Don't,' said Normandie, shuddering.

A bit later, Jude said, 'Does it seem to you that the water's coming through the wall as much as it was?'

They all looked. The gap in the wall was wider than it had been – but yes, the sea was no longer coming through in such force.

The mobile rang. 'Hello?' said Normandie. 'Oh, it's you. No, there's no way we can get to the farm, we're stuck on a roof. Yes, Michael told me he was there.'

She closed the phone. 'That was Andrew Rake, you know, Michael's friend?'

Neither of them responded.

'You two have a cuddle and enjoy yourselves,' she said, standing up. She walked to the far side of the roof and looked towards the Tymoor's farmhouse.

She saw with surprise that it was clear of the water.

On the far side of it, two figures were wading through a field.

'Normandie!' shouted Jude behind her. Turning, she saw a boat nosing its way round a grove of trees by the submerged Holbeach March road.

'OK, Ray. OK, baby,' Jude was saying. 'We're rescued. You can let go now.'

'It's cold,' said Ray, hanging on.

'No, Ray, get off me, Ray. Look, there's a boat and a helicopter.'

The helicopter was skimming over the treetops. Jude struggled free from Ray and stood waving. A man leaned out. At first Normandie thought he was waving back, and then she saw that he was holding a camera.

The boat – low and black with a yellow-coated crew – swept round the concrete roof of the club in a theatrical curve. Then Michael was on the roof, sweeping her into his arms and kissing her. And Jude kissed a sailorman whom she did not know at all. And the helicopter came low and hovered, lovingly, over the scene.

Many who watched the television news that night commented on the lucky rescuers and few noticed the sad hunched figure who was seemingly wrapped in a piece of plastic. But they only had the chance, anyway, to notice him for a fleeting moment. The cameraman – choosing between the man in a huddle of hypothermia and the seamen being kissed by girls – zoomed without hesitation on youth and hope and womanly gratitude.

The helicopter rose and circled. It came down low over the massive breach in the sea wall and tried to get a shot of the American bomber that had, according to the newsroom, crashed in the Second World War. But the tide was only just on the turn and nothing was visible. After a few moments the pilot turned inland again, picking up the rescue boat as it sped northwards.

The cameraman touched the pilot's arm.

He pointed ahead.

A small island, seemingly cut off, although the waters were lapping against a raised track of some kind.

Two figures digging in the mud.

Felix dropped the spade. He plunged his bleeding hands down into the hole. His fingers disturbed the cold worms, guardians all of the King's treasure.

'Look!' the girl was saying. 'Look!'

He looked up briefly but saw only a beaver working in and out of the detritus of rotting logs and branches.

He dug again with the spade.

There had been a royal pallium of purple – it would have rotted long since but the spun gold would have survived if only he could find it. The belt with a gold ring *auri frisio* – the leather would have rotted but the gold was very thick.

Shoes embroidered with pearls – how could he be sure, now, of not missing the pearls? There had been another crown, apart from the great crown – or was he thinking of the crown that John – 'impelled by piety' – had given to the Hospitallers to carry to the poor beyond the seas? Was his memory deluding him after all these years? Maybe, but he was not deluded about the Sword of Tristram, or the *elitrop* and the staff studded with a great sapphire, or the gold mazer with gilded feet and bands that had, as John wrote, belonged lately to 'our excommunicate enemies', meaning the wicked monks of Sibton—

His fingers found something.

'Take it – wait!'

Something else. Something heavy. Water fell away; clods of earth and slime. Wood, perhaps – totally decomposed. It fell apart. He grubbed through the remains.

'Here . . .'

Brown muddy pebbles.

He turned to Alison de Pilche.

'Take them . . .'

She stared at him, frightened, then opened the pocket of her storm jacket and put the brown pebbles into it.

He probed down again with his fingers, deep into the cold slime. It was up to his elbows, then up to his armpits. He strained down into the depths and the water washed over his face – salt in his mouth but cool on his burning forehead. She was shouting at him, but her voice was far away.

'It's all right, it's OK.'

'Let the paramedic get to him . . .'

'Get hold of him!'

He was in the dark water. The blood ran from the cut on his arm, but if he could get across the Raven's Dyke he would be safe in the Deeping Fen. He had the crown still in his grasp. He would take it to Lincoln and see mockery turn to wonderment on the face of the Lady Nicolaa.

Hands were reaching down. Ghostly, smiling faces above them. Salt and mud in his lungs. The singing of monks in his head. They were chanting the *Misericordia Domini*, as they had for John in the church at Worcester. He was being released from this life as John had been released: the fate from which no mortal could escape. There was a moment of precognition, in which he saw the crown being borne through the night by men on ponies, then the mists fell.

They pulled off his sodden clothes, wrapped him in blankets and zipped him into a survival bag. They carried him into the boat and sea water swilled over the side. 'Sorry, but we need to get him back fast,' said the paramedic. 'Can two of you stay here?'

Normandie and Michael clambered out. Jude said, 'I'll stay as well,' and followed them. The boat moved away in a circle of foam. Karen Tymoor waved, but Ray – wrapped in silver foil like a chocolate bear – seemed oblivious to what was happening.

'We walk back to the house, OK?' said Jude.

'They were digging a hole,' said Michael, falling to his knees, feeling down in the mud. 'See if you can find it.'

Normandie also knelt in the mud. 'I don't understand how it could be buried here,' she said. 'This is miles from Cross Keys.'

'It's not miles from where he found the seal.'

'Listen,' said Jude. 'Whatever it was, he can come back for it later.'

'Simon thought it all happened at Wormby. He said it was the Welland estuary and not the Wellstream—'

'Right,' said Jude. 'I'm off.'

'I've got it,' said Normandie, lifting her hands from the mud. 'Here, take it,' she said, as though it were burning her.

It was paper thin for the most part: black rust, flaking, but much thicker at the end where it formed a cross. Michael took it, then knelt, and dipped it carefully in the receding waters.

He rubbed very gently.

A flash of gold, tiny, instantly extinguished by mud, but then revealed again.

He held it reverently, one hand under its hilt, the other supporting its frail blade.

He held it up, over his head.

'The Sword of Tristram,' said Normandie.

42

Spaldynge, Feast of St Michael
and All Angels, AD 1217

The Abbot of Peterborough shivered and pulled his fur cape around him. It was taking a long time, this calling of the dead. The monks of Spaldynge Priory were sticklers to form. They were carrying out the office in all its fussy particulars – perhaps because they had, this day, such distinguished company.

'Jesu's blood,' swore Nicolaa de la Haye, impatiently.

She was sitting on her horse beside him, staring down the hill, her eyes searching for the small procession: for the monks, coffin and cross. The Abbot remembered how she had clattered her way into Peterborough church on that night soon after King John's death. She was impatient then – but patience, of course, was not a woman's virtue.

He muttered an apology for the tardy monks. He could not reprove her, as he would any other gentlewoman who profaned. He did not dare treat her coldly, for she was once again Castellan of Lincoln and Sheriff of Lincolnshire. They had 'relieved her of her burdens' after Lincoln Fair (how the Abbot of Peterborough had savoured the phrase, and how his fellow abbots had chuckled at his wit), but she had gone to London and appealed to the council, reminding the young

King Henry of her ancient, hereditary rights.

'What is this, my lords?' the lad was supposed to have said, staring around him, aping his betters. 'A woman to hold a royal castle?'

Then Fawkes de Breauté had sprung up, as the story went, and told the boy how King John, his father, had given Nicolaa the keys to Lincoln, and had said, 'My beloved, I will that you shall have custody of this castle.'

She had held it safe – de Breauté said passionately – when all of the east had fallen to the French. When St Albans had given way, and Orford, and Berkhampstead. When rebel earls had ruled over Norfolk and Suffolk, and the *Norrenses* had marched south from the Tyne.

Then, through a winter, this *woman* had kept Lincoln for the English crown. Kept it even though King Louis of France and Alexander of Scotland – aye, and Hugh of Arras and Earl Gant – had thrown all their might against her.

And because Lincoln held fast Newark held fast, and because Newark held fast Nottingham held fast. And through those bitter, starving months the white cross of England, painted on the crimson of Christ's blood, had never ceased to fly from Lincoln's walls, never, never, never.

Fawkes de Breauté was an emotional man. Nicolaa de la Haye had proved herself 'in time of need as gold is tried in the furnace,' he had cried, and then had sobbed, and the Earls of the Council had been moved and had sobbed also.

Sir Walter Lacy had spoken for her. Daubney, fresh from his sea victory over the monk Eustace, had spoken for her. And in some manner the Earl of Salisbury had been persuaded to give up his Castellanship of Lincoln. No doubt he had been rewarded elsewhere. They were shrewd enough, the young Earls who now ruled the land.

The French were gone. Peace had been made with Llewellin the Welshman. The Scotch King had retreated to his Caledonian fastness. A new great seal had been made and the Exchequer, it was said, would reopen before Christmas. The justices of a general eyre would soon begin their circuit; cauterising the wounds of war, listing the widows and minors in the King's wardship.

Nicolaa said, 'God be praised.'

The monks were coming up the hill, in procession from the hovel where the man had been kept since the jury had pronounced his fate.

To be taken from his house to church, as though already dead . . .

They made him walk behind the coffin. He was huddled in a coat that had once been a rich, cherry red, but was now filthy and stained, its fur collar matted. On his face the skin was raised in worm-like lesions, the pigment bleached grey.

Nicolaa stared at him as the procession approached.

'Can he speak?'

'Barely,' said the Abbot. The infection in his gums had spread to his tongue, which had swollen and turned black.

The coffin and cross stopped at the church door. The monks shuffled to one side, careful not to let the man wearing the red pelisse stand between them and the wind, which blew clean and salty from the sea.

Nicolaa said, 'Well, Crok. The world turns.'

He turned towards her, and bowed.

'I am again Castellan of Lincoln.'

He again bowed.

She turned to the Abbot.

'Take your monks away.'

The Abbot hesitated. Around him, the monks of Spaldynge Priory looked indignant. But she was the King's Sheriff, this woman, and her greed would know no bounds when the commission to restore displaced lands made its judgements. If she were not placated she would rob Peterborough of half the granges it had so subtly acquired in the confusion of war.

The Abbot urged his horse to one side and then dismounted. The monks of Spaldynge also drew back – they too needed royal favour, their covetous eyes being on Garrock grange, in the wapentake of Elloe, though it would need a royal charter and take a generation to enclose from the sea.

Crok stood and smiled and shivered.

'Idonea is to marry Salisbury's son, William Lungspeea,' said Nicolaa, looking down at him. 'So they'll get my castle in the end. Daubney tells me I am fortunate. Few of John's men are in favour. Phillip Mark has lost Nottingham – he can live on beetles in the greenwood with Will Scarlett for all the Council minds.'

Which was nonsense, Mark had farmed the taxes of Nottingham and Sherwood through half of John's reign. He was a rich man.

'De Breauté grows rheumatic and is mocked by the young Earls, though he will come to my aid at Lincoln, he says, if ever I am in need.'

As always, her own affairs. She cared for nothing but herself. Herself and her castle.

'Well?' she said.

He looked round, vaguely, at the small chapel, the windmill behind it. He wondered what she wanted him to say.

'They tell me you stole a little vessel from the church at Moulton.'

Was that, then, what they told her?

'And that you preyed on a girl, Alison de Pilche.'

He moved uncomfortably.

'She's with child. Not your work, I trust?'

No, not his work.

'The Abbot would put her into a nunnery, swollen belly and all, but she will not leave her cows. She is a ward of the King. She appeals to me, as the King's Sheriff, to let her marry her lover.'

The boy with butter hair.

'Why should this girl marry for fancy? Idonea must marry William Lungspeea, though he is ill-favoured and stupid. As Sheriff for the King I ought to sell this boy his Alison de Pilche for half her dowry – the King's Exchequer will come looking for the money soon enough. But she shall marry for love, all the same, unless you want her for yourself.'

She had ever been a dangerous woman, had ever had a cruel tongue.

'You had pennies from Lincoln. You could have bought her, and her manor.'

The pennies had been few and soon spent, the Earl of Chester's men keeping the cathedral treasure to themselves, the Marshal as rapacious as ever.

'Well? Did you become enamoured of this girl last Michaelmas and dote on her through a winter?'

He shook his head.

'Then what,' she said, briskly, 'brought you back to the sea?'

She knew. It was because she knew, that she was here.

He gazed out past the windmill.

'A necromancer will seek treasure,' she said, softly, leaning down in the saddle, 'as a sergeant seeks a whore. Was that it? Still?'

What else?

'And did you find it?'

He darted a cunning look at her: a wink, perhaps, from a swollen eye.

'Well?' – her voice low, but sharp.

Crok's mouth moved. He snickered and, with his hand, clacked his new wooden clappers. His eyes flitted to the Abbot, Robert of Lindsay.

Nicolaa stared down at him, stony-faced.

'No matter,' she said. 'John is dead. Let his crown lie in the sea.'

'Dame,' called the Abbot anxiously, 'it is the hour of None.'

Her brooding eyes were still on Crok.

'I have given money for your hospital. May God be with you. *Per Dominum nostrum Jesu Christum filium tuum*.'

Her Latin was as vile as ever.

She turned to look towards the estuary. He would have liked to ask if she knew aught of Florence, or of William the *Aquarius*. But the Abbot was looking at him warningly, and

454

the monks were scurrying round him, prodding him with their wands.

The coffin was raised. He shambled into the church behind it.

'You stay tonight at Swinehead?' the Abbot asked Nicolaa, with forced politeness. He himself would sup with the Abbot of Crowland, chew the fat, moan over the King's mercy to this woman.

Nicolaa hesitated and looked at the sky. It was October and the day short.

But Crok had been John's servant.

She dismounted from her horse, gave the reins to one of her men-at-arms, and went into the church.

Crok knelt at the altar, between two trestles hung with black cloth.

Nicolaa found a stool and sat on it. The Abbot sat beside her. The priest started to say mass.

She said quietly, 'He came to you himself?'

'He was found in the Deeping Fen by some of our brothers. He was in the extremity of hunger. He asked for you, dame.'

Nicolaa looked bleakly at the kneeling figure.

'There had been word for some time of a *jongleur* at Moulton Second,' the Abbot went on, 'living in a hovel in the fens, singing stanzas that moved men to lasciviousness.'

'Not him,' said Nicolaa. 'His only song was the Song of the Road, and that moved men only to pity.'

'He crept into houses and stole food.'

'Yet he was wealthy enough once. At Rochester he had a

servant, Adam. They famously killed six Welshmen between them, much to John's delight.'

'He preyed on women.'

'Yes, Alison de Pilche. She has complained against him?'

'She will say nothing,' said the Abbot. 'But women, of course, are peculiarly subject to the cunning charms of minstrels.'

What a fart he was.

'Queen Matilda squandered most of her money on them,' he droned. 'Minstrels, troubadours, fools. She had a delight, as do most women, in favouring those who say scandalous and shameful things concerning men who are not present . . .'

Nicolaa closed her eyes and slept till the mass ended.

Gloria Patri et Filio et Spiritui Sancto. Sicut erat in principio . . .

The Abbot rose and went to the altar. A monk gave him a spade of earth. He turned to the kneeling figure and said gently, kindly, 'Be thou dead to the world, but alive unto God.'

Crok made a little noise that might have been 'Amen.'

The Abbot dribbled the earth over him.

He said, 'Swear by the living Christ . . .'

Never to enter churches, or go into a market, or a
    mill, or a bakehouse.
Never to wash your hands or even your belongings in
    spring or stream of water.
Never to go outside your house unshod.
Never to touch anything which you wish to buy.
Never to touch a child.

> *To wear always your leper's dress that you may be recognised by others.*
> *To give warning of your approach by sounding your bell or wooden clappers.*

Outside, Nicolaa stood and watched as the dead man was taken away, still shuffling behind the coffin.

'Where is the leprosaria?'

'Beyond the town.'

'It has land?'

Robert of Lindsay nodded. 'They keep hogs. There are curative waters.'

'You know of the remedy for leprosy?'

'I know of no remedy but Christ's goodness.'

'Leeks,' said Nicolaa, 'boiled with adders. See that he is told.'

She mounted her horse and, with her men-at-arms behind her, rode north to Swinehead.

Crok in the leprosaria.

Naaman, the leprous captain of the host of the King of Syria, had been cured by dipping himself seven times in the waters of Jordan. The stewing of leeks with adders was a common remedy. Crok also practised blood-letting and purging, and the painful plastering of infected limbs with heated mud, until the other lepers, on whom he tried his medicinal arts, protested in pathetic rage to the procurator of alms.

In time he stopped seeking a cure. Instead he spent his days huddled over his crystal, or staring out over the dykes to Woken's Eye, to the distant sea that sparkled like silver fishes. He was seeking treasure, said the other lepers, who at night listened to his fevered mutterings. He was seeking treasure through his necromancy, through possession of lost souls.

Christe eleison.

Little disturbed the tenor of life in the leprosaria. When an inmate died another leper took his place, thus maintaining the number of twelve, representing Christ and his apostles. Crok was not told – nor would he have cared – about a wedding that took place in Lincoln: Nicolaa de la Haye's granddaughter, Idonea, to William Lungspeea, son of the Earl of Salisbury, the man who schemed to gain possession of the castle. But if Salisbury thought to get the Castellanship through his son he was disappointed. Nicolaa remained constable until the thirteenth year of King Henry, by which time she had a great-granddaughter, Margaret, who was betrothed as a baby to Henry Lacy and in due time married him, and took the castle of Lincoln with her, as her dowry.

Nicolaa took herself to Swaneton in 1231, where the nuns bled her as their sisters had bled Robin Hood in his last extreme, and there she died.

Crok had gone before her, dead in the fourth year of King Henry.

43

London – Cambridge – Peterborough

A meeting in a room in Whitehall: Georgian sash windows, regency wallpaper, a dozen men and women sitting at a dark, highly polished table. Observers from other departments. Rake in a corner with pad and pen.

Trudy Pierce came in, followed by Powell, the physicist from Fort Meade. They were here, at the Wormby Floods Inquiry, because the London Embassy wanted to show that in all its dealings the US government had been concerned, transparent, and forthcoming.

Powell outlined the story of the drone's last flight from Westphalia. Its release from its mother craft as it crossed the Lincolnshire coast. The assumption, by the internal USAF inquiry in 1962, that it had fallen into the sea.

The inquiry Chairman: 'Moving on to the present day. Can you tell us why you only confirmed the existence of the drone, and the nature of its load, *after* it had been discovered on the beach at Wormby?'

'Information was provided as soon as we had it ourselves.'

'Surely the CIA was asked to look into the matter in August, when fragments of metal casing were first found?'

'Yes, but there was no urgency, no reason to believe there was any current danger. Later, when Dr Rake flew to

Chicago, it was given priority treatment. It was, in fact, investigated by Miss Pierce, who is here with me now.'

The Chairman looked through his notes. He looked unhappy. But he wasn't allowed to ask any really important questions, thought Trudy suddenly; this was MoD business, he was going through the motions.

'Miss Trudy Pierce,' he said.

She described how she had found the file in the depository in Kansas. She told them how she had told her superiors immediately, how she had been flown that very night to Fort Meade, thus missing the Tavistock Hog Roast (slip that in, the embassy people told her, it would make her seem naive and cute).

She told how the White House had been given details of file *A-TCAE*377.b in the early hours of the morning, and how she had been sent immediately across the Atlantic.

It was informal and, eventually, friendly.

Afterwards Rake took her to a pub in Fleet Street where she met Mike Lean, a sardonic Californian, and Jennifer McLaren who said, 'Welcome to the Bohr Unit,' in an accent that wasn't remotely Scottish. They squeezed into a dining booth and ate steak-and-kidney pie with cabbage, and drank Beaujolais. Jazz music played loudly and parties of noisy office-workers drank Christmas drinks at a furious rate, and she thought how similar it all was to Dick's Last Stand.

'OK,' Rake said, eating pie with a hearty appetite, 'we've got two years' funding from the NSA and MoD. Trudy will be coming to Cambridge in January for three months, after that she'll be liaising with Gulliford in Boston. The basic brief is to analyse quantum effects on the human brain, with specific reference to electromagnetic leakage. In other words, did Felix Shafto experience genuine retrocognition through the quantum activities that govern the behaviour of neurotransmitter substances transferring signals across synaptic clefts? Or did he just go to the library and cunningly read up on blokes like de Meinnel and Phillip Mark, Sheriff of Nottingham?'

'No way,' said Jennifer.

'Ah, but you're young and innocent,' said Rake. 'Easily deceived.'

'Listen,' she said. ' "To Adam, the man of William Crok, who brought to the King when he was at Rochester the heads of six Welshmen, servants of Cadwallon, six shillings. On the same day, for shoes to Otho the carter, Margaret the laundress, and others, several sums" – that's straight from the Rotuli Litterarum Patentium of 1201–1216, that is. It's straight from King John's household accounts. I've spent three weeks tracking that down with Fisher of Balliol, and I can tell you that no way did Felix get access to the Patent Rolls in Hanger Lane library.'

'According to Felix,' said Rake, 'the King's laundress was called Florence.'

'So what? Can't a bloke change his laundress?'

Despite her aggressive tone, Jennifer was secretly in love with Rake, Trudy decided, eating her pie and drinking her Beaujolais.

'Anyway,' said Jennifer, 'what about physical symptoms – scurvy and something very akin to leprosy?'

'Mind over matter. A form of stigmata.'

'The retrocognition experienced by the two girls at the camp site?'

'Teenage hysteria.'

'The guy who owned the camp site?'

'Pink elephants.'

'I suppose the Cracker was pissed as well, was she?'

Now who, Trudy wondered, was the Cracker?

'The most convincing evidence,' said Rake, unfazed, 'is that Felix found the medieval seal and he found the sword. That was the clincher with the NSA when it came to funding.'

That and the fact, spelt out very clearly by Rake, that the US drone had only narrowly escaped disabling all electro-magnetic systems – including all car engines, computers, hospital-operating equipment, telecommunication and elec-tricity supplies – within a five-kilometre radius of Wormby Beach.

'Was what he found really the Sword of Tristram?' Trudy asked, thinking what a world she was moving in, so full of romance and intrigue.

'We'll take you to have a look,' said Rake.

He and Jennifer took her to the British Museum, to the Anglo-Saxon gallery where a small crowd was gathered round a display cabinet, which had on it a notice:

THE WORMBY FIND

Sword c10th century. There is speculation that this may be the 'Sword of Tristram', which was in the possession of King John and was supposedly lost in the quicksands of The Wash during the Barons' War

(c1216AD). If this is indeed the 'Sword of Tristram'
then King John was deluded about its provenance, this
sword being wrought several centuries after the sup-
posed time of King Arthur.

She stared through the glass at the brightly lit sword
pommel with its shining gold bands, and its blade of flaking
black rust. Once, she thought, it had been strong and sharp,
and had flashed in the bright, pure sunshine of another world.

'Is it true that it belongs to the Queen?'

'Sort of. Any item of gold or silver hidden with the intent
to recover becomes the property of the Crown.'

'What about the person who finds it?'

'They get compensation. In this case around half a million
pounds.'

'Is Mr Shafto going to be able to collect it?'

'The reward money,' Rake said grimly, 'is the least of his
worries.'

Felix in the hospital.

As he lay with his blackened, bruised hands resting
delicately on the coverlet, Normandie tried to stop him
drifting into the past: to free his captured, shattered mind, to
give him something to live for. She told him about the
Coroner's court verdict on the Saxon sword: the decision
that he and Karen Tymoor would share the compensation.

He smiled at that.

'Did you know she's getting engaged? He's a garage
mechanic and they've been in love since they were twelve,
so goodness only knows what she thought she was doing

with that student lad in the summer. They're planning buy a "Magna Charta" starter home in King John's Meadow in Holbeach.'

She had passed the development, on her way to see Ray Monkman in Spalding. *LUXURY HOMES FROM £69000* proclaimed a red-and-yellow flag, flying in the wind like a medieval banner.

'Ray's opening a new caravan site at Skeggy,' she said. 'He told the Yanks that half his caravans were brand-new Winnibegos. He said he'd lost the world's most precious collection of *Negés de Jardinière*. They paid him a fortune before they found out they were gnomes. He doesn't change, doesn't our Ray.'

He had been a bit drunk, actually, and a bit offensive, propping up the bar of Spalding Conservative Club and being anti-American. 'A bloody bomb sitting there for years and years and years! And don't tell me they didn't know it had gone missing!'

'No way,' said his chum, a sprightly old ironmonger.

'We're just like Wops and Dagos as far as the Yanks are concerned.'

'Now, now,' said the ironmonger cautiously.

'Ray,' said Normandie, 'you're disgusting.'

'Ginger,' twinkled the ironmonger, 'you're barmy.'

'Tell me a tale of the days that are gone,' said Ray, 'sing me a song at the past. Of the days when England was mighty, and everyone thought it would last.'

'You're going back a bit there,' said the ironmonger.

'Bloody right I am.'

Then he demanded his share of the reward. 'If I hadn't let

you have my coat I wouldn't have been half-dead from
hypothermia, and if I hadn't been half dead from hypothermia I'd have volunteered to get out of the rescue boat,
wouldn't I? And then I'd have been the one who found the
sword and we'd all have had a divvy – no, flower, no, it was
nothing to do with Spookie. I'm not saying he shouldn't get
something, but it was all down to luck at the end of the day.
You know he made Karen put pebbles into her pocket? He
said they were jewels but they were just daft pebbles – I was
with her when she took them out and chucked them in the
water. He was totally bananas and you had no right to say
that he and Karen could have all the money – what will she
do with a quarter of a million quid? I don't care what your
bearded wazzock said, he should just fuck off and mind his
own business . . .'

Which he was doing.

'Michael's going to the Faeroes,' she said to Felix. 'What
do you think of that?'

He looked at her, puzzled.

'It wasn't ever going to be any good, was it?' she asked. 'I
think I knew that from the start.'

Men, sweetie, his eyes seemed to say.

'Are you feeling any better at all?' she asked forlornly.

He seemed to nod.

His blood tests were normalising, which was a good sign,
but the chemotherapy to his brain, to protect it from external
forces, was being administered at critical levels, and his
heart was under stress, and his auto-immune system was
being weakened by the drugs he was being given to fight the
leprosy. Dr Govindan was still insisting, despite all the

evidence to the contrary, that he must have been to South East Asia to have become infected.

Rake came, daily, and they both sat by him. There was no attempt, now, to monitor his brain. But the camera was still running, she had discovered, and the recording machine was still activated whenever anyone spoke – which meant that Rake knew what she thought of Michael, and all sorts of things.

'I told him once that he could illuminate the world,' Rake said softly.

Felix would have liked that, she thought.

He was drifting away. Despite the drugs, he was going. They both watched over him silently, regretfully, as he fought his last battle with his hidden enemy.

The pneumonia slipped in easily in the end.

King's Lynn crematorium on a dark, damp December day. Could Felix ever have predicted, great seer that he was, the people who would send him on his final journey?

Julia, of course – she who had striven so hard to release the black discarnate attached to his Aura, to send it into the Light, and him to Eternal Peace.

But a government physicist from Cambridge? A young actress he had known for only four months? A marine biologist?

Afterwards, Normandie said, 'We have to go to Peterborough.'

Michael looked at Rake, who shrugged – although he had recorded a multitude of tapes and knew what was in her mind.

'Well, come on,' said Normandie, heading towards her car.

There it was: the great West Front, the most magnificent portico in Christendom, that would have been new stone, half-built, in the days of King John. The afternoon light was fading. Inside, in the quire, shaded crimson lights had been switched on for the choristers, who were practising carols. Normandie walked down the dim nave and found a little medieval tower, built, a notice told her, to house the uncorrupted arm of St Oswald. By it she found the tomb of an unknown Abbot of the thirteenth century.

Cold stone, worn, defaced. He had been a kindly enough man, Felix had told her, during those final, quiet conversations, when she had sat by his bed and drifted with him, so it sometimes seemed, into the Other World. She could see an aura of kindness, now, about the smudged blur of the Abbot's face.

She said a prayer. Michael and Rake were close by. She could sense Michael glancing at her, worried and uneasy, as he had been for several days now. 'The world is but vanity,' said Rake, reading out loud from the tomb of Mary, Queen of Scots. 'And subject still more to sorrow than a whole ocean of tears can bewail.'

Amen.

They joined her and stared down at the tomb.

A moment of silence.

Michael said, 'Felix said that this was Robert of Lindsay?'

She nodded.

'And he had in his possession the crown of Edward the Confessor?'

Again she nodded. 'The monks found Crok in sore distress and he gave them the great crown. They brought him back, in the night, to Peterborough, where the Abbot kept it hidden.'

'Right,' said Michael, after a moment.

'They had a passion, you see, for holy relics.'

Michael looked at Rake, who said calmly, 'What happened to it?'

She shook her head. Hidden in a secret place, perhaps. Lost and forgotten. Melted down.

'OK,' she said. 'We can go now.'

They walked back towards the west door. 'What are you doing in the Faeroes?' asked Rake.

'Investigating activity on the Reykanes Ridge,' said Michael, glancing at her unhappily. He was guilty about leaving her. But something was causing upheavals in the depths, nine hundred fathoms beneath the Atlantic waves where the earth's crust was so very thin. Somebody had to go there. Some poor sod of a marine physicist had to sort it out.

'It's probably the Americans buggering about,' said Rake, comfortably.

'What will happen to Felix's money?' Rake asked as they left the cathedral.

'He made a will,' said Normandie.

They looked at her, interested.

'Julia,' she said. 'He left it all to his friend Julia.'

'After everything he said about her?' said Michael indignantly.

'He didn't have anybody else.'

She set off towards the cathedral teashop. Michael wanted her and cared for her, but would go to the Faeroes, and would not be back for six months. He was a marine physicist, with his PhD and his little area of special interest, and in another ten years he'd wake up and wonder sadly why he didn't have much in the way of a private life.

Rake was a bastard and she didn't suppose she'd see him again, which maybe was a pity but probably wasn't.

She looked back. They were still standing under the West door. What were they talking about?

Her, probably.

The last light had fled the winter sky. The cathedral spires stood stark in the floodlights. She pictured the winds as they flowed from Peterborough's island, out over the fens to Crowland, over the Christmas lights of Holbeach and Spalding to the lonely lands beyond Whaplode Marsh and the Fosdyke Wash. Out over the bubbling waters of Black Buoy with its treacherous sands and its secrets.

'Michael's just making a phone call about his flight,' said Rake, coming across the cathedral close to join her. 'He says I'm to take care of you while he's in the Faeroes.'

'That's nice.'

'I'll need to check up on you anyway.'

So she would see him again.

'Are you all right?'

'Of course,' she said. 'Why shouldn't I be?'

'Come on,' he said gently, opening the teashop door. 'Let's have some tea, then I'll run you back to London.'

'Listen . . .' She hesitated. She'd hoped to find a priest to talk to – but Rake, after all, was a priest of a kind. 'Felix was free at the end, wasn't he?'

'Free?'

'His soul was at peace? His mind wasn't still possessed?'

'At the end,' he said, after a moment, 'I think they were both at peace.'

Felix Shafto and William Crok.

She looked back, up at the cathedral. It would soon be the shortest day, the winter solstice. A time of mystery, when the heavens moved darkly to the chimes of celestial music.

> *The rising of the sun*
> *And the running of the deer . . .*

For an instant she saw a huge red sun over the fens, the trees black against it, fallow deer started from their hides, splashing in alarm through the shallow waters.

The sound of the drum.

An army passing.

Nemesis

Bill Napier

According to a shock CIA report, Russian cosmonauts have deflected a giant asteroid onto a collision course with the United States – presenting the President with an impossible moral dilemma: either he must wait passively for almost certain annihilation, or retaliate first with a massive nuclear strike.

The only hope of averting catastrophe lies with an elite team of the world's top astronomers and astrophysicists, gathered secretly at Eagle Peak Observatory, Arizona. They have five days to identify the asteroid – codename Nemesis – and stop it. If they can't, the President will have to assume the asteroid is going to hit and make his appalling choice.

But as time begins to run out and the search for Nemesis becomes increasingly desperate, British asteroid expert Oliver Webb has an extraordinary idea – that the key lies in the dusty pages of an obscure seventeenth-century Latin manuscript, a manuscript which has just gone mysteriously missing . . .

'The most exciting book I have ever read' Arthur C. Clarke

'Napier has put a lifetime's knowledge into a stomach-churning thriller . . . a gripping read' *Scotsman*

0 7472 5993 3

HEADLINE
FEATURE

Dead Headers

James H. Jackson

Officially the British Intelligence organisation known as Executive Support doesn't exist. But for its far-from-innocent victims it is all too real. Its aim: to terrorize the terrorists, to eliminate them before they can act. Its nickname: the Dead Headers.

When a sadistic mortar attack turns the streets of Paris into a charnel house, no group claims responsibility and there are no clues to the killers' motives. But the attack is only the first piece of a terrifying jigsaw that leads the Dead Headers from a secretive German pharmaceuticals company to an Iraqi biological weapons base in the Libyan desert, from a gruesome sex-murder in London's Hammersmith to a power struggle at the heart of the Iranian revolutionary regime. And by the time the final piece is in place, the fate of millions will have been decided . . .

'Tense, well researched, fast-paced and hard-nosed' Frederick Forsyth

'Hair-raising' *Guardian*

0 7472 5771 X

HEADLINE *FEATURE*